EVERY DUKE HAS HIS DAY

ALSO BY SUZANNE ENOCH

Something in the Heir

Hit Me with Your Best Scot
Scot Under the Covers
It's Getting Scot in Here
A Devil in Scotland
My One True Highlander
Hero in the Highlands
Some Like It Scot
Mad, Bad, and Dangerous in Plaid
Rogue with a Brogue
The Devil Wears Kilts
The Handbook for Handling His Lordship
A Beginner's Guide to Rakes
Taming an Impossible Rogue
Rules to Catch a Devilish Duke

EVERY DUKE HAS HIS DAY

SUZANNE ENOCH

ST. MARTIN'S
GRIFFIN
NEW YORK

First published in the United States by St. Martin's Griffin, an imprint of St. Martin's Publishing Group

EVERY DUKE HAS HIS DAY. Copyright © 2023 by Suzanne Enoch. All rights reserved. Printed in the United States of America. For information, address St. Martin's Publishing Group, 120 Broadway, New York, NY 10271.

www.stmartins.com

Designed by Omar Chapa

Library of Congress Cataloging-in-Publication Data

Names: Enoch, Suzanne, author.
Title: Every duke has his day / Suzanne Enoch.
Description: First edition. | New York : St. Martin's Griffin, 2023.
Identifiers: LCCN 2023017090 | ISBN 9781250842541 (trade
    paperback) | ISBN 9781250842558 (ebook)
Subjects: LCGFT: Romance fiction. | Novels of manners. | Novels.
Classification: LCC PS3555.N655 E94 2023 | DDC 813/.6—dc23/
    eng/20230421
LC record available at https://lccn.loc.gov/2023017090

Our books may be purchased in bulk for promotional, educational, or business use. Please contact your local bookseller or the Macmillan Corporate and Premium Sales Department at 1-800-221-7945, extension 5442, or by email at MacmillanSpecialMarkets@macmillan.com.

First Edition: 2023

10 9 8 7 6 5 4 3 2 1

For everyone who shares a home with a furry, scaled, finned, or feathered friend. And especially for Tiki, who slept against my side and kept half of me warm the entire time I wrote this. Good dog.

And as always, a special thanks to Monique, Mara, Marissa, Kejana, and Sara—and all the great team at St. Martin's. You guys are magicians.

EVERY DUKE HAS HIS DAY

CHAPTER ONE

MICHAEL BROMLEY, THE DUKE OF WORITON, SET THE THIN, round-trimmed sheet of zinc on the halfpenny, then pulled a circular piece of paper from the bowl of salted water on the table in front of him and placed it atop the two metals. Another piece of zinc went on top of that.

"Your Grace?" Huston rapped a knuckle against the door.

"Working," Michael said, and placed another coin on the stack.

Mumbled conversation from beyond the door tickled at his concentration. Rolling his shoulders, Michael continued stacking—halfpenny, zinc, saltwater paper. Seven layers ought to suffice for his purposes today; he only needed a spark, and that didn't warrant pulling out the troughs or the larger zinc plates.

"I understand, Your Grace," the butler's voice came again, "but your aunt is here. Lady Mary wishes to speak with you."

"The sign is on the door, Huston." Michael looked up for a moment. "The sign *is* on the door, isn't it?"

"Yes, Your Grace."

Ha. He'd remembered it—or more than likely, neglected to take it down yesterday. "And what does it say?"

"It says, 'Do not disturb,' Your Grace."

"Thank you, Huston. I'll take luncheon at one o'clock."

More hushed conversation whispered through the closed door of his study. His aunt knew he was generally occupied in the mornings, so she had no one to blame but herself for choosing a morning to call on him. Michael lifted the stack enough to place the end of a copper wire between the bottom coin and the wooden disc beneath it.

The door opened. "You will ruin your eyesight, spending all your time looking at such little things," Aunt Mary stated, swishing into the room and leaving the door ajar behind her.

"The world is composed of little things," he returned, finishing off the stack with a last piece of zinc, another copper wire, and a top wooden disc. "Smaller even than most people realize."

"That sounds impressive, Michael, but it looks as if you're just sitting there counting money."

"This," he said, sitting back to look at his aunt and noting that she was dressed rather fancily for a cup of tea with her nephew, "is a voltaic pile. A 'battery,' if you wish to go by Benjamin Franklin's definition."

"And what does a voltaic pile do, then?"

"It makes electricity."

"Hm. Much more practical than attaching a key to a kite and flying it in a storm, I suppose. Silly Americans." She removed one glove to slap it against her hand. "I won't be back in London until mid-June, at the earliest. I've left instructions about Lancelot with Huston, as I don't imagine you're listening to anything I'm saying, but for God's sake take him for a walk once in a while."

"I am not going to take my butler for a walk," Michael countered, frowning. "He can damned well walk himself. And be careful of that receiver. It took me an hour to fill it with hydrogen."

"For heaven's sake, Michael. Not your butler. Lancelot. My poodle."

Because she didn't seem to be listening, Michael stood to move the upside-down glass receiver and the water-filled saucer upon which it sat to the other side of his large worktable. While hydrogen wasn't difficult to collect, it wasn't a quick process, by any means. "What about Lancelot?"

"Take him for a walk. Daily, if possible."

"You take him for a walk. He's your dog."

"I won't be here. Have you paid attention to nothing I've been saying to you for the past month?" Sighing, she dragged a stool up to the table and sat down opposite him, still managing to make the motion look ladylike. "I am going to visit Violet, Lady Penderghast. I can't take Lancelot with me, as her husband Gerald is allergic to dogs."

"I've been occupied, Aunt Mary," he stated. "I haven't become senile. You're going to Cornwall and leaving Lancelot in my care. Is that today, though? I thought you weren't leaving until the middle of May."

"I changed my mind. A woman's prerogative."

Michael sent her a brief grin. "Indeed. Give my regards to Lord and Lady Penderghast, then." Leaning over the table, he kissed her on one pale cheek. "And yes, I or someone else will walk Lancelot daily. And I'll make certain Mrs. Fellows bakes oat biscuits and a boiled egg for his breakfast every morning."

Aunt Mary threw her arms around his shoulders, nearly upending the table. "You *do* listen, Michael."

"On occasion." Craning his neck to see around her, he slid the voltaic stack into a safer position. "Now please go away. I *am* working."

Clucking her tongue against her teeth, Lady Mary Harris released her hold on him. "I wish you would phrase that differently.

'Working' is *très gauche*, especially for a gentleman. You do recall that you're a duke, don't you? I concede that at your station being thought of as eccentric is tolerable and possibly expected, but it's a very few steps between your fellows thinking the Duke of Woriton unique, and those same people deciding you're mad as a hatter and deserve to lose all your holdings and your title. There is avarice in the government, you know."

"I'm aware." Reaching behind him for a dish with a minuscule quantity of black dust on it, Michael set one of the copper wires into it. "Let them say whatever they wish. I have a great many solicitors on retainer." Leaning back a little, he touched the other copper wire to the powder.

It exploded in a loud puff of flame and black smoke. Aunt Mary shrieked and jumped backward, her hands flying to her chest. "Michael! You nearly scared the life out of me!"

"My apologies. It was just a bit of gunpowder; a simple trick." He sighed. "Much easier than measuring the heat of burning hydrogen gas, which is what I'm meant to be doing this morning."

"Just how many of the chemicals and . . . things you store in here are explosive?"

"Most of them, if combined in the correct proportions."

"You are being carel—"

"I am not being careless," he interrupted. "I put a sign on the door, and my staff knows not to enter the room unless I'm present. Nor do I ever leave the door open when I have equipment on the table, as you've done. I'm not some boy playing with fire, Aunt Mary. If I can adapt an Argand's lamp to burn hydrogen, and if it burns hot enough, it'll . . ."

Michael took a breath, trailing off. They'd had this conversation before, but like many of their peers, she plainly found it impossible to believe that an aristocrat's scientific work was anything more than dabbling. A hobby. Pointing out that he'd had papers published in respected scientific journals, that he'd given lectures before the City Philosophical Society, even that some of the most brilliant scientific minds in England had voted him a Fellow of the Royal Society—to her that was just proper scientists humoring him.

"I shan't bore you with the details," he modified, "but it will be significant. And useful."

"Very well," she said, sighing. "But I sometimes think you value that 'F.R.S.' after your name more than you do the 'Duke' in front of it."

"Nonsense. One provides me with the means and opportunity to delve into the other." He avoided using that "work" word this time, but given the responding flare of his aunt's nostrils she'd heard it nonetheless. Yes, the way he'd chosen to spend his ample spare time annoyed her, but a hotter-burning lamp with a controllable flame would be of considerable use not just to him, but to a great many of his fellows.

"Oh, do as you will, Michael. Just please do not poison or set fire to my lovey boy Lancelot, and remember to eat—and to re- move that silly leather apron before you go out in public. You look like a shopkeeper."

Michael glanced down at the light brown leather apron, filled with convenient pockets and rather effective at keeping his proper clothes from being splashed with acid or whatever else he happened to be working with. "Very well," he said, motioning her toward the door and sending her another smile so she would know he wasn't angry, "for you, I shall attempt to look other than shabby in public."

"Thank you. I will see you in six weeks. Pray do not burn down Bromley House in the interim. I'm rather fond of it. And you."

"Yes, my dear. Likewise."

Michael spent the rest of the morning working on tubing and valves; the immediate problem in working with a combustible, lighter- than-air gas was convincing it to travel from one vessel to another in a controlled manner that wouldn't leave him with one large, pretty fireball and singed eyebrows.

When a soft rap sounded on the door, he pushed away from his worktable, walked over, and pulled it open. "Yes?"

Huston blinked, taking a half step backward. "Your Grace. It is one o'clock."

"I own a pocket watch and several clocks, Huston. There's one inside this very room, as a matter of fact."

"You said you would take your luncheon at one o'clock, Your Grace," the butler said in what Michael recognized as his patient tone.

"Ah. So I did."

"Do you wish it brought in here, or to the small dining room?" The servant glanced past Michael at the chaos of equipment sprawled across the worktable.

"The small dining room will be fine. I'll be there in a moment."

With a nod, the butler stepped backward. "Very good, Your Grace."

Shutting the door again, Michael returned to the table, blew out the flame of the Argand's lamp, shifted a pair of combustible vials farther away from each other, and shut the window at the back of the room to prevent a stray breeze from knocking anything over. That done, he paused to read the note he'd nailed to the inside of the door. No flame, no open acids, no open windows, and no active decompositions of combustibles currently underway. Tapping the note with one finger, he opened the door again, stepped into the hallway, and shut it behind himself.

The table was set for two, and he scowled as he took his seat. "Who's joining me? I don't recall—"

With an elegant hop, Lancelot took the chair at the far end of the table. The poor thing had been groomed within an inch of its life, and looked like nothing so much as a collection of black balls of yarn. A ball of black fur at the tip of its tail, one over each hip, and four at its feet and obscuring the paws, with a close-shaven back half and legs.

The head, though, he didn't even know how to describe. A sort of overhanging pompadour on top thickened as it covered the chest and the top of the forelimbs and extended halfway along the animal's frame; the effect seemed to be a combination of smooth lion's mane and lady's cowl. Only the ears were straightened, long, thick paddles hanging down either side of his head.

"Good God," Michael muttered. "What the devil has she done to you this time?"

"Lady Mary said he'd been groomed in the very latest style," Huston supplied. "She left a comb and instructions on how to maintain the . . . smooth bulk of the crown."

"That is not a crown. It's a schooner. Possibly a galleon."

The butler cleared his throat. "A very fashionable schooner, Your Grace."

"Poor lad. I'd take scissors to you in the study, but I don't believe even a surgeon as skilled as Dr. Frankenstein could help you, Lancelot."

The dog woofed at him. Footmen set out luncheon, and he and the large poodle ate while engaging in a rather one-sided debate over the merits of oxygen versus hydrogen as a fuel. *Hm.* Anyone listening would think he'd strayed beyond the acceptable side of eccentric, but at least Lancelot didn't interrupt him with random tales of eligible females or who'd slighted whom at the latest soiree.

As he set his utensils aside, the butler approached again. "Your Grace, Bradley and myself have been attempting to lure Lancelot into the garden for a . . . constitutional since his arrival, but the animal refuses to step outside. Do you think—"

Michael sighed. "She told you to take me walking, didn't she?" he asked the poodle, who jumped down from his chair and padded over to stand at attention beside him. "Very well. You may take me for a walk. But if anyone asks, we don't know each other."

Lancelot barked and wagged his poof of a tail.

Retrieving a study about the recombination of the elements from his office, Michael made his way to the front door and waited as Huston attached a lead around the poodle's neck. "Thank you. We'll return shortly."

"Your Grace? Your apron."

Looking down, Michael sighed. "Ah. I did give my word, didn't I?" Pulling off the garment, he handed it over to the butler. "Please don't attempt to wash it this time. I have notes in several of the pockets."

Huston inclined his head. "We're not likely to make that mistake again, Your Grace."

"Don't be cruel, Bitsy! Come down and walk with us!"

Elizabeth Dockering grinned. "I'm sorry; I can't quite hear you," she teased, putting a cupped hand to her ear.

Another of the young gentlemen surrounding her barouche gripped the low carriage door and rose up on his toes. "Come down and join the rabble before we all expire from yearning, O goddess."

"I simply want to know her opinion of the new modiste," Anne Caufield commented from the crowd, tapping Peter Cordray's shoulder with her parasol. "Do stop trying to suffocate my friend."

Laughing, Elizabeth leaned forward. "You may as well stop here, William," she said to her driver. "We're making no headway in the barouche, anyway."

"Yes, Miss Bitsy." The driver pulled the carriage to a halt, a barely perceptible change from the slow walk they'd been forced to since entering Hyde Park.

Elizabeth stood, taking the upstretched fingers of the nearest gentleman—which was, of course, Lord Peter Cordray. "Thank you, Lord Peter," she drawled with a smile, tugging on the lead wrapped around her left hand.

"I've begged you to simply call me Peter, Bitsy. You must—"

Peter's plea cut off as the big black poodle leaped to the ground beside her and jammed its nose into the crotch of the Marquis of Plasser's younger brother. The dog snorted, and Lord Peter yelped, jumping backward.

"No, Galahad," Elizabeth ordered, making what she hoped was an apologetic chuckle as she pulled her poodle back to her side. "You naughty boy." She squeezed Peter Cordray's fingers with her free hand. It would never do to have her foremost suitor in a sulk all afternoon. "I'm very sorry. You know he never listens."

"No need to chastise him, Bitsy," Lord Peter said, tugging at his trousers and favoring her with a smile that didn't reach his eyes. "Though I am surprised you brought Galahad along at all. He is somewhat . . . unpredictable, and as you can see, the park is quite lively today. You might send him home in the barouche."

"He's a brute," Elizabeth agreed as she ruffled the poodle's coiffure, "but he's also my protector and champion. And William could never both drive the carriage and manage Galahad. Go on, William."

"Galahad's a very effective protector," Anne Caufield commented, grinning. "My father's been talking about getting a large dog for my sister Alice for the very same reason."

"For God's sake," Tom Hillstead exclaimed, "at this rate we'll all be dog-bitten by the end of the Season."

"And shot by the ladies' fathers, if we get past the dogs," Tom's brother Geoffrey added.

"You all know 'the course of true love never did run smooth,'" Elizabeth pointed out, laughing.

"Oh, now you've quoted the Bard," another friend, Florence

Pickery, said, the baron's daughter wisely keeping her fingers well away from Galahad. "You know what that means, Bitsy—you must deliver us a soliloquy."

"Yes! Who will it be, Bitsy? Lady Macbeth?"

"Cleopatra, of course!"

Elizabeth cleared her throat. Of course she had a soliloquy to hand that would suffice. Every one of them did, she would have been willing to wager. "'What's in a name? That which we call a rose, By any other name would smell as sweet; So Romeo would—'"

Tom groaned. "Not *Romeo and Juliet,* Bitsy. For God's sake."

She grinned. "'So Romeo would, were he not Romeo call'd, Retain that dear perfection which he owes Without that title.'"

"You can't think she would choose Lady Macbeth," Anne stated. "That woman is such a schemer."

"'Romeo, doff thy name; And for thy name, which is no part of thee, Take all myself.'"

"Bravo," Lord Peter cheered, as the others laughed and applauded. "Perfection, even with such savage interruptions."

With a curtsy, Elizabeth chuckled. "That's all part of the challenge, as I recall. I'll have to memorize another one now, on the chance I accidently quote the Bard again."

"I always say, 'The greater the challenge, the greater the reward,'" Peter added, offering his arm. "Though I don't think that's Shakespeare. Shall we?"

Galahad growled, and Elizabeth tugged on the lead again to distract the poodle from his fixation with Lord Peter Cordray. Yes, her friends and suitors tolerated Galahad, and even pretended to like him, but the poodle could be a handful even on the best of days. Still, he didn't care if she snored, or if she wore the same walking dress for two Tuesdays in a row—not that she would do such a thing. Not in London and not during the Season, anyway. He did give her the excuse of a few moments' thought and distance when she required it, and he never failed to cure her of an ill mood. And he always, always, watched out for her.

"Have you seen Lady Prudence Fulton's new dog?" Lord Peter asked, sending a glance over his shoulder when Elizabeth's petite maid, Peggy, nearly bashed him with the parasol she was attempting to hold over the two of them. "A delightful little thing she carries in a basket over one arm. She calls him Cricket."

"Don't worry about shading me, Peggy; the trees will suffice," Elizabeth said. "I promise I won't burn."

"I . . . Yes, miss." Collapsing the parasol, the lady's maid fell back to mingle with the rest of the companions trailing close behind them.

Elizabeth glanced at the light-haired man walking beside her. "Are you suggesting I should give away Galahad in favor of a smaller dog, then, my lord?"

"I am only sharing information with one dog lover about another," he said smoothly. "You know I adore you, which means I adore Galahad."

On her other side the poodle growled, and she tugged the lead again. "Well, we're both very flattered to hear that, my lord, though you should be glad Galahad doesn't understand enough English to know you suggested he be replaced."

"I've begun to fear the same for myself," he commented. "We've known each other for better than a year, and despite my pleas you still won't address me more familiarly."

"I rarely call any gentleman solely by his given name, Lord Peter."

He pulled her to a stop, shifting to face her. "Bitsy, I'm not jesting. You must give me some small measure of hope that you feel at least a fraction of the passion for me that I feel for you." The marquis's brother lifted a hand toward her face, as if to cup her cheek. "Please say you'll call me Peter, and I can die a hap—"

Oh, this was too much, especially in front of all her friends. Elizabeth took a step backward. Apparently sensing her abrupt discomfiture, Galahad jerked out of her grip, reared into the air, and snapped his jaws around Peter Cordray's outstretched sleeve, barely missing his arm.

"Galahad!"

With a yelp the poodle sprinted away, leather lead flapping behind him and a good portion of fine cloth and a cuff link hanging from his mouth.

"That damned—"

"Galahad! Oh, you frightened him!"

Hiking her skirts, Elizabeth ran after her poodle. *Oh, dear.* It wasn't the first time he'd taken a bite from the vicinity of one of her suitors, but he couldn't go about biting the brothers of marquises. Not even if he'd been attempting to protect her. Lord Peter Cordray should never have tried to be so familiar with her, of course, but now no one would be gossiping about that. They'd all be wagging their tongues about how Bitsy Dockering had allowed her evil, slobbering villain of a dog to nearly bite someone. Well, she was fairly certain that if Galahad had intended to draw blood, he would have done so.

When she considered it, what the poodle had actually done was deliver a warning to all gentlemen present not to attempt to take liberties with her, and if even one of them hesitated before they attempted to loom over her with love poems or demands for a walk or a dance, then she would call Galahad a hero. Not aloud, of course, because a man finding an appropriate bride, and a bride accepting the suit of an appropriate gentleman, was, quite logically, the rule of the day. A dog standing in the way of the marriage market was unlikely to be tolerated for long.

"Miss Bitsy!" Peggy called from behind her. "Please come back!"

"As soon as I retrieve Galahad!" Retrieving Peter Cordray's cuff link would also help to ease his bruised sense of . . . whatever it was that kept men in pursuit despite the odds against them.

She caught sight of the poodle, head up and blue sleeve dangling from his mouth, trotting close by the near bank of the Serpentine. Thank goodness he hadn't gone far. Slowing to a more dignified walk, she crossed a riding trail and then a walking path that bordered the water. Her relief caught in her throat, though, as Galahad lurched into a run again—this time making straight for a black poodle nearly his size. Its owner stood by the pond, the lead loose in his hand and his attention clearly on a handful of papers rather than the impending disaster.

"Galahad!" she yelled again, ignoring the startlement of the crowd around her. "No!"

The two dogs came together in a flurry of barking, black, curling fur and flying slobber, splashing into the shallow lake . . . and dragging the man still attached to the second poodle with them. *Oh, good heavens.* He kept to his feet, one hand clutching the papers and the other holding on to his blue beaver hat—no easy task with the lead wrapped around his arm.

"Let go of the lead!" she yelled at him, before he could get himself drowned or something equally horrible.

He turned, pinning her with a glare. For a heartbeat, despite his expression, the perfect . . . symmetry of his face, the deep brown eyes beneath long lashes and curved brows, even his flattened, annoyed mouth—all struck her with the force of a blow to her chest.

"Adonis," she breathed.

"What?" he asked. At that moment both dogs barreled into his legs, knocking him onto his backside. The papers, hat, and lead all went flying, and he splashed into the water up to his neck. "Damnation!" he cursed, standing again and plucking pages out of the water rather than wading to dry land as any sane man would have done.

Now one of the poodles seemed to be attempting to mount the

other, and while with their wet fur and wrestling about she couldn't tell which was Galahad, she could certainly guess. "Galahad! Leave that dog alone!"

The man swept up his wet hat and jammed it on his head. One hand clutching the mess of papers, he reached out with the other and snagged the collar of the top dog. "Off, you brute," he growled, dragging the two poodles onto the shore.

Now that he was out of the water and not tangled in poodles, Elizabeth could see that he was well, if plainly, dressed. But as she didn't recognize him—and she knew practically everyone of note in Mayfair—she couldn't imagine who he might be. Perhaps a solicitor, or a clerk of some sort, though neither of those would be likely to appear in Hyde Park during strolling hours. Even in his soggy cravat and dripping coat he seemed more annoyed than embarrassed and still ridiculously well-favored, his gaze direct and remaining on her as he and the dogs slogged onto the pathway in front of her.

With a bark Galahad twisted sideways, nearly escaping the man's grip as he grabbed up the torn, sodden sleeve again. Well, at least Lord Peter hadn't lost his cuff link. Elizabeth held out one gloved hand, and the man slapped the end of her dog's lead onto her palm.

"Thank you," she murmured with her most charming smile.

"Your animal needs to learn some discipline," he snapped, water dripping from the brim of his sagging hat.

Elizabeth blinked. People—men—didn't rebuke her. "If you'd paid more attention to your animal than your . . . love letters, you might have seen him coming and prevented this mess," she shot back at him.

He lifted one curved eyebrow. "'Love letters'?" he repeated, ignoring the snickering of the crowd around them. "I'll have you know this is a scientific treatise on the composition of base elements."

"Well, I'll have you know that I don't care what it is, and you look ridiculous."

Brown eyes narrowed. "At least I have an excuse for my appearance. If not for your lips moving, I would have thought you a dressmaker's mannequin. And your speech is that of a spoiled child attempting to evade responsibility for something clearly her fault."

"A dressmaker's . . . Oh!" Men as a rule didn't insult her, either. Too many of them wanted to marry her. But now, while his insult had several interpretations, she'd evidently just been called pretty and empty-headed. And spoiled, though that one didn't take any interpretation. He'd just come out and said it. "You are rude!"

"Bitsy," Peter Cordray said, trotting up to her, one arm exposed to the elbow.

If he meant this to be a rescue, he should have arrived much more quickly, she decided, though it did seem rather uncharitable of her to think so. At the least, he hadn't insulted her. "My lord."

"There's no need for fisticuffs, either of you. I'm certain that more than anything else Woriton wishes to go home and don a dry set of clothes, and you've the Sommerset ball to prepare for."

Woriton. "*You're* the Duke of Woriton?" she asked as she spun back to pin the tall man with a glare. "Well. You certainly live up to your reputation, Your Grace."

"And you are?"

Peter cleared his throat. "Ah. Allow me. Woriton, Miss Elizabeth Dockering. Bitsy, Michael Bromley, the Duke of Woriton."

The duke regarded her for another moment, then tugged on his poodle's lead. "Come along, Lancelot. I've had enough of madwomen today."

They walked away, the poodle balking only to be sternly spoken to before falling in beside his master. Elizabeth watched them for a moment, tugging back against Galahad's pull as her poodle attempted to go after them again. "Oh, no, you don't. You've made

enough trouble today, Galahad," she muttered, facing Peter Cordray.
"*That* was Woriton? I'd heard he was old and walked with a cane and
an ear trumpet." He had certainly had neither of those things with
him, and she wouldn't have put his age anywhere over thirty, if that.
His manners and madness, though, were something else entirely.
"How do you know him?"

With a frown, pulling at the frayed end of his sleeve with his
other hand, Lord Peter glanced after the duke. "He and my brother
went to school together. Don't worry about him; he's a complete
Bedlamite."

Well, he certainly was that. If she'd initially thought him handsome, it had only been because he was standing quite a distance
away. Yes, that must have been it. "How is it he's allowed to be out
in public, then?"

The frown became a grimace. "He's a smart Bedlamite. And a
very wealthy one. Anyway, I find it more amusing that your dogs'
names mesh, and that Galahad handed Lancelot a bruising."

"Galahad handed *you* a bruising, as well," Tom Hillstead pointed
out, gesturing at Peter's missing sleeve as the rest of her friends
regrouped beside the lake.

"Yes, I'll forgive that, though, since he put that stiff-spined
Woriton into the Serpentine." The marquis's brother eyed Galahad. "I would appreciate getting that cufflink back, however. It was
a gift."

Oh, yes, that. Elizabeth squared her shoulders. "Give it, Galahad,"
she ordered in her most confident voice, holding out one hand. The
poodle, fur still drooping and water running off him in rivulets,
looked up at her, lowered his tail, and dropped the sleeve onto her
palm. *Well.* That almost never worked. Not unless she had a bit of
beef to offer as a trade.

Trying not to look surprised, she straightened, handing the

torn cloth and attached gemstone to Peter. "There you are, my lord. Please send me the bill for your coat's repair or replacement; my father will certainly recompense you."

He nodded. "I appreciate the gesture, but it's unnecessary, Bitsy. Your company is recompense enough."

"Smoothly done, Peter," Geoffrey Hillstead put in. "That may even get you a dance with our diamond at the Sommerset ball this evening."

As much as Elizabeth disliked promising dances before the actual event, Peter had certainly earned some consideration. "It will get you a waltz, Lord Peter," she decided, smiling.

"I say, Bitsy," Tom protested. "What about a dance for me, then?"

"And me?" his brother added.

She put up her hand. "Oh, no, you don't," she said, keeping her smile to show that she knew they were jesting. Mostly. Over-eager gentlemen seeking an advantage were nothing new in her experience. "I owe Lord Peter an apology. As for the rest of you, I will wait to see who makes an appearance at the Sommerset fete, and then I will decide with whom I care to take a turn about the room."

"And what if Woriton makes an appearance?" Anne Caufield suggested, giggling behind her hand.

"Considering I've been out for two Seasons and today is the first time I've set eyes on the Duke of Woriton, I wouldn't wager a penny that he would join his fellows at a dance. If he were even invited. A soiree is hardly the place for a madman." Elizabeth recovered her parasol from her maid and opened it, appreciating again what a handy tool it was in keeping any overeager gentlemen from taking her arm. "If he did, I would certainly never dance with him." She sniffed. "I might stomp on his foot, though."

Her friends laughed, as she'd known they would. Yes, that was her, the witty one with hordes of admirers and suitors and hangers-on, and one rude man with whom she was barely acquainted but who evidently thought her nothing more than a spoiled, empty-headed, addlepated ninnyhammer.

CHAPTER TWO

HUSTON PULLED OPEN THE FRONT DOOR OF BROMLEY HOUSE. "Welcome back, Your Gra—Good heavens! What's happened?"

Michael handed him the end of Lancelot's lead and brushed past him into the house. "The Serpentine and I had a disagreement," he muttered, setting his soggy mass of papers on the hall table before removing his hat. Then he peeled off his coat and dropped it to the floor, following that with his cravat and waistcoat. "And Lancelot met another lovely black poodle who attempted to bugger him. Give the poor lad a biscuit, will you?"

"Shall I summon Jarrett, Your Grace?" the butler asked, picking up the wet garments with two careful fingers.

Untucking his shirt from his trousers, Michael nodded. "If you please. And have Bradley attempt to dry Lancelot before he drowns in his own coiffure."

"I'll see to it at once."

Michael retrieved the papers and detoured to his study before heading upstairs; the pages would be a complete loss, but he'd made notes on several of them. All he could do was set them out to dry and then copy over his work as best he could. "Love letters," he grumbled, separating each page and laying them across his work-table. "As if I would make critical notes all over a love letter and then take it outside for everyone to see."

Silly, pretty chit. And *Bitsy*? What sort of nickname was that for any self-respecting female? Perhaps if she'd bothered to apologize for her dog's ill behavior, he might have been less . . . sharp with her, but his notes were ruined, damn it all.

What had she called him? Oh, yes. Rude. And ridiculous. He did tend to be direct, he knew, so perhaps "rude" wasn't far off the mark. The other one stung a little. Aunt Mary had asked him to be more careful with his dress, and he'd worn all the proper accou-trements this afternoon. He imagined, though, that anyone who had been dragged into a lake would look ridiculous coming out of it. That part hadn't been his fault. A true gentlewoman wouldn't have pointed it out.

"Your Grace?" his valet said, sticking his head through the door-way. "Huston said you'd . . . Oh, dear."

Michael set out the last page and turned around. "Never mind the clucking, Jarrett. My boots are still full of water, and I reck-oned the two of us could remove them with less mess than I could do alone." Cracking open the study window enough for air but not enough for a breeze, he left the room and headed upstairs to the master bedchamber, squishing with each step.

"Did Lancelot run off on you, Your Grace?" Jarrett asked, kneel-ing to pull off one boot and then the other as Michael yanked off his soaked shirt. Water dripped on the floor and seeped into the blan-ket he'd set between himself and the chair. "I thought him so well-mannered."

The most ridiculous thing about all this wasn't his appearance; it was that he'd lost a good hour of time when he might have been working. "He didn't run off. He was accosted by another poodle.

The two of them decided to take their disagreement into the Serpentine."

The valet stood, picking up the boots and carrying them over to an open window, where he turned them over and dumped them out. "I'll have to put these by the fire and hope the heat doesn't shrink them. I've always said, people shouldn't have pets if they can't mind them properly."

Michael imagined the valet had never said such a thing in his life, but he appreciated the sentiment. Bitsy Dockering shouldn't have been walking her animal in the park if she couldn't keep hold of its lead. It was that simple. If anyone was ridiculous, it was her. "I find your logic sound," he said aloud.

Nodding, the valet handed over a dry shirt, which Michael pulled on over his head. "I hope you gave the culprit a stern talking-to, Your Grace."

"I daresay Miss Dockering will be more attentive in the future." At the least, if she allowed her Galahad to escape again, she would hopefully apologize for the disruption she'd caused.

Jarrett straightened. "A Miss, Your Grace?"

"Yes. Elizabeth Dockering. They call her Bitsy, apparently, which is a ridiculous nickname and makes her sound like a plump child, which she isn't." He bent his head, buttoning his own waistcoat. "A rather attractive thing, actually, if hopelessly spoiled and . . . helpless." And sharp-tongued, which didn't quite fit with the rest of his assessment, but as he wasn't entirely certain he'd won the volley of words, he left out that part.

"I see." The valet cleared his throat. "Do you require a cravat and coat this afternoon?"

"No. I'm not going out ag—"

Something downstairs crashed and broke to the accompanying sound of shattering glass. Before Michael could close his mouth over his words, a man's scream echoed up the stairs.

"Good Lord," Jarrett muttered.

Michael barely heard the comment as he charged out of his room and up the hallway to the main staircase. "Huston!" he bellowed.

Another shriek, and more things crashing. He vaulted down the stairs and whipped up the hallway toward the sounds, more servants falling in on his heels as he ran. The butler skidded into sight from the direction of the kitchen just as Michael reached the servants' part of the house.

"Your Grace! That—He's bitten Bradley!"

The plump cook charged past the butler and flung herself into Michael's arms. "It's a murder! He's gone mad!"

Extricating himself from Mrs. Fellows, Michael handed her into the care of the butler. Lancelot looked like a silly, black, carved shrubbery, but the lad didn't have a mean bone in his body. Once Michael had turned the corner and made his way over the fallen table and tea set, he strode into the kitchen.

Bradley stood on the wide worktable as close as he could get to one end, crushed carrots and eggs around him and plopping onto the floor, while Lancelot reared up on his hind legs and growled at the footman from the other side.

"Your Grace!" The servant gulped, a red-stained cloth wrapped around one hand. "I don't know—he went mad! All I did was bend down to pick up the slab of beef he'd knocked to the floor, and—"

"Steady, Bradley," Michael interrupted. Explanations could wait. "Lancelot! Down!"

The poodle dropped to all fours and lowered its head to growl at Michael. Then the animal picked up the chunk of meat to bound past him and up the hallway, accompanied by more sounds of panicked household staff. *Damnation.* He'd been the one to gift his aunt with Lancelot five years ago when he'd returned to London after giving a lecture in Prussia, and in all that time he'd never known the poodle to show the slightest sign of aggression. Something was very wrong.

"Get down from there and let Huston and Mrs. Fellows take a look at your hand," he ordered the footman, then went in pursuit of the dog again.

Following the sounds of shrieking and things breaking, he reached the main hallway again and strode toward the back of the house. Aside from his annoyance with the hand-wringing and panic, this didn't make sense. And if he'd learned one lesson, it was that *everything* made sense. If a known conclusion didn't follow from the formula, then the formula was wrong. This formula, then, began and ended with a young lady who owned a nearly identical poodle to Lancelot.

"Your Grace, your study," a maid rasped, even as Michael realized he hadn't closed the door. *Bloody hell.* He'd failed to follow his own rules.

Something else broke inside, and he stepped into the room. His carefully collected dome of hydrogen had been overturned and cracked. His voltaic pile lay in pieces and a puddle of water. And one of his ruined pages, one of the group he'd been attempting to salvage, drifted down to the floor in a flurry of torn, shaken paper.

He shut the door behind him. Then, distracting the poodle with a tossed block of iron into the corner, he dove forward and grabbed the leather collar. With a yelp the animal tried to twist around on him, teeth bared, but Michael kept his grip still and hard.

"Galahad," he said, in his most commanding voice. "No."

The poodle looked up at him, gave a sad whine, and sat on his haunches.

That was it, then. Instead of calm, well-behaved Lancelot, he'd come home with mad, angry Galahad. Yes, both dogs had been groomed in the same very latest style and were of a similar size *and* had both been disheveled and dripping wet, but for the devil's sake he should have recognized his aunt Mary's companion.

"Huston!" Michael called, and the study door cracked open.

"Your Grace?"

"I need to send a note to Miss Elizabeth Dockering's home." He frowned. "We seem to have traded poodles."

"Oh, thank God, Your Grace. I thought Lancelot had acquired hydrophobia. Or worse."

"Rabies," Michael corrected absently. "Hydrophobia is only a symptom." He shook himself. "Please discover Miss Dockering's address for me."

"I shall inquire, Your Grace."

Yes, he attended sessions of Parliament as his station dictated, but socially he had very little to do with his so-called peers. A bunch of gossipers and wastrels, they were, and attending parties and dinners with them would only take time away from experiments and discoveries of actual import. So no, he had no idea where Elizabeth Dockering resided or who her father might be. What he did have was her dog.

And she had his. Or Aunt Mary's, rather. His aunt had trusted him with Lancelot, and he was damned well not going to disappoint her. Not on the first bloody day, certainly. He looked down at the dog whose collar he still gripped.

"You are going to behave, Galahad. I won't have my staff terrorized and my home destroyed because your mistress allows you to get up to whatever devilry you choose."

The black poodle woofed at him. Sighing, Michael left his wrecked study to find a leash. Evidently the dog was going to have to remain attached to him until it could be returned to its owner. His hydrogen burner would have to wait; something else for which he could thank Bitsy Dockering.

By the time a runner returned to Bromley House it was well

past dark, Galahad had eaten his way through a good quarter of beef flank, and Michael had begun to wonder if he could somehow obtain a vicious dog of his own that could be trained to stay away from his experiments. The presence of this dog had certainly kept the household well away from him for the remainder of the day. It might work wonders for his productivity.

"Your Grace," Huston said, taking a single step into the morning room, where Michael and the poodle had settled. "The runner has left your missive, but evidently Miss Dockering has gone out and isn't expected to return until early morning."

"I don't require her," Michael stated. "I want Lancelot."

"I interrogated the runner, Your Grace, and I gathered that no one in the Dockering household dares to venture close enough to the dog to discover whether it is Galahad or Lancelot. We'll have to wait until tomorrow." The butler sent a wary look at Galahad. "What shall we do with this one tonight? Lancelot has a bed in the east room, but I fear what this beast might do to it."

"So do I. Nor do I wish to go through this again tomorrow. I've already lost half a day." Closing his book and pushing to his feet, Michael tugged on the leash. Galahad stood, stretched, and favored Huston with a low growl. "I'll stow him in the music room," he decided. "Have Bradley put a bowl of water and the rest of my dinner in there for him, and ask Jarrett to join me in my dressing room."

The butler cocked his head. "You're . . . going out, Your Grace?"

"As I recall, Miss Dockering is attending the Sommerset ball. I received an invitation to the very same fete. I'll go, have a word with her, and arrange for her to return Lancelot to me in the morning. Then she can have her own demon back, and in the meantime perhaps I'll be able to finish setting up the tubing for my restructured lamp."

"Of course, Your Grace." The butler backed up so quickly he nearly fell out the door. "I'll fetch Jarrett immediately."

Michael led Galahad out to the garden again, and then upstairs and down the hallway to the music room. The dog could eat the pianoforte, he supposed, or the chairs, but beyond that there wasn't much available into which the poodle could sink his teeth. Since he'd deduced the animal's identity it had at least listened to him, but as no one else would go near it, this mess needed to be resolved quickly. Certainly before Lancelot could be induced to mimic the other lad's poor behavior. That was only one of several things about which he didn't wish to have to inform his aunt.

"Is your dance card filled yet?" Anne Caufield asked, giggling as she dashed between Lord and Lady Fellbrook to take hold of Elizabeth's forearm.

"I've only just arrived this minute," Elizabeth answered, grinning. "Good heavens, how is anyone supposed to dance in this crowd? We'll all have to move in the same direction at the same time like a school of fish!"

"I know! It's glorious, isn't it?"

"I'm only glad I wore yellow, so if I fall to the floor someone might notice and not trample me." Elizabeth chuckled, swirling to make the green and blue beads on her yellow skirt sparkle and shine. It was only at the very largest of the Mayfair houses that grand balls such as this could even be held, and the Duke and Duchess of Sommerset had outdone themselves this year—quite a feat in itself.

Sprays of flowers decorated every surface of the ballroom and neighboring rooms, while each of the dozens of candles in the four chandeliers had been placed in holders of crystal glass that sent sparkles of light in every direction. More crystal teardrops dripped in strands from beneath each of the gigantic fixtures.

The orchestra sat above one side of the room on a balcony draped with wisteria flowers, and footmen dressed in yellow and red carried about trays laden with glasses and sweets. Chairs lined the walls and stood around the two fireplaces, but most young ladies avoided sitting—no one wanted to be labeled a wallflower, especially by accident.

"Let me see your card," Anne demanded, handing hers over. "Oh, you truly did just arrive! Only two dances spoken for! Bitsy, I may faint."

"You only have three dances taken, Anne. Shall we stroll in the direction of the desserts table? No doubt we won't make it three steps before we're swarmed by so many young gentlemen we'll have to swat them away."

When Anne nodded, her round face lighting up with another excited smile, Elizabeth took back her card, removed the pencil from her reticule, and put her arm around her friend's.

Her parents had already vanished into the crowd, but she had no doubt Lord and Lady Mardensea would leave her to her own devices tonight. She never lacked for partners, or suitors, and if anything, she'd been proving to be even more popular during her second Season than she had during her first.

It all took a great deal of effort, of course, but she could see the worn bits of fabric, the mechanisms by which the *haut ton* measured their own. And the less mystifying it was, the easier she found it to navigate. All the while making it look as effortless as possible, of course.

Within two minutes every space on her dance card had been taken by an eligible gentleman. Thank goodness for the card, for on nights like this she would never have been able to keep straight which young man she would be partnering with for which dance. As Geoffrey Hillstead handed Anne's card back to her friend, Elizabeth smiled. Unless she was greatly mistaken, Geoffrey would be offering for Anne in the next few weeks—and obvious as his infatuation was, she would have been willing to put money on that wager.

"Who has your first waltz, Bitsy?" Anne asked. "Though I don't know why you've given Lord Peter the second one. The second one is always more memorable."

"Every dance is equally memorable," she quipped, "though not always for the best of reasons. But I've given Lord Danton the first waltz, as he was the first one to get hold of the pencil."

"That's not very romantic," her friend noted. "I'm beginning to think you don't care at all for any of the men so ardently courting you."

Elizabeth smiled, taking Anne's arm in hers again. "I'm certainly not head over heels for any of them," she whispered, hoping her friend would take the hint and keep her own voice down, "but there's always the chance that in becoming better acquainted with one gentleman or another, I might become so."

Anne sighed. "Yes, I agree. Several of them are not so very impressive on first acquaintance. But I overheard you chatting with Diane the other day. I hope you truly don't think marriage is *all* a matter of commerce. Not for young ladies like us, who don't have to wed in order to support our families or ourselves."

"Oh, Anne. It's not commerce for *us* in those instances, but it still may be so for the man who requires our family's income to keep himself in cravats and ponies, or a father-in-law's good name to get him invitations to the best gentlemen's clubs." She shrugged. "So, yes, generally some sort of trade or exchange is involved."

"That may be true, Bitsy, but I intend to be mad for whichever gentleman offers for me. Then the commerce part won't matter."

That seemed both silly and darling, so Elizabeth only smiled as a trio of young ladies pranced up to join them. Sometimes she wished she could see it as simply as Anne Caufield did. And be as content with it. That nagging question, though, remained—how could she know, if she fell in love, that it was reciprocated? That one or the other of them, somewhere, even in the smallest place at the back of the most fleeting thought, didn't have a second reason for a union? Or even if that reason *was* secondary?

Oh, dear. Now her head would begin aching, and she would never sleep tonight no matter how much dancing and visiting and laughing she did. To Anne such things didn't matter, so long as she could be in love. It shouldn't matter to Elizabeth, either, and she should be grateful and thankful that her family was well-off enough that she could even be tormenting herself this way. And yet there she stood, tormented.

"Ah, I just realized what the trouble was here," Lord Peter Cordray said, slipping into the middle of the circle of young ladies. "I was over there." He pointed toward the main hallway. "Now I'm here, and all is well."

"I see you have both sleeves attached this evening, my lord," Florence commented, and everyone laughed.

Lord Peter laughed, as well, but he didn't seem all that amused. Elizabeth put her fingers on his arm. "I apologize again for Galahad. I've locked him in my bedchamber with the barest of suppers as punishment."

He smiled at her. "I do find it wondrous, that you and Galahad could be such close companions and yet so completely opposite in temperament. Have you saved me a waltz?"

Anne leaned forward. "Oh, yes. The second waltz of the evening."

Lifting one eyebrow, he swept Elizabeth an elegant bow. "I am honored. And very pleased."

She eyed him. "You please easily."

"Or perhaps he's feeling bolder because your guard isn't about," Anne's sister Alice suggested.

"Galahad is formidable," Lord Peter conceded, his smile stiffening just a little, "but I have made it my goal to win him over. We'll be fast friends before you know it."

"I will wager anyone ten quid that Cordray gets bitten in the next fortnight." Tom Hillstead pulled the money from his coat pocket and waved it in the air.

"I am not taking that wager," Humphrey James countered. "That's throwing away good money."

"Very amusing, the lot of you." Peter faced Elizabeth again. "You wouldn't, perchance, have another dance for me this evening, would you? A quadrille, perhaps?"

"I'm afraid my dance card is full. If any gentleman should fail to appear or be forced to dance with his sister instead of me, I shall look upon you as his second."

Lord Peter inclined his head. "You wouldn't care to give me that list for a moment, would you?"

She chuckled. "I would not."

"Ah. Well, you can't fault me for trying."

After that the first dance began, and she hopped about for ten minutes with Humphrey James. Thank goodness the Duchess of Sommerset had divided the dancers into three groups, or by the time everyone had their turn at prancing through the line they would have been well into tomorrow. Panting, Elizabeth applauded with the rest of the mob, then stepped backward before Humphrey could offer to bring her a ratafia and she would be stuck chatting with him until the next set began.

The next hour proceeded like that, swirling and hopping and stepping and clapping until she felt quite dizzy and her toes began to hurt. They'd been stepped on at least four times, but only twice by dance partners. By now the heat in the room had become stifling, too many people all crammed into one space, most of them dancing and all of them chatting and eating and drinking. There were moments she felt like the head of a drum, thumped and rattled and reverberating with noise.

Turning around, she made for the refreshment table. As she glided through the crowd, to her left an odd, low-pitched murmur began. Someone unexpected had arrived at the Sommerset ball, then. Prinny, perhaps? Or the Duke of Wellington? If it *was* Wellington, her father would keep them there all night while he and the duke reminisced about their time together in India. Poor Mama.

A smile to a harried-looking footman earned her a fresh glass of Madeira, and she hummed a little as she went to find her circle of friends. The waltz with Peter Cordray would be next, followed by another country dance, a cotillion for the older set, and one more quadrille. And then she could return to her parents' coach and take off her shoes, thank goodness.

"Miss Dockering."

She blinked away her daydream of stretching out her toes and looked up. At first glance the tall, fit gentleman with the brown hair, its waves rendering it both disheveled and at the same time attractive, looked familiar if not quite placeable, in a way that made her breath catch a little. His gray coat was well-fitted, as was his fashionable green waistcoat embroidered with peacocks, and as were his black trousers. Dark brown eyes, one of them presently narrowing a touch as he regarded her from beneath curved brows . . . Oh, she recognized *that* look. Quickly she dipped a curtsy. "Your Grace."

"Miss Dockering," the Duke of Woriton repeated, inclining his head.

What in the world was he doing here? She'd been out for two years now, and couldn't at this moment recall a single party she'd attended where he'd also been present. This didn't seem at all like a coincidence, then. As he continued to look at her and not speak, evidently she was supposed to figure out the circumstances all by herself. Well, *she* hadn't taken herself somewhere unexpected and then confronted a young lady who happened to be having a very pleasant evening. "Your Grace," she repeated, keeping her expression mild.

"Miss Dockering. I have something of yours in my possession," he stated in a clear, deep voice. A group of ladies behind him immediately lifted their fans and began chittering to each other.

Good heavens. "You can't say such things," she hissed.

"Whyever not? You are also in possession of something very dear to me. Have you not yet deciphered what it is?"

The music for the waltz began, and she grabbed his hand to pull him to the dance floor. "I am sorry Galahad was too familiar with your dog, and that you fell into the Serpentine," she said, keeping her voice low.

The duke glanced at the people around them. "Are we dancing now?"

"Yes, we are, Your Grace," she returned, her teeth still clenched. "Put your hand on my waist. It's a waltz. Do you know the step—"

"Ah."

His warm hand cupped her waist, his long fingers closed over hers, and abruptly they were waltzing—in the correct direction, and with the correct steps. He wasn't by any means old, but given the rarity of his presence at soirees, she expected him not to be familiar with anything more modern than the cotillion. "You cannot go about saying we've exchanged gifts or that I've won your heart, for heaven's sake. We are not betrothed."

His brows lowered. "What? My heart remains in my own chest. You have my dog, Miss Dockering. Lancelot. Or my aunt's dog, rather. Haven't you noticed?"

He'd been walking his aunt's poodle. It didn't signify, of course, but for the briefest of moments she thought that very kind of him. "You're mad, Your Grace. I'm sorry to say it, but that is a very poor ruse if you wish to pay . . . court to me, or something." She felt her cheeks warm, though she had no idea why. "I will not—"

"Lancelot is a very well-mannered dog who sits, lies down, and stays on command," he interrupted. "When I returned home with the poodle I assumed to be Lancelot, he bit a footman, ate my steak dinner off the table in the kitchen as it was being prepared, and then found his way into my study, where he knocked over a return full of hydrogen gas, tore apart my voltaic pile, and ate my notes on the decomposition of chlorine gas. What conclusion would you draw from that evidence?"

That did sound somewhat familiar. And now that she considered it, Galahad had been on his best behavior all afternoon and evening. She'd put it to his being embarrassed about the mess at Hyde Park, but he'd only wagged his tail even when Peggy had dropped the hairbrush close beside him. "I know my own dog," she said anyway, because anything else would mean that she'd put Galahad in the hands of a complete stranger.

"I admit that I assumed Lancelot would be the victim rather than the aggressor in their mounting-and-domination performance, but at least I have admitted my error. Don't be bird-witted about it, Miss Dockering."

Bird-witted. "I am not bird-witted, Your Grace," she snapped. "Galahad has his faults, but he also has every right to them. He was stolen as a puppy, and the thief who took him beat him horribly. I therefore accept his idiosyncrasies, even if they occasionally involve him being unexpectedly pleasant. If only you suffered from that same malady, yourself."

He looked at her. "I concede that an unexpected pleasantness is easier to accept than an unexpected malice," the duke said after a moment, keeping his gaze on hers in a way that felt like he listened to and assessed every word she spoke, every sound and movement she made—looking for additional ammunition for their sparring match, no doubt, except that his words now seemed . . . kind. "And that perhaps it's even something to be welcomed. I cannot fault you for that."

That, it had been, she realized, shaking herself free of other, less helpful thoughts. Yes, she'd confined Galahad to her bedchamber, but he hadn't seemed to mind. In fact, he'd curled up on his large pillow in a rather contented manner. Of course, now she knew why; it hadn't been Galahad. "I still think you are very likely mistaken," she said anyway.

"The two animals are almost identical." The duke lifted his gaze from her face for a moment to look past her. "Lord Peter Cordray does not look happy," he stated. "Did I take his dance?"

Oh, dear. She'd actually forgotten about the marquis's brother for a moment—but who could blame her after she'd just discovered that Galahad was in the Duke of Woriton's custody? Even if her poodle was the reason Lord Peter Cordray had been promised a dance and was currently standing to one side of the ballroom as he glared at them. "You did," she admitted, "but I couldn't have you talking about you possessing something personal of mine in front of everyone."

"I was discussing dogs," Woriton countered, as if that sufficed as an explanation. "And you said I was ridiculous this afternoon, while I called you a dressmaker's mannequin. That does not seem to me to be the language of courting. I don't know why you would think otherwise."

"True enough, but not everyone knows what we spoke of during our earlier encounter. Only that some . . . unusual events occurred. And your appearance tonight will only cause that talk to spread."

"I suppose a man being dragged into the Serpentine isn't an everyday occurrence," he conceded.

Humor? She thought perhaps she'd misunderstood, until his mouth curved up at the edges just a little. "Falling into the water amused you?"

"It would have amused me less if the acid vial I had in one pocket had broken and dissolved my trousers."

"I'm certain the ducks and fish are also grateful."

He tilted his head a little. "You are unusual."

She didn't know if that was a compliment or an insult, but considering the source, it would seem to be the former. "Thank you."

That led to a moment of silence between them, which gave her time to note that his brown eyes had tiny flecks of green in them, and that a faint stubble shadowed his cheeks, as if he'd neglected or forgotten to shave for the ball. Elizabeth took a deep breath. *Stop looking at him.* "To return to our earlier conversation, you have to be aware that you can't say things to a young lady that sound as . . . intimate as claiming you have possession of something precious to her. There's nothing the wags love more than taking a silly moment and using it to tear a proper young lady down. I will not take that risk."

"I have a direct manner," he stated. "It's a flaw of mine, I'm told. I find all the talking in circles around a subject to be exhausting. And wasteful, when one has better things to do than suffer through two hours complimenting a dowager's bird-covered hat."

Surprised yet again, Elizabeth snorted, swiftly covering the sound with a cough. "You sounded very offended," she noted. "It must have been a supremely unattractive hat."

"It was hideous, and resting on the head of my aunt's dearest friend. I had no means of escape. Haven't made that mistake again, though. I try to learn from those."

It wasn't just his conversation that seemed intimate. His grip on her hand and his palm on her waist made her feel more . . . aware of him than she was accustomed to. The typical politeness of manners provided a barrier of sorts to a more personal connection, she supposed, and he possessed none of that.

"Do you wish to exchange animals in the park tomorrow?" he asked, the abrupt change of subject making her blink, "or should I call on you at Dockering House? I sent you a note earlier this evening, but your butler said you'd gone out. I surmised it would be here, after your discussion with your fellows."

"You were listening to my conversation with my friends?"

He lifted an eyebrow. "Wasn't it meant to be overheard? I assumed you wished everyone nearby to know that you would be attending the Sommerset ball."

Her cheeks warmed all over again, this time from embarrassment. "Of course that was the reason, but no one is supposed to admit it."

"Ah. A confidence for a confidence, then. I'm only here tonight because I neglected to send my regrets, though I imagine Sommerset wouldn't have shut the door on my face." He gave a swift grin. "Hydrochloric acid decomposes iron."

Elizabeth stared at his transformed countenance, stunned at the difference a full-on smile could make even on someone as pleasantly featured as he was, then cleared her throat when she realized she must look like a gawping pigeon. "That's very interesting, I suppose."

"It is, when you're a general on the battlefield in France and wish quietly to disable the enemy's cannons."

"I . . . Oh." She'd heard that tale, of course, the one where the Duke of Sommerset had had an entire French brigade surrender to him without a shot being fired because their cannons had somehow melted overnight. "That was you?"

He shook his head. "That was Nicholas. Sommerset, rather. I only sent him some well-packed bottles and a letter."

"Even so."

"I have some cleaning of my laboratory to do this evening," he said, evidently tired of the subject of his sideways heroics. "I mean to leave after this waltz is finished. So, Hyde Park or Dockering House, and at what time?"

Previous to this dance she would have chosen the park, of course; duke or not, she didn't know him well enough to grant him a privileged place among her gaggle of suitors by inviting him to her home—even if he was a great deal more interesting than she'd expected. And even if he said things for which she hadn't already rehearsed an answer.

Dancing well and having unexpected and stimulating conversation didn't make him a beau, of course, but it was an improvement over the off-putting madman he'd been that afternoon. "Considering how our last meeting at Hyde Park went, I think you should call on me at Dockering House. At eleven in the morning, shall we say?"

Woriton nodded. "That will give me adequate time to separate more hydrogen for my lamp modification, so, yes. Eleven o'clock, Dockering House."

He repeated the facts as if he was committing them to memory, which made her wonder whether he would forget to make an appearance at all. Or, even more interesting, if he wouldn't forget.

CHAPTER THREE

GALAHAD WAS CLOSED IN BITSY'S BEDCHAMBER. LORD PETER CORDRAY took in that bit of information as Miss Dockering promised him the second waltz and then glided off for a country dance with the unimpressive Humphrey James. He could stand and watch, of course, or do a good turn by one of the wallflowers looking about so hopefully for any man to show them the slightest bit of interest, but he didn't wish to look like either a lovestruck idiot or a desperate one.

He opened his pocket watch. It was early in the evening for the rendezvous he'd arranged, but hopefully the weasel would be there waiting, looking for scraps. Peter left the ballroom and made his way through the less-crowded solarium. Those doors stood wide open to the garden, no doubt in the hope that some of the cool air outside would find its way inside to the overheated revelers. Padding down the trio of stone steps, he stopped by a torch to light his cheroot and take a puff.

The Sommerset garden was large, as was everything about the property. It even had a pond with goldfish swimming about in the far corner, beneath an overhanging vine of wisteria and beside a set of benches. Making his way down the length of the garden, he sat on the stone bench facing the house and its bright, welcoming windows.

Peter didn't want a fish pond. Or even a gigantic town house that would mean hiring thirty servants just for its upkeep. All he wanted was a diamond, and the more modestly sized Mayfair home her dowry would provide. "Are you here?" he said into the air, smoke curling around the words.

"We agreed you was supposed to say something about the moon, so's I would know it's you." The male voice came from somewhere in the undergrowth to his right.

"I'm the only one out here," Peter replied with a deep breath. "And you already know it's me, because I spoke to you this afternoon. Come out of the shrubbery, you half-wit."

Leaves rustled and shook, and a tall, thin man unfolded himself to lurk just outside the edge of the firelight that the scattered torches provided. "There's no call for you to insult me, Yer Lordship," Jimmy Bly said, keeping the brim of his tweed cap low to shade his eyes. "You came to me, if you'll recall."

"I do recall." Pulling a pencil and paper from his pocket, Peter wrote out an address, then handed it over.

Bly looked down at the note. "I don't read, Yer Majesty."

"Oh, for God's sake." Taking a breath, he reclaimed the paper. No sense leaving evidence lying about unnecessarily. "Do you know where Chesterfield Hill is? The street, I mean."

"I can find it. I found here, after all, and Mayfair ain't my usual go-about."

"Dockering House is on Chesterfield Hill, between Hay's Mew and Hill Street. It has white roses all along the front, and a large letter 'D' over the door." He drew the letter and held it up. "This is a 'D.'"

"So it is."

"The dog is in one of the upstairs bedchambers. Go up the

staircase leading from the kitchen, turn left, and it's the third door on the right."

"A poodle, you said."

"Yes. A vicious, black one, nearly the size of a sheep. I suggest you bring one stout rope to bind its muzzle, and a second one to tie it up like a hog. Don't kill it yet; I may need to perform a rescue or something later."

"If I don't get the rest of the money from you like you promised, Yer Lordship, I reckon I'll do whatever I want with the beast. I know some fellows who'll take a dog and sell it back for twenty quid or more."

Peter was not about to have this ruined over twenty pounds. He pulled a bank note from another pocket. "You'll hear from me," he said, handing it over. "Do nothing with that dog but keep it alive. Do you understand me, Mr. Bly?"

Bly pocketed the blunt. "I understand you. I get the dog, you get the girl, and I get another twenty quid, because this money don't count."

"It doesn't? I don't think you kn—"

"It's just some goodwill, from you to me. I'll be off, then, before any of you fine folk head for home. Jimmy Bly, he don't get caught."

Jimmy Bly, he did talk a great deal. Peter watched the man shove back into the bushes and then presumably over the back wall of the garden. Remaining where he was, he finished his cheroot and watched the goldfish swim aimlessly about. A faint quadrille played inside, and with a sigh he pulled another smoke from his pocket. Everyone would be talking about his torn sleeve this evening, laughing and teasing about how he'd never make any headway with Bitsy while she had that blasted poodle around.

He'd been courting Elizabeth Dockering since midway through last Season. She wasn't in a hurry to wed, which made sense given her social and monetary status. Neither was he in a rush, but with several young men now making entries in the betting book at White's as to the odds of their success in marrying the chit, he couldn't afford to do nothing.

In fact, he would have settled it already, except for one thing he hadn't anticipated. The main obstacle between him and a marriage with Bitsy had become her damned poodle. He'd brought treats for the dog. He'd thrown sticks for the beast. He'd gone out of his way to be pleasant and good-natured to bloody Galahad. And still the poodle never missed a chance to bark or growl or bite at him. As a result, he'd begun a slow slide away from the position of most-favored suitor to object of pity and ridicule. That could not stand.

Therefore, a wander through Covent Garden and chancing to witness one mop-haired Jimmy Bly picking someone's pocket had felt like providence. It was simple mathematics; Galahad subtracted from Bitsy equaled a marriage between Bitsy and Peter. He could play the hero, supportive of her as she mourned the loss of her dog, becoming her de facto protector against the circling men of Mayfair. Hell, he could even offer to pay a reward should Galahad be recovered.

For a time, he mused on the very pleasant prospect of adding Bitsy Dockering and her family's wealth and reputation to his own. Finally, dropping his second cheroot into the fish pond, Peter returned to the house. As he reached the ballroom, a flourish of music announced the second waltz of the evening. Perfectly timed, then. She would be to one side of the dance floor with her usual gaggle of friends and admirers, waiting with a clever word to chastise his near tardiness.

Except that she wasn't waiting for him to one side of the ballroom. She was on the dance floor, gabbing with a tall man who then put his hands on her and stepped with Bitsy into the dance. His dance. Peter narrowed his eyes as the couple turned and her partner came into view. Michael Bromley, the Duke of Woriton. *Bloody hell.*

Yes, she gave away dances if her partner was tardy. Everyone knew that. But the music had just begun. Couples were still making their way to the floor. Peter glared at them all for a moment. He'd wager none of them had pesky dogs, or eccentric lords, standing between them and happiness.

Even so, it might have been worse, he reminded himself. Bitsy might have chosen to dance with one of the Hillstead brothers, and both of them had been paying her attention nearly as long as he had. Whatever the devil Woriton was doing in public, this wasn't the duke's world, and Peter doubted even Bitsy's popularity could make his rude manner more palatable to their fellows.

He hadn't lost anything. This was merely a delay. And he'd have cause to ask another favor of her, since she'd given away his waltz. Perhaps he'd arrange to call on her tomorrow, so he could be surprised and angry that someone had dared make off with Galahad. He would be the first shoulder on which she could cry. With that in mind, he was willing, albeit reluctant, to miss a waltz.

Hands in his pockets, head down, Jimmy Bly walked up Chesterfield Hill past the quartet of houses between Hay's Mew and Hill Street. He paused for a moment as a coach rolled past, then turned around and retraced his steps.

Housebreaking. He'd thought about it, from time to time, mostly when he set eyes on some fancy cove and his missus all covered in shiny jewels as they left Vauxhall Gardens or Drury Lane Theatre. So many jewels, when just one or two could keep him in bread and beer for months. It was damned tempting, especially when anyone could see they had more blunt than they knew what to do with.

The street cleared again, and with a quick breath he dodged into the shadows close against the house with the white roses along the front and the big "D" over the door. A few of the upstairs windows had dim light behind them, and those no doubt belonged to the fancy folk out dancing tonight and not yet returned for the evening. Downstairs was dark, so the servants likely had gone to bed or at least down to the kitchen until their master returned.

Cordray had told him to use the stairs by the kitchen, but that was because only guests and other important folk used the front door. The back door was for servants and delivery folk and house-breakers. Jimmy Bly, though, wasn't going to walk into the kitchen just because His Lordship thought that was where he belonged, and because grand people never thought about those who worked for them.

Stepping onto the portico, he slowly pushed down on the front door handle. It gave way, because even worse than a butler not getting to the door in time to welcome home his master would be a butler who locked the door against the owners. Aye, this wasn't dipping into pockets, which was the crookedest he'd cared to get until now, but the things that made sense *always* made sense. And forty quid, plus that goodwill twenty quid, to nab a dog for a few days made a lot of sense.

A nice silver tray sat on the side table as he slipped inside and shut the door behind him. Cordray had said not to take anything but the poodle. He likely wouldn't have anyway, because trays or jewelry could be recognized, while a few coins from some cove or other's pocket couldn't be. Dogs would be easy to spot, too, but tonight he was a dog taker, anyway.

He waited for a bit; then, not hearing anything, he continued up the curved staircase to the first floor. Just the foyer was the size of the room he rented from Widow Vixing, and it looked nicer, too. Mary Vixing would have a place this size rented out to fifty or sixty people, he imagined, though his estimate might have been low. A frugal woman, Widow Vixing was.

It took him a minute to find the top of the servants' stairs, but that was where he had directions from, and he didn't want to be wandering about opening doors when there could well be a younger daughter or son who'd stayed home from the soiree. That was territory he didn't want to be treading in.

He stopped at the third door on the right. Information about dogs had never been of much importance to him. Mostly he knew that a dog could hear and smell better than a man, was faster than a man, and would eat just about anything. And that they had sharp teeth and strong jaws. Blowing out his breath, he pulled the cloth from his pocket and unwrapped it. The damned thing had cost him three shillings, but Cordray, as he'd introduced himself, had said the poodle liked beef, and he'd reckoned that a dog in such a household would be spoiled, and so he'd gotten the best cut of beef the butcher had had to hand.

The laudanum he'd poured over it had cost another small fortune, but a barking dog in a quiet house would never do. Jimmy took another breath, held it, then cracked open the door, threw in the beef, and shut it again.

On the far side the dog growled, then huffed, and toenails padded across the wooden floor. Some licking and swallowing sounds followed, and Jimmy sank down to sit against the door. How long this would take, whether it would work at all—well, that was a set of wagers he'd made with himself. Ten minutes or so, he'd guessed, and he'd used a substantial amount of the laudanum because Cordray had said the poodle was the size of a sheep and meaner than the devil.

They hadn't discussed the how of making off with this Galahad, but as he was supposed to be unseen and the dog unharmed, this was the best that had occurred to him. He was no educated nobleman, but by his thinking, this was a sound enough plan. Or so he would discover in another few minutes.

After he'd waited a bit and then said the Lord's Prayer to himself twenty times to be sure he wasn't rushing things, he reached up over his shoulder and rattled the door handle. Nothing stirred on the far side of the door. "Here we go, Jimmy," he murmured to himself, standing again and crossing his fingers against an angry dog lying in wait, teeth bared, just inside the room.

Little by little he edged the door open—until he bumped against a pile of black, curly fur. Jimmy bumped the dog again, but it only snored. Grinning, he closed himself inside the room and pulled the coil of rope from around his waist. As he tied the jaws closed the dog opened one eye, shiny in the faint candlelight, then snuffled and shut it again. The poodle might wake enough to know he was being tied up and moved, but hopefully with the laudanum it wouldn't give a damn where it was going.

Once the legs were bound, he squatted down, bent and heaved the heavy animal across his shoulders, and staggered to his feet again. Before this, the biggest thing he'd ever plucked from someone's pocket had been a snuff box. Now he was a cracksman, sure enough, breaking into a fine house and making off with a proper lady's dog.

At least it paid well, and no harm would come of it. The lady would be without her dog for a time, and he guessed that was so Cordray could court her proper, but the poodle was to be kept safe by him so they could all be reunited. He did favor a good romance. "Come along, Galahad," he whispered, and slipped back into the hallway. One job done, three days to wait, and another twenty quid to collect. Well done, Jimmy Bly.

If Michael Bromley had had any doubts about the poodle's true identity, the way Galahad barked and his puffball tail wagged with ludicrous speed as the Woriton coach stopped before Dockering House would have laid them to rest. The dog knew where home was, and he was ecstatic to return there.

Now that he knew the boy had been stolen and abused previously, a great deal of his so-called vicious nature made more sense. Strangers, nervousness, aggression, unexpected movement—all those things meant danger to Galahad. This morning he'd made an effort to calm the dog and gain a little trust, and while he wouldn't say he and the poodle had become fast friends, they had certainly reached an amiable understanding.

"Let's go, my boy," he said, taking a firm hold of the lead and letting Galahad exit the coach ahead of him.

He started to tip his hat as two young ladies crossed his path, then realized he'd forgotten to wear one. The things were a damned bother, anyway. With his hand halfway to his head already, though, he settled for a half salute that made the women giggle as they continued on their way. *Hm.* At least he'd remembered his pants.

The door remained shut as he and Galahad reached it, which didn't make the dog at all happy. As the big boy scratched and whined at the heavy oak, Michael lifted the brass knocker, shaped like a horse's head with a bit in its teeth, and tapped it against the door.

Nothing. Frowning, he pulled out his pocket watch. Miss Dockering had said eleven o'clock, and it was precisely that. Knowing he had a tendency to arrive far too late for any given appointment, he'd even left Bromley House early and then had to order the coachman to drive around the block once in order to manage it.

This morning he'd separated another bowl of water into its separate elements thanks to a stronger voltaic pile and assigning Galahad a pillow in one corner of the study, and the receiver of hydrogen presently sat upside down in a shallow plate of water waiting for him to resume experimenting on a hydrogen burner. If this worked, he would need a better way to store the hydrogen, and a method to continue producing the gas so as to extend the length of time the burner could be used. Perhaps a continuing supply of water being separated by electrical charge might—

The front door yanked open. "Oh. *Oh!* Galahad. Miss Bitsy!" the butler called, taking a step back into the foyer, "Galahad is returned!"

Miss Dockering herself appeared at the top of the stairs, her blue gown flowing around her as she glided down to the foyer. Last night her light-colored hair had been bound in a tight bun with ringlets at her ears and green ribbons twined throughout, intricate and perfect. This morning, though, her long hair was held in a single ponytail, and wisps had come loose to land across her forehead and be tucked behind her ears, and for a moment he forgot why he'd arrived on her doorstep. Certainly she should always wear her hair in this simpler style, because, well, she looked very fine. Very fine indeed.

"Galahad!" In the doorway she sank to her knees, and the dog leaped into her arms, squirming and whining and licking and vibrating with palpable joy. Elizabeth wept, as well, her eyes red and one kerchief clenched in her hand.

"If Galahad's absence leaves you so distraught," Michael said, scowling at her obvious upset, "you should have asked me to come earlier. I would have, you know." Intense emotion generally made him uncomfortable, but this morning, with her, he had the oddest desire to squat down beside her and offer comfort. Or a hug. Or something kind and warm.

"No, it's not that," she countered, sniffing as the butler offered her a hand and she stood again. "It's . . . Oh, I don't know how to tell you!"

Michael tilted his head. "Miss Dockering, I am much more comfortable with facts than with speculation. What's amiss?" In the back of his mind he wondered if something had happened to Lancelot, but he dismissed the thought as soon as it arose. It was natural to immediately jump to the worst possible scenario, but a far more likely answer would be that his aunt's poodle had whined all night, or had refused breakfast.

She took a visible breath, holding the door open herself. "Please come in, Your Grace."

He stepped into the foyer, handing her Galahad's lead as he did so. Her fingers felt warm as they brushed his, and he stifled the abrupt urge to grip her hand. Whatever had gotten into him today, he well remembered that according to his aunt he was not adept at commiserating, and the odds of him saying something appropriate were less than optimal.

When the butler closed the door behind them, Michael glanced over his shoulder. He hadn't intended on an extended chat; this entire mess had set him back more hours than he cared to contemplate. "If you please, Miss Dockering, I would like to collect Lancelot and be on my way."

"Oh, dear," she breathed, sniffing again. "I'm . . . I arrived home last evening after the ball, and when I opened my bedchamber door, Lancelot was . . . gone."

Something hard thudded in his stomach. "'Gone'?" he repeated. "You mean deceased?"

"No! No. Missing. I'm afraid he's been stolen, my lord."

Stolen. That was unacceptable. "Have you looked for him? He is adept at opening doors."

"Yes, we've looked for him. We've turned the house upside down. And in my chambers, we found a half-chewed piece of beef that smelled like stringent alcohol. No one here gave that to him."

"Please take me to the room where he was kept, and I would like to see that piece of beef." Michael didn't know if that was the most logical thing to say, but at the moment the look that would be on Aunt Mary's face when he told his closest relative—the woman who'd practically raised him—that he'd lost her dog took up most of the space in his mind.

"Y—You want to visit my bedchamber?"

"I would wish to visit the cellar, if that was where you kept him. The ownership and usage of the room is irrelevant."

She blinked at that, but nodded. "Certainly, then. This way. Crawford, where is the meat? Fetch it for us, if you please."

The butler grimaced. "I asked Vincent to see to it, miss, but I'll recover it if I can."

"At once, please. The Duke of Woriton wishes to examine it."

The older man sent Michael a glance that very clearly said gentlemen did not visit ladies' bedchambers. "Of course, Miss Bitsy. And I'll fetch Peggy, as well."

The butler was incorrect about men being in women's bedchambers, but as this visit concerned not animalistic urges but an actual animal, Michael only nodded. "After you, Miss Dockering."

Walking sideways to keep him in view, Elizabeth Dockering started up the stairs. "We have looked, Your Grace," she said.

"I don't doubt it." And now he seemed to be making her nervous, which was odd both because he'd noticed, and because he disliked the idea of it. He cleared his throat. Chatting. Talking about unimportant, trivial things comforted people. "Galahad doesn't obey your staff?" he asked, noting the dog accompanying them upstairs.

"Generally, they don't get along at all," she said, reaching down to scratch between the poodle's ears. "Oh, I should have realized I had Lancelot rather than Galahad the moment I walked in the door. He looked at Crawford and wagged his tail. Galahad has never done that. And then I should have set the entire staff to watch over Lancelot because he wasn't my dog, and it was my fault in the first place that Galahad got loose in the park yesterday." She frowned. "Well, actually it was Lord Peter Cordray's fault, because he reached for my face, and Galahad doesn't condone that sort of thing."

"I appreciate that in retrospect you would have seen to it that

Lancelot didn't go missing, but your logic involves several things that you couldn't have known before this—whatever it is—happened."

"Whatever logic dictates, I feel very guilty about it," she stated, wiping her cheek again. "And I suppose I feel even worse because my first thought when I couldn't find Lancelot was that I was thankful Galahad hadn't been here to be stolen again. Because if we hadn't gotten our dogs tangled, it *would* have been Galahad who disappeared. And we've already gone through that once, and it was horrible."

"*If* Lancelot was stolen. I still posit that he might have wandered off, trying to find his way home. Speaking of which, I need to send a note to Harris House, to alert my aunt's staff that Lancelot might be on his way there. Do you have pen and paper I may use?"

"Certainly." She looked at him, then shook herself and opened the second left-hand door in the long upstairs hallway. "My bed-chamber. How is it that you're caring for your aunt's dog?"

"Aunt Mary, Lady Mary Harris, has gone visiting, and her host-ess's husband is allergic to dogs."

"I see. It's very kind of you, then. And I suppose it shouldn't make me feel any better that Lancelot isn't yours, but it does." She made another face. "But I'm sure your aunt is very fond of him, so I don't feel any better, really."

Michael had never noticed that one female could have so many expressions, and all of them look so attractive. "Thank you."

He paced about the edges of the room, stopping by each of the three windows to look for any scratches, any signs of tools being used to open the latches, or drag marks, or whatever else he pre-sumed a thief might leave but a household staff would not. And he looked at the back of the door, checking for any teeth marks in the iron door handle or along the edge where Lancelot might have tried to get purchase. It all looked pristine, though, neat as her dark green bed with its surprising number of pillows.

The maid lurched into the room, nearly knocking him backward as he examined the door. She yelped, eyeing him as if he had poison fangs.

"Calm down, woman," he said. "I'm looking for clues, not female underthings."

Miss Dockering snorted, though she once more tried to make it sound like a cough. "Just so, Peggy. We're trying to discover how Lancelot was taken."

"But can't His Grace look somewhere that isn't your private rooms, Miss Bitsy?"

"What purpose would that serve?" Michael asked, shaking his head as he took one last look at the doorframe. "I don't think Lancelot left on his own," he announced, "as long as the door was properly shut with him inside."

"I made certain it was well-closed," Miss Dockering answered. "After his—or what I thought was his—misbehavior yesterday, I didn't want to risk him getting out to frighten the staff."

"And none of us opened the door to give him this," the butler added, stepping into the room, as well. In his extended hand he held a cloth, and atop that a very sad-looking, mangled piece of meat. "Here it is, my lord. I had to rescue it from the bin, I'm afraid."

"No matter." Taking the cloth and its contents, Michael lifted it toward the light from the window. Galahad grunted, pulling against the lead that Miss Dockering held. "Not for you, my boy," he said sternly. Chewed, definitely, and at least partly eaten, despite Lancelot's preference for oat biscuits and baked chicken. Leaning over it, he sniffed. Alcohol, as Elizabeth had said, and something else. Interesting. He brushed a forefinger across the beef, then touched the pad to his tongue.

"Oh, good heavens," Miss Dockering exclaimed, and the butler made a gagging sound. The maid took an abrupt seat.

Michael looked up to find them all staring at him. "What?" He glanced down at his finger. "Oh. Unsavory, but useful. There's a medicinal bitterness about it. Laudanum, if I'm not mistaken."

"Laudanum?" Miss Dockering put her free hand over her mouth. "Oh, no." She tugged on Galahad with her other hand. "You stay away from that."

Though he'd only taken laudanum once, for a toothache when he'd been twelve, the taste, the way it lingered not on his tongue but in the backs of his eyes, was unmistakable. "Someone did take Lancelot, and they planned for a way to keep him from raising a ruckus."

"They meant to take Galahad," Miss Dockering said in a very quiet voice. "Dog takers, housebreakers, in my home. In my bedchamber." She took a shaking breath. "This is awful."

Michael agreed with that. Aunt Mary doted on Lancelot. *He* doted on Aunt Mary. And he owed her a great deal. Losing Lancelot the same day she'd entrusted the poodle to his care . . . No. It couldn't be allowed. "I need to go speak to Bow Street," he said, and inclined his head. "Excuse me."

Damn it all. He wanted to blame Miss Dockering, because Lancelot *had* been in her care whether she'd realized it or not. It wasn't at all logical, but annoyance, impatience, were easier and more familiar than his odd . . . concern over her hurt feelings even though she hadn't actually been injured.

All of that, though, was secondary. Someone had known what he or she was doing, breaking into a house full of servants and drugging a dog to remove him without a single bark. He'd heard of dogs being stolen before, and then being ransomed back to the owner for a steep price, but he'd never given the news much attention.

If this was one of those situations, he could wait to be asked to pay the ransom, go home and work on his burner until summoned. And then he and Lancelot could stay on the grounds of Bromley House until his aunt returned from Cornwall. Or, he could take steps to stop this nonsense that was supposed to have happened to someone else in the first place. For *that,* he could blame Miss Dockering. Stepping outside, he strode for his coach.

"Your Grace?" Elizabeth Dockering, Galahad's lead still securely knotted around her hand, hurried out the door. "I want to help."

"That's not necessary. It was a sad bunch of tangled coincidences, but I certainly don't blame you for it, Miss Dockering." Except for the bit where she'd lost control of Galahad in the park yesterday and allowed all this to happen in the first place, that was, but he seemed to keep forgiving her the second after he blamed her for something. Very indecisive of him, really.

"But listen. Someone took my friend Kitty Parsen's dog, Rex, a fortnight ago. They sent a note asking for twenty pounds. She paid it, and a day later she found Rex tied to her front gate. It could be the same people, couldn't it?"

He paused. "Does Kitty Parsen live in the area?"

"Yes. Just two streets over."

"Then yes, I suppose it could."

She put a hand on his sleeve. "If it *was* the same people, they'll send a ransom note here, for Galahad. I can get it to you, and then we can get Lancelot back." Elizabeth took a half step closer, looking up at his face. "I want to help."

"That isn't necessary," he repeated, his attention arrested by her slender fingers gripping the dark blue cloth of his coat, and the dark green of the irises of her eyes as she gazed at him. *Clover.* Her eyes were the color of new clover. "This should have been your dilemma, but circumstances have made it mine. And I don't intend to wait about. I *will* suggest that in the future you take more care in locking up your home."

With a sigh, she released his sleeve. "Very well. Be angry with me if you wish. I am, as well. But please let me know what happens. And I will certainly inform you if a note arrives."

Even as he turned back for the coach, he had to acknowledge that her offer of assistance, while he didn't actually see how she could possibly help, had been both unexpected and . . . kind. And her tears over Lancelot's loss had seemed genuine. At the least none of her admirers had been present to note her soft heart or the attractive flush of her cheeks, so arousing their sympathies couldn't have been her goal, and he had no sympathies to be aroused. "Bow Street, Adam," he ordered his driver as he climbed into the coach and shut the door.

He knew the location of the City Philosophical Society, with its lecture hall and myriad labs and warren of residences. He knew how to find Parliament, though he tended to avoid the general speech-and-argument sessions, preferring to read any material for himself and without the accompanying bombast, and of course he could find Hyde Park and Boodle's Club where they served a fine beefsteak and he could meet on occasion with fellow science-minded gentlemen like the Duke of Sommerset and Sir John Soane.

Bow Street north of Covent Garden, however, might as well have been on the moon for all he knew about it. The Runners chased down lawbreakers, though, and that seemed to be what he required.

When the coach stopped and he stepped out, the building didn't look anything like he expected—which he supposed was something more . . . stately, or official. Instead, it stood unnoticeable and nondescript as any home or shop on the street, except for the stream of men in their simple workmen's coats, small clubs in hand and shackled prisoners in tow, and a magistrate or two in his silly powdered wig.

Michael walked inside to stop in front of a desk, one of a dozen or so in the main room of the converted manor house. The man seated on the far side of the cheap oak didn't look up, instead paging back and forth through a litter of papers and drawings.

"I require your assistance," Michael stated, once it became obvious that simply looming there wasn't going to accomplish anything.

The man, ten or so years his senior, he would guess, somewhere in his late thirties or early forties, looked up. "The . . ." He trailed off, Michael watching as the fellow took in his expensive coat, polished Hessian boots, and neatly tied cravat. "Your name, sir?"

"Woriton."

The arm-wrestling match the next desk over stopped, along with a good portion of the head-rattling chatter. They'd been paying more attention to his arrival than it appeared, and he counted that in their favor. The mustachioed man stood up. "Woriton. As in the Duke of Woriton?"

"Michael Bromley. Yes."

"Well, have a seat, then, Your Grace. Excuse the gawking. Most of your ilk send someone else here when they have need of our services." The Bow Street Runner pulled a sheet of paper from the top drawer of his desk. "Stephen Everett, at your service. How can Bow Street help you?"

Michael seated himself. "My aunt's poodle has been stolen."

The pencil scratching out his name and title stopped moving. "I didn't quite hear that. Could you repeat it, Your Grace?"

"My aunt, Lady Mary Harris, entrusted me with the care of her black poodle Lancelot, while she is traveling. Last night Lancelot was taken."

"Are you certain he didn't just leave your house and wander home?"

"He wasn't at my home. He was at Dockering House on Chesterfield Hill, in the custody of Miss Elizabeth Dockering, and yes, I'm certain he didn't wander off."

The scratching resumed, this time with more names and arrows. "How did your aunt's poodle, Lancelot, entrusted to your care, end up at Miss Elizabeth Docking's residence?"

"Dockering. The home of Viscount Mardensea. It was an accident, actually. Her poodle, Galahad, attacked Lancelot in Hyde

Park yesterday, and as we untangled them, we each went home with the wrong dog."

"'Wrong dog.' Write that down, Everett," someone behind Michael urged.

In fact, he seemed to have attracted a great deal of attention, now that he looked about. "When Miss Dockering returned home from a soiree," he explained, "she found Lancelot missing and a chewed-on cut of beef doused with laudanum on the floor of her bedchamber."

Everett looked up. "How did she know it was doused with laudanum?"

"She didn't. I discovered that when I tasted it."

"You tasted it." The Runner made another note. "Of course you did." Blowing out his breath, he set down the pencil. "Here at Bow Street, Your Grace, we look into murders, coach robberies, thefts of valuables, arsons, and a dozen other things. There are about seventy of us, all told. Dognappings ain't on the list."

"And why is that?"

"We'd have time to do nothing else, honestly. Dogs run off, get nabbed by neighbors tired of barking, children who want one for themselves, some hungry passerby or other, and, if you're lucky, get grabbed by professionals who send ransom notes and return the pooch for more than it's likely worth. Any of those but the last means the dog don't get found. The last one, well, you're better off not letting anybody know you came to us. At best it'll end up costing you more, and at worst, well, the dog's already been killed so they don't have to risk returning it to you."

That was alarming. Michael dismissed all of the possibilities except for the last one, himself, since Lancelot had clearly been taken by someone who knew how to go about it. At the moment, the dog thieves thought they had taken Galahad, and that they would be dealing with the Dockering family. His trip to Bow Street was therefore unimportant, as far as the lawbreakers were concerned. As they refused to help, he would not be mentioning them again.

The key to all of this, though, remained Miss Elizabeth Dockering. She'd as much as said so, *and* offered her assistance, and because he'd been annoyed that Lancelot hadn't been guarded more carefully and he found her . . . distracting, he'd dismissed her. Another mistake. He seemed to be making a plethora of them today.

Standing, he nodded. "I understand. Thank you, Mr. Everett."

The Runner stood, as well. "If you do happen to discover a ring of dog stealers, I would appreciate you letting me know, Your Grace. But it is best just to wait, I've found."

"Waiting is certainly the easiest course of action," Michael returned. "I doubt whether it's the most effective."

CHAPTER FOUR

PETER CORDRAY LOOKED AT HIS REFLECTION IN HIS FOYER MIRROR, then pulled the daisy from his buttonhole and set it aside. It was tricky, being prepared to be solemn and comforting without looking either too frivolous or too grave beforehand.

"If you're offering marriage today, I would go with the daisy," his brother said from the doorway down the hall. "And a bigger smile." The Marquis of Plasser handed over a satchel to the butler as he reached the foyer. "Or are you going to church? You look very solemn, Peter."

Damnation. "Yes, I do look solemn, I suppose," he agreed, turning for the stairs. "Perhaps a yellow waistcoat would better suit." On the other hand, the daisy added lightness, and could be strategically removed at the correct moment. Frowning, he turned around again.

His older brother chuckled. "What the devil are you so nervous about? You didn't even claim your waltz with the chit last evening, and after you told us to watch for it. I'd say you have several more steps to climb before you venture a proposal." Arthur Cordray pulled on his gloves and set his hat on his head before reclaiming his satchel. "And for God's sake, don't ask until you're assured of the answer. No other woman wants to be a second choice, and popular as Miss Dockering is, everyone will know what's occurred."

"Yes, thank you so much for the advice. Without you saying the obvious, I certainly never would have considered any of this on my own."

The marquis tipped his hat as the butler opened the front door for him. "Don't be petulant, Peter. And Lady Plasser would like you to join her for luncheon, as I have a meeting."

"I have an appointment," Peter countered, jamming the flower back into his lapel.

Arthur stopped halfway through the front door. "My wife has asked you to join her for luncheon," he repeated. "Need I remind you that she prefers the country to London, and familiar company to that of mere acquaintances? Or that while you're under my roof, you are my second?"

Peter hid his grimace; it would only cause more trouble. "No. And I appreciate your generosity in allowing me to live at Cordray House with you and Millicent." And he would be even more appreciative when he had his own house in Town and his own wife—and no damned poodle.

By limiting his responses to "yes" and "of course," he managed a quick luncheon with Millicent, though he didn't have much of an appetite as she droned on about how she longed for the peace of a Derbyshire afternoon and time for her precious embroidery.

He managed to do nothing but nod as she found fault with every eligible young woman in London who enjoyed dancing and taking walks, even when she got around to Elizabeth Dockering and how shamelessly that female waltzed about with a carefree smile and men draped all over her. The marchioness was another reason he'd set his gaze on Bitsy—Miss Dockering was the exact opposite of Millicent in every possible way.

With the abuse he'd handed the buttonhole daisy it had become rather sad-looking by the time he rode up to the front of Dockering House, and he pulled it free and dropped it to the ground as he dismounted. Overly somber would have to do, then. No doubt Bitsy would be too overset by the theft of Galahad to notice his attire, anyway. It was only him, and his obsession with every step of this little theatrical endeavor. Peter stifled a smile as he dismounted, handing his gray gelding Shadow over to a groom. A little play in which he would be taking on the role of hero. A part written by him and for him.

The door opened as he topped the pair of shallow steps—and a big black dog darted out at him only to be pulled to a halt just short of his very vulnerable crotch. Yelping, Peter jumped backward, stumbling back down the steps and onto the drive, just barely keeping to his feet and covering his manly parts with both hands.

"Galahad, don't be so naughty," Bitsy chastised, following the dog out the door at speed and hastily winding another length of the lead around her wrist. "Good afternoon, my lord. I'm just going for a stroll. Would you care to join me?"

"I . . . Yes, of course," he stumbled, risking a glare at the dog as the skinny maid followed her mistress outside. *What the devil?* He'd paid Jimmy Bly twenty quid thus far to take Galahad out of Dockering House, plus the additional twenty the idiot had demanded from him last night. And now he couldn't even ask if anything had happened at all. *Damnation.*

"You're lucky to catch us," Bitsy went on with a smile. "Ordinarily we would have been all the way to Bond Street by now, but today has been rather . . . unexpected."

"'Unexpected'?" he repeated, grabbing on to the word and hanging on for all he was worth. "In what way?"

"Someone broke into my home last night, and stole Lady Mary Harris's poodle, Lancelot. It was dreadful."

Peter put on a confused expression, which wasn't at all difficult. "What was Lady Mary Harris's poodle doing here? And isn't Lancelot the name of Woriton's poodle?"

"Yes. Well, Woriton has been looking after his Aunt Mary's Lancelot while she's out of Town, so it's actually not his dog at all—though it was very kind of him to care for Lady Mary's poodle while she's away. When we—or our dogs, rather—became entangled at the park, I inadvertently left with Lancelot, while the Duke of Woriton took Galahad." Her mouth pinched in a grimace. "It should have been Galahad stolen last night, but he spent the night safely at Bromley House. Isn't it all horrid?"

So that was what had happened. *Damnation.* At least Bly had done as he'd been told—though he might have bothered to notice that he had the wrong dog. "Yes, of course it's horrid. I don't know what you could have done differently, though," he said, hoping he would still have a chance to be consoling. "As you said, it was only a mix-up that saved Galahad."

"Yes, but that doesn't change the fact that Lancelot is lost. And there's been no ransom note, which is why the duke drove off to Bow Street, trying to find some assistance."

"He went to Bow Street?" The last thing Peter needed was the constabulary becoming involved. And damnation, was he going to have to come up with a ransom note now, too? This mess was getting worse and worse by the moment.

"I offered to help him, but I don't think he's very pleased with me right now."

"I'd hardly let that fact trouble you, Bitsy. Woriton is rarely pleasant on the best of occasions." He gestured for her to proceed, falling in beside her with Galahad yanking on the lead ahead of her. "And you did offer, which is all anyone could expect."

"It is truly the least I could do. Except that I did give my word to pass the ransom note on to him when I receive it, which I expect to do any time now. At least, Kitty Parsen had her note within a day of her Rex being taken." She frowned, slowing her pace. "Why is he—the duke—so . . . determined to be unpleasant? Which is not to say unkind, but rather more . . . blunt, I suppose. The way a hammer is blunt, though."

Peter shrugged. "I don't know him that well. From what my brother has said, he's been that way for some time. If you have nothing of scientific value to offer him, he simply isn't interested in conversing with you, or in pulling you out of a hole if you should fall into one."

Finally, a smile touched her mouth. *Ah, success.* He'd much rather be thought of as clever and a steady arm on which to lean than as the pitiable victim of Galahad's aggression. He would work toward being thought of as a potential spouse, next. Or rather, restore his status and make another attempt at it.

"I think he might well pull someone out of a hole, if he noticed they fell in," she countered, her grin crinkling the corners of her eyes.

If she kept that up, she'd develop wrinkles. Not for some time though, at least. "I say if he doesn't want your help, waste no more time thinking about him."

Her shoulders lifted and lowered. "Yes, of course you have the right of it, my lord. An all-around unpleasant man."

"And you still owe me a waltz," he reminded her, smiling so she could consider it a jest if she chose to do so.

"I do, don't I? So much has happened since last evening, I'd nearly forgotten. Which soiree do you attend next? Weatherby's?"

"Yes, I've been invited."

"Then I shall save you the first waltz."

He would have preferred the second waltz, but then again there weren't always two. "Thank you, Bitsy."

"I do try to pay my debts." She waved at an acquaintance on

the far side of the street. "I just wish there was something I could do for—" Abruptly Galahad turned to the left, pulling hard on his lead. Bitsy sped into a trot, falling in behind him. "I seem to be going this way, now."

Speeding his own steps, Peter caught up to her. "Perhaps you should hire a groom to keep Galahad's lead. I hate the thought of you being pulled to the ground."

"I haven't gone over y—" The dog leaped up through the open door of a coach. Bitsy grabbed on to the door to keep from landing inside, herself. "Galahad!"

"A fortuitous coincidence," the Duke of Woriton said, leaning forward from his seat inside to pet Galahad—who didn't seem at all bitey toward the duke, damn it all. "I appear to have need of you after all, Miss Dockering."

"Oh! Well, good."

Peter scowled. "We're in the middle of taking a stro—"

"Come along, then," the duke interrupted. "And Peggy, as well," he went on, indicating the mousy maid. "That makes things proper, if I recall correctly."

"Well, as Galahad has already decided, I suppose I shall come along for the ride." With a deeper grin than the one with which she'd favored Peter, Bitsy took Woriton's outstretched hand and stepped up into the coach. Muttering something insensible to herself, the maid followed.

Woriton thumped on the ceiling. "Toward Hyde Park, Adam."

As the coach rolled away, Bitsy inclined her head at Peter through the window. "Good day, Lord Peter."

Peter looked after them. *The wrong damned dog.* He needed to go find Jimmy Bly, arrange to have a ransom note delivered from a man who couldn't read or write, and figure out how to get past blasted Galahad. Again.

* * *

Jimmy Bly looked at the tied-up dog lying on his floor. The poodle looked back at him and made a pitiful whimpering sound. "Stop that, now," Jimmy said, and went back to hammering.

It wouldn't do for him to keep Galahad stashed elsewhere and risk someone else stumbling across him, but neither could he keep the dangerous beastie fed and watered in his tiny rented space as it was, the problem being that it was just one room.

"I know you must be thirsty," he went on, standing up another of the planks he'd taken from the fence up the street, the one that used to separate the rear of Frank Gardner's blacksmith's shop from the alleyway. At first he'd worried the wood might smell of horses or cattle and drive the poodle mad, or more mad, rather, but he couldn't detect anything himself except for perhaps a bit of general outdoors manure and piss—though that smell swept through the Rookery, as Widow Vixing called the building, with every breeze. "I've nearly got your quarters finished, Your Highness."

A dog with its own room. It seemed preposterous, and especially so for a dog living temporarily on Maudlin's Rents in Smithfield, but Cordray had warned him at least twenty times how vicious the beast was. And Galahad couldn't be bound at all times; that wasn't fair, or very practical, considering he'd already peed on the wood floor once.

Luckily Jimmy was a fair hand with a hammer, if he said so himself, and as the nails had come with the planks, he'd nearly gotten it finished. The trick was a door, or a way in and out, where he could put food inside without getting his fingers bitten off, and where he could get Galahad in and out as needed when it was time to return the beastie.

His door rattled. At first he thought he'd knocked it loose with the hammering, but then it shook again. "Jimmy Bly? What the devil are you up to in there?"

"Shite in a bucket," he muttered, tossing aside the hammer

and immediately running a hand through his hair. With the Season begun already, he'd nearly given up looking for his downstairs neighbor. His heart beat two times faster. "That you, Sally Pangle?" Grabbing up the poodle, he carried it into the nearly finished pen and then tipped some boards across the remaining opening.

"It is me," Sally answered. "Wondering why you have something that smells like pee dripping from my ceiling and onto my clean wash."

Damn it all. Wiping his hands on his trousers, Jimmy smoothed his hair again, straightened his shirt, and unhooked the metal latch holding his door closed. "I'm sorry for that," he said, leaning into the opening he'd made. "I kicked over a bucket. I'm glad to see you, though."

The tall young lady with a tangle of hair black as a raven's wings piled up at the back of her neck narrowed one gray eye and then crossed her fingers. "Kicking over a bucket's bad luck, Jimmy Bly. And even worse luck for me, because now I have to wash my unmentionables again." She tilted her head, trying to look past his shoulder. "And what are you hammering? You know Widow Vixing don't like us making improvements to our rooms."

Jimmy shrugged, wishing for a moment he could invite Sally inside and offer her some tea. For that, though, he'd need tea. "As a man likes his privacy now and then, I reckoned I'd put up a just a small wall for myself. I'll take it down if it gets her bonnet in a twist."

"You live alone, Jimmy. And if the Widow catches you taking in a tenant, she'll double your rent."

"It's not—I just wanted to fancy the place up a bit, is all." That sounded like something he might do. And if he could avoid it, he didn't want anyone knowing he had a large, well-groomed poodle tied up in his room. He had no idea how many people might start chatting about Miss Dockering's Galahad going missing. The wealthy set seemed to spend most of their time gossiping about each other, from what he could make out.

Sally grinned at him. "Well, let me see it, then."

She did have a lovely smile, warm as sunshine. "Not until it's finished. What say I fetch you a pie this evening to make up for the tipped-over bucket and to buy your silence. Will that do?"

"That'll do. Widow Vixing'll hear no word from me. She'll be back from the market before long, though, so you'd best finish your hammering before then."

Jimmy smiled back at her. "I will. Thank you for the warning."

"Ah, you know how it is, Jimmy. Neighbors have to look out for each other."

He leaned deeper into the doorframe. "Well, this neighbor's glad to see you back again for the Season. I was beginning to wonder how much longer Widow Vixing would keep your room for you."

"I paid her to keep it for me. The last thing I want after traveling up and down the countryside all winter is to come back and have no place to rest my head. Or worse, to find the cove she rented it to while I was gone was a smelly old fishmonger." With a wink she backed away from the door, then, humming, headed for the staircase at one end of the building.

Her hips in her green muslin dress kept his attention until she swayed out of sight. Jimmy shut his door to lean back against it, one hand over his heart. "Sweet, sweet lass," he murmured, reaching back to fasten the latch again.

He jumped as the boards blocking the unfinished opening of his makeshift jail tumbled forward. Muzzle still tied shut and rope tangled around his back and one front paw, Galahad stepped carefully over the pile of wood. His black gaze on Jimmy, he padded slowly forward.

"Oh, no, you don't," Jimmy warned, backing toward the corner.

"I'm bringing a pie to Sally Pangle this evening. You can't murder me before that, Galahad."

With a soft whoomph the poodle sat, then sank onto the floor with his muzzle over his front paws. He still looked huge in the small room, but not even on a dark night would Jimmy have been able to call his pose menacing.

"Are you being clever, then, trying to make me let you loose so you can eat me?" he asked, straightening a little. The poodle's gaze shifted to keep him in view, but it didn't move otherwise. "Hm. Are you thirsty, boy?"

The poodle lifted his head, then lowered it again.

"Well, then. We can try being friendly, I suppose. I'm a reasonable fellow. As long as you mind yourself." Pulling a bowl off the small table that served as his kitchen, he set it on the floor, poured part of a pitcher of water into it, and nudged it toward the dog with the toe of his shoe.

Galahad didn't move until the bowl bumped his nose. Only then did he lift his head, sniff, and then whine again.

"Of course. You need your tongue for drinking, don't you? Just mind your manners, dog. I've no wish to be bit." Moving slowly, he reached out with one hand and tugged at the knot around the animal's muzzle. Another tug, and one of the loops slipped off. "That's enough for a drink, I think," he went on, backing up again. "No teeth, or we're going to have a disagreement."

The dog bent over the bowl and began lapping up the water, not stopping until the container sat empty. Then it looked up at him and whined again.

"More? I'll have to go fetch another bucket from the well or I'll have none for myself. And I'd prefer you go back into your room while I'm gone." He gestured at the half-finished enclosure. "Go on. Get."

The poodle stood up. With a tilt of its head, it walked slowly back toward the corner, tail down, and stepped carefully over the fallen lumber where it went in and sat down again.

"I'll be damned," Jimmy Bly muttered. "I'm beginning to think that that Cordray fellow just don't like dogs. You seem gentle enough to me, boy. But I'm still keeping my eye on you." Bending down, he retrieved a spare bucket. "I'll be back with the water. You stay there. We'll talk about some scraps from the butcher if we're both still alive after."

"Where are we going, Your Grace?" Elizabeth Dockering asked, noting that Galahad had sat on the coach's opposite seat and presently had his head on one of the duke's knees. *Remarkable.*

"You mentioned someone who had a dog stolen and received a ransom note. I would like to speak to this person."

"Kitty Parsen?"

"Yes. Her."

"Did you not have any luck at Bow Street, then?" She'd suspected he wouldn't, but then he'd seemed very certain the constabulary would have Lancelot recovered by nightfall.

He sent her a sideways look. "No, I did not. If Lancelot had been wearing a diamond collar I might have found some cooperation, but alas, he's not a murderer or a smuggler."

"There have been a great many dogs taken over the past year or two. Particularly among our fellows."

"Have there been? I hadn't noticed."

Elizabeth tilted her head, eyeing him, as he sent his gaze out the coach's window. It was a very nice coach, leather well-oiled and body well-sprung, the Woriton coat of arms painted in red on the doors and the coachman in proper red-and-black livery. "Am I wrong in assuming that you haven't noticed a great many things in Society?"

That earned her a pair of keen, assessing brown eyes locked with hers. She liked that; men generally spoke to her bosom. "I suppose I haven't," he said after a moment. "Society is a distraction. A well-walled pasture full of bored people trying to pretend they're doing something important instead of just being loud and colorful." He lifted one eyebrow. "How many more dog thefts have there been?"

"Since you've just called me a brightly garbed sheep, I'm not certain I wish to answer you," she returned, not as offended as she would have been yesterday at hearing his opinion of "her" kind. Galahad liked him, after all. And thus far every sentence he'd spoken to her had been a surprise, when she could carry on both sides of most conversations she'd ever had with her eyes closed and her mind daydreaming about sweets or something.

"Hm."

"'Hm,' what?"

"I keep expecting simpering and blushing, and you don't do it." Brief amusement crossed his lean face. "You have a sharper mind than most of those in your circle, I imagine."

She sat back, crossing her arms, half exasperated and half pleased that someone had noticed something other than her oft poetically praised figure. "That is the worst compliment I've ever been handed. What in the world makes you think I wish to help you any longer?"

"Empathy," he returned promptly, mimicking her pose. "You've experienced Galahad going missing, and as Lancelot was in your care when *he* was taken, you feel some responsibility. And you can well imagine how distraught I—or at least, my aunt—must be at the ordeal."

Perhaps he wasn't quite as obtuse as she'd initially thought. "Very well. And it so happens that I know four people who've had their pets taken over the past few weeks. I will take you to see Kitty, and then you must say something genuinely nice to me if you wish to go on to the next one."

"I'm to pay you in compliments."

"Yes."

"With the caveat that speaking with any additional victims may turn out to be pointless and unnecessary, I agree."

That had been almost . . . sweet? He'd made a space to explain that if he didn't hand her a compliment, it might only be because her assistance was no longer needed—not because she didn't deserve one. At the same time, no man had ever spoken so bluntly or unflatteringly to her before. Ever.

"Kitty resides at Parsen House on Cork Street, then. I will accompany you, because Kitty becomes a watering pot at the slightest provocation. Try not to make her cry, will you?"

His lips flattened. "I'm not a fiend."

No, he wasn't a fiend. Just what he *was,* though, was going to take a bit more conversation and observation to figure out. Yesterday she would have gone out of her way to avoid having to do either. Today, however . . . Well, he made for a very interesting diversion. At the least she meant to discover whether he would make Kitty Parsen cry now that he'd been warned against it.

CHAPTER FIVE

"PERHAPS WE SHOULD LEAVE GALAHAD LOCKED IN THE COACH," Miss Dockering suggested as Michael stepped to the ground in front of Parsen House.

Turning around, he held a hand up for her. "Galahad was evidently the target of the thieves last evening. I don't think you should leave him where he could be snatched, but that's your decision."

One green eye twitched. "Of course. It's only that, well, you've seen how he acts around other dogs. And Kitty's Rex is . . . small."

Michael cracked a grin. "A mouthful, eh?"

"Barely that."

She curled her fingers around his as she stepped down to the ground. Their hands together felt . . . something he couldn't quite describe even to himself, but the search for a word made him forget to offer to take hold of Galahad on her behalf. He shook himself as she released him again. A distraction was what it was. An unasked-for distraction, wrapped around a quest to recover Lancelot so he could return to his work.

"Warmth, or caloric," he said aloud, still after a way to put a name to the odd connection he'd felt, "always gives of itself to a cooler object, cooling itself as it gives warmth away. Caloric cannot help itself; it must always warm others."

"Caloric seems a very generous fellow, then," she said, her brow dipping for a bare moment before she recovered her expression again.

Ah, so he was being odd again. "I only mentioned it because your hand was warmer than mine, so you have given me a bit of your warmth. And that made me wonder if I've also become more pleasant, albeit temporarily."

"I shall let you know if I notice anything," Miss Dockering returned, her mouth quirking.

"Be sure you do."

"The newspapers may even take note," she continued.

Michael cleared his throat. The woman had no fear, and was clearly happy to stand toe-to-toe with him. He could count on one hand the number of people willing to do that. *Fascinating.* "In the meantime——"

"Parliament may declare a holiday," Miss Dockering went on.

"Very amusing. I assume this is retaliation for me dismissing your offer of help and then requiring it again?"

"Oh, yes." She grinned.

"Well, thank God I'm a duke and above feeling embarrassment," he said mildly. "Now. Shall I hold Galahad's lead for you?"

"Yes, thank you." She held up the strip of leather. "Do not allow him to eat Rex."

"You have my word."

The house's butler showed them into the morning room, where a moment later a petite blond woman with a cherubic face and very pink cheeks glided in to greet them. "My word, Bitsy," Kitty said, taking Miss Dockering's hands in hers, "I never expected to see you today."

"Kitty, this is the Duke of Woriton. Your Grace, Miss Kitty Parsen."

"Oh!" The girl dove into a deep curtsy, her pink cheeks deepening to a mottled red. "Your Grace! I certainly didn't expect you!"

"I didn't expect this either, but here we are," he commented, keeping Miss Dockering's warning about her friend's penchant for tears in mind.

"Of course! Well, it's just delightful. Do you wish some tea? Hiddles, tea, if you please!"

Tea meant conversation. He had two or three damned questions to ask. Anything more would be a waste of time when he had one dog, myriad experiments, and an unwritten speech to attend to. "I don't—"

"Yes, please, Kitty," Miss Dockering interrupted him with a smile. "The duke has been the victim of a dog theft, and he wishes to ask you a few questions about your own experience. Tea should fortify us all, I think."

"Oh, that." Tears welled up in their hostess's eyes. "It was horrible. I never thought I'd see my Rexie again."

As if on cue a small brown dog pranced into the room, bounced to a stiff stop, and started a high-pitched barking at Galahad. The big poodle's head went down, and he lunged forward.

"No," Michael stated in his firmest tone, and refused to give an inch of lead. "Sit."

Galahad looked over his shoulder, grumbled, and sank onto his haunches.

Miss Dockering looked from the poodle to him and back again, but didn't say aloud whatever she might be thinking. Instead, she gestured him toward a couch and took a seat beside him. Not close enough to touch, of course, but just thinking about the "close" part annoyed him. A great many things annoyed him where Elizabeth Dockering was concerned. More than made sense, actually.

He looked sideways at her as the butler and a footman hurried in with a pot of tea. Nineteen or twenty, she was, a good nine years younger than himself. That didn't matter, of course, because they were together due only to happenstance and ill luck—which also annoyed him, because he didn't believe in luck, ill or otherwise. He had no other excuse to hand, however, to explain the mix-up of Lancelot and Galahad.

Yes, she was lovely, in a far more elegant and subtle way than her friend Kitty was with her loud colors and rouged cheeks. The only fault Society could possibly find with Miss Dockering would be her tongue, and he had a good idea that she didn't unleash that for any reason—except, perhaps, when a man insulted her. Or asked for her assistance.

"How may I assist you, Your Grace?" Kitty asked, her voice whispery and breathless now that her startlement was over with.

"How was Rex stolen?"

"Well, you see, I took my baby boy shopping with me, and I set him down on the floor of the coach so I could help Georgia, my maid, put my purchases inside. I turned to take a hatbox, and when I turned back, the opposite door of the coach was open, and Rexie was gone." A tear ran down her cheek, carving a canyon through her cheek rouge.

"That's not at all similar to a housebreaking," he said, favoring Miss Dockering with a frown.

"It's still the theft of a dog, when other items were available," she insisted. "And I didn't say this was the same; only that speaking with Kitty might be helpful."

Very well, he could concede that Miss Dockering's reasoning made sense. "You said you received a ransom note, Miss Parsen. How did that come about?"

The girl took a sip of tea, her hand shaking just a bit too much to be nerves. "Yes, Your Grace," she answered in that idiotic whispery voice. "It was on the front step when I returned home."

"How soon after the theft was that?"

"Oh, I have no idea. I ran up and down the street calling for him, on the chance that the door had opened on accident. I was completely overset, but Georgia talked me into returning home, and there it was. Written in a very gauche hand, too."

"Gauche how?" Miss Dockering asked.

Miss Parsen waved her fingers, evidently forgetting that she was shaking with nerves and delicacy. "Full of misspellings and grammatical errors. And very poor penmanship."

God save him from silly females and posh, pocket-sized dogs. "Do you still have it, by chance?"

"Rex and I threw it in the fireplace the moment I got him back," she breathed.

"Where did they want the money to be sent?" Miss Dockering asked, her tone still infinitely patient. "It was twenty pounds, yes?"

"Yes," Kitty whispered. "Twenty pounds. Which was very dear, but Papa knows how I dote on Rex, and I daresay he would pay any amount to see my wittle one safely returned."

Oh, that was enough of that. Michael tilted his head. "Do you have a tender throat, Miss Parsen? Perhaps you should put some honey in your tea."

Red blotched the young lady's cheeks again. "Oh, no, Your Grace. I am in very good health. I rarely suffer ailments."

"Is there a family member nearby who is ill and attempting to sleep, perchance?"

Kitty's delicate brow furrowed. "No, Your Grace."

"Then why do you insist on whispering like a naughty schoolgirl in church?" he asked, scowling. "You sound like a simpering infant."

Miss Dockering spit out her tea and began coughing. Before he could reach over to pound her on the back she sat forward, grabbing Miss Parsen's hand. "Do not mind him, Kitty," she soothed raspily, giving her friend a warm smile. "He is very worried about Lancelot, and I fear that has made the duke impatient."

He did not need her to explain him. Kitty Parsen was an idiot, and he had merely pointed that out. "I do not—"

"Isn't that so, Your Grace?" she cut in, beaming at him. "You're very worried, or you would of course be more sensitive to Miss Parsen's delicate nature."

Michael looked from her to the other female again. The two ladies might have been the same age in years, but Kitty Parsen seemed very much the younger of the two of them. Some men preferred women who fluttered and acted helpless, he supposed, but for God's sake, what a dull life that would be. "I apologize, Miss Parsen," he said aloud, deciding he didn't want one of them weeping all over him, either. "I am indeed . . . worried to distraction." And he'd promised the other blasted female not to cause tears.

Miss Parsen immediately smiled again. "Of course you are, Your Grace. I was quite beside myself when Rex went missing. I don't think I breathed until he appeared tied to the front gate three days later."

"It still doesn't sound at all like what occurred with Lancelot." And they were therefore wasting their time and his limited patience with any further conversation. Michael stood. "Good day, Miss Parsen."

Galahad, evidently also pleased to be out of Rex the tiny menace's territory, paced with him up the hallway to the front door. Behind them, Miss Dockering and her maid fell in, as well. "That was interesting, but unhelpful," he commented as they reached the street again.

"But we couldn't have known that without speaking to her," Elizabeth pointed out. "You should be more politic with people who might be helpful to you."

"Up," he said, and Galahad hopped onto the floor of the coach. "I spoke with her. And despite her ridiculous affectations, I attempted not to offend or upend her sensibilities. Most importantly, Rex was not eaten and his mistress did not cry. As promised. Now. Who do you recommend we interview next?"

She folded her arms across her chest, head tilted a little to one side. While she and Miss Parsen would both be considered blond, Miss Dockering's hair had more of a honey hue to it, richer and far more attractive. For once in their admittedly short acquaintance she didn't speak, but instead continued to eye him, her expression expectant.

"What? I know you haven't been struck mute."

Tapping one toe, she took a breath. "We agreed I would bring you to see Kitty. And that if you wished more help, I would require something in return."

Oh, that. "I thought you were jesting."

"I wasn't. A genuine, unnuanced compliment, or I'll bid you good day and take a hack home."

Michael pulled out his pocket watch. The day had long since passed into afternoon, and other than a quick decomposition of water into its component parts, he'd done nothing about his hydrogen torch experiment. And given the increased traffic in Mayfair, he could deduce that most everyone who meant to spend the afternoon out visiting was presently out doing so. "Galahad, come," he said, tugging on the lead.

The dog appeared in the coach doorway, then jumped back to the ground. As she watched, eyes widening a little, Michael handed the poodle's lead back to his mistress and stepped up into the coach. "If you should happen to hear from whomever took Lancelot, I trust you will inform me," he said, and pulled shut the door. "Home, Adam."

As he sat back, he caught sight of Miss Dockering and her expression of utter bafflement. No doubt she was unaccustomed to anyone naysaying her, or refusing to hand her a compliment when she'd asked for one. Her suggestion to question Kitty Parsen had been soundly reasoned, but it had left him no closer to finding Lancelot. Logically, his next step would be a reconnaissance of the Dockering House neighborhood, and asking any residents if they'd seen a black poodle being carried off in the night. Having Miss Dockering present might provide him some quicker answers, but she also insisted on chitchat and drinking tea and other nonsense. He didn't need her for that. In short, he didn't need her.

That, though, hadn't been the sole reason he'd left her behind. He'd gotten in the last word just now, and he'd surprised her. And that felt . . . amusing. Hilarious, even. Every man of science knew not to take an unproven theory as fact. And the theory for Miss Dockering had been that every man in London would bend over backward to please her. Well, he'd just disproven it. Factually.

"You said I was to keep him for three days." Jimmy Bly frowned at the man in the blue beaver hat and blue coat and fancy gray breeches. With his overcoat and cane, even a blind man could tell Cordray had dressed for an important evening of being entertained. His waistcoat had been embroidered with tiny blue birds, for God's sake. "I built a room in my own room to keep him from eating me while I sleep."

"And I said, you took the wrong dog," Cordray stated, his fingers tightening on his cane.

"That ain't my fault. I went *where* you said, *when* you said, and did exactly *what* you said." He took a half step backward into the deeper shadows of the alley behind him. If the fancy man meant to start some fisticuffs, well, Jimmy knew how to be out of reach and out of sight in three or four steps. "Don't you be trying to not pay me what I'm owed for this."

Cordray frowned. "What I'm trying to tell you is that your job isn't finished yet. To begin with, I've written out a ransom note, which you will copy on a fresh piece of paper and place somewhere the residents of Dockering House will be certain to find it."

"I have to write something?"

"Just copy the shapes of the letters. I am not going to risk Bitsy recognizing my handwriting." He pulled two sheets of paper and a pencil from his pocket. "I assumed you would have neither pencil nor paper."

"I have some paper from the butcher's shop," Jimmy countered, "but I reckon it smells of beef."

"Use mine. I don't want Galahad eating your note before Bitsy reads it."

"But I thought I had Galahad. That's what I've been calling him."

"Oh, for God's sake," Cordray muttered. "No. You were supposed to take Galahad, but because of an idiot mix-up, it was Lancelot staying in Bitsy's bedchamber, and that's the dog you took."

"Lancelot. And Galahad. They're King Arthur's knights, ain't they?"

"I am not here to deliver history and literary lessons." This time the cove frowned. "Deliver the note, and meet me here again tomorrow night at the same time. I need to decide whether we can risk taking Galahad after this mess, or if he needs to have an accident."

"So, I have Lancelot right now. Not Galahad. That explains why I ain't been eaten, I suppose." This Lancelot, he seemed to be a proper and gentlemanly dog. "What does Lancelot like to eat? It was Galahad you said liked steak and beef stew."

"How the devil should I know? You figure it out."

"When do I return the lad, then?"

"The note you're writing says three days, but just hold on to him for now. I don't want Bow Street lying in wait for you."

"That's kind of you." Except that it wasn't; Cordray didn't want Jimmy caught, because Cordray didn't want Jimmy to flap his gums about who'd hired him. If not for the twenty quid he was still owed, mayhap he wouldn't be so quick to head back into trouble. And as to not returning Lancelot after getting the ransom? That was pure meanness. If dog thieves did that, after a time no one would pay for the animal's return, knowing it would make no difference. This could cause him some trouble if word got out that he'd been involved. He was far from the only dog stealer in London, after all. "I reckon I could sneak him back without anyone being the wiser."

"I'm paying you to do as I say, Jimmy. Not to walk about following your whims. Deliver the note by morning. I will see you tomorrow night to inform you if we will be returning Lancelot or not, and to let you know what I've decided about Galahad. Do you understand?"

"I understand. And when you hired me, you didn't say nothin' about delivering notes. So that'll cost you another quid." He grinned. "And we both know you'll pay it, because I complain when I'm not happy. You want me to be happy, you know."

With a muttered curse the cove pulled a coin from his pocket and tossed it. "Yes, Jimmy. Be happy, and do what I told you to."

Jimmy touched the brim of the shapeless hat he'd donned against the evening chill. "And I snatched a dog from a house and am holding on to him. I earned the last twenty pounds."

"You haven't taken the correct dog."

"Then give me ten now, and another ten tomorrow night after I've delivered the note."

"This is outrageous," Cordray sputtered.

"Without that blunt I might not be able to eat tonight, and then I might not remember where Dockering House is located."

Swearing under his breath, Cordray slapped the money onto Jimmy's palm. "Ten. Do not ask me for anything else."

"Not tonight, anyways. Good night to you, then."

He didn't wait for a response, because Cordray wasn't likely to give him one. Instead, he ducked into the depths of the alley and then headed south and east toward Smithfield. It was near a mile to get from Maudlin's Rents to Cordray's meeting place off Charing

Cross Road, but that alleyway was likely as uncivilized as the gentleman was willing to get.

Tonight he'd made eleven quid, which was a very fine workingman's wage, and was owed ten more. That was good, and the forty quid he'd already made for taking the poodle was even better. If Cordray did want Galahad as well, he would have near enough to tell Widow Vixing to go shove her wagging finger in her ear, and he would go rent himself a nice couple of rooms farther from the Thames and its constant stench.

As he neared Smithfield, he crossed the path of a butcher's boy selling off the leftover scraps of the day. The poodle hadn't eaten much today, and now that he knew he had an entirely different dog than the one he thought he'd taken, he felt a little guilty. He spent an entire quid on different cuts of meat, on beef bones and pork and half a chicken. He'd have to do some cooking tonight, but Lancelot seemed a fine dog who had only accidentally been pulled into this mess.

He wasn't supposed to have his small, wood-burning stove in the building, but it gave him a bit of heat in the winter, and it warmed his teapot on the mornings he had tea to hand. And now he could cook some chicken and pork while Lancelot sat close by and watched. "Does this smell good, boy? I should call you Lancelot now, I suppose. Are you Lancelot?"

The poodle wagged its tail, then went over and nudged the bowl where he'd put a bit of pigeon meat earlier. The pigeon bits remained.

"You might have made an effort," Jimmy complained, picking up the bowl for a sniff and then dumping it out. "I can't be feeding you pheasant and venison, you know."

His door rattled, and he nearly dropped the bowl. Damnation. If Widow Vixing had smelled the chicken, she'd put him out onto the street—or worse, double his rent. Generally he hid the stove behind a pile of tools and an old chair, but if he tried that now he'd send the entire building up in flames.

Clearing his throat, he unlatched the door and cracked it open. "Yes?"

Sally Pangle, her nose lifted, gazed at him. "You're cooking," she announced, thankfully keeping her voice down to a whisper.

"Couldn't leave it sitting all night," he responded, wishing now that he'd got some tea while he'd been out. "Go away."

"Oh, no, you don't. That's chicken, and it's making my mouth water. You don't want me telling the Widow that you have a dog in here, do you?"

Jimmy lifted both eyebrows. "What makes you think I have a dog?"

"I live below you, Jimmy Bly. You think I don't recognize the sound of dog's nails on floorboards? Or barking? Widow Vixing came by, and I had to set my three off to cover the sound of yours."

That made him smile, and he leaned against the doorframe. "You did that for me?"

"Of course I did."

With a quick breath he opened the door wider. What he had wasn't as fancy as tea, but if the woman wanted to join him for it, he wasn't about to naysay her. "Then come in and have some chicken and pork, and meet Lancelot."

She grinned, the expression lighting her gray eyes. "I brought my brood with me. Chicken, you know."

Jimmy grinned back at her, because his face would have broken if he'd tried to do otherwise. Sally glided into his room, her three dogs on her heels. Two little white balls of fluff, and one large black poodle with much longer, shaggier fur than Lancelot's. "Pickle, Bob, Jenny," he greeted them. "How is training going?"

"Well. By the end of summer, I'll have Jenny jumping through a flaming hoop and walking a rope." She looked toward the stove, and her eyes widened. "You've a poodle, yourself! This is Lancelot, you said?"

"I'm more just watching him for a bit than owning him."

She squatted in front of Lancelot and held out her hand. "Hello, Lancelot. Do you do any tricks? Can you lie down?"

The poodle shifted and settled onto the floor, his head on his front paws. "Well, I'll be damned," Jimmy said, chuckling.

"He's a well-cared-for beastie," Sally commented, leaning down to scratch him behind the ears. "That haircut alone costs a quid, you know. A proper barber does it. All the fur balls he's got are supposed to make him more buoyant in water, if you had him trained to fetch ducks and other game. And they're very fancy." She looked over her shoulder at Jimmy. "Tell me you're not doing something you shouldn't be doing."

"For your information, I'm helping a fancy fellow win a young lady. He and the dog don't get along, so I'm watching the dog for a few days." He grimaced. "Except that this is the wrong dog, so I may have to do it all again."

"'The wrong dog'?"

"I still can't figure out how that happened."

"Jimmy, you have to stop doing things like this. I could help you with your rent for a month or two if you're having trouble finding an honest day's work."

Jimmy shrugged. "Sometimes the only work available ain't that honest. But I'm truly only looking after him." He pulled the note and the blank paper from his pocket. "I'm to copy out this note tonight, and deliver it tomorrow, and after that, old Lancelot will be back where he belongs."

"Let me see it." Standing, she held her hand out to him, much as she'd done for Lancelot.

"Don't be preaching at me," he grumbled, and handed it over.

She unfolded it, her lips moving as she read. "Oh, Jimmy."

"What? What does it say?"

"'To whom it may concern,'" she read aloud. "'We have your dog. Put twenty quid in a sack and set it behind the butcher's shop on Radley Street by midnight if you want him back again. If you do as we say, you'll see him in two days.'" She sighed. "'Your,' 'butcher,' 'midnight,' and 'you'll' are misspelled."

"Well, I reckon if I could read and write, I'd be misspelling words. Give it back. I have to copy it."

Handing it back to him, she sat on one of the pair of small wooden chairs in the room and primly crossed her ankles. "I thought you were looking for honest work, these days."

"I am. I just haven't found any, lately. Lots of men asking for not so many jobs. And some of them have wives, and babies. This ain't so bad, and Lancelot looks happy, don't he? And it's for a good cause. True love."

"Hm. In my experience, if a dog doesn't like someone, it's for good reason." She snapped her fingers, and one of the white dogs sprang onto her lap. "Isn't that so, Pickle?"

"I'll be making it right in two days, Sally. You have my word on that. And in the meantime, chicken and pork for the lot of us. Unless Lancelot doesn't like that, either, and then I'll have to try cake and biscuits."

Lancelot woofed at him, his tail wagging. And then the poodle walked over to sniff Jenny's backside. Everyone was getting along tonight, and Jimmy preferred to view that as a good sign of things to come for everyone concerned. Even for Cordray and his lady, if he deserved her.

"Galahad, sit."

The poodle turned around to eye Elizabeth, but then resumed sniffing about the bedchamber, no doubt for traces of Lancelot. Refusing to give in, she picked up a piece of cheese and shook it at him.

"Sit, Galahad. Sit. Sit, and you may have this yummy cheese. Mm mm."

That made the black dog look around again. He trotted up to her and gave her hand a solid lick.

"Yuck! No, sit, Galahad. Then you may have the cheese."

He nuzzled at her hand again.

"I don't understand," Elizabeth complained, glancing over her shoulder as Peggy pulled two walking dresses out of the wardrobe and held them up for her perusal. "The blue and green one, I think. Woriton doesn't have sweets, or cheese, in his pocket. All he does is say, 'sit' in his man voice, and Galahad listens to him."

Peggy giggled. "You might try using his tone of voice, then, Miss Bitsy."

Elizabeth rolled her shoulders and tucked in her chin. "Sit, Galahad," she said in her lowest, most commanding voice.

The poodle ignored her in favor of the cheese.

"You see? It's useless. At one point he listened to me, but now I have to bribe and cajole everything. I know I blamed his theft on frightening him out of his manners, but since Woriton proved that Galahad does listen to someone, he should be listening to me."

"Well, I'm no expert," her maid returned, "but it seems to me that when the duke says something, it's as if he expects to be listened to, and no one dares contradict him."

Hm. "You make a good point, Peggy. He does have a rather unsufferable air of confidence about him." Was it possible that if the duke believed he would be obeyed, he somehow conveyed that tone in his voice, and it caused Galahad to listen to him without question? She cleared her throat, telling herself that she was the dog's mistress, and that he was going to sit down because she told him to. There was no other alternative. "Galahad. Sit."

With a soft whumph, the poodle sank onto his haunches. *Oh!* Swiftly she stopped herself from cheering or being overly effusive.

She was the mistress. Cooing over him would ruin the miracle she'd just managed.

"Good dog," she said calmly, and ruffled his ears.

"My heavens," Peggy breathed.

Elizabeth waited a moment, then gave Galahad the bit of cheese. "Well." She gave a short laugh, still half wondering if she hadn't dreamed that little exchange. "I wonder if I would find Woriton more amenable if I treated him the same way. Confident and expectant of obedience."

"I can think of several other gentlemen, at least, who would no doubt sit the moment you asked them to."

"Peggy."

"Well, they would, don't you think?"

"Quite possibly. And without any offer of cheese." Laughing into her hand, Elizabeth stood up, turned a circle, and sat again. The idea that men would respond to being treated like dogs—well, it was silly, but Peggy had the right of it. Men fetched her punch, chairs, wraps, anything she asked for just because she asked for it. Sometimes even before she asked for it. Of course, they had their own expectations in return for their kindnesses, but the idea of her being in the lead and them following her whims had a great deal of appeal to it.

As for Woriton, well, she didn't know that he wanted anything from her, except perhaps a bit of assistance with finding his dog. His aunt's dog, rather. And all evidence pointed to the idea that he didn't think he needed her any longer even for that. In fact, considering that he'd driven off without her yesterday rather than handing her a compliment, she should have felt insulted. It had left her flat-footed, but in light of Galahad's new compliance, it got her thinking.

Woriton wasn't one of those dogs—men—who required treats in the form of dances or strolls or conversation in exchange for their considerations. What, then, *would* motivate him? Perhaps the very air of confidence and unshakable belief that her words would be listened to and her orders followed, the things he used on Galahad, would also work on him.

Not that she foresaw having anything further to do with him, of course. He'd just been an odd, handsome, unexpected diversion from the rigors and stresses of the London Season. For all she knew he would have found Lancelot by daybreak this morning, and their paths would never cross again. She should have waved goodbye yesterday, and thanked him for showing her a new way to interact with Galahad.

Her bedchamber door opened. "Bitsy," her mother, Victoria, Lady Mardensea, said with a broad, excited smile, "we've found a note. Your father has it downstairs."

"Oh, thank goodness." Rising, she tied her dressing robe around her waist and hurried down to the breakfast room. "What does it say, Papa?"

The viscount offered it to her. "The spelling is atrocious, but it says that we'll have our dog back in two days if we leave a sack of money in an alleyway."

"I imagine His Grace will be much relieved," her mother said, still smiling. "I certainly am. He might have made a large row and had everyone blaming us for not guarding his dog when it was our guest, inadvertent or not."

"He only wants it back with the least possible fuss," Elizabeth countered. She read through the short note herself. "But yes, I imagine he will be quite pleased."

"Shall I have it delivered to Bromley House?" her father asked.

"No. I think I'll deliver it myself." When both parents eyed her, she pretended a sigh. "This disaster isn't my fault, but a personal delivery seems a much more proper ending to it, don't you think?"

"Yes, I suppose so." The viscountess kissed her on one cheek.

"You do somehow manage to turn every possible misstep into part of a lovely dance, my dear."

Elizabeth gripped the note, flashing her mother a smile. "I do like to dance."

And Woriton was going to have to do some dancing himself, to apologize for abandoning her on the street yesterday. And he would have to do it with something much more significant than cheese as a reward—though cheese might not be a poor idea. *Ha!*

CHAPTER SIX

MICHAEL TIGHTENED THE APERTURE OF THE TUBE FEEDING hydrogen to the burner, then lit a match and, with the aid of a pair of tongs, reached out to hold the flame over the burner's mouth. With a pop, a small blue flame flickered into life.

"There you are," he murmured, exchanging the match for a thermometer and using the tongs again to hold the instrument into the top of the flame. The mercury in the narrow tube shot up its length, slowing as it passed two thousand degrees, and finally hovering just below twenty-five hundred.

That wasn't hot enough. He'd personally measured pure, burning oxygen at over five thousand degrees. Shifting, Michael opened the valve, and the blue flame pulsed upward, deepening in color. That looked better, but he wanted facts. Once again he lowered the thermometer into the flame. This time it reached just over three thousand, five hundred degrees before the blue sputtered into orange and then went out.

He replaced the upturned receiver with a fresh one full of hydrogen gas and repeated the experiment, this time moving the thermometer around the outside of the flame. Now, that was interesting.

Oxygen-fed flames radiated heat in all directions. Hydrogen flame, though, barely heated the air beside it. A more concentrated flame, then. Perhaps something could be done with that.

Sitting back, he eyed the flame for a moment, then closed the valve and sighed. "Huston!" he yelled, pulling out his pocket watch.

The butler cracked open the study door. "Your Grace?"

"Any word regarding Lancelot?"

"No, Your Grace. Per your instructions, I will notify you the moment anything changes." Huston cleared his throat. "Do you intend to send word to Lady Mary about the incident?"

"I do not. I intend to resolve the incident, at which time I will instruct you and the rest of the staff not to say a damned word about it. Ever."

A muscle in the butler's cheek jumped. "We will follow your instructions, of course, Your Grace."

"Good. Now have Romer saddled. I feel the need to speak with Miss Dockering."

"Very good, Your Grace." Not even bothering to hide a smile, the butler turned on his heel and hurried out of sight.

Clearly his staff had become nonsensical idiots. No, he didn't actually *want* to leave his worktable and go talk to Elizabeth Dockering again. Yes, she had been hovering at the edge of his mind all morning—and halfway through the night, if he was being honest with himself. The fact simply was that he remained worried about Lancelot. And even though her first suggested interviewee had been a useless, fluttering, bat-witted ninny, Miss Dockering did claim to know other people whose dogs had also been taken. He didn't know the identities of any of them. Looking through back issues of *The Times* could resolve that, but considering he had a much handier source of information living just a few streets away, he would be foolish not to make use of her.

Likewise when he'd taken a ride this morning in the area im-

mediately around Dockering House, everyone had seen a black poodle, and everyone knew it to be Bitsy Dockering's ill-mannered
dog. That made the information useless; even if someone had seen
Lancelot being removed from the house, they would have thought
it Galahad and seen no reason to come forward to speak with him.

Michael went upstairs and changed into an appropriate coat
and riding boots, then clomped back down to the foyer again. As he
reached it, Huston lifted the tray that habitually sat on the hallway
table, awaiting calling cards, missives, and the mail. "You have a note,
my lord."

"Miss Dockering?"

"No, my lord. His Grace the Duke of Sommerset."

For the briefest of moments, Michael felt . . . deflated, as if he'd
opened the door expecting to find a garden, and instead discovered
nothing but old rocks. Not that Sommerset was an old rock—though
he could be stubborn as granite. Taking the note, he broke the wax
seal and unfolded it. "Hm."

"Anything pressing, my lord?"

"No. Nicholas noticed my presence at his soiree the other night.
He's invited me to join him at White's this evening if I still have any
civility remaining."

"Ah. Very good. Will you be joining him, then?"

"It's still too early in the day to assess my levels of civility." And
his tolerance for idle chatter.

He pulled on his gloves. Huston took hold of the door handle,
but didn't open it. "Your Grace," he said, just as Michael was about
to ask him if he'd fallen asleep standing there, "you mentioned that
you and Miss Dockering had a . . . disagreement yesterday. If I may
be so bold, might I suggest that flowers might be a salve to soothe a
young lady's wounded pride?"

Michael tilted his head. "I am not in pursuit of Miss Dockering,"
he stated, raising his voice so any other servants in the area could

also hear him. "We met by accident, and Lady Mary's dog was stolen while in her custody. She is a source of information. That is all there is to her."

Huston inclined his head. "Of course, Your Grace. My suggestion was only due to the fact that in my experience, females do not like to be considered mere reference material."

"Give me my hat." Michael jabbed a forefinger at the butler. "There are times, Huston," he said, setting the chapeau onto his head, "when I think you have been in my employ for too long."

"I well agree, Your Grace."

Walking out the front door, Michael took Romer's reins and swung up onto the bay's back. *Flowers.* It was ridiculous that a handful of vegetation had become so meaningful in polite society. The only practical use of flowers was in certain medications and to provide pollen for bees, who in turn produced honey. As he enjoyed honey, he approved of the flowers in his small rear garden. Flowers currently just sitting there, waiting to be noticed by bees.

Damnation. Still swearing under his breath, he turned the gelding up the carriageway to the back of the house. Dismounting, he grabbed a handful of yellow daisies and orange chrysanthemums, and returned to the horse. *There.* Damned interfering butler.

As he reached the end of the carriage drive once again, he pulled up. Just to the right, at his own front door, Miss Dockering herself stepped down from a barouche. She removed her bonnet, revealing honey-colored hair coiled into a loose knot. Strands escaped to be tucked behind her ears and drift across her forehead, no doubt with the intent of making a man wish to brush them aside. It worked; his fingers twitched. She'd worn a green and blue walking dress with a deeper green pelisse, a color which he had to admit looked well on her, and deepened the clover green of her eyes.

"Good morning, miss," Huston said, pulling open the front door. "How may I help you?"

"I'm looking for the Duke of Woriton," she said. "I believe he may be expecting me."

"His Grace has just left," the butler returned. "Might I have your name? I will inform him that you called."

"Oh," she said, glancing down at her hands for a heartbeat before her shoulders squared and she lifted her gaze again. "Yes. Please tell him Miss Dockering received the note for which he's been waiting."

"You did?" Michael kneed Romer forward, swinging down again as he reached the lady and her maid. "Let me see it."

She put her hands behind her back. "Good morning, Your Grace," she said, inclining her head.

He eyed her. "Good morning. The note?"

"Were you calling on someone?" She indicated his fistful of flowers.

Ignoring the self-satisfied grunt coming from the direction of his front door, he took a step closer. Considering that she seemed reluctant to pass on the ransom note, evidently he did need to make some sort of amends. "Yes, you. I believe I was rude to you yesterday. Here." He held them out to her.

"You know, it's customary to wrap a bouquet with a ribbon," she stated.

"I didn't have a ribbon."

"Then I'm afraid you'll have to wrap them with an apology."

He scowled. Impossible female. "I just did apologize."

"No, you didn't. You said you believed you were rude, which you were. A statement of fact is not, in fact, an apology."

Blowing out his breath, Michael looked at her. At the slight upturn of the corners of her mouth, the tiniest squint of her eyes, all signs that she was greatly amused. At him. Or rather, at the circumstance in which he had placed himself by discounting her—twice now. And by God, she had every right to be, clever woman. Nor would he make the mistake of underestimating her again. He sketched a deep bow,

doffing his hat and adding it to the flourish. "I apologize, Miss Dockering, for my rude behavior yesterday when I drove off in my coach
and left you behind. It was inexcusable."

"Well. Very plainly said, which I quite appreciate. Thank you."

She held out her hand, and he placed the flowers into them.
Their fingers brushed, and for an odd, inexplicable moment he was
angry that they'd both worn gloves. He'd felt the spark, the last
time they'd touched. And yes, skin-to-skin contact obviously had
its benefits, but this was just hands, for the devil's sake. *Her* hands.
"The letter, if you please?"

She pulled it from her reticule and handed it to him.

"Was it so tightly folded when you received it?" he asked, counting at least four across-the-middle folds as he opened it out.

"No. I had to fit it inside my reticule. It was folded in quarters.
Does that matter?"

"I don't know." He read through it, noting the misspellings and
the awkward hand, the timeline and the place of exchange. "Radley
Street," he muttered to himself, trying to place it.

"I looked it up on a map before I headed over here," Miss Dockering offered. "It's just off Drury Lane, in Covent Garden."

Michael nodded. "An odd place to find a circle of dog stealers."

"Well, I'm certain they don't live in the butcher's shop. Perhaps
that's merely where they purchase meat for all the dogs they steal."

That made a certain amount of sense, and perhaps he was men-
tally nosing into things that weren't of any importance, but he hated
unanswered questions. All of them. "He misspelled all the words
which one might misspell," he noted, half to himself, "but he used
'whom' correctly. And even with writing clearly a labor, he bothered to begin with a salutation."

"It's a ransom note. Are you going to pay it?"

"Of course I am." He turned back to Romer. "But first I'm going
to go look at the butcher's shop on Radley Street in the daylight."

"Then I'm going with you."

Michael stopped. "Why?" he asked, turning around.

"Lancelot is your aunt's dog, but was taken from my home," she stated. "I am an interested party. I can either follow you and your horse in the barouche, or you may ride with me. I daresay conversation, queries, and reading are better suited to the carriage."

"I . . . Yes, I suppose so. Huston, have Romer returned to the stable."

"Yes, Your Grace."

Miss Dockering handed the butler her flowers. "Please see these put in water, will you?"

"And tie a damned ribbon around them," Michael added. "We don't want them mistaken for weeds, do we?"

Opening the low carriage door, he handed Miss Dockering and her maid in, then joined them, taking the front-facing seat beside the young lady. She retied her bonnet over her hair, and he set his hat back over his. "Radley Street in Covent Garden, William," she instructed the driver.

"Yes, Miss Bitsy."

"Does everyone call you Bitsy?" Michael asked. "It doesn't suit you."

"It doesn't?"

"No. It sounds . . . flighty. Scatterbrained. Which you don't seem to be."

A smile that made him absurdly think of ripe strawberries and warm brandy curved her mouth. "Thank you, I think. I'm one of three sisters. Being an Elizabeth, and being the youngest, I became Bitsy. The nickname has just stayed with me, I suppose." She furrowed her brow. "I always thought it sounded friendly."

"It might cause a stranger to attempt to take advantage of you, if you welcome that sort of thing."

She folded her hands in her lap, blinking long eyelashes at him.

"You mean that people might underestimate me? That they might expect a smiling fool, and be surprised when I'm not an idiot?"

That made him frown. "Your barbs are rather pointed, and they seem to be jabbing at me. I never thought you an idiot. Just . . . glib, I suppose. Always ready with the proper set of words for the proper moment."

"Whereas you always use the fewest possible words at every moment. Are you worried about wasting them? That you only have a certain number to hand, and you don't wish to run out at an inopportune moment?"

"Yes, that's it." He pulled a notepad from his pocket and pretended to make a notation. "And I only have . . . seventy-one words left for today."

She laughed, the sound warm and pleasant and tickling down his spine. "That was a joke! You made a jest!"

Michael sighed, pretending that her laughter hadn't pleased him. "I don't know why that always surprises everyone."

"It was a pleasant surprise. Feel free to indulge at any time." Sitting back, she played with the ends of her bonnet ribbons for a moment. "Your horse's name is Roamer? Does he wander?"

"No. It's spelled differently. He's named for Ole Christensen Rømer, the Danish astronomer who measured the speed of light."

"Light has a speed?" Miss Dockering asked, and her maid giggled behind her hands. "It must be very slow indeed, because I never see it move."

"It's incredibly fast, actually. Faster than sound." At their skeptical looks, he held up his hands as far as he could stretch out his arms from each other. "For instance. If I'm over here," and he balled his right hand into a fist, "and I shoot my gun, you over here on this hill, will hear it a few seconds after I actually pull the trigger, yes?"

"Yes."

"That is the speed of sound. The speed at which it travels from its origin to a given point elsewhere."

"Oh. That's . . . fascinating," Miss Dockering said, her eyes widening a little. "I've never thought of it that way. At all."

Michael nodded. "Light is the same. If I'm over here again," and he waved his right hand, "and I strike a match, you will almost instantly see it from your place on that second hill. That is light's speed." He smiled, reaching out the tips of his fingers. "It's so fast that we can only measure it at great distances. From the sun to here, for example, or the light of a very faraway sun, which we call a star. The light we see from a star was actually produced hundreds or thousands of years ago. The light a distant sun produces now," and he clapped, making both ladies jump, "we won't see for decades. Centuries."

She looked up at the sky, presently blue with a few scattered clouds floating across it. "So, a star—or a sun, rather—I see at night might not even be producing light any longer, but we wouldn't know until a hundred years later that it's gone out."

"Yes. That. Exactly that, Miss Dockering."

Miss Dockering lowered her gaze to look him in the eye for several beats of his heart, an imprecise measurement, but one that felt appropriate this morning. "I find that both remarkable and . . . supremely moving. Call me Elizabeth," she said, and grinned again. "I won't have you calling me Bitsy, and that's for certain."

"Woriton," he replied. "Or Michael, if you prefer."

"What do *you* prefer?" she asked.

"Michael."

"Michael it is, then."

Light had a speed. Stars were suns, and they were far older than Elizabeth had realized. She hoped the sky would remain clear, because tonight she meant to go outside and look up, and see light that was hundreds of years from its creation. *Goodness.* It made her feel small and young, and at the same time, ancient and wise. Anxious and serene. How very odd.

Woriton—Michael—had taken the ransom note from his pocket and was reading it again. When he'd first begun picking it apart for clues, she'd thought the idea silly. They had their instructions, and it made sense, then, to put the money in a sack, leave it where they'd been told to do so, and wait for Lancelot to be returned.

Now, though, she wondered if the tiny things were how Woriton saw . . . everything. If clues and information invisible to everyone else simply sat up and waved at him, waiting to be ac-knowledged and catalogued and solved. It was fascinating, actually. *He* was quite fascinating.

Several things flipped on their heads as she thought about their conversation. He'd said her nickname sounded silly and the actual her seemed slightly less so, and of course that was far closer to an insult than a compliment. Or it had been. Now she almost felt flattered that he considered her competent enough to listen to and speak with—which he had done, and on several occasions now.

"Radley Street, Miss Bitsy," William said, slowing the horses to a walk. "Is there somewhere in particular you want me to take you?"

"Just continue along for a bit, if you please," she answered.

Beside her, Michael leaned closer. "That would be a butcher's shop," he muttered, gazing past her side of the barouche.

He felt pleasantly warm and solid beside her, and more than a little distracting. "Yes, it would. I don't see another. Shall we stop here?"

"Let's visit the bakery there, instead," he suggested, gesturing at the small shop three doors past the butcher's, "and then take a stroll."

"You think someone might be watching?"

"I doubt it. But you, at the least, will cause a stir. Let's give the gawkers a moment to gaze upon you before we stomp into the butcher's shop and the alleyway beyond."

"Now you're being silly. A stir?"

"Of the three of us," he said, stepping down to the street and offering his hand, "which one looks dressed appropriately for tea with the Queen?"

He was dressed well, if plainly, for riding. But no, nothing other than his eyes keen as a hawk's and his handsome face stood out from the shopkeepers and vendors and lady's maids and seamstresses presently walking up and down Radley Street in the middle of the morning. Peggy had on a good-quality muslin, but it was a rather unspectacular brown and cream. "I could never wear this to see the Queen," Elizabeth stated. "I'd never be invited again if I did."

Taking his hand, she stepped down. All around her hats were being doffed, women were eyeing her attire, and children simply stood and stared. Michael leaned down to murmur in her ear. "A stir."

Very well, it might be a stir. A small one. "I told you," she commented to no one in particular, "I have heard that the bread at . . ." She glanced past Michael's broad shoulder. ". . . Rabini's Baked Goods is delightful. Let's see, shall we?"

She wrapped her hand around Michael's arm as he fell in beside her, Peggy behind them. "You've just increased Rabini's sales," he murmured, reaching out with his other hand to open the bakery door. "Well done."

Elizabeth couldn't imagine Lord Peter Cordray or any of her other suitors firstly noticing that her endorsement might have an effect on a shop's sales, or secondly complimenting her for it. "It's not measuring the speed of light or anything," she returned, pitching her voice to keep them from being overheard, "but it does no harm."

"No, it doesn't. And I don't measure the speed of light. Nothing that bold, I'm afraid."

"What do you do, then? I remember you had papers about chlorine or something with you when we had our accident."

He lifted an eyebrow at that, but didn't dispute her description. "At this moment, I'm attempting to modify a lamp into a burner. One that burns long and hot enough to be useful in a laboratory, with a gas that isn't prone to explode or poison the air. I've been working with hydrogen, which can be explosive, but I'm finding that pure oxygen both burns hotter and is easier to collect. Thus far the only benefit to the hydrogen is in the way the heat of it is directed. That may have some applications, but I still need a better way to deliver the gas to the burner."

"That sounds very complicated."

The duke shrugged. "Of course, this is all in the ultimate pursuit of combining chlorine in both its gaseous and liquid form with as many different elements as possible. Thus far we have acids, a way to whiten textiles, salts, and a dozen other derivatives from chloride, but at the moment this still feels like tinkering. Measuring out all the wood before I can begin building a house, as it were. What I'm ultimately aiming toward is being able to use a chlorine or chloride combination as a medical cleanser, to prevent infection in someone with an open wound. And without poisoning the patient, of course."

"It sounds quite impressive to me," she said, meaning it.

"Well, I find your manner of dealing with people rather impressive."

It didn't sound impressive. Especially not when compared with finding the benefits of chemicals and measuring the speed of light. Through a judicious use of her charm and wit, she could persuade people to like her and enjoy her company. That benefited her, certainly, but if there was a larger, grander, more important application for that, she had no idea what it might be.

He left the requesting of samples of bread to her, and Enzo Rabini turned out to be both a talented and loquacious bakery owner.

The shops here, close by the Drury Lane Theatre and a handful of other places frequented by the gentry, had well- or adequately heeled clientele. Clerks and day servants, craftsmen, and professors.

"What do you make of that?" she whispered, dividing her attention between the various types of bread slices and the tea set before her.

"Of what?" Michael asked, examining a slice of bread infused with a cheddar cheese.

"You were listening to my chat with Enzo, I hope. He and any of the shopkeepers here would be shocked and dismayed to see the sort of men who steal other people's pets hanging about or even buying scraps of meat. Such customers would hurt their businesses, just as you claimed that my endorsement has aided his."

"Sound reasoning," he said, taking a bite of the bread and then examining it all over again. "This is quite good."

So he wasn't overly impressed with her deductive reasoning. Fine. "You think that perhaps our thief chose this street because it wouldn't be too uncomfortable or dangerous for a member of the aristocracy or one of his servants to come sneaking about here at midnight. That perhaps this location is somewhere between us and wherever they're keeping Lancelot."

"That makes sense," the duke agreed. "Both suppositions do."

"You're not going to set someone to watch the alley tonight, are you? If anyone is seen, it could be very bad for Lancelot."

"I'd considered it," he said, taking more bread from the platter they'd ordered. "But as you said, here is nowhere near wherever Lancelot is. I, or whomever I send, would be unlikely to recognize the thief on sight, and would therefore have to keep him *in* sight for an unknown distance without being seen. So, as much as I would prefer to bloody the dog snatcher and his cohorts, I will have to settle for doing as they instruct and waiting two more days."

The stroll they took down the alleyway to Drury Lane confirmed that setting anyone to keep a lookout and then follow the culprit who came to collect the money would be a very difficult task. At night it would be very dark, and crowded with crates and wagons and probably rats and other unsavory things.

"You truly want to . . . punch the thief?" she asked, looking up at his profile in the shadowed alley.

"They broke into your home, Elizabeth. Into your bedchamber. What if you'd elected to return home early, or stayed in that evening? That idea displeases me. And that doesn't even take into account the theft of my aunt's beloved dog."

"But you seem too civilized to be bloodying noses. Or too cerebral."

He laughed. It was the first time she could recall him laughing in their admittedly short acquaintance, and it surprised her, hearty and deep and loud. "My dear Elizabeth, what in blazes have I done to make you think me the least bit civilized?"

"Well, you . . ." She trailed off, frowning as she reviewed his speech and behavior since the moment they'd met. "Oh, my, you're not civilized at all, are you? I mean, you did show me the respect of calling me Miss Dockering until I urged you to do otherwise, and you dance well, but you really are very rude and direct."

"Generally, yes," he agreed.

"Do you like being so?"

He sent her a sideways glance. "My aunt says I can't be bothered to be otherwise. I suppose that could be true, but the politic way of conversing, the talking around a subject or avoiding it when information about it may be important—or at the least, interesting— bedevils me. I find it frustrating and illogical."

For a moment she hesitated to speak. It wasn't that he intimidated her, but rather that she sensed now that she hadn't yet felt the full brunt of either his ire or his intellect. "I have to point out that we've been conversing nearly constantly for two days."

"*You* make sense."

Now *that* seemed like a compliment. A large one, coming from the Duke of Woriton. "Thank you. You have insulted me several times, though."

A grin cracked his face, lighting all the way to his dark brown eyes. "Likewise."

"I'm glad we understand each other." It was more than that, but she had no intention of admitting that firstly his insults both stung and were rather insightful, and secondly, that she enjoyed conversing with him far more than she would ever have expected.

Being seen with him would do nothing for her continued popularity, though at the moment she couldn't see any sign that he was damaging it, either. It would happen, though, the first time someone she knew approached for a chat while he was occupied with discovering clues and the science of the world. Michael would insult her friend, and that friend would complain to other friends, and soon she would be that odd Bitsy, spending time for no discernible reason with the mad Duke of Woriton.

"Are we finished here, then?" she asked, annoyed with her own thoughts. Petty, they were. And selfish.

"I believe so. Originally, I thought I would need you to introduce me to other dog-theft victims," he said, stretching, "but with the note received, I don't think it's necessary any longer. So, I suppose I should return home to tinker with my burner, arrange to deposit the ransom tonight, and wait for you to send word that you've received Lancelot. I've been invited to White's by Sommerset this evening, and since I seem to be feeling chatty, I may take him up on the offer. You?"

"Oh." He was discussing the end of their partnership, not just the bakery outing as she'd meant. What, though, if she wasn't ready for these unique conversations to be finished? *Dash it all.* "Quite busy, as well. Tonight, my parents and I are dining at my sister Madeleine's home, and tomorrow is the Evenson soiree." Since she'd only ever seen Michael at one party and that had been so that he could inform her about Lancelot, the odds that he would make another social appearance this Season were very small. As small as a grain of salt, which was partly composed of a derivative of chlorine.

So in their short acquaintance no one's reputation had been damaged, and she'd found a diversion the like of which she'd never encountered before, and with a man unlike any other she'd ever met. Therefore, she could call this a pleasant, interesting set of days and then return to her very busy schedule and her very full life.

"Each to our specialties, then," Michael noted, and turned to watch the passing traffic.

She continued gazing at his lean profile for a long moment. Previous to meeting him, her specialty, the way she navigated Society, her quest to put herself in the most optimum position to find a husband who best suited her, had seemed paramount. Today, she wouldn't have been willing to wager that she had any idea what was truly important. She *would* wager, though, that *he* did. And once again finding herself outside of his circle of interests didn't feel like it would be all that flattering. Or satisfying.

CHAPTER SEVEN

"ANOTHER, IF YOU PLEASE," MICHAEL SAID, GESTURING AT HIS empty glass as one of White's liveried footmen walked by.

"Right away, Your Grace."

The Duke of Sommerset wrote something on the edge of the newspaper he'd brought with him. "That's four," he muttered.

"Four what?"

"Words, Woriton. Add two more for that outburst, and thus far tonight, you've uttered thirty-seven of them."

Michael scowled. "Why is everyone today counting the number of words I use?"

"'Everyone'?" Sommerset repeated.

Ignoring that, Michael accepted his new glass of whiskey.

"Would you care for another, Your Grace?" the footman asked, facing Sommerset.

"I'll have a brandy."

"Yes, Your Grace."

"Make that two," Michael put in, more out of amusement than anything else.

"I'll see to it, Your Grace."

"Thank you," Nicholas added.

The footman nodded, beginning to back away. "Your Grace. Your Graces."

Michael waited until the poor man had fled. "I speak when I have something to say, as you well know, Nicholas," he commented. "You asked me here, leading me to believe *you* had something to say, so I've been sitting here, waiting patiently, while the staff and other club members 'Your Grace' the two of us to death. It is somewhat entertaining, but not particularly useful."

"Not everything has to be useful." Sommerset tapped the pencil against the edge of his glass. "Very well, I suppose I do have something to say. You attended my party, and didn't bother even to say hello. And that's after you declined to answer the invitation in the first place."

"I went for a specific purpose. I'm watching Aunt Mary's poodle, which was accosted in the park by another black poodle. In the confusion, Miss Dockering and I left with the wrong dogs. I needed to inform her."

"Ah. Hence the waltz with Miss Dockering. You have it all straightened out, then?"

"Yes. No. That is to say, she has her own poodle now, but mine was stolen from her home before I could retrieve it. I just delivered the ransom, so now I wait for two more days for Lancelot's return."

"I almost liked it better when you weren't talking. That's some impressive chaos you've stumbled into." The duke swirled his glass, his gaze on the amber liquid. "Did you enjoy yourself?"

"Trying to find Aunt Mary's dog and slogging about London looking for clues?" Michael thought about it for a moment, about the difference between a typical morning spent looking for answers to yet-unasked questions in his study, and this past afternoon spent trying to find a particular butcher's shop in Covent Garden. "I did, actually."

"I meant at my soiree. And I only ask because if you *did,* perchance, enjoy yourself, I could discreetly whisper a word or two and all those invitations to parties you used to receive would come flooding back in again. They only stopped because you never bothered to answer them. Or worse, you wrote 'NO' in large letters across their lovely, embossed works and had them returned."

Michael had enjoyed the dancing at the Sommerset ball, but that had had nothing to do with the party. "Nicholas, I'm a duke. And wealthy. And an eccentric. And rude. A conundrum of troublesome opposites. I like that despite the first two, people are afraid to invite me to parties because of the latter two."

"So you mean for it to be you and your voltaic piles for the rest of your life?"

Ah, so that was what this was about. "That sounds both lewd and painful. Don't try to marry me off. I would not be a good husband. I can't even manage a civil drink with an old friend without arguing."

"I am not old. And as I quite like being married, I thought you might enjoy it, as well." Sommerset finished off his drink. "Ask that Miss Dockering if she knows anyone who might suit. She's a diamond of the Season. I'm certain she's acquainted with at least one female who's surly and silent and doesn't like parties."

Michael had no trouble believing Elizabeth was sought-after, though he did wonder who among this year's herd of bulls such a witty woman could regard with even the slightest bit of interest. Cordray had been in her company, but he didn't know the others. There'd been no one the slightest bit like him, certainly.

Abruptly he didn't want to discuss Elizabeth Dockering or her social standing or how well-suited to life in Mayfair she was. Michael stood. "I am twenty-nine years old, Sommerset, set in my ways, and a terrible bore. I don't like most people. I like being stodgy and not leaving my house. Leave me be."

"Yes, but you're not dead, Michael. And I suggest you not wait that long to discover if there's anything more you want in life."

"So says the man who spent half *his* life wandering about the world and getting shot at. Good night, Sommerset."

"Woriton. And I believe you made it past two hundred words there. Remarkable."

Michael snorted. "You're the devil, you know."

Outside he reclaimed Romer and headed home. Only John, the youngest and least senior of the footmen, remained awake, opening the door for him and accepting his hat and gloves. "Shall I fetch Jarrett for you, Your Grace?" he asked, stifling a yawn.

"No. Go to bed."

"Yes, Your Grace."

Upstairs, Michael stripped out of his coat, cravat, and waistcoat. Tomorrow he would have time to run a full set of hydrogen experiments, because he had two more days to wait for Lancelot to be returned to Dockering House, and no clues to follow with Elizabeth Dockering. Life would more or less return to its old schedule, just the way he preferred it.

He glanced at the bed, then with a grimace headed back downstairs to his study. Generally, on nights he felt restless, any one of his multiple tasks sufficed. On occasion he neglected to go to bed entirely. He already had his receivers full of hydrogen ready for the morning, and another three of oxygen on the chance he felt like doing some experiments with heat intensity. He could always make more, or prepare more of the pure chlorine samples for combination.

Numbers, chemicals, measurements, compounds—they'd always been a balm to his restless mind. Why the devil he needed some scientific comfort tonight, though, he had no idea. His mind was all odd . . . feelings and thoughts, along with some nebulous questions he didn't care for. At all.

Tomorrow everything would be back to normal. It had best be, damn it all. A sharp-tongued young lady had no place in his life, and however much he'd enjoyed the distraction she'd provided, he had other things to do. Myriad other things that *didn't* leave him restless and unsettled, thank God.

"Are you certain you weren't seen? Or worse, followed?" Lord Peter Cordray glanced over his shoulder, half expecting an entire company of soldiers to appear at the head of the alley.

"I told you," Jimmy Bly replied, "I spied some proper types hereabout earlier in the day, but they left well before nightfall. And I've kept an eye on that damned alley for hours. No one saw me; no one followed me. If you'd make your next demand for ransom somewhere closer to Smithfield, though, I'd be a happier fellow. And give me better directions. Took me near an hour to find that butcher's shop you made me write the note about."

Peter strode back and forth up the alleyway. This was not what he'd envisioned when he'd hired the idiot Bly. The wrong dog, the wrong victim, and him nowhere closer to an engagement with Bitsy Dockering than he'd been before this fiasco. "And the money is in the sack?"

Bly shook it. "Sounds like it. I wasn't sure if it was to be yours or mine, but I reckoned that since we're partners, I should have half, at least."

"Give it to me."

"Are we sharing?"

Oh, for God's sake. "Yes, we're sharing. I want to see if there's a note inside. Or anything to be wary about."

Untying the mouth of the cloth sack, he opened it and looked inside. Enough coins to equal twenty pounds, certainly, and beneath them, a folded paper. Ah. He'd thought so. The Duke of Woriton seldom let an occasion pass him by without some witty, scathing commentary or other.

"What's it say?" Jimmy Bly asked, taking back the sack and dumping the coins into one hand. "Twenty quid, pretty as anything. How much for each of us?"

"Five for you, and fifteen for me," Peter said absently, unfolding the note.

"That ain't so. I know it's ten apiece. I just wanted to see if you'd try to cheat me. Which you did."

"Since our agreement was for you to earn a total of forty pounds, and since we have already exceeded that, anything more I choose to hand over is a bonus, Mr. Bly. This is not a partnership."

"Well, it ain't a bonus, either. That Lancelot won't eat nothing but baked chicken and oat biscuits. That's better than what I generally eat." He gestured at the paper. "And I need to know what it says, too, so I'll know if Bow Street's heading my way."

"Yes, yes. It says, 'To the dog stealers, I've done as you asked. If the dog in question is not returned in good condition and as promised, know that I will find you.' It's not signed, but as far as they know that we know, it's Bitsy's poodle we've taken. Not Woriton's. Or his aunt's, rather."

"The Duke of Woriton? Wait a minute, now." Jimmy dropped the empty sack and backed into the alleyway's deeper shadows. "I didn't know we was taking from a damned duke."

"You knew we were taking from a viscount's daughter."

"Just don't tell me next that royalty's involved. I might drop dead of fright, right on the spot."

This was not at all how he wanted to be spending his evening, standing in a blasted alleyway chatting with a criminal. "Take all twenty pounds, then," Peter stated. "And I want Galahad gone from Dockering House tonight. They won't expect that. Not when we've given them a two-day deadline."

"But they just gave us the blunt. They won't give anything for Galahad if we take him without returning Lancelot first."

Taking a deep breath, Peter gripped his walking cane—and the sword hidden inside it—as hard as he could. "We are not dog thieves, Bly. Or I'm not, anyway. I am arranging to marry a desirable female of fine appearance, birth, and standing. Getting the poodle out of the way is my best means to succeed. It's not about the damned dogs, or the reward. Do you understand that?"

"Maybe for you it's about a lady, but for me it's about the blunt. If I'm stealing a second dog, that'll cost you the same as it did for the first one. And that's forty quid." Bly folded his arms across his chest.

"You stole the wrong dog the first time. That wasn't my doing."

"And it wasn't my fault. Forty more quid, Cordray, or our business is concluded. And this twenty pays me the rest of what's owed me for the first dog, plus the first ten of that forty." He showed his teeth. "I can add just fine."

Peter cursed under his breath. He could do it himself, he supposed, slip into Dockering House and make off with Galahad. The trick would be doing it quietly—a near impossibility considering how much the damned poodle disliked him—and doing it without being seen. *He* would be recognized.

There were a plentitude of thieves and robbers and lawbreakers and dog stealers in London. He didn't need Jimmy Bly, except that Bly already knew where he was going, how to go about it, and he'd clearly managed to remove the first dog without being detected. "Agreed, then. Thirty more pounds when you have Galahad."

Bly tilted his head. "I'll be taking half of what you owe me, which means another ten now."

"I don't have any cash with me. Tell me anywhere else you think you can earn eighty pounds for a few days' work, Mr. Bly, and I'll call you a liar to your face. Thirty once you have Galahad."

The thief eyed him. "You've got me there, Cordray. So, where's the lady tonight? It's close to dawn now, and I'd rather her not be home when I sneak back into her private rooms."

"A sister's home for dinner." Taking a breath, Peter glanced down at his pocket watch. Nearly two o'clock in the morning. Bitsy could well be home from her sister's already. By the time Bly gathered his supplies and reached Dockering House, servants would be stirring. Too little time, considering the consequences of failure.

Damnation. Another day gone by with that blasted dog standing between him and Bitsy. "Do it tomorrow night, then. She'll be at Lord and Lady Evenson's soiree. As will I. Do it between midnight and two o'clock." Sidestepping, he took hold of Shadow's reins and climbed into the saddle. "We'll meet the next afternoon so I can tell you what we'll be doing with the dogs. Be here at four o'clock. That'll give me time to chat with Bitsy first, lend her my sympathies, and determine her reaction to Galahad's loss."

"Dog tomorrow after midnight, and you the next afternoon at four o'clock," Bly muttered. "I'm going to have to get myself a pocket watch, if this keeps up."

"It won't," Peter stated. He kneed Shadow; then, as something else occurred to him, he pulled up again. "And Bly?"

"Yes?"

"If you speak about this to anyone, if you attempt to implicate me in anything, I will see to it that you hang. Do you understand?"

"I do. I've never met you, Cordray, don't you fret. And we'll have this all tied up prettier than Christmas by the end of the week."

They'd better. Evidently Woriton had been in Bitsy's company on and off all day because of the mistake with the poodles, while he'd managed perhaps fifteen minutes. If Bly didn't get it right this time, Galahad was going to have to fall into the Thames or walk beneath a wagon's wheels or something. And that would mean encouraging Bitsy to go for a walk, finding a moment, and not getting caught, which seemed extremely unlikely.

In the meantime, a visit to Woriton might suit. The correct amount of concern over a missing poodle and a subtle reminder of how very eccentric Michael Bromley was, compared with how very popular Bitsy was, could serve to make certain that the madman wouldn't be creating an additional muddle for him to have to wade through. The duke wasn't an idiot, after all. Just humdrum and something of a looby.

"Ouch! Damnation," Michael swore, as another shock of electricity jangled up his right arm, making his muscles jump.

The large voltaic battery had its uses—particularly in helping to separate certain bonded elements from each other—and it was equipment with which he was well acquainted. But this was the fourth time he'd been electrified within twenty minutes.

His study door rattled. "Your Grace?"

"I'm unhurt, Huston," he grunted, shaking out his fingers. "Just clumsy, evidently."

"Perhaps a cup of tea, Your Grace?"

"No, I don't need a cup of tea. Go away, Huston."

"Yes, Your Grace."

It was the waiting, he was certain. The sitting about waiting for an unknown someone to perform the task for which he'd been very generously paid—even though trusting the same thief who'd taken Lancelot to return him as promised seemed like the height of naïveté. And Michael was not naïve.

Neither had he gotten much sleep last night, but that was his own fault. Sitting back on the stool, he pulled the ransom note from his pocket and unfolded it again. As long as Lancelot was returned, he had no reason to delve further. No reason to wonder why the note read like someone trying to hide their education. One "whom" did not an education make, anyway. The writer might simply have heard it said, and used it without thinking. And even though he couldn't spell "butcher" with a "t," he'd known that "whom" had a silent "w" and no "u." That didn't make the misspellings intentional.

Blowing out his breath, Michael dropped the note onto his worktable. It was entirely possible that he was imagining conspiracy where only a poor, spotty education stood. "Stop wandering about," he muttered to his brain.

He could attempt to blame his distraction on the Duke of Sommerset for using his decision to attend one party in two years against him. For God's sake, it had been one dance. That in no way meant he wanted to begin receiving invitations to every damned party and recital and cheese tasting in Mayfair. Nor did it mean he was lonely and wanted to get married.

Or it might have been the *way* Sommerset had decided he should be in pursuit of a wife, and that he'd immediately discounted Miss Dockering as lively and lovely and not at all the sort of woman who would suit the Duke of Woriton. No, he was evidently to find someone surly and silent, and without a multitude of friends and acquaintances and suitors.

Not that her social or marital status signified to him, anyway, any more than his own status did. Michael rolled his shoulders. He had a burner and a medical cleanser and a half dozen other things to occupy him. Important things, including writing up the lecture he was to give next month at the Philosophical Society. And not one of those things had honey-colored hair and a sharp tongue.

It came down to logic, then. Elizabeth Dockering had set his life into a tumble by her inability to control her dog. And then, after a mishap that *hadn't* been her fault, she'd been of use, like any component in a task. And like a spent receiver of hydrogen, she wasn't required any longer. Except to receive Lancelot and return the poodle to his care tomorrow, of course.

The door of his study rattled again. "Apologies, Your Grace. Yes, your sign is up, and yes, it says you are not to be disturbed."

"That smacks of insubordination and sarcasm, Huston," Michael stated, setting the positive and negative wires of the pile aside again.

"I apologize again, then, Your Grace. You have a caller."

He stood up. "Miss Dockering?"

A pause. "No, Your Grace. A Lord Peter Cordray."

Ugh. Plasser's younger brother. Elizabeth's suitor, evidently. Disconnecting the voltaic battery entirely, he made his way to the door. "This is why ever attending social events is a mistake, Huston," he told his butler, pulling off his apron and shrugging into his coat. "One time, and now everyone in London is beating down my door. It's ridiculous. And unacceptable."

"Yes, Your Grace. Two visitors within a week *is* inexcusable."

Michael glanced sideways at his butler. "You're being sarcastic again. I do recognize it. I even utilize it, from time to time. Morning room?"

"Yes, Your Grace."

"Do not come in and offer us tea or any refreshment whatsoever. In five minutes, enter and inform me that the item I've been awaiting has arrived. Is that clear?"

"Certainly, Your Grace."

From his glance in the foyer mirror he looked fairly well put together and his hair, while it needed a good trim, wasn't smoking or standing on end, so he pushed open the closed door and stepped inside his large, comfortable morning room. "Cordray," he said, nodding, and shut them in, leaning beside the door to make it clear that he didn't intend to settle in for a long chat. "What can I do for you?"

The younger man rose from his seat on the couch. "Woriton. Thank you for seeing me. I apologize for not sending over a calling card first."

"No matter. What do you need?"

"It occurred to me that while I have spent sleepless nights contemplating what horrors might have happened should Bitsy Dockering have been home when her bedchamber was broken into, I haven't spared much thought for you. Your dog was taken. Or your aunt's, rather. Lady Mary Harris, yes?"

"Yes. Everything is being resolved, thankfully. Was—"

"Bitsy mentioned that you'd gotten a ransom note. A return in two days, yes? That would be tomorrow, I believe? I wonder at the delay, but I'm relieved that this awful incident looks to be over with soon." He smiled, starting to take a seat again and then clearly changing his mind when Michael didn't move. "Bitsy and I are . . . Well, we haven't yet come to an agreement, but we've definitely been negotiating toward a union, you know."

Michael wanted to respond that Elizabeth hadn't mentioned Cordray once yesterday, that her interest hadn't seemed to have been caught by any one gentleman in particular, and that this appearance seemed more like a male declaring his territory lest another fellow step into it, unnecessary as that was, but neither could he argue against the man's statement. Lord Peter seemed to know all the most recent information about Lancelot's ordeal, at any rate. "Are you looking for my congratulations?"

"No. Of course not."

"Then why are you telling me?"

"It's just conversation. We haven't spoken in quite a long time. I tell you about my life, you tell me about yours, and we part as friends once again."

"I've never been your friend. I was better acquainted with your brother, but he wasn't a friend, either. So, thank you for your kind wishes about my aunt's dog, but I'm in the middle of something."

Cordray opened and shut his mouth. "Very well. You're not interested—that is to say, you're not in pursuit of Bitsy, then?"

"Did you come here with a puffed-out chest and a coiled fist ready to fight over a lady's favor?" Michael retorted, forcing a grin. "Sorry to disappoint. Do go away now."

It irritated him a little when Cordray barked a laugh. "I shall.

I have no idea what I was thinking, anyway. Bitsy is a diamond, beloved by Society. She enjoys the theater, and parties, and picnics, and most of all, I believe, the company of her friends. You're very nearly a hermit and an automaton."

Generally, when someone interrupted what he was doing with something trivial or silly, it annoyed him. As Michael contemplated the man cheerfully insulting him in his own morning room, however, he didn't feel annoyed. He felt angry. Not a general aggravation, either, but a specific ire pointed directly at Peter Cordray.

"As I just informed you that Miss Dockering and I have no connection, I can only assume that you had this speech about our mutual incompatibilities already memorized and didn't wish to waste the mental effort it's clearly cost you. Well done, then," he said crisply, nodding. "In return, I suggest you try a friendlier tack when you next meet Galahad, or it may not be just your sleeve he removes."

"Ha. Bitsy had the right of it when she called you rude, the other day. Adieu, Woriton."

Cordray reached the morning room door just as Huston flung it open to make his announcement. The edge of the door caught the viscount's brother across the nose, and he stumbled backward.

"You idiot!" he screeched, touching his nose, seeing blood, and his face turning an equally bright red as he reached for a handkerchief. "Sack this fool, Woriton. I demand it!"

"You have a delivery, Your Grace," the butler said, his stoic expression admirably unchanged despite the squawking. "The item for which you've been waiting."

"Thank you," Michael returned. "And thanks to the door for saving me the effort of bloodying Lord Peter's nose myself. Get out of my house, Cordray, or I'll send a table after you, next."

"Bah. I don't know why I tried to be civil to you, Woriton. You don't deserve it." Handkerchief held tightly to his nose, the marquis's brother stalked past him and the butler and into the foyer. A moment later the front door opened and then shut again, hard.

"Your Grace, I apologize for my clumsi—"

"Oh, shut it, Huston. That was splendid timing. Tea and luncheon, if you please."

The butler bowed. "At once, Your Grace."

Michael walked back to his study and closed the door behind him. Nothing Cordray had said rang false. He knew perfectly well that he had a reputation for oddness and eccentricity, because as he'd told his aunt, he wasn't deaf or blind. Neither did he particularly care what Society thought of him; he didn't need them, and they got on perfectly well without him.

Just once, though, it would have been nice to stand up and say in a very loud voice how useless he considered most of his fellows. An exceptional few of them ran charities or contributed to them. A single percentage point of them understood that the power they wielded in Parliament could be used to better conditions for the least privileged. Other than that, the lot of them could fall into a volcano and the only thing anyone else noticed would be the loud hissing sound and a dearth of carriages during the afternoon promenade.

Except.

Yes, Elizabeth Dockering was pretty, and yes, he'd enjoyed his several conversations with her—even the more barbed ones. Especially the more barbed ones. It didn't make him wish to reassess his overall opinion of the aristocracy, but at the moment she did stand out as the one exception to the morass of uselessness.

Huston knocked at the door again, and Michael shook himself. "That had best be tea and luncheon."

The door opened. "It is, Your Grace. And a letter from Professor Davy."

"Humphry? Hand it over."

The butler did so, and while he set out luncheon and a pot of tea on a clear section of worktable, Michael unfolded the missive. It wasn't so much a letter as it was a confirmation of a theory. Sitting back on his stool, he read through it again.

"Good news, my lord?"

"Very good news. The liquefication of chlorine gas I demonstrated to the Royal Institution last month has been duplicated and confirmed. Chlorine now has two states of being." And he'd been credited with one of them. That, however, fell far behind the real news in the note. He glanced up at his half-constructed experiment. "As a liquid, its possible uses have expanded exponentially."

"That's wonderful, Your Grace. Sugar?"

"Yes. Two." And that was that. Later, as the news spread, congratulations would trickle in from his scientifically minded friends and compatriots, his presentation next month would receive more publicity and attract a larger audience, and everything else would continue as it had, because there was always more to do, more to attempt, more to learn.

And for a brief, damned moment, he wanted to go find Elizabeth Dockering and tell her that he'd discovered a new state for an element. And no doubt she would congratulate him, and then ask why he hadn't bothered to put on a cravat before he ventured out of doors and whether all scientists could be mistaken for fishmongers or if that was just him.

"Something amusing, Your Grace?" Huston asked, adjusting a fork and then straightening.

"Possibly, Huston. Possibly."

"Another one?" Sally Pangle repeated, not even trying to hide the skepticism in her voice.

"I told you there was a confusion, and I ended up with the wrong dog. Now I'm to fetch the right one." Jimmy Bly broke the small lump of sugar into even smaller pieces and took a third of them for himself. "Here."

He always did that, giving her extra sugar for the weak tea they shared when either of them managed to scrounge some up, and she remained appreciative. She did like sweets, but neither her costume nor her purse allowed her to indulge very often. "When is this supposed to happen?"

"I'm to retrieve Galahad tonight. Lancelot goes back tomorrow, and Galahad two or three days after that. That'll be the last of it. I swear."

He kept his eyes looking at his cup of tea, a sure sign that he was lying. She knew Jimmy tiptoed on the wrong side of legal, as did most of the tenants of the Rookery. Most stayed on that side. Jimmy, at least, took the odd job when he found it, from chimney sweeping to errand running to toting cargo to shops from the ships along the Thames that delivered it. But he also dabbled in other things, and that worried her.

A paw tapped on her foot, and she looked down to see Lancelot pretending not to look at her, his pointed nose in the air. "It's biscuits you like, isn't it?" she asked, breaking one in half and holding it so he could see.

He gave a low whine.

"You're spoiling him, Sally," Jimmy said, his grin countering any chastising he might be doing.

"I'm making him work for it," she returned, turning in her seat to face the poodle. "If you want this, you're going to have to sit up and beg." She snapped her fingers twice, and her own poodle approached. "Ask me, Jenny," she commanded.

The smaller poodle raised up on her hind feet, put her front paws together, and lifted them up and down.

"Good girl." Sally gave Jenny a quarter of the biscuit, then looked at Lancelot. "Ask me, Lancelot."

The big black poodle cocked his head at her and barked.

"No. Try it again." Squatting, she put him in position. "Ask me, Lancelot," she repeated, holding up the piece of biscuit.

With a whine he waved his front paws at her.

"Good boy!" She gave him the rest of the biscuit, and he chomped it down in one bite.

"I'm not sure you should be teaching him that," Jimmy cautioned.

"Why not? Someone's already taught him to heel and sit and lie down on command. A couple more tricks, and he could join the fair with Jenny and the boys and me. You could join, too. Sally Pangle and Her Amazing Animals and Jimmy Bly."

He laughed. "Pickle and Bob know more tricks than me, I'm afraid."

She looked over at the two white fluff balls, presently making one, slightly bigger, snoring ball of fluff. "Well, I've been training them for three years, now. Of course, I've only had Jenny for a year, and she can do more tricks than you, too."

"I am a slow learner." Ruffling the now-lopsided coif on Lancelot's head, he sighed. "Would you watch Lancelot for me while I'm out this evening?"

"You know I will." If Jimmy Bly hadn't had a pair of blue eyes with long lashes and a straight nose and square chin, if his mop of brown hair didn't almost constantly make her want to run her fingers through it, she might not have been so willing to aid his criminal activities, but they all had their weaknesses. Jimmy Bly was hers.

"Thank you, Sally. You're a rare one."

"And don't you forget it." She swirled her teacup with one hand, instructing Jenny to roll over with her other. "I *could* find you some work with the fair, you know. It might be shoveling horse shite or dragging benches about, but you wouldn't have to fret that the constabulary is looking for you."

He shook his head. "My pa said I'd be fit for nothing but shoveling manure. I'd rather risk all of London's magistrates than take a penny for moving shite about."

"Jimmy."

"I know, I know. I'm stubborn." He flashed her a grin. "But neither do I smell like the backside of a horse."

Sally snorted. "All I can tell you, then, is don't get caught. And keep in mind there are other dog stealers out there, ones who aren't as kindly as you. Stay away from them, as well."

It wasn't just the dog stealers, either. So far Jimmy had merely gone about scamping, snabbling something minor when the opportunity presented itself. He'd avoided the gangs and the counterfeiters and the more lucrative and dangerous armed robberies, but eventually everyone got noticed. Taking dogs from viscounts' daughters and dukes, for heaven's sake, was a good way to be seen by the even less savory residents of the Rookery and its environs. From there, being pulled into worse would only be a matter of time.

"You're frowning mightily, Sally Pangle," Jimmy said.

She took a breath. For the three years she'd lived downstairs from him she'd wanted to have this conversation, but in her daydreams he'd been the one declaring himself to her. And she wouldn't do anything as softhearted as declare love to him—not when he might end up in jail at any moment, or worse, leave her a widow. Not even a widow, because of course they weren't married. "I like you, Jimmy Bly. You don't have to be a wealthy man to impress me."

For a long moment he looked at her. "Aye. But for you, I do have to be better than what I am. I'm trying, you know. After this, I'll be swimming in blunt for a year, maybe, if I'm careful. I might even have the time to find myself proper work."

"I can't wait forever," she said, touching one finger to the back of his hand, then standing. "But I can wait a bit longer. Come along,

Pickle, Bob, Jenny, Lancelot. Papa Jimmy has somewhere to be this evening."

The dogs fell in behind her like a parade as she headed down the hallway and down the stairs to her near-luxurious set of two rooms that lay just below Jimmy's place. She couldn't ask him to give up his life of petty crime and odd jobs and share her rooms, because she couldn't afford to feed another mouth together with herself and the dogs. The reality of it, though, didn't stop her from wanting to do precisely that.

CHAPTER EIGHT

WHILE THE EVENSON SOIREE WOULDN'T BE CONSIDERED A GRAND ball—with only a hundred guests, it didn't even come near to qualifying for that exalted title—it was still lovely and loud and crowded with friends. Elizabeth swept into the ballroom and gave a twirl, making the silver beads on her midnight-black gown twinkle in the candlelight.

Peggy had woven black ribbons through her light-colored hair, and even though her mother said the colors were too dark and gloomy, Elizabeth thought them dramatic and romantic. With the elbow-length black gloves and the black onyx necklace and earbobs added, well, she felt nearly Shakespearean.

That marked a large improvement over the rest of the day. She'd overslept, and then forgotten to send out calling cards for visiting. Almost no one would object to her arriving somewhere unannounced, but she was generally much better organized than that.

When Lord Peter Cordray and Anne and Alice Caulfield had come calling she'd begun to feel more like herself, even if the sarcastic questions about the Duke of Woriton had annoyed her. For heaven's sake, he might be blunt, but he hadn't forgotten to wear shoes or comb his hair or put on a cravat.

Thus far the consensus remained that she was merely humoring him, that after the unfortunate tangle of their dogs she'd been kind and gracious and patient in assisting him with Lancelot's return. At one point she'd evidently defended his character too vociferously, however, and then the insinuations had begun. Was she fond of Woriton? Had she overlooked his ape-like manners and possible depravity because he had deep pockets? Had she been to see his study and his mysterious experiments? Did he have bits of people lying about and ready to sew together like some Dr. Frankenstein?

Such nonsense, it was. She'd told them so, and she hadn't as much as mentioned driving about Covent Garden yesterday and how entertaining it had all been. Nor would she, because she was Miss Bitsy Dockering, a diamond of the Season, and she wished to remain that way. She took a dance card and a pencil from the table, smiling as Tom and Geoffrey Hillstead approached her. "My, aren't you two gentlemen looking very fine this evening?"

"Why, yes, we are," Tom said, sketching a bow. "Dance card, if you please." He held out one hand.

"Just a moment. I need to put Lord Peter's name by the first waltz."

"Ahh. Still making amends for the torn sleeve, are you? He's wrung that out past anything reasonable." Geoffrey glanced about the crowded room, though she doubted he was hoping to see Peter Cordray.

"It's not his doing; I missed my waltz with him at the Sommerset ball."

"That's right! I forgot you got dragged onto the floor by Woriton," Geoffrey commented. "It must have been a full moon that night. I can't explain it, otherwise."

"Geoffrey," she commented, handing Tom the card and pencil, "you know we all do our charitable deeds. That was mine."

As she looked up, she caught sight of the Duke of Sommerset passing by, his wife Lydia, the duchess, on his arm. Sommerset and Michael were friends, Michael had said. Her chest tightened a little. The room had been very loud, though. It was entirely possible he hadn't heard her being uncharitable with her, well, charity comment.

The duke continued on his way, and she let out her breath. "One dance, Tom. I will not be monopolized."

"A quadrille is barely a dance. Surely—"

"One," she repeated, smiling to take any sting from her words.

She'd said something uncharitable in public about Michael Bromley, though, and that continued to irk her. He'd insulted her to her face on multiple occasions now, but she'd done the same to him. Talking about him when he was likely home trying to find a way to save lives felt . . . both unkind and unfair.

"Did you know that light has a speed?" she asked aloud.

Tom gave her a sideways look as he handed her card to his brother. "I beg your pardon?"

"Light has a speed. Just as a horse or a man on foot have speeds at which they can run."

"Well, it must be very slow, because I have yet to see a candle move on its own." Geoffrey wrote in his name and handed back the card and pencil. "Is that something Woriton told you? I believe him to be a bag of hot air. Cordray says his brother used to talk about how Woriton went about Oxford with ink stains on his fingers and a pencil behind his ear. Like a clerk."

Anne Caulfield hurried up and grabbed on to Elizabeth's arm. "Stop frowning," she whispered. "You'll make wrinkles."

Elizabeth smoothed her expression. "Anne, have you met these two rascals?"

"Oh, yes, but neither of them has asked a dance of me this evening! Isn't that odd?"

Thank goodness for friends. It remained on the tip of her tongue to say something more . . . supportive of Woriton, though, so she announced that she would be by the refreshment table and swirled away.

Defending him wouldn't help anything, because everyone had already made up their minds. He wouldn't approve of her interference, either, firstly because he wasn't even there, and secondly because he didn't care what anyone else said. And it could hurt her reputation. If word got about that she enjoyed conversing and dancing with odd persons, she would have every clod with a rock collection and every country bumpkin in Mayfair lining up to speak with her.

"Miss Dockering?"

She turned around at the low voice to see the Duke of Sommerset looking at her from the far side of the sweets table. "Your Grace," she said, curtsying. *Dash it all.*

"You are a friend of the Duke of Woriton, are you not?"

"I . . . We are acquainted, Your Grace."

"Yes, friendship with Michael can be a bit hard to quantify," he said, half to himself. "Anyway, he said you've been helping him look for Lancelot and that you didn't run away when he began talking about science. I thought you might wish to know that earlier today he was credited with being the first to render chlorine gas into a liquid. He devised a method, which he tested multiple times and then put in writing, and as of this morning his paper has been confirmed and the experiment successfully duplicated."

That sounded significant. "He did say he was working with combining different elements with chlorine, looking for a way to prevent infection."

"Indeed, he is. Anyway, he more than likely won't say anything about it, so if you see him again, you might congratulate him." He leaned over the table, sorting through a tray of biscuits. "And if you know of any lady who doesn't mind a brusque and . . . surly fellow, there are those of us who would appreciate your assistance. The man needs a wife to encourage him to lift his head from his work now and again, whatever he may think, and I'm aware that you know nearly every young, eligible lady in Mayfair." He straightened again. "I will, of course, deny we ever spoke if he confronts me about it."

She lifted her eyebrows before she could stop herself. "I—As will I."

"Good."

Well, her literal collision with Michael Bromley continued to grow more and more mad. A duke had just asked her to help find a wife for another duke, a feat evidently to be managed while she was in the middle of returning said duke's dog to his custody. That was all that remained of their temporary partnership—Lancelot arriving tomorrow and her taking her carriage to Bromley House to return the poodle to Michael's care.

The odds of her discovering a suitable spouse for him in that amount of time were abysmal, even if she actually wanted to help. Which she didn't. For heaven's sake, she didn't know any woman rude enough to match Woriton. Most women would likely scream and run away—or faint—after he uttered a single sentence to them.

In addition, he'd made it clear that he needed her for only one task. She doubted he would bother to find another reason to cross paths with her after Lancelot was returned. Not that she would have time to go about looking for him, either, of course. She had a spouse of her own to find, and it didn't matter that time sped in his company, or that his praise of her intelligence and wit had seemed the best compliments she'd ever received.

"Ah, there you are."

Lord Peter Cordray stopped beside her, a smile on his handsome face. He *was* well-favored, and tall, and had a fine pedigree. At times it seemed as if he was performing, acting the part of a suitor rather than actually being one, but that could well be nerves, or awkwardness, or her own tendency to look for flaws.

"Here I am," she answered.

Sending an exaggerated look around the room, he bent toward her a little. "Woriton is absent, I trust? I don't wish to lose another waltz to him."

"If he did appear, I would inform him that this dance is taken," she said firmly. Then he would likely have some argument or other about that, and by the time she'd finished making her point, the waltz would be over entirely.

"I am pleased to hear that, Bitsy." Peter held out his hand. "Shall we?"

She took his fingers in her gloved ones just as the music for the waltz began. He bent his arm and she spun with some force into his chest, so that she had to splay her free hand across his breast to catch herself. His grin deepening, he put his other hand on her waist and moved into the dance. A bit aggressive, that, but she let it pass as Anne and Tom swung by, both of them smiling.

"I have waited what feels like an age to dance again with you, Bitsy," the marquis's brother said, curling his hand around her fingers.

"We danced on Saturday, did we not?"

"Every moment not in your company feels endless, I'm afraid."

Elizabeth smiled. "Well, that's very kind of you to say, my lord, even if you are exaggerating."

"But I'm not." He met her gaze and then seemed to refuse to blink, which made her own eyes want to water. "I have a house in mind," he went on, "a medium-sized one on Old Burlington Street. With your dowry and a gift from my brother, we could manage it quite easily. It has a lovely large drawing room, perfect for entertaining, and a small garden at the rear with red roses."

Oh, dear, a proposal right in the middle of a waltz, right in the middle of a soiree with her friends and peers all around them, practically drooling for gossip. "I appreciate your enthusiasm," she said, keeping a smile on her face. "What of Galahad, though? You two don't get along. At all."

One eye twitched. "That is so. I believe, however, that with time, Galahad and I will become great friends. I have said so before."

"So you have. And it was mere days ago that he ripped off your sleeve, and very nearly your arm."

"It doesn't signify, Bitsy. Don't let a dog dictate your future."

"I'm not," she protested. "But neither will I be rushed into a decision that affects me, and my family, and yes, Galahad."

Finally, he closed his eyes, and she blinked hard. Intensity or bullying, she didn't much like either. Not when he had her trapped on the dance floor. Still, he wasn't the first to imagine a life with her that didn't require any suggestions from her, and he likely wouldn't be the last.

"You're correct, of course," he said, nodding. "Perhaps tomorrow you will come and see the house with me—without any questions from me other than whether or not you like the look of it."

"My lord, I—"

"Peter, please. For God's sake, Bitsy."

She took a breath. If it would calm him down, though, give her time to think, she could give him that one thing. "Peter, then," she said.

His smile deepened. "Come see the house with me, Bitsy. I will be a perfect gentleman. I swear it."

He was relentless. "If you will make it tomorrow afternoon, I shall agree. I have something to see to in the morning." At least, she hoped Lancelot would be returned in the morning. If not, she would have to put Peter off, and she didn't imagine he would take that well, at all.

"Very well, then. Tomorrow afternoon."

After that the evening went smoothly. A few other men waxed poetic over her virtues, which were apparently innumerable, but she accepted their compliments with a smile and managed to avoid encouraging them toward yet more proposals. She danced, she laughed, she drank, and perhaps for one, small moment she wished the Duke of Woriton would make an appearance and set the entire room on its ear and then insist on dancing with her. Now, *that* would be fun.

It was well after midnight before she and her parents returned home. The moment she passed through the front door into Dockering House, she sat on the foyer bench and took off her shoes. "Ahh," she breathed, wiggling her freed toes. "That is so much better."

"I would call you scandalous," her mother said with a smile, "but my feet feel like they've walked from London to York."

"But Mama, if you remove your shoes, as well, Crawford might faint."

The butler finished latching the door before he faced them, his spine straight. "I will attempt to remain upright, my lady," he said, nodding at the viscountess, "and I further offer to fetch you a basin of hot water if you wish to soak your feet."

"Thank you, Crawford, but that won't be necessary. Please send up Lois, Peggy, and Eastley, and go to bed."

"Of course, my lady." He nodded again. "My lord, Miss Bitsy."

"Good night, Crawford." Lord Mardensea offered an arm each to his wife and his youngest daughter. "Shall we, ladies?"

"Thank you, Papa." She took his arm, with her mother on the other side, and they clumped up the stairs to the first floor and the north hallway with its row of bedchambers.

"I happened to notice," the viscountess said, as they stopped outside the master bedchamber, "that Peter Cordray looked quite serious as you danced with him this evening. Has he offered for you again?"

Elizabeth sighed. "Yes. And tomorrow he wants to show me a house that's caught his interest."

"You're joining him?"

"It doesn't mean anything, Mama, and I told him as much. He says it will indicate whether our tastes are in alignment."

Her mother kissed her on the cheek. "You are going to have to choose someone eventually. Don't wait until all the most eligible gentlemen propose to other young women because they've gotten tired of waiting for you to decide which of them you like the most."

"I know. And I am considering."

Lord Mardensea snorted. "Is your hesitation still because Galahad doesn't like him?"

She grinned. "Perhaps. A little bit."

"Never ignore a dog's sensibilities," he commented, and with a wink opened the door, holding it for his wife.

Her own door was down one more to the left, and with a yawn, swinging her dancing slippers in one hand, she made her way there. "I'm home, Galahad," she said, opening her door.

She dumped her slippers onto a chair, her shawl following them. And then she stopped, caught up by the absolute silence in her bedchamber. No clicking toenails, no panting, no quiet half bark welcoming her home. Swallowing, Elizabeth turned to face the room. A low fire in the fireplace made yellow flicker dimly up the walls, but nothing else moved.

Oh, no. "Galahad?" Hiking up her skirt, she knelt to peer under the bed. A small mound of something caught her attention, and she bent further, reaching out to get hold of it.

Behind her, her door opened again. "Miss Bitsy? What's—"

"Tell me you took Galahad downstairs to bed with you, Peggy," she ordered, finally touching the thing. It was damp and soft, and as she pulled it into view, she already knew what it would be. Meat, dosed with laudanum.

"I didn't," the lady's maid whispered, as if her breath had left her in a rush. "Oh, no. Not again."

Elizabeth sat down on the floor, the chunk of steak in one hand. "Please go fetch . . . everyone," she said, a tear running down her face and plopping onto her arm.

It didn't make sense, unless the thief had decided that her willingness to pay had made her worthy of another robbery. But as far as the dog stealer knew, he'd taken her one dog already. Another one wasn't supposed to be here. Unless he'd been watching the house. Unless he'd heard a rumor that he'd taken the Duke of Woriton's dog by accident and wanted to make another go of it.

But whatever it meant, whatever had caused this to happen, Galahad had been taken out of her home. Again. And the poor dear still whined in his sleep after the first time. *Damnation.* Her parents would offer her sympathy and of course to pay any ransom. They would rail at the housebreakers and make certain that at least one footman remained awake all night from now on so something like this would never happen again. None of that would help Galahad, of course.

Oh, and did this mean that Lancelot wouldn't be returned tomorrow? Surely the thief would realize that people would be watching for him if he so much as entered the street with a poodle in his care. As her father burst into the room, profanity falling from his lips, she looked up at him.

"I need to send word to Woriton," Elizabeth stated. "This concerns him, as well."

"It's three o'clock in the morning, Bitsy. We'll send a note before breakfast."

She shook her head, the half-eaten steak still clutched in one hand. "He knows things. I want to see him now."

"I . . ." As her mother put a hand on her father's shoulder, he nodded. "Of course. I'll see to it."

Michael sat back, picking up his snifter of brandy and swirling it as he read the last few lines of the parliamentary paperwork in front of him. Prince George wanted another loan—or rather, a forgiveness of his previous three loans—and of course Parliament would give it to him.

A Prince Regent who defaulted on his loans was a very bad look for a country, and every Tory and Whig in the House of Commons and the House of Lords knew it. The vote would be Friday, which meant another day lost to idiotic arguments over an idiotic topic where the conclusion was already foregone. Politics lay in the arguing, though, and for most of his fellows, *that* was the important part of all this nonsense.

Sighing, he pulled the next document off the waiting stack that cluttered one corner of his desk. For his official work as a duke, he retreated to his small downstairs office; him, frustration, drinking, and glass vials of acids did not go well together. And when it came to legislating, the first three were unavoidable.

Someone thumped on the front door. Frowning, he set aside his glass and stood. Huston would be along to see to it in a moment, but at this point any excuse to avoid reading about more taxes on grain was a good one.

Glancing at the cane set in the stand to one side of the door as he reached the foyer, he unlatched the sturdy lock and pulled open the thick oak door. "Yes?"

A liveried footman, his dress somewhat careless, stood on the front portico. "A message for the duke," he said, panting as if he'd been running.

"Thank you."

The servant didn't relinquish the paper in his hand. "I'm to give it directly to the duke."

"I *am* the duke," Michael said, as Huston, clothed in his proper jacket over a nightshirt, cleared his throat from the far end of the foyer. "*He's* the butler."

"Oh. I—I beg your pardon, Your Grace. Here you go." The footman handed over the missive.

"Are you to wait for an answer?" Huston asked, hovering as close to the door as he could without shoving Michael out of his way.

"No. Just to deliver it with all possible haste." The young man bowed. "I'd best get back. Good evening, Your Grace."

Nodding, Michael turned away from the door and left Huston to close and latch it as he unfolded the note. He didn't recognize the handwriting, but he was damned familiar with the subject of the missive. "Have Romer saddled, Huston," he said, striding back to the office for his coat. He'd have to forgo a cravat.

"Your Grace, it's the middle of the night. And you shouldn't be opening your own door. Could be hooligans or housebreakers about."

"Romer, Huston. Now."

His hurry wasn't because there'd been another dog theft, or because Lord Mardensea had personally sent over a note requesting his presence. No, he shrugged into his coat and trotted down through the servants' area of the house and out the rear door because the viscount had written that his daughter had specifically requested Michael's presence. "At once," the note had said, following that with an apology and a comment about young women and their frailty.

Perhaps he didn't know Elizabeth Dockering well, but he had learned two things about her: Firstly, she felt guilty over Galahad's first kidnapping; and secondly, she wasn't frail. The woman had spleen aplenty, and if she'd asked for his assistance, or even just his presence, then she would have it.

The groom was cinching the saddle around Romer as he strode

into the dimly lit stable. "If you'll give me another moment, I'll saddle Celsius and accompany you, Your Grace."

"Not necessary, Dobbin. I'm capable of looking after myself."

Michael swung into the saddle as the groom stepped back. "Please inform Huston that I'll be at Dockering House, if he should need to find me."

"I will, Your Grace, after he finishes thrashing me for letting you go alone."

"Thrash him back, then."

The ice and milk wagons had begun appearing on the streets, but it was too early for most other honest folk. He passed a few other types, the ones lurking just outside the lamplight, or in the deep shadows between buildings, but other than noting their presence, he mostly ignored them.

Galahad had been taken. Had it been the same thief or thieves who'd made off with Lancelot? If so, how the devil had they known they would find another black poodle—another dog at all—in residence? Had they been watching Dockering House? Elizabeth had mentioned the poodle mix-up to several of her friends, as had he to his; had one of them been overheard by the wrong person?

It all smacked of something even more suspicious than a simple dog theft, and he didn't like that. He preferred theories that could be proven with facts, and so he refused to speculate further. If Elizabeth thought his presence would be somehow helpful, perhaps she had some of those same questions herself. A very logical bent, Miss Dockering had. It had initially surprised him, but he appreciated it about her. It was one of several things he'd begun to appreciate about her, actually.

As he reached Dockering House, he noted that most of the windows upstairs and down shone with light. The whole house was turned out, then. A sleepy-looking groom took Romer from him, and the front door opened as he reached it.

"Your Grace," the butler said, "you'll find the family in the morning room. This way."

The butler's guidance wasn't much needed, since the morning room door was but three steps beyond the foyer, but Michael stood in the doorway and allowed himself to be announced to the half dozen people in the pretty, green-walled room.

"Thank you for coming, Woriton," Lord Mardensea rumbled, stepping forward to offer his hand. "I don't know that there's anything to be done, but Bitsy insisted you would be the one to figure something out."

"What am I to figure out, then?" he asked, shaking hands and then moving around the trio of tired-looking servants to stand in front of the tired-looking Elizabeth seated on one end of a long blue and brown couch.

"I found the remains of meat with, I assume, laudanum," she said, her hands twisted into her lap and her voice not quite steady. "No other sign at all of someone being in the house. Except for Galahad being missing, of course."

"The same thief, then? That doesn't make sense." Frowning, he sat beside her. "That is, it doesn't make sense if we go by the assumption that the thief initially saw you and Galahad together and decided to take him for ransom. He did so. He therefore had no reason to break in again after another dog."

"That was my thinking, as well," she said, lifting one hand for a moment to brush at her eyes. "It's so stupid, me being hysterical over a dog, but this seems intentional, you know? A vendetta, almost. And I cannot think of who might wish to be so cruel to me."

"Crawford, a pot of tea, if you please," Lady Mardensea ordered, and the butler left the room. "We'll all think more clearly after a hot cup of tea and some breakfast, I imagine."

She and her husband were both in their dressing robes, presumably over their nightwear. Elizabeth wore a gown of midnight, over which a fine netting of innumerable silver beads lay. Black necklace, black ribbons in her hair—it should have been funereal, but it wasn't. And then, peeking from beneath her black skirts, bare toes. She was barefoot.

"Most crimes are, I believe, ones of opportunity," he said, because her feet distracted him and he wanted to compliment her appearance, neither of which was the least bit helpful. "Someone looking for money finds an unlocked door or a man who's removed his coat with his purse inside. It's entirely possible that taking Lancelot was easy, so the thief decided to take a second look through your house and to his surprise found another black poodle with which to abscond."

Elizabeth sniffed. "Any reason for it is horrible, but I much prefer that it be something random. It doesn't explain the meat with laudanum, though. That says to me that he came here with the intention of taking a dog."

"Yes, it does. A good catch, that," Michael complimented her. Developing theories only worked when all the facts could be taken into account. And the laudanum—that definitely spoke of planning and intent.

"Don't fret, my dear," Elizabeth's father said, patting her on the shoulder. "It will be difficult, but we'll only need to wait another day or so for a ransom note, and then Galahad's return."

Michael considered that, as well. "How could he possibly expect to return Lancelot when he's got the entire household in an uproar over Galahad? Either this man is an idiot, or he has no intention of returning either dog."

"That was what worried me," Elizabeth said. "Lancelot was supposed to be returned later today. And now . . ."

"Where's the bait he used?"

She gestured to the table beneath the window. "I pulled it from beneath my bed, but didn't let anyone else touch it in case you're able to discover something."

Standing again, he walked over to take a look. Assuming the cut of meat was the same size as the first one, Galahad had eaten a great deal more of it than had Lancelot. Galahad did have a weakness for beef, however. He would have been docile as a lamb by the time the thief was ready to carry him from the house. "Was the front door left unlatched again?"

Lord Mardensea cleared his throat. "Crawford claims to have kept it locked all evening, up until three o'clock—which was when we expected to return. We were here forty minutes after that."

"Hm. Drugging Galahad would have taken twenty minutes at the minimum. Sneaking in here, bundling him up to carry him out . . . It makes me wonder if the dog thief coincidentally arrived the moment after the door was unlocked, or if he did enter through a window this time, and left via the front door after Crawford unlatched it." He turned around. "I'm going upstairs."

"Your Gra—"

"I'm going with you," Elizabeth said, cutting off her mother's gasp. As if he meant to do anything untoward up there.

"Bitsy—"

"We're looking for clues, Mama. Please."

Without waiting to hear more of the nonsense, Michael left the morning room and trod up the curving staircase. Behind him he heard the viscountess wondering aloud how he could possibly know where her bedchamber was. "Did you not tell your parents that I was here after Lancelot was taken?" he asked over his shoulder.

"I told them you were here at the house. I may not have mentioned specifics."

"Why not?" Pausing, he turned to face her on the stairs below him.

Elizabeth looked up at him, her eyes large in the predawn gloom. "Because I didn't wish to have to explain why I permitted a man to enter my bedchamber."

The explanation seemed simple enough to him, but abruptly he realized what she meant—he was a male, and males weren't supposed to be in the private rooms of unmarried females. Which meant he was a candidate to ruin her. Which meant he was . . . a potential suitor? That she saw him as a potential suitor?

"Why are you still staring at me?" she asked.

Michael shook himself. "I haven't slept yet tonight, either," he muttered, continuing up the stairs. "Damned parliamentary papers to read before the next session of the House of Lords."

"That would put me to sleep," she commented, clearly aiming to regain some of her usual composure.

"Hm. You should try sitting through one of the sessions where they read it aloud and argue over every word."

"No, thank you."

"Your gown is lovely, by the way. Very striking."

"I . . . thank you."

At least she wasn't crying any longer, which had bothered him far more than it should have. He much preferred when she had her wits about her and noticed things he might have missed. "How *was* the soiree this evening?"

"Like every other soiree. Though if I'd known in advance that Peter Cordray meant to propose to me again, I might have stayed home, and then Galahad would still be here, safe and sound."

"Or you might have found yourself face-to-face with the thief." Abruptly furious at that idea, but not, of course, at hearing about the proposal, he opened her bedchamber door and strode inside. "Cordray proposes to you often, does he?"

"It's the fourth time. There's nothing wrong with him, I suppose, but I keep hoping for . . . a spark. It's silly and girlish, I know, but I still want to feel my heart beat faster when my beau walks into a room."

Michael lit the lamp, noting that the pair of windows were both shut. "Sparks are caused by friction," he noted. "Perhaps you're seeking someone who ruffles your feathers, so to speak."

"Cordray and I are too much in harmony, you mean? I would think that a good thing."

Shrugging, he lifted the lamp and moved it over to the first window. "You're the one who wants a spark. A spark is the result of an irritation. Not harmony. Did you agree to his offer?"

"No. Not yet."

Good. "Ah. Was either window open last night?"

"I cracked the right one an inch or so, to give Galahad some fresh air. There's a rosebush below, though. No one could climb the wall without being badly scratched."

"It's shut now," he observed, moving sideways. "Peggy, perhaps?"

"I don't remember her shutting it." She walked to the door. "Peggy!"

The lady's maid appeared so quickly she must have been poised just outside in the hallway. "Miss Bitsy?"

"Goodness. Do stop lurking. Did you close my window this evening, before or after I returned home?"

"No, miss. Galahad likes to smell who's coming and going outside."

Michael set the lamp on the floor in front of the window and squatted down to examine the oak floorboards. "Look at this," he said, leaning closer.

She knelt opposite him. "What is it?"

With one finger, noting and then attempting to set aside the awareness that she smelled like cinnamon—perhaps a tea?—he outlined a partial heel mark made of a minute scattering of still-damp earth. "He came in this way. No doubt he used his toes for the climb up, which is why he only had dirt left on the heel."

"I . . . My goodness." Putting a hand to her chest, she stood again and pushed open her window, leaning out to look down. "How?"

He joined her, holding the lamp outside so he could see the ground. "I'd wager he used that plank, there," he said, gesturing with his free hand at the piece of wood lying against the bottom of the brick wall, "to push the roses away from the wall and flatten them so he could get to the drainpipe."

"Outsmarted, then," she murmured, turning her face to look at him. "And it's my fault Galahad was taken. If I hadn't opened the window, the thief wouldn't have gotten in."

"Your argument is unsound," he returned, noting that her green eyes looked black in the lamplight. "Galahad was only taken because someone broke the law in order to do it. Housebreaking is illegal. Opening a window for night air is not. Nor is owning a dog."

"Thank you for saying that, but I should have realized Galahad was still a target. They came here after him the first time, after all."

"You don't know that. You know they came here and took a dog they likely thought was yours. Why would they come back and do it again when they still have custody of that dog? You had no reason to suspect any such action would be taken, because it's illogical."

Elizabeth blinked, leaned closer to give him a quick kiss on the cheek, and ducked back into the room.

Lips soft as a feather, and warm as a sigh. A handful of even more illogical thoughts entered his mind, and it took him a moment to brush them away. Happenstance, circumstance, had brought them together. He'd thought to be done with her after today. The idea that their alliance would have to be extended, though, didn't annoy him as much as logic said it should.

Both Galahad and Lancelot remained missing and were now unlikely to be returned. That made him angry, both on Elizabeth's and his aunt's behalf. At the same time, while everything seemed a bit fuzzy and mixed with tiredness, he also felt a sense of renewed opportunity—though for what, he couldn't precisely say.

Belatedly he pulled his head back in from the window and straightened. "I think we have to assume that Lancelot will not be returned, and that there will be no ransom note for Galahad. And that makes me wonder why he would take Galahad before returning Lancelot. He has to know we won't trust him again. Therefore, we have to wonder what will happen to the dogs."

"I'm already wondering that," she said quietly, another tear running down her face. "How certain are we, then, that it's the same person who took both boys?"

"Fairly damned certain. A chunk of steak, laudanum, utilization of convenient forms of entry into the house, no ransom note at the time of theft . . . It adds up to the same individual. Or the same gang, at least."

"A gang? Oh, my. That's even worse." She clenched her fists. "I will not have Galahad lost to some . . . evil people, no matter how unsound their reasoning."

"Then we are going to have a busy day tomorrow."

She looked up at him, her expression hopeful. "'We'?"

His heart stumbled a little. Too much brandy and not enough sleep, no doubt. "Yes. We."

CHAPTER NINE

"FOR GOD'S SAKE! DON'T MURDER ME!"

Snatching his hand back, Jimmy Bly slammed the board into place and leaned his spine against it as the big black poodle lunged at him. Those bared teeth and that snarl were going to haunt his nights for a time, if he ever slept again.

Now he wished he'd hired a carpenter to construct his little room within a room. Some nails and boards stolen from behind a shop, a bit of rope to help secure the makeshift door—it seemed a disaster waiting for the worst possible moment to happen. Mayhap he should move his bed into the hallway until he'd rid himself of the dogs.

Lancelot sat down in front of him and stuck out one paw. "That's a good lad," Jimmy said, when he felt fairly sure his heart wasn't going to pound itself out of his chest, "but I don't have any biscuits in my pockets."

Snorting, the poodle shifted, sat down again, and held out one paw.

"Are you offering me a handshake, then?" Jimmy leaned down, took Lancelot's paw, shook it, and straightened again. With a wag the dog stood again and wandered over to stick his nose into a crack between the boards.

"Did you teach him that?" he asked, turning to the doorway as another black poodle and two fuzzy white dogs traipsed into his room, Sally Pangle behind them. No matter the time of day or night, when Sally walked into his room it always felt like a sun-shining morning. He smiled even though he probably looked like a half-wit doing it.

"I think someone had already been attempting it," she said. "He caught on far too quick for it to be his first try." She joined him by the homemade fence and peeked through another gap in the boards. "I can see how one could be mistaken for the other. They even have the same haircut. It makes them look a bit silly, doesn't it? I would never tell that to Lancelot, though."

A growl from beyond the temporary wall didn't sound very happy about the conversation. "No, Lancelot's a fine lad," Jimmy agreed, patting the poodle on the head. "Galahad, though, he's something else entirely."

"He's backed himself into the far corner," she reported, peering inside again. "I reckon he's more scared than anything, poor lad."

"I'm scared, too. He nearly took my hand off. Where's your sympathy for me?"

Chuckling, she took his hand and patted it. "You poor dear. Though I might suggest if you stop stealing poodles, they won't try biting you for it."

"This is my last one. I swear it." That had been a close one; the family carriage had driven right past him where he'd jumped into the shrubbery just down the street from the house. Carrying sixty pounds of sleeping poodle over his shoulder, only a blanket to keep it from looking like what it was, had had him thinking that he should be asking for even more money from Cordray.

"Do you still return Lancelot later today?"

He winced. "I'm to keep him a bit longer, until the household gets tired of looking for anyone lurking about the property. I may just give 'em both back at the same time, if I can put a lead on Galahad without being murdered."

That made sense to him, anyway. Much more sense than Cordray's plan—which contained a great deal of "I'll figure it out later" and "keep them until I say otherwise." Cordray didn't have to feed the beasties, or clean up after them, or sleep beside them.

"Give him something to eat," Sally suggested.

"I need to go to the butcher's again. He won't open his door for another two hours."

"Some water, then. Something that's not frightening."

"Give him Jenny, then. She won't frighten him."

"Oh, Jimmy Bly. Men are frequently scared of women." With a slight grin she sat on the floor, leaning back against the boards, and motioned him to join her.

He sat down. "What are we doing?"

"We're talking. Letting him get to know our voices, and our smells, and to figure out that nothing terrifying is happening. Come here, Jenny. Down."

At her command, the female poodle lay down beside the make-shift cage. A moment later he heard sniffing coming from the far side of the wood. "I told you so. He likes *her,* at least."

Lancelot shoved himself in between Jimmy and Sally, and put his head on Jimmy's knee. "And Lancelot likes *you,*" Sally pointed out. "Well done, Jimmy."

"Lancelot and me could never be happy together," he commented, giving her a sideways glance and hoping that was affection he still heard in her voice. "He's too fancy for a sneaking budge like me."

She met his gaze, gray eyes level. "Then don't be a sneaking budge."

Well, *that* wasn't affection. Or if it was, it was the kind that came with telling a fellow how he should be behaving. "I was telling a joke, Sally. For God's sake."

"I know you were. But I worry about you, Jimmy. I'm gone for a good six months of the year. The last two winters I was away, I wondered every day if you'd still be here when I returned, or if the magistrate had shipped you off to Australia. Or had you hanged. A lady—a female—doesn't appreciate when a man whose friendship she enjoys could disappear at any moment."

Friendship? Was that what this was? Part of Jimmy liked that she considered him a friend, but the other half, the one that had been pining after her for three years, wanted to yank the arrow out of his heart. "You thought of me every day?"

She scowled. "Most days. Maybe. Don't make me regret it."

He hated the idea that he caused her worry. Because he considered it a friendship, too, heading toward something closer if he could manage it. "I will do better. I just need to find my feet, Sally."

"So you keep telling me. I'd like to see some proof. I'll stay here to keep an eye on the dogs while you go to the butcher's. Then I need to go show Mr. Happley our new routine." She gestured at her three dogs. "Every year we try something new, and something that's a little trickier. Sooner or later some lightskirt will make an appearance with a horse that can serve tea, and I'll be out of work."

"Not likely. You'd just teach Jenny and Pickle and Bob to have their own tea party."

Her eyes narrowed just a little. "You may have something there, Jimmy Bly."

"You're the one who suggested it." He grinned. "Happy to take a little credit, though, if it earns me another meal or two in your company."

"We'll see about that. I *will* see if I can make friends with Galahad, here. Don't want you getting an arm bitten off."

"No, we don't want that."

Lord Peter Cordray trotted up the street toward Dockering House.
He had the uncomfortable sensation that he'd done this very same
thing before, with these very same expectations, and had nearly lost
his balls to Galahad the moment the front door opened.

This time, though, there couldn't possibly be a third black poodle
spending the night in Bitsy's bedchamber. This time she would be
distraught, and he would offer comfort.

He would take her to see the house on Old Burlington Street,
tell her there would always be a place for Galahad there when he returned, and then propose marriage. She would be so intent on planning her betrothal ball and wedding and reception that she would
forget all about the damned dog, and then he could instruct Bly to
get rid of the poodle. Both of them.

Perhaps he would get her a kitten. No, with his luck it would
scratch him at every opportunity and he would die from infection.
No pets, then. Just children. They would have to mind him, or he
would cut them off from their inheritance.

He'd wanted to arrive earlier, to be among the first to comfort
her after Galahad's theft, but an afternoon assignation would save
him from the worst of her blubbering. It could also place him in
the role of hero or savior, for taking her mind off her troubles with
both the possibility of a home of her own and a marriage proposal.

Peter patted his breast coat pocket. There, next to his heart,
he carried his grandmother's betrothal ring. His sister-in-law, Millicent, had claimed it should by rights belong to her, but Arthur
had purchased a shiny new diamond ring when he'd proposed to
the marchioness-to-be. But oh, the flattery and groveling he'd had
to give his mother before she would part with the damned thing.

It had best be worth the effort. He took a deep breath. It *would* be worth the effort.

Dockering House looked its usual self from the outside, and he took that as a good sign. No servants running about looking for the missing poodle, no constabulary pretending they would do something to find a single dog in all of London. And no horse or carriage belonging to another visitor who could stomp all over his moment and rob him of the opportunity to spend the afternoon with Bitsy.

Handing off Shadow to a stable boy, he trotted up the pair of steps to the front door. Generally it opened before he reached it, but not this time. He tapped the brass horsehead knocker against the door, waited a moment, then did it again. And once more.

Finally, the butler, Crawford, pulled open the door. "Good afternoon, my lord," he said, nodding.

That seemed . . . supremely calm. Had Jimmy Bly failed to snatch Galahad from the house, after all? If he had, Peter was going to take a whip to that ne'er-do-well. For the devil's sake. "Crawford. Bitsy is expecting me. Would you please inform her I've arrived?"

"I'm afraid Miss Bitsy is gone from the house."

Peter blinked. "But I'm to spend the afternoon with her." Taking a moment to consider how he could word an inquiry without putting suspicion on himself, he furrowed his brow. "Is something amiss?" he ventured. "Lancelot was to be returned today, was he not? Perhaps she's gone to deliver the dog to Woriton?"

The butler cleared his throat. "I am not at liberty to say, my lord. I shall inform Miss Bitsy that you came by to see her."

Oh, that was not how this afternoon was going to go. "Surely you could tell me where she's gone, Crawford. If she forgot our appointment, I will certainly forgive her, but I arranged for the property I want to show her to be available only for the next two hours."

"I'm sorry, my lord, but I have not been given leave to inform anyone of Miss Bitsy's whereabouts."

Damn it all. "Would Lord or Lady Mardensea be available, then?"

The butler took a step backward into the foyer. "If you would care to wait in the morning room, I shall inquire."

Good. At least one of them was home. Nodding, he walked past Crawford into the well-appointed morning room. No sounds of a dog barking from inside the house, at least, and Galahad *always* barked when he entered Dockering House. He couldn't ask yet, though, because if Bitsy was gone, Galahad could presumably be with her.

As he stood there, his hat in his hands, the viscount entered the room. "My lord," Peter said, inclining his head.

"Cordray. Crawford told you that Bitsy isn't to home, did he not?"

"Yes, my lord. But last night we arranged to meet here this afternoon, so that I could bring her to see the house I've been eyeing for the two of us." He cleared his throat. Bitsy wasn't precisely traditional, but it couldn't hurt to have her father on his side. "And I actually wanted to see you anyway, to ask your permission to marry your daughter." He put a hand over his chest. "I have my grandmother's ring with me, as a matter of fact."

"You were assuming I would agree to this, then?" Mardensea lifted both eyebrows. "I do have to admire your confidence."

Peter put a smile on his face. "With all due respect, I've been courting Bitsy for nearly two years. I imagine you would have sent me away months ago if you didn't approve of me."

The viscount looked at him. "I cannot disagree with that logic. You have *my* permission. It's up to you to gain Bitsy's. She's more critical than I am."

"I am aware of that," Peter returned with a smile. With her father's permission, easy to gain and reportedly meaningless or not, his pathway became much smoother. "Now it only remains for me to discover where she is so I can show her the house while it's still open to us." He pulled out his pocket watch. "Which will be for another hour and forty-seven minutes."

The viscount sighed. "Galahad was taken last night. The same way the bastards got hold of Lancelot. Bitsy insisted we send for Woriton, even though it was the middle of the night. Evidently, he has an eye for clues and a mind for puzzles. They've gone to Covent Garden to have a look about. I can't tell you more than that."

Inside, a large herd of profanity went stampeding through Peter's head. Outside, he allowed his smile to drop, but replaced it with a look of concern and—hopefully—mild consternation. "Bitsy does have a soft spot for eccentrics. She's probably ready for a rescue by now, though. I'll just go see if I can't locate her before Woriton tries to deliver a lecture on hot air to her."

The viscount's mouth quirked. "He's an unusual man, I'll admit, but she sent for him, not one of her thousand other friends, and he came here. In the middle of the night." He inclined his head. "I don't pretend to know what any female is thinking, but I do know that actions speak louder than words. If you'll excuse me, Cordray, I need to return to my paperwork."

"Of course."

Woriton. Again. That first mix-up of the poodles seemed determined to haunt him forever after. Returning to the drive, he collected Shadow and cantered off toward Covent Garden. Thankfully, it made sense that after spending much of the day with the duke, Bitsy would welcome both Peter's rescue from the stodgy stick-in-the-mud, and his distraction from the realization of Galahad's loss.

No, he hadn't lost anything. It had only been delayed. Again, but for the last time.

The Duke of Woriton—Michael—unwrapped the piece of beef he'd kept with him all day, and held it up to the butcher. "This would have been purchased yesterday afternoon at the latest," he said. "It's about half the size it would have been originally. Do you recognize it?"

The butcher, his apron splattered with old, brown blood, snorted. "You expect me to recall one piece of beef, Your Lordship? I sell dozens of 'em every day."

"Do you? Dozens of orders for three pounds of prime beef? You must have quite a wealthy clientele. How much would three pounds of fresh beef cost, anyway?"

He already knew the answer to that, of course, because this was at least the tenth or eleventh butcher they'd visited today. But he had asked a very similar set of questions each time, and thus far he'd received a very similar set of answers. What that meant, Elizabeth didn't know, but it clearly meant something to him.

"Thirty pence, I reckon, depending on the cut." The butcher held out one hand. "Let me see it."

"It's been soaked in laudanum," Michael said. "Don't touch it with your fingers unless you're ready to spend a long, drowsy afternoon."

"Christ." Shifting his hand, the man took the beef, careful to keep the cloth between it and him. Elizabeth had touched it this morning, and didn't recall any ill effects. Was Michael lying? Exaggerating? Attempting to make one of his clever deductions? It could be any of the above, and she didn't care if it helped them find Galahad.

"My cuts generally have less fat than this," the butcher said after a moment, handing it back. "I'd say the butcher's shop you're after takes whatever meat comes their way and doesn't ask too many questions about it."

"And where might such a butcher's shop be located?"

"Hm. I'd have to ponder that for a bit."

"Ah." Reaching into his pocket, Michael pulled out two coins and set them on the counter. "I'm taking your time away from your work. You should be compensated for it."

"Two quid would put me at my leisure for the rest of the week." The butcher swept the money off the counter and dropped it into one of his questionably clean pockets. "You might try east of here. Somewhere toward Vine Street, would be my guess. Too much fat, but a good quality, and cut thin enough to be easy to divide into smaller portions. Near the cattle yards. That's just a guess, mind you."

"A well-considered one," Michael commented. That sounded like a high compliment from him.

"Is there truly that much difference in how each butcher cuts meat?" Elizabeth asked, watching as Michael folded away the beef again.

"Different as penmanship, I reckon."

"We need to head east, then," Michael said, turning to leave the shop. Elizabeth sent the amused butcher a last, quick smile and hurried after him.

"How many butcher's shops are there in London?" She stepped into the barouche, Michael and Peggy following her.

"Hundreds."

"So our odds of finding the exact one where this . . . bait was purchased are abysmal."

He sat beside her. "South toward the Thames, William," he ordered her driver. "Yes. They are abysmal. I therefore find it fascinating that we've located him."

Elizabeth blinked. "What?"

"You didn't notice?"

"For heaven's sake, Michael, he's what, the fifteenth butcher with whom we've chatted? Other than being far more knowledgeable about cuts of beef than his fellows and having an idea where less expensive selections can be found, I didn't notice any . . ." She trailed off. "He sent us away without trying to sell us anything. And who the devil would know if one cut of meat was meant to be thin enough to divide, or not?"

A smile touched his mouth. "Too much detail. It's my belief that he made up several facts in order to send us in a different direction. He didn't do a bad job of it, though."

"If you're correct, he's lying to protect a dog thief. Don't admire him."

His brown eyes met hers. "I apologize, Elizabeth. In my defense, I enjoy chatting with clever people."

She smiled despite the overall disaster of the day. "Are you calling me clever? Was that a compliment?"

"A statement of fact." He faced forward. "Stop here, William."

She looked about them. Carts, vendors, orange girls, chimney sweeps, soldiers, washerwomen, rag-and-bone men—they clearly weren't in Mayfair. "Do we sit and wait? Watch to see if someone comes to collect a cut of beef and then follow that person? The butcher said he sells dozens of them every day."

"I doubt that he does, but I was actually going to suggest that I go keep an eye on his shop while you and Peggy return home to see if, by some chance, our thief is confident enough of his skills that he does send you a ransom note. Or even better, that he does that *and* returns Lancelot."

"I can't leave you here on your own," Elizabeth countered, even though what she wanted to say was that she didn't want to leave his company. With his logic and his razor-sharp thinking, he made something as outlandish as finding a singular dog thief in the middle of London seem . . . possible. Even likely.

"I'm safer with you about to protect me, you mean?" he asked, sitting back. "That's rather absur—"

"Miss Bitsy?" Peggy interrupted.

"It's not absurd to think anyone would be safer with a second person to help in keeping watch," Elizabeth shot back, motioning at the maid to wait a moment.

"And what would you do if you did spy something dangerous? Run straight at it?"

"Miss—"

"Pull you away from it," she insisted.

"M—"

"Bitsy," Lord Peter Cordray's voice came.

She looked up to see him on his gray gelding beside the barouche. The setting together with the man was so unexpected that it took her a moment to put it all back together in her mind. "Peter. What on earth are you doing here?"

"I came looking for you. We had an assignation this afternoon. But—"

Drat. "Oh, my goodness. I forgot. Surely someone at the house informed you that—"

"Yes, that Galahad was taken. I was so sorry to hear that. People are barbarians." He swung down from the horse. "After I heard, I expected to find you at home, waiting for a ransom note. Not here practically dockside and wandering about in . . ." Peter looked at the loud, dirty crowd passing around them. ". . . less than ideal surroundings."

"We're not wandering. We're looking for clues."

"I see. Perhaps we should leave that to the professionals, though, and allow me to see you home. Or to view the house on Old Burlington Street, where you agreed to accompany me, if you'll recall. You'll be much safer there, certainly."

There were times Elizabeth wished she could simply growl at and bite someone when they annoyed her. Life would certainly be much simpler and more straightforward. At the least it seemed to work well for Woriton. "I apologize for forgetting about the house tour you wished to give me," she said, putting one of her warm but tired smiles on her face, "but at this moment I can't think of anything but getting Galahad back. And as the Duke of Woriton is my best chance for doing so, I will be remaining in his company for now."

Finally Peter Cordray looked over at the duke, seated beside her and watching the exchange with obvious interest. "Being seen in his company will do nothing but lend you his reputation for eccentricity and rudeness, Bitsy. You know this. Allow me to escort you home. We can await word about Galahad together."

She took a deep breath, reflecting for a bare moment that she wasn't even tempted. "Thank you, my lord, but I mean to listen to my own counsel today, and to continue my efforts with the assistance of His Grace. He has proven to be very helpful, thus far. Nor has he suggested I run home and cower beneath my bed, hoping someone else will miraculously rally to my cause."

Michael shifted a little, no doubt preparing to inform all and sundry that he *had* been attempting to send her home. That, at least, had been for a useful reason, but she wasn't about to let him announce it in front of Peter Cordray.

"We have already discovered the butcher's shop from where the thief has been purchasing food," she went on. "Have we not, Michael?"

"We have." He tilted his head at Cordray, the expression on his face reminding her of a bug collector eyeing an insect stuck on the end of a pin. "If you're so intent on being helpful," he drawled, "you might wander about and ask if anyone has spotted a black poodle. We're missing two of them now, which makes the odds of one of them being spotted twice as good."

Peter swung back onto his horse. "Tomorrow, I will forgive you, Bitsy, for being so sharp with me. I recognize you are under great strain. Pray do not allow yourself to be compromised to the degree that he becomes your best and only hope for a match. What a misery—and a waste, and a very bad joke—that would be." With a stiff nod he turned and trotted away.

Well, that was nonsense. At least she hoped it was. Peter Cordray perhaps wasn't as sought-after as she was, but he did have a large circle of friends and acquaintances, many of whom also traveled in her orbit. It wasn't even so much that people might make fun of her for being the object of Woriton's affections—as if that were so—as it was that either she'd been lowered to fortune hunting, or worse, something as yet unknown had occurred and she was being forced to court the duke as a result of it. "Oh, dear. Was I too sharp?"

Michael shrugged. "You told him to leave you be, and he ignored your wishes in favor of his own."

"Yes, he did do that, didn't he? That would annoy anyone. And yes, I am under a great deal of stress. I'm very worried for Galahad."

"Is that why you declined to mention that you were practically on your way home even before his idiotic counsel?"

She shook a finger at him. "I was *not* on my way home. You tried to make me leave either so you could track down a lead about which you haven't told me, or so you can go engage in something dangerous. You should consider that I would feel terrible if something happened to you. You're out here because of me, after all."

"Th—"

"Don't you dare tell me that none of this is my fault," she pressed. "Perhaps a dog being stolen wasn't my fault, but it being Lancelot was. I haven't forgotten him, or the fact that the odds of you finding him again have become much worse. Or that you're a renowned scientist who discovered chlorine is also a liquid and that you certainly have better things to do than escort me about Covent Garden and Smithfield."

He blinked. "Who told you about the chlorine?"

"The Duke of Sommerset." Abruptly, though, she wished she

hadn't brought it up at all, because she had not sounded very nice at the outset of that conversation. "He overheard one of my friends commenting on your absence at the soiree last night after your rather spectacular appearance at the Sommerset grand ball. Perhaps he felt the need to offer an alibi for you."

"Nicholas frequently attempts to render me more palatable to my peers," he commented, standing up and leaning over to open the barouche's low door. Before she could say another word, he'd stepped into the street.

"Where are you going?"

He held out a hand to her. "If you're not going home, we have to send someone. I would suggest Peggy, but you would only frown and inform me that I know nothing about propriety, so I think it should be William. We—you and I and Peggy—will surveil the butcher's shop."

"I . . ." She stood up, following him to the ground. This was not the moment to marvel that he'd changed his mind, evidently at her insistence. "Yes. William, please find us right here at five o'clock. In the meantime, return to Dockering House. If a poodle has been returned or a ransom note discovered, we will need to know."

The driver doffed his hat. "I'll see to it, Miss Bitsy."

Peggy scampered out of the carriage, and William sent the pair trotting down the street and around the corner, back toward Mayfair. "Miss Bitsy, you have a dinner and recital to attend this evening," the maid commented, worry putting lines across her forehead. "And it's not safe here," she went on, lowering her voice to a muted whisper.

"We will be cautious, Peggy. We're only surveilling; not confronting. Not unless the thief appears with the poodles in tow."

"Which isn't likely to happen." Michael motioned them back in the direction of the butcher's shop. "As I consider this, the fact that the butcher seemed to know who purchased the meat may well indicate that it wasn't a single purchase. That the thief has made several appearances there, possibly paying more than the meat was worth in order to gain an unspoken ally. Hence the butcher sending us away."

That made sense; if they didn't expect the thief to return, watching the butcher's shop would be useless. If she'd learned one thing over the past few days, though, it was that some things that were obvious to Michael Bromley were more than opaque to others. Multiple purchases and the butcher's ongoing loyalty meant the thief could well return, but what else did it mean? Oh. *Oh.* "You think Lancelot, at least, is still alive," she announced. "That he's being fed regularly."

Michael nodded. "It could also be that this person is simply feeding his family more beef than most in the area enjoy as a result of the twenty-pound ransom payment, but the butcher didn't seem to think anything unusual about the obvious bite marks on raw beef."

"Which makes it more likely that this person *is* feeding a dog. Or dogs, now."

They entered the rear of a general mercantile shop across the street and several doors down from the butcher. The proprietor looked stunned, and the duke nodded at him. "Our maid, here," he said, indicating Peggy, "has made the foolish decision to marry. We have agreed to furnish her kitchen as a wedding gift." He glanced at Elizabeth. "Or rather, my wife decided we should do so. *I* have decided it shouldn't bankrupt me."

"We've got every pot and pan and spoon you'll ever need, sir," the older man crowed, practically leaping up and down on his stumpy legs. "How may I be of service?"

"I would suggest following her about and helping her carry things."

Peggy sent him a bewildered look, then wandered off to look at the myriad shelves and barrels when he gestured at her to proceed. Elizabeth wanted to burst out laughing, but that would ruin everything, so she put a hand over her mouth, pretending to cough, and joined him at the front window. "That was spectacular."

"I dislike lies, but it's simpler this way, and less likely to lead to the butcher being warned that we're watching his shop." He offered his arm, and she wrapped hers around it.

"So we're married, are we?" she pursued, then realized she sounded like a nodcock just out of the schoolroom. *Daft girl.*

"A marriage of convenience, I've no doubt," he responded, looking down at her, his keen brown eyes . . . amused? It was that, certainly, but also something that made her pulse flutter.

"For the sake of our poodle offspring, the ne'er-do-wells," she added, smiling and then making a show of looking for Peggy because suddenly everything felt very significant and she didn't quite know how to respond.

Michael took a breath. "A pair of scamps, they are." He took a breath. "Elizabeth, th—"

"Goodness, I had no idea so many pans existed," she interrupted, forcing a chuckle. "Peggy is much better at subterfuge than I expected."

His arm beneath her fingers flexed. "So I see," he commented after a moment. "What the devil I'm going to do with a hundred pots and pans now, I have no idea."

Thank goodness. They needed to keep in mind that this was a poodle rescue. Any other . . . tangles of thought or feelings, well, they were quite possibly caused by the circumstances. Or something that she had no intention of contemplating in a Covent Garden general goods shop. "Could you use them for your experiments?"

Michael glanced down at her again. "I don't bake chlorine," he stated, narrowing his eyes a little.

She scowled at him. "How was I to know that?"

"You couldn't have." He turned his attention to the street beyond the shop window. "But I prefer the idea that I use pots and pans to the rumor that I have body parts lying about ready for stitching together."

Elizabeth had heard those rumors herself. "Oh, please. You don't sew."

Snorting, he grinned. "No, I don't. Perhaps one day you should come see my study," he said after a moment. "Lots of glass vials and receivers; very little kitchen crockery."

"I might enjoy that. Scientific studies are a rarity in Mayfair. And I almost never visit anyone's study."

At that he laughed. "You prefer their ballrooms, I suppose?"

Abruptly she was in good humor again herself. "I do like a good ballroom. And a comfortable morning room, especially if it has a view of the street or the garden. I should say libraries, I suppose, but most of them smell like mold and they all have the same books, most of them never read." She turned to look out the window, noting at the edge of her view that his mouth quirked again at her latest comment. "Music rooms are tolerable," she went on, "though entering one is generally enough invitation to cause someone to sit down to play or sing, and then one is rather trapped."

She liked when she made him smile or laugh. He liked cleverness, so a grin felt like a compliment to her wit. Why that should matter she had no idea, because while he did have a title and wealth and even looks to recommend him, her favorite room remained the ballroom, and he had only stepped inside one of those in the past two years.

But how had he escaped her notice, despite that? A duke, in his late twenties, unmarried, well-favored, rich—why wasn't he on every young lady's list of potential husbands? The fact that he wasn't, that she couldn't recall any more than a passing word or two about him that had made him seem old and mad as a hatter, almost felt like another sort of robbery.

"How is it that you're not actually married?" she whispered, since for the moment he *was* married—to her.

"I suppose I'll have to eventually, to keep the family line from dying out, but honestly I've never met a female I find more interesting than a voltaic battery pile or a full retainer of nitrogen." He shifted a little. "And I don't have to imagine that most females consider me as dull as both of those items, and something of a lunatic, to boot. They forget sometimes that I in fact hear quite well."

"Well, I'm glad we've become friends," she declared with a bit too much enthusiasm. "I have never before visited fifteen butcher's shops in a day, or purchased cutlery in Covent Garden."

"'Friends,'" he repeated in his low voice, then stood for a moment in silence. "And searchers for poodles."

CHAPTER TEN

"WHERE IS HE?"

"Keep your voice down, for God's sake." Jimmy Bly glanced up the alleyway. Angry about something or not, a fellow like Cordray attracting attention to himself hereabouts was not a wise idea. For either of them. "Galahad, you mean?" he asked, keeping his own voice low. "He's where the first one is. Safe. Ready to be returned for ransom, just like you said. Though how you mean for me to get either of them back where they belong, I have no idea, because I ain't going near Dockering House right now. They'd see me for certain."

"I don't give a damn about that," the lordling snapped. "Evidently I've traded one damned mongrel for another. I thought getting rid of Galahad would clear my path, but I've only managed to make room for a bloody duke to step in."

Jimmy couldn't quite follow all of the ranting, but as it didn't seem to be aimed at him, he let Cordray go stamping about and snarling. For now the only one other than them who could hear it would be Mary, the lady who fed all the cats, and she was half deaf and three-quarters blind, and a portion mad.

Cordray kept swearing, kicked a wooden box into kindling,

and finally squared up on Jimmy again. "I will deal with Woriton," he growled. "You will dispose of Galahad."

Narrowing one eye, Jimmy took a half step backward. "I need a bit more direction of what you mean by 'dispose.' Turn him loose? Find him another family? Sell him to a butcher?"

He'd been jesting about that last one, but the glint in Cordray's eyes said that the fellow liked the idea. "A butcher would be interesting," he said slowly, "but there's always a chance the beast might get free. Or make friends with his captor. No. I want you to tie a stone around his neck and throw him in the Thames. At high tide."

"We agreed on a ransom for Lancelot, and I reckoned we'd do the same with Galahad," Jimmy said, frowning. Drowning dogs. Didn't seem a man could get much lower than that. But that was the sort of man he was, according to Cordray. "Not on murder."

"It's a dog, Bly. You can't murder a dog, any more than you can murder a rat or a deer. And once I get rid of Woriton, I do *not* want Galahad returning to ruin what I'm building. You've been well-compensated, and now it's time for you to earn your wages."

"I—"

"I'm not arguing with you, Bly," he snapped. "Get rid of him. Both of them, as far as I'm concerned. Less chance for error, that way." He dug into a breast pocket and handed over thirty pounds in coins and paper. "Our business is completed. We will not meet again."

He turned on his heel and stalked off to where he'd left his horse. Climbing into the saddle, he wrenched the animal around, dug in his heels, and set off at a fast trot. Jimmy watched after him, half expecting him to turn around and give him more orders anyway, or at least remind Jimmy to check the alley regularly for a secret mark detailing another meeting date and time.

Out on the street wagons rolled by, lads and ladies called out their wares, and someone yelled at a cat. Dogs barked, pots and pans clattered from inside open windows, and everyone went about their day. Except for him. No, he was supposed to murder a dog. Because you *could* murder a dog, he reckoned, when it looked up at you and wagged its tail and you turned around and drowned it.

"Devil's sake," he muttered, kicking a rock out of his path. He and Galahad weren't friends, but he and Lancelot had a good understanding. And neither of them had actually ever injured him, even if Galahad had come near to making him shite himself, that first night.

It took him half an hour to walk back to the Rookery, but by the time he climbed the old stairs and opened his door, he'd come up with no other ideas or plans. Damn his lack of imagination.

"Did he give you another ransom note to copy?" Sally asked, glancing up from where she knelt in front of the boards dividing Galahad from the rest of the room. She made a damned fine sight, a lovely, bright addition to his room. As he watched, she held a strip of beef up to a hole in the wall. "Come on, Galahad. That's a sweet boy," she murmured.

A few seconds later the tip of a muzzle and teeth appeared, and with surprising care the poodle took the meat out of her fingers. "Be careful, Sally," Jimmy cautioned. "You could lose a finger doing that."

"I think he's mad at *you,*" she commented, standing. "Not me."

"Or you're a fine hand at training dogs, which we both know you are."

She grinned. "Thank you for saying so, Jimmy. May I see the ransom note before you copy it?"

Jimmy took a breath. "He didn't give me one. He's furious because he thought getting the poodle away from the lady would let him step in to marry her, but the duke—the one whose aunt owns Lancelot—beat him to it. He wants me to tie stones to Galahad and Lancelot and throw them both in the Thames. I think he means to do the same to the duke."

Gasping, she put a hand to her chest. "Jimmy Bly! You can't!"

"You don't truly think I could do such a thing, do you?" he responded, reaching down to pat Lancelot on the head as the poodle meandered over to greet him. "I make some questionable choices, I admit, but I ain't a killer. Not even of dogs."

"Thank goodness." With a relieved smile Sally sprang forward and threw her arms around his shoulders. "*I* know you're a good man, but sometimes I think you forget that."

Well, anything that caused Sally to embrace him couldn't be all bad. He hugged her back before she could regain her senses and back away. "You never let me forget it."

"Are you going to keep them, then?"

Jimmy looked from Lancelot to the cage made of boards. "They eat dainty little biscuits and prime beef and expensive, smelly cheeses. I can't afford to feed 'em all that. I mean, I'm flush now, but buying a couple of pounds of meat and a tin of biscuits every week means the blunt I got for taking them won't last very long." One hundred and one pounds, he'd gotten from Cordray, all together, equal to what he would have brought in by taking and ransoming five dogs on his own. It had sounded like a fortune, but he didn't like what the job entailed, any longer.

"Perhaps you could lend them to me for a small fee, and I could make them part of my act," Sally suggested, backing away from him again. "Three big, black poodles walking on their hind legs while the little white ones ride a ball? That would be amazing."

He already knew he was going to agree, because she'd suggested it. "Well, training 'em can't hurt. I can't put 'em out on the street, and nobody's going near the Thames. It'll give me a bit of time to consider things, anyway."

She kissed him on one cheek, then clapped her hands together. "Oh, this is exciting! But you have to promise me you won't have anything more to do with that horrible man who wanted you to drown them."

"He's finished with me, even if I wasn't finished with him, which I am. Feeding 'em and sheltering 'em is up to us now, for certain."

"Well, then. Let's begin with you and Galahad making friends."

"Ha. That ain't likely. And we can't keep calling 'em those names, either. Someone might figure things out."

"I hadn't considered that." She pursed her lips. "Lad for Lancelot, and Louie for Galahad."

Jimmy chuckled. "I'm glad you had something in mind. If it were up to me, it would have been Dog and Poodle, or some such."

"No. Lad, Louie, Jenny, Pickle, and Bob. The Amazing Pangle Pack." She giggled. "That may change, of course."

"I don't know why. I like it."

She looked over at him. "I think I do, as well."

One by one the lights went out in the butcher's shop, and a hand in the growing gloom turned over the sign that said OPEN so that it read CLOSED. "We either missed him, or he didn't come by this afternoon," Michael said, rolling his shoulders.

"Or he did come by, and didn't purchase enough meat to make us suspicious."

"It's the same result; no poodles. I'm sorry, Elizabeth, that I couldn't be of more help."

She squeezed his arm. "And I'm sorry *I* couldn't be of more help in finding Lancelot. We both have dogs in this hunt. Isn't that the saying?"

"Something like that."

The idea that she wouldn't ever see Galahad again, that he could be frightened and alone and lost—or worse—somewhere, made her want to begin crying all over again. If they hadn't been in a very public place with curious shoppers eyeing them, she would have wept. "We should offer a reward to anyone who brings us the dog thief," she stated. "That would show him what it feels like."

"Sir, ma'am," the shop's owner said, approaching them and bent nearly double in a bow, "it's past time I shut the doors here tonight and get myself home. My wife and little ones will be expecting me."

"Oh, yes," Elizabeth said, "we're sorry to have kept you so long."

She had to tug on Michael's arm twice before he stirred to walk with her to the counter and pay for the large pile of pots, pans, copper teapot, utensils, several very large ladles, a straw hat, and a few other things that she didn't even recognize. They'd been there for quite a while, and evidently Peggy had chosen at least one of everything in the shop. Well, the church would be happy to have so many charity items this week, since Michael didn't seem to want any of them any more than she did.

"Give me a moment to check my totals again," the proprietor said, licking the end of his pencil and scrawling out numbers.

She half expected Michael to have done all the figures in his head and announce the total before the shopkeeper could do so. When she glanced up at him, though, his gaze had returned to the window. His reluctance to leave made sense; he wouldn't want to have to inform his aunt that her dog was missing any more than she wanted to accept that she'd lost Galahad.

"Is there nothing else we can do?" she whispered.

"Actually, there is," he murmured back. "We're not beaten yet."

That announcement lifted her heart a little, and she smiled. Making a partnership with quite possibly the sharpest man in London had some definite advantages. And if they weren't finished with the search for the poodles, then she could continue gazing at his lean face and pleasant features without feeling like she was simply prolonging their friendship for no good reason.

"I'm afraid it's seventeen pounds, four pence, sir," the owner said. "I'll make it an even seventeen; I haven't had a day like this in quite some time."

Michael took a breath. "We've taken up more of your time than we should have," he said, pulling twenty pounds from his pocket. "If you'll remain open while I find our carriage and if you'll assist me with loading our purchases, we'll call it even."

"With pleasure, sir."

Freeing his arm from her grip, he inclined his head. "Wait here. I'll be back with William and the barouche in a moment." He paused in the shop's doorway. "Don't leave this shop, even if you see Galahad trotting up the street."

Generally, she didn't like being told what to do. Neither, though, was she an idiot. "I'm aware that we're not in Mayfair, Michael."

He nodded. "Good."

While Peggy and the shopkeeper piled kitchen items into a wooden crate he'd retrieved from the back of the store, she tried to figure out what his plan might be. Perhaps continuing to keep an eye on the butcher's shop, but neither of them could spend their days doing that. And anyone else . . . Well, she doubted there were many people about who were as observant as he was.

As she gazed outside, a black poodle trotted past the window and on down the street. Elizabeth blinked, her breath catching. *What?* she mouthed, no sound coming out.

She started for the door. With one hand on the handle, though, she paused. As she watched, two little white dogs took turns running beneath the poodle's stomach and jumping onto its back. Directly behind them, a young woman dressed in a harlequin's colors, her black hair loose about her shoulders, skipped. "Steady, Jenny. Hup, Pickle. Hup, Bob."

Elizabeth blinked, and when she looked again, the quartet had vanished up the street. That . . . She didn't know what the devil that was. A waking dream? The result of an unsettled stomach? Another in the series of odd things that had happened around her over the past few days?

Michael reappeared on the other side of the door's glass, and she jumped. "What?" he asked, as she pulled it open and admitted him back into the shop.

"You didn't see that?"

He glanced over his shoulder, back toward the street. "See what?"

"I . . . Nothing. Never mind. You found William?"

"Yes. Right where you asked him to meet us. Let's load our bounty and get you home, shall we? You'll be late for your dinner."

She helped carry items to the barouche, and then climbed in with Peggy seated to her left, and Michael to her right—the facing seat being loaded with a crate and sacks of kitchen items. "I hope you don't think you're going anywhere until you tell me what your new plan entails," she said as the barouche joined the rest of the early-evening traffic, most of it headed east rather than west toward Mayfair.

"It's your plan, actually. A reward. I would suggest one for our dogs, though, rather than for the thief."

Elizabeth looked at him. "Do you really think a few pounds would entice the thief to return Galahad and Lancelot to us? Because I don't."

"I don't think so, either. But a large reward might convince one of his friends or neighbors or family members to remove the dogs from his care and return them to us." He frowned. "It has a very small chance of succeeding, but it would also have the dogs, any witnesses, and possibly the thief or thieves, coming to us."

"How would we manage it?"

The duke reached over to move a strand of hair off her forehead, and a pleased shiver went down her arms. His fingers were surprisingly gentle for a man who felt more comfortable with chemicals than people. "I'll post an advertisement in the newspaper, and have a few of my staff put up flyers in the area of Covent Garden and that butcher's shop." He sighed, sitting back again. "I suppose they'll have to come to Bromley House to gain their reward; we don't want more suspicious types hanging about your residence."

"That's . . . That's very kind of you, Michael."

"I'm after a missing poodle, as well. This, hopefully, benefits both of us. And while I'm waiting for news of Lancelot and Gala-had, I'll be home and able to work."

She'd taken him away from several days of working, now. He'd grumbled about it on occasion, but had also been in her company without a word of complaint since approximately four o'clock this morning, when she'd sent for him and his sharp mind. He could say it was because he wanted Lancelot returned as badly as she wanted Galahad back in her care, but the little tremors running down her spine wanted his reasons to be more personal.

Not that they had anything in common *but* the poodles, of course—and his poodle wasn't even his, really. He was no doubt happiest when he was in his own home, doors closed, and his nose buried in an experiment. She, on the other hand, adored nothing as much as a crowded ballroom and a lively waltz. The word "incom-patible" might as well have been invented by someone who'd seen the two of them interacting.

"When will you post the notice?" she asked.

"It's early yet; I'll have it in tomorrow's *Times,* and the notices posted by eight in the morning, the reward offered for tomorrow only. If Lancelot and Galahad are still alive, I'd like to keep it that way. Speed would seem to be of the essence, and I will be offering a rather substantial reward. Hopefully enough to make anyone think twice about doing what might be easier and disposing of them." He cleared his throat. "I will, of course, notify you of anything significant."

And now she was unnecessary again. "Oh. Of course."

Silence. "Unless you'd care to come by and have luncheon with me. Bring your parents if you wish; I know you prefer not to cause a stir. Or come in through the garden so no one will know you're anywhere near Bromley House. Whatever suits you."

"You must think me a great coward." And from the mix of anticipation and uncertainty that began yanking on her from the moment he'd suggested she call on him, he wasn't far wrong.

"I'm perfectly capable of expressing myself," he retorted. "I don't require you to put words in my mouth. Particularly false ones."

So, he didn't think her a coward. She wanted more details than that, but he obviously had no intention of elaborating. "Thank you," she said instead. "I will call on you tomorrow. Whatever else I may have on my calendar, I want Galahad back."

Going solely by memory she had a dress fitting, a luncheon, a stroll in the park, and a soiree all scheduled for tomorrow. Her friends would understand her canceling an outing in the wake of Galahad's theft, of course, but she didn't wish to sit at home and cry as she imagined all the horrible things that might have befallen the poor dear. With Michael's assistance, she could actually do something about it.

Therefore, calling on Michael Bromley, the Duke of Woriton, *did* make the most sense. And that was good, because she wanted to see where and how he lived, anyway. Because with every moment it became more and more clear that she'd never met anyone like him in her entire life, and that her fascination bordered on . . . obsession.

"I cannot promise we will succeed, Elizabeth," he said, turning from the view to gaze at her again, "but I can promise that I will do everything within my power to see Galahad—and Lancelot—back where they belong. I have no intention of giving up."

Now she wanted to hug him. That wouldn't be at all proper,

though, and there were people about who might notice. "I'm certain your aunt will appreciate that," she said instead.

"I'm not planning on saying a word about any of this to my aunt. Mary Harris is my nearest relation, and I happen to adore her. She will never believe that I didn't just wander off somewhere and forget I was walking Lancelot, and that will break her heart as much as the loss of the dog."

"But you did no such thing," Elizabeth protested. "Nor are you anything near as absent-minded as you seem to like to pretend." She turned sideways in her seat to face him. "Why *do* you pretend to be absent-minded and obtuse? You are no such thing."

His mouth curved. "Elizabeth, my dear, there is nothing our peers dislike more than thinking their barbs have gone astray, or worse yet, have not even landed. I ignore them, and they go away to be noticed somewhere else. It's actually because of the times when I couldn't resist, when I decided to fling a barb back at some idiot or other, that they've decided I'm both mad and eccentric." He shrugged. "In all honesty, there *are* moments when I have completely missed someone's conversation because I've lost interest. So, it's not precisely an act."

That was a great deal of information he'd just delivered to her. She understood enough about him by now to realize that he didn't just say things for no reason. And the best reason she could conjure for what he'd confided in her was that he trusted her. They were partners in this mess. Friends.

She smiled back at him. "Please never put on an act with me, then. The actual you is rather more interesting than most other people. Even with the insults."

"I haven't insulted you in better than a day. You're not an idiot."

Hm. A rather unusual compliment, again, but she'd take it. She almost looked forward to sorting them out, now.

* * *

"Your Grace," Charles Huston said, half bowing as he pulled open the Bromley House front door for his master, "we were near to sending a search party after you."

The Duke of Woriton paused on the way to his office. "Why?"

"You fled the house at four o'clock this morning, Your Grace, and we haven't had word from you since. It's been fourteen hours."

"I left word where I was going. Please have Mrs. Fellows find me something to eat, and ask Bradley and Tim to be ready to head out. I need one of them to deliver a note, and the other to keep watch on a butcher's shop at the edge of Covent Garden."

The duke disappeared into his office, and a moment later Huston heard him shuffling through papers. "Odd" was a relative term, the butler had discovered several years ago, and that realization had served him well as the Bromley House butler. The most frequent visitors here were bookish types, many of them with no refinement and no experience at having servants about to pour tea or fetch refreshments, or how to properly address a duke.

He'd thus become accustomed to ill-dressed men wandering the hallways or asking for directions to the kitchen or digging through the library looking for blank paper. Some of these same men had names he recognized, John Tatum and Sir Humphry Davy and Baron Jöns Berzelius and Jean-Baptiste Biot, and some of them looked as if they'd lived most of their lives in an attic somewhere and survived on birdseed.

Most of the past week, however, had been outside his experience. Taking a deep breath, Huston went to find Bradley and Tim in the kitchen. "Tim, you're to deliver a message. I don't know where, yet, but I doubt it's to the Royal Institution. Bradley, you're to go to Covent Garden and surveil a butcher's shop. I shall be providing you with a warm coat, a whistle, and a pistol."

"What the devil is he about now?" the senior footman asked, shoveling the last few bites of dinner into his mouth. "I've delivered papers and vials of God-knows-what to professors' homes in the middle of the night, but I've yet to be ordered to keep watch on a butcher's shop."

"There's a first time for everything, as I've often said," Huston reminded him.

"Does this still have to do with the lady who summoned him this morning?" Tim downed a cup of coffee and pulled his jacket back on over his slim shoulders.

"I damned well hope so. And that is why we are going to perform our duties, no matter how . . . unusual they may be, without fault and without complaint. He's spent more time out of this house over the past few days than he has over the past year. If some lady has finally managed to pull him out of his study, we are going to do everything possible to encourage it to continue."

"Huston!" echoed up from the main part of the house.

"Come along," he said, and led the way back up the hallway.

The duke, several folded notes in his hand, stood in the foyer again, only the stubble on his chin and cheeks giving away the fact that he'd been awake for better than a day and a half. His excessive waking and working hours were something else that Huston had long ago ceased to view as unusual—it was simply the way things went, here at Bromley House.

"Tim? I assume you're the messenger. This is to go to the address I've written on it, the editor at *The Times*." The duke held up a second note. "This is to go to a printer at the address noted. You are to wait for fifty flyers to be printed. I want you to post them throughout Covent Garden, Smithfield, and the surrounding area. Hire persons to assist you if you deem it necessary."

He held out a third piece of paper to Bradley. "This is the address of the butcher's shop. Find a location from which you can keep an eye on the front door, but from where you won't be noticed. Remain there until Tim comes to collect you after he's posted the flyers. If you see anyone, make a note of what they look like, which direction they go, and what time this occurs."

"*Any* customers, my lord?"

"Any who look like they might have stolen two big black poodles. Any walking away with large quantities of meat or being furtive."

Huston saw the two men off with enough blunt for hiring hacks and getting a meal, and something to hire some of the local street urchins to help post flyers. If he'd had a moment, he would have taken a look at what it was, exactly, His Grace wished posted all over the east side of London, but the duke was clearly in a hurry to put all his plans into motion.

"Mrs. Fellows roasted some lamb, Your Grace, in the hope that you would be returning home for dinner," Huston said after the footmen had left the house. "Would you like to dine in your study, or the dining room?"

"My study. I suggest you take yourself to bed early tonight, Huston; we may have callers fairly early tomorrow."

"May I ask who we're expecting?"

"Lancelot and Galahad, if we're lucky. If not . . ." The duke squared his shoulders. "I have some plans to figure out."

"Is there anything I might do to assist you, Your Grace?"

To Huston's surprise, the duke sent him a brief smile. "You should certainly hope not, Huston."

Yes, "odd" and "unusual" were relative terms, and he had the uneasy feeling that he would be expanding their definitions yet again tomorrow.

CHAPTER ELEVEN

MICHAEL BROMLEY AWOKE FROM A DREAM IN WHICH HE AND Elizabeth Dockering were dancing in his study, tubes and vials and bottles flying onto the floor and shattering in liquid arcs of color and light, and all in time with the waltz being played by an unseen orchestra—which was good, because he and she were both naked.

"Huh," he muttered, sitting up to see the small German-made clock on the wall across from his bed. Eight o'clock. He'd slept later than he'd meant to, but at least his eyelids didn't feel like they were made of sand and weighed ten pounds each any longer. His nether regions were at least as awake, and had nearly begun the day without him.

Standing, he splashed a good deal of cold water on his face before he rang the bell for Jarrett and sat down to shave two days' worth of stubble from his chin and cheeks. Generally, a few days of beard growth didn't bother him, but he had something to attend to today. And unless Elizabeth Dockering had come to her senses overnight and decided to allow him to conduct this part of the search on his own, she would be calling at Bromley House today— quite possibly with her parents in tow.

He'd only suggested that because it seemed like something a gentleman concerned about preserving a lady's reputation would say, but he didn't actually wish to spend any part of his day explaining his thinking, his house, his work, or this latest hobby of his to Viscount Mardensea and his viscountess. Particularly when his latest hobby seemed to be their daughter.

Jarrett knocked at the bedchamber door and entered the room at his acknowledgment. "Have Bradley and Tim returned?" Michael asked, as the valet dug into the wardrobe for attire.

"Not as of yet, Your Grace. Is this going to be a working day, or an out-in-public day?"

"I'll require a coat and cravat, if that's what you're asking."

"It is." Jarrett pulled out a waistcoat, then with a frown returned it to the wardrobe. "I do need to know if you'll be seen by your peers, or by your fellows at the Philosophical Society."

"That makes a difference?" Michael asked, glancing in the mirror at the servant behind him.

"Certainly, it does. Your good daywear does not accompany you anywhere you are likely to encounter acids or other corrosives."

"I had no idea my clothes were divided into categories depending on the likelihood of me being near science."

"Well, they are. Though it seems we need a new section for when you decide to go walking in lakes or rivers."

Michael stifled a grin. "Enough of that, Jarrett. The blue coat with the gray and yellow waistcoat, I think."

He caught the servant's stare in the mirror's reflection. "Yes, Your Grace. And the buckskin trousers, if I may suggest?"

"You may."

"I may weep with joy," Jarrett muttered under his breath, just loud enough for Michael to overhear.

He decided to ignore that, as he knew himself to be a careless dresser. And whatever happened today, whoever came to his door, he had a sudden wish not to embarrass himself. It was odd, this caring what several—one—of his peers thought about him. And it made his day infinitely more complicated and full of distractions, which was the main reason he'd decided several years ago that he simply didn't care about the fashions or conversations of his fellows. He had no time for that sort of nonsense.

Except that today, obviously, he did. And it wasn't only because the Dockering parents might be visiting. Elizabeth's appearance, her reputation, meant a great deal to her. He disliked the idea that she was willing to be seen in his company *despite* her caution over those things. For the devil's sake, he could at least not make a difficult few days worse for her. It wasn't much of a sacrifice, after all, to look like a proper gentleman for a few hours.

"Your Grace?" Huston knocked at the half-open door.

"What is it?"

"You have callers, Your Grace."

For a second his breath caught. "Well, who is it?"

"You'd best come see for yourself."

Michael stepped into his boots while Jarrett knotted his cravat. Shrugging into his blue coat, he padded down the curving staircase behind the butler. "You might just tell me," he said. "I do pay you for that sort of thing, do I not?"

"I don't believe I can answer that question appropriately, Your Grace."

Rather than heading into the morning room, the customary waiting place for guests, the butler continued on to the front door. With a quick breath Huston pulled it open.

A group of people stood outside. Seven, no, eight people, in a ragged sort of line trailing from the front portico down to the street. Two were women, one in a leatherworker's apron and the other in a plain gown that made her a governess or perhaps a clerk at a shop. The men were similarly dressed, shopkeepers, a milk cart driver, a laborer or two—folk likely to be found in Covent Garden and its environs. Most telling of all, five of them had dogs with them.

"What do you wish me to do with these . . . persons?" Huston asked, only his fingertips touching the door.

"Keep the line orderly, I suppose, and discover if any of them require refreshments." Stifling a grin at the butler's obvious discomfiture, Michael stepped into the doorway. "Good morning. My flyers have begun circulating, I assume."

"Aye, Your Grace," one of the men said, pushing to the front of the line. "I have your dog, right here."

Michael looked down at the beast standing at the far end of a frayed rope. "That is not a black poodle."

"I think he's just rolled in flour. I'm sure he's black."

"Even if that were so, flour would not turn a bulldog into a poodle. I'm afraid you've come all this way for nothing."

"Worth a go, I reckon." Shrugging, the man jerked on the lead and pulled the dog down the street with him.

"I don't have a dog," the next visitor, one of the women, said. "I seen one, though. A black poodle, just like you said on the paper."

"Describe it to me, then, will you?" Michael glanced over his shoulder. "Fetch me a paper and pencil, Huston. I may have cause to take notes."

"I'd like to note that you've gone mad," the butler grumbled, stepping back from the door.

"Well, it were a poodle, and it were black."

"A little more detail, if you please."

The woman shifted. "Describe the poodle?"

"Yes."

"Well, it had a nose, a pointy one, and a long, shaggy tail, and long black hair."

"No. Thank you, madam."

"Damnation," she muttered, kicking at the threshold as she turned around and descended the shallow steps of the portico.

He rid himself of the other six just as quickly, and retreated into the foyer as Huston reappeared with paper, a pencil, and a tray. "Your Grace!" the butler exclaimed, taking charge of the front door and shutting it.

"It's been dealt with," Michael said. "I'm expecting a few more who either hope I'm an idiot, or do have something useful to offer. Just inform me when any of them appear, and I'll manage it."

"How many more are you expecting?"

"I don't know. A dozen or more. And if they're bothering to come here from Covent Garden, I'll take a moment to speak with them. Someone somewhere is bound to have seen at least one black poodle over the past week."

Huston sighed. "Yes, Your Grace."

"And send Bradley and Tim in to see me when they return."

"Of course, Your Grace."

He started for his study, not that he expected he'd be doing much work this morning. Hopefully a dozen more possible witnesses would appear, though he'd be happier with twice that number. And he needed to take down names and addresses in some instances; someone for certain *not* seeing a poodle could eliminate a street or two, potentially. Not realizing that immediately had been a mistake, of the sort he didn't generally make. And once he'd noted that, he realized he didn't want the other someone who might be calling today to be left to wait on the portico.

"Huston," he said, turning around. "Miss Dockering may be coming to call. Her, you will please show to the morning room and then inform me."

The butler's spine snapped straight. "You've had a great many callers this week, Your Grace. Will you describe her again for me?"

"She won't have a dog with her, to begin with." Michael considered the question for a moment. "Honey-colored hair, a slender figure, attractive features, green eyes, and she prefers to wear blue or green."

"I shall keep a watch."

"Then stop staring at me and do so. What, were you expecting poetry from me? She's a female, not a Grecian urn. I do remember you've already encountered her at least once."

"I . . . Yes, Your Grace. I mean no, Your Grace."

After yet another hesitation the butler went to stand at his position by the front door. The man was going to have a long day, but Michael continued to be annoyed at the way every mention of Elizabeth Dockering's name sent his staff into wide-eyed frenzy and his own pulse into a race. He'd pursued women before. Half-heartedly, perhaps, but he wasn't a damned virgin. And he wasn't pursuing Elizabeth. Peter Cordray was pursuing Elizabeth, and so were perhaps a half dozen other young men. *He* was pursuing an easily produced, easily stored, effective medical disinfectant.

What he was doing was important. He'd already made some great strides toward it by figuring out how to render chlorine into a liquid. A solution could save lives. Countless lives. Seating himself at his stool in the study, he pulled over his latest notes to read through them again. With his discovery of liquid chlorine recognized, he needed to make a few changes to his presentation in front of the Philosophical Society, as well.

"Then do it," he grumbled at himself, "and stop the bloody daydreaming."

He couldn't even say what it was that kept pulling his mind away from his chemistry. Something nebulous and warm and utterly impossible, he knew, but chose not to delve further than that. Such an exercise was useless and ultimately self-defeating. The—

His door rattled. "Your Grace?"

Taking a breath, Michael pushed away from the table. "What is it?"

"Tim has returned. You wanted to s—"

"I remember what I wanted, Huston. I just said it ten minutes ago. Send him in."

The door opened, and the young footman stepped in. Behind him, Huston sniffed and shut the door again with unnecessary firmness. "Your Grace," Tim said, bowing.

"Where's Bradley?"

"He said I should tell you that he wanted to stay watching the butcher's shop a bit longer—no one came to the door until it opened at six o'clock, and he's set his eyes on one or two possibilities, but nothing for certain."

Michael nodded. "I appreciate his initiative. The flyers were posted, I assume, since we've already had a few callers."

"Yes, my lord. And the advertisement will have gone into the morning edition of *The Times,* that fellow with the thick glasses told me last night, and he said to thank you for your generous payment."

"Good. Get something to eat and then some sleep."

The footman bowed again. "Thank you, Your Grace. I hope this helps you find Lancelot. He's a good dog."

"Yes, he is. Thank you, Tim."

Blushing, the young man strode back to the door, fumbled to open it, and hurried back into the hallway, shutting the door behind him. Michael looked at it for another moment. Did he actually express his appreciation to his staff so rarely that it turned them into bumbling loobies? They didn't generally comport themselves like idiots.

"Back to work, Woriton," he ordered himself, stretching out his arms and returning to his notebook. As keen as he'd been on a hydrogen burner, at this point it wasn't worth his time any longer.

Not when all of his experiments showed that oxygen burned hotter, and was easier to collect.

The door rattled again.

"What?" he barked, slamming his pencil down.

"There are more . . . persons outside. In a line." Huston's voice was muffled, as if he was speaking into the keyhole.

"I'll be there in a moment."

He'd sent out a request for information about or for the return of a black poodle, with a reward offer for both, if it or they could be proven to be true. And while it wasn't a medical advancement, it *was* important—to him, to Aunt Mary, and to Elizabeth Dockering. As he rose and blew out the lamp by his elbow, he could admit that he wanted to give her good news, and if at all possible, he wanted to be the one to hand Galahad back to her.

It had nothing to do with visions of heroics—or of naked dancing—of course. It was only that it seemed the best and most poetical conclusion to this mad episode. The metaphorical ribbon tied around a series of actual mishaps.

When he reached the foyer, Huston pulled open the front door for him as he always did.

Michael glanced at the orderly line arranged by Huston, a string of people and dogs that began at the top of the portico and turned up the carriage drive, back down the carriage drive, and up the street as far as he could see. "I'm going to need a chair," he told the butler. "And a pot of tea. Have Mrs. Fellows make biscuits."

"Where are you off to?" the Viscountess Mardensea asked as she entered the foyer.

Elizabeth finished tying on her bonnet. "The Duke of Woriton has arranged to have flyers posted, offering a reward for information about, or the return of, Galahad and Lancelot. He is expecting that several potential witnesses may call at Bromley House, and he's invited me there to listen. And assist."

She added the last part because he'd made her feel quite useful several times over the past days, and she liked feeling that way. It was one thing to be held up as pretty or a paragon of manners, but those were both temporary and . . . silly, when she considered it. They were things she was good at, of course, and certainly she'd never thought of them as silly before, but for heaven's sake, the man who'd discovered liquid chlorine had called her clever. And his eyes danced when he smiled.

"He's posted a half-page advertisement in the newspaper, as well," her father said, exiting the breakfast room with the paper in his hands. "A hundred pounds for the safe return of a black poodle, and fifty pounds for any verifiable clues leading to its recovery. That's exceptionally generous. Only one dog, though?"

"I imagine he offered enough to make certain the thief or thieves would find out about it. They know how many dogs they have. And hopefully they will see it's worth more to them to keep the dogs alive than . . . to do something more drastic with them." She pulled on her gloves and took her parasol from Peggy. "I shall return before dinner."

"Just a moment, Bitsy. This way, if you please." Her mother gestured her toward the morning room.

Elizabeth sighed. "If you're going to warn me that being seen with Woriton will make people think he's courting me, and that all of our acquaintances will begin to think me as odd as he's believed to be, I don't care," she stated. "He's doing something to help, and he may well be the most intelligent man I've ever met." She wrinkled her nose. "Except for you, of course, Papa."

Her father snorted. "I have no illusions on that count. The man is brilliant."

"But people *will* begin to think you're smitten with him," her mother took up. "Do you truly understand what that could mean? Do you recall two years ago when Miss Prudence Berry allowed that pastor to call on her, because she claimed they shared a fondness for Egyptian history? She *had* a duke courting her. And now she has a pastor with a small London parish, a very limited income, and parents who won't even speak to her."

"Michael's not a pastor, Mama. He's a duke. A very wealthy one, from what I hear."

"So you *are* smitten with him? Goodness, Bitsy. You—He—People laugh at him behind his back. To his face, practically. And he detests his peers. You love everyone. Everyone loves you. It's not—"

"I am not smitten with Michael Bromley," she stated, folding her arms over her chest and not for the first time wondering if she was lying or not. "I do admire him, and he's helping me find Galahad. That is my first and only connection with him." And that was by far the safest thing to say, and the one least likely to give her complications later.

"I understand how important Galahad is to you," the viscount said. "You should know, though, that yesterday Peter Cordray came by and very properly asked for my blessing. It seems he wants to propose to you again, and this time he's done all the things he should, in advance. I gave him my approval, but told him he would have to earn yours."

Elizabeth opened her mouth, then shut it again. Her father's announcement was so far from what she'd been thinking that it took her a moment to absorb what he'd said. She'd known that Lord Peter Cordray meant to propose to her again; a man didn't spend two years taking her on walks, dancing with her, escorting her to shops, and sending her flowers for no reason. Apparently, he considered his previous proposals and her kind rejections as rehearsals, and now he meant to do it for real.

"Well," she said aloud. "I suppose I shall answer his question when he asks it of me."

"You are fond of him," her mother said. "If you weren't, you would have turned him aside ages ago, as we've seen you do with countless other men."

"He is a steadfast companion," Elizabeth agreed. "All I can think of right now, though, is Galahad."

"I understand, but that doesn't explain why you intend to call on a man at his home."

"I've done it before, Mama, when we received the ransom note for Lancelot. This is all the same venture, except for the fact that two dogs are missing now. If any of my friends don't understand that I intend to do whatever I can to get Galahad back, they must not be the friends I supposed they were."

Her mother took a breath. "Very well. I won't tell you that it's not just your friends who notice what you do, what you say, and to whom you say it, because you know all of that. Thus far, you've navigated Society with grace and skill. I will only suggest that you not toss away your two years of hard work simply because Galahad tangled with the dog of a man who likes puzzles."

"I will keep that in mind, Mama," she said, nodding at Crawford and silently noting that there was nothing simple about meeting Michael Bromley. Maddening and fascinating, yes. "Perhaps I will only stop by to see how his plan is progressing, and then continue on to Bond Street. I do need a new hat."

The viscountess smiled. "A lady can never have too many hats."

There. Everyone was comforted, and she could go see what Michael had discovered since last night without her parents worrying overmuch about her reputation. She supposed *she* should be more concerned about it, but it hadn't been Peter Cordray, for all his proper manner and impeccable reputation, who'd gone out of his way to help her find Galahad. It had been the rude, self-confident

Woriton. In his company, actions seemed more important than what the wags like old Lady Appleton, for example, thought of the comportment of a young lady whose nickname she couldn't even recall. The dowager countess had called her "Bitty" on more occasions than she cared to remember.

Bromley House lay close enough that she and Peggy might have walked there. She decided to take the barouche anyway, since Michael had a tendency to jump into her vehicle and take her on an adventure somewhere. Or rather, a hunt for clues as to the poodles' whereabouts, which amounted to the same thing.

When the barouche turned up Mount Row, Elizabeth sat forward. The streets of Mayfair were generally full of wagons making deliveries, vehicles of residents, riders, and those who scavenged off of rich households—rag-and-bone men and the like. That, though, didn't explain what she saw lining the street in front of her. People stood about everywhere. Well-dressed and barely dressed alike. People with dogs in tow, people carrying boxes, barehanded people—but mostly people with dogs. The noise . . . She couldn't even describe the cacophony of barking and yelling and trading insults, everyone pushing closer to the large white and gray house halfway along the street.

"My goodness," Peggy breathed, moving closer to the middle of the seat opposite Elizabeth.

"Indeed," Elizabeth seconded. "Bring us as near to Bromley House as you can, William."

"Miss Bitsy, I don't think it's safe, leaving you here."

Part of her agreed with that, but at the same time she wanted to know precisely what was afoot. "We'll be fine," she said. "See if you can turn up the carriage drive, though. The street's already blocked."

Even from behind him, she could see the driver's jaw clench. "Yes, Miss Bitsy."

"The back of the line is that way," a man shouted at them, gesturing down the street as they maneuvered closer.

"Just because you're pretty-dressed don't mean you get to move to the front!" another one yelled.

"You, there!" A stout man in Woriton's black and green livery jabbed his finger at the gaggle of people and dogs directly in front of the barouche. *Huston.* Thank heavens. "Make way!"

"Hey, Yer Lordship," someone else contributed, "I been here for an hour. I ain't moving till I see the duke!"

"Yes, you are," the butler stated, gazing levelly at the complainer. Grumbling, the fellow stepped sideways, pulling his very large mastiff with him. Huston walked up to the barouche. "Good morning, Miss Dockering."

"And to you as well, Huston."

"His Grace told me to expect you. Please follow me, if you will. Driver, around the corner there's a second drive up to the stable. I think you'll find it less crowded."

"Thank you, Huston. You have impeccable timing."

"As I have on occasion been told." He handed her down, and Peggy behind her, and Elizabeth followed the swath he cut through the crowd as he led the way to the front door of Bromley House.

"Was this expected?" she asked.

"That's not for me to say, Miss Dockering."

The door stood open, and a few feet inside the foyer she spied Michael sitting on a chair, a small desk in front of him, a wooden bench facing that, and a plate of biscuits on the table. A footman stood at the duke's elbow.

"Madam," the duke said, eyeing the older woman seated on the bench opposite him, an even older man folded up beside her, "that is clearly not a dog, much less a poodle."

The woman petted something round and orange on her lap.

"Of course Turnip is a dog. A good dog. But you say he belongs to you, so for that hundred quid you mentioned, we'll hand him over."

Michael glanced up, his mouth quirking as his gaze met Elizabeth's. "Turnip is a cat, and I believe you are well aware of that fact. Now please each of you have a biscuit and," and he reached into his coat, "a quid to hire a hack to take you home."

The woman snatched the coin out of his fingers. "If you say so, Your Lordship, but I reckon you're mistaken." She stood while the man unfolded himself, bones audibly creaking, freed two biscuits from the platter, and hobbled past Elizabeth and outside.

"That was kind of you, to give her money," Elizabeth said, taking a step closer when he stood.

Michael inclined his head. "I'm doing it to protect the biscuits."

She snorted. "Has it been like this all morning?"

"No. John, fetch the other chair, if you please." He looked back at her. "If you care to sit, that is."

"I insist on it."

As the young footman carried a second, matching chair from a side room into the foyer and set it down beside Michael's, the duke himself shifted the table over so they shared it. "This morning I had perhaps ten callers, none of whom offered anything of value. That was evidently before the morning edition of the newspaper began circulating. It's been like this for the past hour or so."

"The line just keeps getting longer and longer, Your Grace," the butler commented, peering through the curtains to one side of the open door. "Soon they'll overwhelm us. And who's most likely to be killed? The butler. It's always the butler."

"If they assault the house, Huston, I will hold the door," Michael stated, handing Elizabeth into her chair. "You will flee with Miss Dockering and go fetch the dragoons."

"I will do that, Your Grace. You may be certain of it."

"Then show in our next visitor."

A young man, perhaps ten or eleven, crept through the door, a small black dog on a lead he held tightly in one hand. "Your Majesties," he whispered, his face bright red.

"Tell me your name, sir," Michael said, his voice rather less intense than she was accustomed to hearing.

"Robert, Your Grace."

"And are you a witness to something, or have you found something?"

"I found something, I reckon." He lowered his head. "My ma says this is your dog, so's I can't keep him any longer. And the money's to keep us in bread and poultry for a year."

"What's this dog's name?" Elizabeth asked, aching to go hug the young man, who was clearly being forced to give up a beloved pet.

"Scratch, 'cause that's what he does." He held out the lead. "Here."

"I'm afraid, Robert, that Scratch is not the dog we're looking for," Michael said. "He is, however, a rare mix of beagle and bulldog, I believe. The perfect animal for a young man. I therefore cannot offer you the reward posted in the flyers."

If it was possible to look relieved and worried all at the same time, the boy achieved it. "My mama won't be happy," he said, pulling the lead tight against his chest.

"Hm. We can't have that. What say, in exchange for your word that you'll look after the very rare Scratch, I put twenty pounds toward his—and your—upkeep?"

"You would do that? But he ain't the proper dog!"

"He's a very proper dog. And you are a bright young man. Do you accept?"

"That's smashing! O' course I do!"

The duke held out his hand, and the boy shook it. Then young Robert received a biscuit and twenty pounds, carefully placed in a breast pocket of his thin jacket. "Straight home, now," Michael said.

"And look sad, as if you expect your mother will tan your hide for failing her."

Immediately the boy slumped, the very portrait of dejectedness. "Like this?"

"Perfect. Off with you."

"Are you giving everyone money?" Elizabeth asked, once Robert had exited the house again. "I daresay you'll be to-let by the end of the day."

"I've had to send one of my solicitors out for more ready money," he admitted, "but this isn't going to send me to the poorhouse. Patents, income from three estates, a very generous inheritance from a family with an ever-narrowing number of heirs . . . Well, suffice it to say that I'm obscenely wealthy," he said.

"It's still exceedingly generous."

Michael shrugged. "I don't generally like people. This exercise, though, is not unpleasant."

"You mean it feels good to help people."

"I suppose so."

"But with your work, your discoveries, you help more people than anyone else I know."

"That's abstract. And long-term. This is more immediate." Digging into his pocket, he handed her a fistful of money. "Here. You try it. John, find Miss Dockering a cloth bag or a biscuit tin for that."

"You don't have to—"

"Huston. Next, if you please."

Their next "guest," as he referred to them, was a portly man who claimed to have information on where a great many poodles could be found. Michael started to write down his information, then stopped as the fellow continued listing every borough in London.

"If you think to cheat me by naming every square foot of London and then later claiming you told me a poodle could be found there," he said, "I will call you a buffoon and wallop you. And no, you may not have a biscuit."

For the next three hours they met with one Londoner after another. Most of them seemed either sincere or desperate, and the duke soon gave Elizabeth all his ready cash and allowed her to donate to the guests as she saw fit. Some received a few pence; others, with better tales or sadder circumstance, received a few pounds. He'd been correct about donating even a small amount to someone in need. It felt glorious. And just before the last of the biscuits could vanish, someone from his kitchen replaced them with a fresh platter.

An older, thin man limped in, a bunch of ragged feathers cradled in his arms. "I've got 'im for ye," he rasped, once he'd given his name as Smith and his place of residence as Cheapside.

"Sir, that is a chicken," Michael stated.

"It's a rooster, lad. A doodler, just like ye wanted."

Elizabeth frowned. "I beg your pardon?"

"You asked for a black doodler. Cock-a-doodle-do. Here he is. Reggie. One hundred quid, and he's yours."

The duke stifled a cough. "Ah. We were actually looking for a poodle. A dog."

"Bah," the old man said, and limped back out the door. "That's rich folk for ye, never sayin' what they mean."

Once he was out of earshot, Elizabeth let go of the laugh she'd been holding in. "A doodler?" she managed, covering her mouth with her hands. "He brought us a black rooster! Oh, I shouldn't find this amusing, because it's actually not helping us find Lancelot or Galahad, but good heavens."

Grinning, Michael took a biscuit for himself. "It's all helping," he said, gesturing at the rough map of London he'd made on one of his sheets of paper. All around the dot marked as Bromley House were X's, interspersed with a few triangles. Some overlapped, some had a distance between them, but they lay in every direction—and especially to the east. "We know where two large black poodles have *not* been seen. Which leaves us mainly here," and he circled an area encompassing the butcher's shop and east, "or here." This time he marked a large area south of the Thames. "The triangles are possible sightings."

"I admit, I'm impressed," she said, turning the map so she could see it more clearly. "That's rather brilliant."

"Thank you. It's not foolproof, though. There's always a chance that either the dogs have never been let out of doors, or they're . . . not anywhere."

"Dead, you mean. You might as well say it. I've definitely thought it. Endlessly." She sighed. "Do you think any of those people could have been the thief, trying to discover if we've figured him out or not?"

"It's possible."

"The two triangles directly beside the butcher's shop might well be the black poodle I saw last night," she offered, indicating the marks with her fingertip.

He looked at her, his eyebrows diving together. "What?"

"Oh." Well, that was something she should have shared with him. "I saw a black poodle last night."

"Why didn't you say anything then?"

"I almost did, but then I saw two little white dogs jumping over and crawling under it, and a woman dressed like a harlequin walking behind them."

"A performing poodle, then."

"Clearly one better-trained than Galahad, at least." She sighed. "For a moment I thought I'd gone mad and had imagined the entire scene."

He gazed at her for a long moment, though his thoughts were clearly on this poodle puzzle. "That might explain the other two triangles, but it also puts a twist into my theory. Any of these sightings," and he gestured at the scattering of triangles, "might have been the harlequin's poodle, rather than one of ours."

"Poodles are not inexpensive," Elizabeth countered, not liking the idea that she might have made things worse by not saying anything last night. "And they are not common here. How many could there possibly be in London? Ten? A dozen?"

"If that. At least half of our guests today didn't know what a poodle was." He looked at the map again. "That was actually quite a coincidence, wasn't it? To see a black poodle prancing down the exact street where we were watching for any black poodles to appear."

"Almost as if it were trying to say, 'Look at me! I'm the poodle any possible witness will have seen. No need for you to bother searching this area any longer.'"

"That's quite an eloquent poodle," he noted dryly. "And a rather vain one."

"I've always wanted to speak to an eloquent yet vain poodle," Elizabeth returned.

"As have I." He glanced over at the butler. "How many more, Huston?"

"A dozen, maybe. I chased two away that were already here this morning."

"Let's see what they have to say," Michael stated. "And then I owe Miss Dockering luncheon and a tour of my study." He looked back at her. "If you're still interested in one."

Oh, that she was. She was far too interested in anything that allowed her to spend time in his company. And far too pleased that she could continue to blame their interactions on the search for the dogs. It was rather like sneaking a sweet and not getting caught, and then developing a taste for the subterfuge. "I would like to see where you do your work, yes," she said aloud.

"Good. I tidied it up, just in case you did."

CHAPTER TWELVE

"SIT, BOYS," SALLY COOED, HOLDING A TIDBIT OF MEAT IN ONE hand and part of an oatmeal biscuit in the other. "Good boys. Now, up." She lifted her fingers.

Lancelot sank onto his hind legs, his front feet pawing at the air. He was a smart beastie, this Lancelot. Someone had taught him manners, and adding to those was fairly easy once Jimmy had discovered his weakness for biscuits of all kinds. Oatmeal, especially.

Galahad grunted and lay down, chin over his paws. He was trickier—or just more stubborn. The way he flinched whenever Jimmy came too close, though, made her think that a man had struck him somewhere in the past. His owner was a lady, Jimmy said, so perhaps she'd rescued him from somewhere.

Giving Lancelot his reward, she turned to lie on her stomach, nose-to-nose with Galahad on the scarred wooden floor. "What's the matter, Galahad?" she asked, paying close attention to his ears. When a dog was angry or frightened, ready to fight, he dropped his ears back along his head to keep them from getting torn. This fellow had growled at her a few times, but she'd trained animals since she could walk, practically, everything from ducks to dogs to horses. If she couldn't tell what they might be thinking by now, she deserved to get bitten.

The poodle looked at her, huffing out its breath.

"Not in the mood for dancing about, are you? How about a crawl, then?" Hiking her bottom in the air, she scooted backward, keeping her face low. "Come on, Galahad. Crawl. Show him, Jenny."

Her own poodle padded over and sank down, creeping forward with her belly just brushing the ground. She barked at Galahad and continued forward.

"Come on, Galahad. Crawl." Sally waved the chunk of meat she still held in one hand.

Eyeing the meat, he wiggled forward a few inches and stretched out his neck.

"Good boy!" she praised him, handing him the reward. "Good crawl."

"I don't know what the devil's afoot here, but I definitely approve," Jimmy said, slipping in through the door and eyeing her backside.

Sally stood up, brushing at her skirt and feeling heat in her cheeks. "Everybody does their share of work in this family," she stated, not certain whether she was embarrassed or pleased at him noticing her rump.

Galahad sprang to his feet again, growling and ears back. "Here," she said, handing Jimmy another morsel of beef.

"Are you trying to get him to murder me, Sally? Take it back."

"No. Stretch out your hand, palm up and open with the snack in the middle, and say, 'Here, Galahad. Good boy,'" she instructed.

"He is going to eat me."

"He most likely will not."

"What? 'Most likely'?"

"Just do it, Jimmy. For heaven's sake. And then don't move a muscle."

"Fine. Fine. I'm using my off arm, though, just in case." With a deep breath he did as she said, putting the meat on his palm and stretching his arm out as far as he could. "Here, Galahad. Good boy."

The poodle barked at him, lunging forward and snapping its teeth just short of Jimmy's fingers.

"For Christ's sake," Jimmy breathed, but to his credit he didn't move.

Galahad grumbled again, his ears twitching. One more bark, and he leaned forward to snatch the meat from Jimmy's fingers.

"Well done!" she congratulated him.

"Wait. I'm counting my fingers," he said, a combination of relief and amusement touching his face. "Is that how *you* made friends with him? You're a madwoman, Sally Pangle."

"I'm a wise woman, Jimmy Bly," she countered, pleased that he'd trusted her. "What did you find?"

He pulled a piece of paper from one pocket and unfolded it. "They're everywhere. Bernard at the butcher's shop had the right of it. The Duke of Woriton himself was in there asking about me and poodles and cuts of beef, and the lady, Miss Dockering, was with him."

"I'm glad he warned you," she said, taking the flyer from him. "Do you trust him, though?"

"No. Which is why I won't be visiting his establishment again. He only has my first name, and he doesn't know where I lay my head. So even if he decides he wants that reward, he can't tell anybody much, thank God."

"Woriton's offering a hundred quid for the safe return of his black poodle," Sally said, reading through the flyer, "and half that for good evidence of the dog's whereabouts or who made off with him." Her heart skittered. "This isn't good."

"Bernard would definitely hand me over for fifty quid," Jimmy said, nodding as he took the paper back to look at it again, though since he couldn't read, she didn't know what he might be searching for. "He only says one poodle?"

"I imagine he didn't want folk knowing too much, so they tell him what *they* know, and not what they think he wants to hear. That's why he didn't give many particulars. Doesn't even say if he's looking for a male or female dog."

Jimmy ruffled Lancelot's fur. "It'd be safer to do what Cordray wanted. I wish I was the sort of fellow who could just do what was easiest or best for saving his own hide."

"I don't. If you were the sort of man who could drown a dog, we wouldn't be conversing right now."

Sighing, he dropped into a chair. "You're devilish hard on a man's conscience, Sally. Making me want to do the right thing, and all."

She sat in the other chair while the herd of dogs padded around them, barking, sniffing, playing, and generally making a mess of what had once been a neat little room. "You're doing that on your own, which makes me quite proud of you." She cleared her throat. "I took Jenny, Pickle, and Bob out for a bit of rehearsal last night," she commented.

"Did you? How's the act coming?"

"Well. The folk out on Radley Street seemed to enjoy it. We only did a few jumps and some front-leg walking, but we made nine shillings on it." She grinned. "Just for passing by on the street."

He sat straight up the second she mentioned Radley Street, which she'd figured he would. "Why Radley Street, Sally? Are you trying to get me caught?"

"Just the opposite, nick-ninny. Even if Bernard tells tales about you, there are plenty of folk about that butcher's shop who'll swear they did see a black poodle. One that walks on two legs and was in the company of a harlequin and two little white dogs."

Jimmy continued gazing at her. "Well, then," he finally said. "That very nearly makes me want to give you a kiss, Sally Pangle."

Oh, my. "I'd very nearly let you, Jimmy Bly."

"I suppose I expected it to be more cluttered," Elizabeth said, practically tiptoeing as she followed Michael into his study. "The sign on the door is quite direct."

"The last thing I want when I'm trying to do something that takes a little delicacy is Huston or one of the footmen pounding on the door because I haven't requested tea for an hour." That made him sound like a curmudgeon, so he smiled. "I sometimes neglect to take the sign down, however, so they tend to ignore it."

"All this glass and wire. How does one make tubes like that?" She ran a finger along one of the tubes he used for carrying gas from one container to another.

"A glassblower. I give him a sketch, and he makes an apparatus for me. The tubes where I need some flexibility are rubber, but rubber is susceptible to corrosives, so I can only use it under certain circumstances."

"And the upturned glass . . . bowls set into plates filled with water?"

"Those are receivers, filled with various gases. The water stops any substance from leaking beneath an imperfect edge."

She glanced up at him—which he knew, because he'd been watching her since they walked into the room. "I feel like I'm asking stupid questions. I'm not certain I would know a glass tube from a vial, and you . . . use these instruments like a conductor before an orchestra."

"Wanting to know something outside of your experience is not stupid, Elizabeth. I read somewhere that the greatest mark of intelligence is curiosity. I appreciate curiosity."

Her cheeks reddened. "Thank you for saying so."

"I also liked your analogy. There are times I feel like I have an entire orchestra in here, every instrument playing a different tune at the same time. Then it becomes a cacophony of smoke and broken glass, at which point I burn my composition and start all over again."

She laughed. "This is fascinating. Science sounds very exciting when you add in explosions."

Snorting, he gestured at the back wall. "These are my various samples. Acids, alkalines, et cetera. I've had a second sink put in the kitchen, so the dishes don't get washed with benzene or something." Michael stopped, listening to what he must sound like to a person with a limited science background. What the devil was he doing? Showing off his collection of pinned butterflies to a pretty girl and hoping she liked dead butterflies? *Good God.* "Are you hungry? I've had luncheon set in the garden."

"You don't entertain very often, do you?" Elizabeth commented, tapping her finger against a vial of vinegar.

"Of course I don't. What sort of question is that?" He took a breath. "I know I'm an oddity, Elizabeth. I'm content to be so. If you find what I do as boring and silly as the rest of our peers, I certainly can't fault you for it. Th—"

"Show me how you remove hydrogen from water," she interrupted. "Then we'll have luncheon. Peggy, please go compliment the cook on her biscuits, and ask if she can provide me a glass of lemonade, will you?"

The maid looked from her mistress to Michael, then shrugged as if she'd realized that her presence or lack thereof made no difference at all to him or his conduct. "I'll see to it, Miss Bitsy."

Elizabeth wanted to know more. He hadn't expected that. "It involves a battery, a bowl of water, two tubes and two receivers—one for oxygen, and one for hydrogen. I'm afraid it's not very exciting. Just oxygen bubbles attracted to the batteries' negative charge, and hydrogen bubbles attracted to the positive charge. The bubbles travel up their respective tubes and fill the receivers with gas."

"Show me anyway," she said.

"Very well. If you fall asleep, don't snore."

He set up his voltaic pile, the water, tubes set directly over the positive and negative wires, and the rounded receivers beyond the tubes. Though he'd done this same thing so many times he could probably manage it with his eyes shut, he made an attempt to explain the steps, the way water conducted electricity to complete the circuit, so that she would understand without being insulted. It was tricky; generally, he didn't care whether he insulted someone or not. Or rather, he didn't pay any attention to whether he'd done so.

"So one wire is positive and the other is negative? Who decided which is which?"

"I . . . have no idea. The electrical current flows out from here, which we've designated the positive side, and flows back into the battery to complete the circuit here, and we've deemed that the negative side."

"Do I conduct electricity?"

"The human body does conduct electricity, though not well. If you're asking about you, specifically, I would say that's a matter of opinion."

She faced him, leaning back against his worktable. "And what is your opinion?"

Michael knew what he wanted to say. He wanted to tell her that he practically saw sparks when he looked at her, and that in her company over the past few days he felt positively enough charged that the hairs on his arms lifted.

Instead of answering, he took a half step forward, leaned down, and kissed her on the mouth. Her lips molded against his, and while he'd expected another of those pleasant, enticing shivers, the heat spearing down his spine took him by surprise.

Elizabeth slid one arm around his neck, the other hand splayed against his chest. He noted it distinctly, because everywhere she touched him felt like fire. Slipping his arms around her waist, he tugged her closer. The days he'd spent in her company—if they'd been an experiment, he was now reaping the very successful results. And she kissed him back.

He blinked as down the hallway Huston said something to one of the other servants, his voice echoing. Whether or not he thought himself a suitor, or suitable, he was certainly capable of ruining Elizabeth's reputation. And she was nine years his junior, and popular, and she enjoyed dancing and being around people—things that made him cringe. The social niceties at which he failed. Miserably.

Releasing her took all his willpower. Lifting his head, he stepped back again. "Science doesn't have opinions," he commented, turning to pull the wires out of the water and disassemble the pile to render it inert. "Luncheon?"

She straightened, lifting her gaze from his mouth to his eyes and her expression slamming shut to that mask of politeness he frequently saw on those occasions he mingled with his peers. "What was that, one of your experiments?" she demanded.

Yes. And there had definitely been combustion. "Curiosity," he said aloud. He had no business interfering with her life. None. And they both knew it. "Luncheon?" he repeated.

"I . . . suppose I knew from the beginning that you have no manners," she stated, an edge to her voice.

Michael inclined his head, trying to keep his gaze off her sweet, soft mouth. "I did warn you. Are you going to stomp off, then?"

Elizabeth cleared her throat. "If flight is what you expect, then of course I will stay for luncheon," she said, moving to put the worktable between the two of them. "I'm famished, and not a coward."

"Good," he said, though he almost wished for a few minutes

to gather the shambles of his thoughts back together, himself. "We need to refine our search area for Galahad and Lancelot. The sooner we find them, the better."

No, she wasn't a coward. He felt like one, though. Rather than offering his arm, Michael led the way back into the hallway. Huston glared at him, clearly disapproving of his manners. The servants could say he was being obtuse again, his mind on nothing that didn't have tubes and wires attached to it. More often than not, their assessment was correct. Today, though, the kiss had been the accident. What followed had been on purpose.

Circumstance had literally thrown them together, and she required his assistance. Her beginning to feel some . . . affection for him made sense from her point of view.

As for him, well, she wasn't a vial or a voltaic battery. She was unique. And unique had always interested him. That didn't make them compatible. It didn't even make them friends, though at the moment he was loath to let go of that title—because they still had two dogs to find, of course. It had nothing to do with the arousal he felt from being in her presence, much less kissing her. That was just emotion, and emotion was unreliable.

While all he'd told Huston was to set luncheon in the garden, the servants had outdone themselves. A proper table, tablecloth, candelabra—supremely useless given the light breeze—a vase of garden roses, the best silverware and china, and a footman standing behind either of the two chairs. "Good God," he muttered.

"This is lovely," Elizabeth noted, gliding to a seat before he could even think of holding a chair for her.

"I suggested sandwiches. The rest is none of my doing." Michael sat opposite her.

She kept her gaze on her plate. "No, we don't want anyone thinking you like me."

"*You* shouldn't like *me*," he stated, then cleared his throat. *Civil-*

ity. He could be civil for a few bloody minutes, even if he did want to peel off all her clothes and claim her for himself. "I believe it's more about my servants wishing to remind me that I have good silverware and should entertain more often." It was actually far more likely that his staff wanted him to make a good impression on a female in whose company he'd been seen, but he'd ruined that by losing what little self-control he possessed.

"You know, if you don't want me here, I can go," she said, lifting her napkin and then setting it down again. "I feel like I've been foolish, and you've just handily pointed that fact out to me. I *should* go. This is a mistake."

"It's not—" Michael swallowed the awkward lump of what he'd been about to say, and attempted to weigh the fact that she was quite right against the fact that he didn't want her going anywhere. And the fact that he was not going to apologize for kissing her. Ever. "Perhaps view it as me making a point of my own impropriety. Not yours. Aside from everything else, we're partners until the poodles are found, Elizabeth, and we both did quite a bit of work this morning. Eat a damned sandwich."

She narrowed one eye, gazing at his face intently, then nodded, settling the napkin across her lap. "Very well. You are provably objectionable."

Well, that hurt, but it had been his misstep. Not hers. "Thank you."

"Thank *you* for continuing to state that the dogs will be found. I've thought of the other alternative, endlessly, but I don't want to hear it said by anyone else—by you, specifically—until every other possible path has been explored."

A roundabout way of saying she believed in his abilities, even if she wanted to slap him. "Agreed," he said. "They are alive and well until we have proof otherwise. And as of this moment, given that we've offered a great deal of money and no one's seen or found anything in the Thames or some alleyway somewhere, I do believe both dogs are still alive."

"I hope so. Very, very much."

Tim and Bradley served more of the ridiculously tiny sandwiches, fresh-sliced peaches, and champagne. "I hope there are more of these," he muttered, sending Huston a glare as he lifted a delicate cucumber sandwich between his thumb and forefinger and then popped it into his mouth. It could barely be considered a mouthful.

"What do you mean to do with the information you gathered today?"

All business now, she was. Well, that was his fault, so he'd have to live with it. "I'll look into the half dozen sightings that seemed credible, and then I intend to go for a walk in the area your performing poodle was spied. You're welcome to join me, of course."

"I'll have to consult my calendar. Lord Peter Cordray evidently means to propose to me again, this time with my father's blessing, so I'll have to give him the opportunity to do so."

A bit of bread went down his windpipe. Coughing, Michael grabbed for his glass of champagne and tried to wash it down. She said it very matter-of-factly, which should have had his approval, but he didn't like the damned content. At all.

"Do you want me to pound you on the back?" she asked, sipping at her own champagne.

"No, thank you." He coughed again. "Do you mean to accept Cordray's suit, then?"

"I haven't decided. We do enjoy many of the same things, and though Galahad detested him, well, logically I cannot have my life dictated by a dog's whims. But ignoring Galahad's very strong opinion doesn't sit well with me, either. And now neither of them can attempt to make amends."

"So your main objection is due to your affection for Galahad?"

She blinked long lashes at him. "Of course."

Even a failed experiment contributed an opportunity to gain knowledge, and Elizabeth was presently handing him a very sharp lesson over what he thought had been a rather spectacular—if poorly timed—kiss. "Hopefully we'll find Galahad quickly, and you *will* be able to take his wishes into account."

"Does science believe in hope?" she asked.

Well, that struck its mark. "Elizabeth, I . . ." He stopped, not certain what he could say to take his insult back without making it clear how much he liked her. *Him. The curmudgeon.* "Science doesn't care what anyone believes. It simply is," he finally said. "Not always sufficient, that, but it's the main rule."

"Science can't explain everything."

"It can."

"Then explain this." She stuck her tongue out at him, and went back to eating her tiny sandwiches.

Michael snorted. "I stand corrected. Science cannot explain you." Or his damned attraction to her.

"Good."

Peter Cordray paced in front of Cordray House's stable while a groom saddled Shadow. All day he'd rehearsed what he meant to say to Bitsy when he rode to her home this afternoon. He had several things for which to apologize, to begin with, and while he didn't remember precisely what he'd done or said—and *she'd* been the one to miss their appointment in the first place—he had it on good authority that as long as he sounded sincere, whatever he'd done wouldn't matter. As far as he was concerned, half the time women simply invented offenses in order to receive an apology, anyway.

"Going out again, are you?" his brother asked, pulling on his gloves as he approached the stable.

"Yes."

"Proposing finally?"

"That is my goal, yes."

"A bit King Richard of you, don't you think?" The marquis lifted an eyebrow at the groom, who immediately let go of Shadow's saddle and disappeared into the stable.

Peter barely noticed the servant's departure. If there was anyone with whom he didn't wish to be compared, it was Shakespeare's crooked, hunchbacked Richard. "How do you mean?" he asked.

"Well, you might not have taken her precious poodle, but you're certainly willing to propose to her over its grave. And that is classic King Richard."

"Firstly, a poodle is not a husband," Peter retorted, reflecting that observant as his brother was, Arthur Cordray could not read minds. Or deeds. "And secondly, we don't know for certain that her poodle is deceased. Therefore, husband versus poodle, deceased husband versus missing poodle, ergo, not King Richard."

"Hm. You've given this scenario far more thought than I expected." His brother resettled the blue beaver hat on his head. "What did she think of the house on Old Burlington?"

"She hasn't seen it yet. Evidently, she heard a rumor that her dog might have been seen, and she rushed off to investigate. I'll show it to her after I've secured her hand."

The marquis snorted. "So even without the poodle present to bite off your fingers you still haven't been able to manage a conversation with her? Perhaps considering all of this, you should find another lady. Or at least be the one to rescue her dog so she'll feel grateful to you. Hell, buy her a new dog. You might wish to wait a fortnight or so before you attempt that, though."

So full of ideas, Arthur was. None of them helpful, but that didn't stop the marquis from giving voice to all of them.

The groom emerged with Lord Plasser's mount, and the marquis stepped forward and mounted. "Well, best of luck anyway, of course. Don't embarrass the family."

"Thank you for your wholehearted support," Peter sent after him.

If Bly had made off with the correct dog the first time, Bitsy would already have had three additional days to adjust to Galahad being absent. In a way, though, perhaps Lancelot going missing first had softened the second blow, so it had all been easier on her. He didn't think anyone else would hesitate to propose simply because a dog had gone missing. Dogs were stolen all the time, or they got lost, or had unfortunate accidents. One didn't refuse a marriage proposal simply because of a missing dog. Even the idea was preposterous.

As for waiting, he wasn't the only one pursuing Bitsy Dockering. No one else had seemed much of a rival—until Woriton had stumbled onto the scene. Peter wouldn't have taken him seriously, either, even with his title and his money, except for the fact that this dog disaster had thrown them together. That had been a matter of pure bad luck, but he couldn't ignore it any longer. Not when the duke and Bitsy seemed to be spending every waking moment in each other's company.

Before long that could become habit, and then he would have lost her to a wooden, single-minded oaf simply because he'd waited too long. *Not bloody likely.* "Finish saddling my damned horse," he snapped.

"Yes, my lord. Of course, my lord." With mollifying alacrity, the boy jumped forward to fasten the cinch and make a few last adjustments to the bridle. "There you are, my lord. All finished."

"I should hope so."

As he headed to Chesterfield Hill, he decided that he'd learned from his previous mistakes. This morning he'd gone to see each of Bitsy's close friends and verified that she had no luncheons, shopping excursions, charity outings, walks, drives, or anything else happening between two o'clock and six o'clock. He'd asked that they not seek her out, or accept an invitation from her. They'd all smiled knowingly, wished him well, and agreed.

She would be home, she would be available, and he would apologize for his rudeness, telling her it was concern for her that had made him speak out yesterday. He would take her for a stroll, and then get down on one knee in front of witnesses and propose to her. As correct and polite as she was, she would have no choice but to accept.

Careful as he'd been with discovering her schedule for the day, he was still relieved not to see Woriton's horse or coach at the front of Dockering House. The man had no respect for appointments or other people's calendars.

The front door opened as he reached it, and Crawford nodded at him. "Lord Peter. Good afternoon."

"Good afternoon. I would like a word with Bitsy, if she's to home."

"If you'll wait in the morning room, I shall inquire," the butler said, stepping to one side and gesturing at the first door on the right.

"Certainly."

He'd been admitted into the house, which meant that Bitsy *was* home. If she agreed to see him, everything would fall into place. If she didn't, well, he would have to convey his apologies for his behavior via the butler, and then she would have to see him in order to accept his remorse, because that was the polite thing to do. Peter liked it when the rules worked in his favor.

In the past Galahad would already have begun barking from wherever in the house Bitsy was. The silence this afternoon felt almost blissful. Knowing that the dog had been drowned in the Thames by now made the quiet even more peaceful. Nowhere else could he imagine a dog preventing his mistress's marriage to a perfectly eligible young man. And so he'd put a stop to it. Simple, clever, and effective.

"Good afternoon, my lord." Bitsy strolled into the morning room, her maid on her heels.

"Ah, back to formalities," he said smoothly, sweeping a bow. "I came to apologize, Bitsy. I was rude yesterday. Unforgivably so. I blame my concern on your unusual lapse in common sense. I mean, I understand it—you're worried about Galahad. I would think less of you if you weren't. But as a friend, I felt, and I still feel, it is my duty to say something when I see you allowing someone into your life who may cause you lasting damage. You've always been so care—"

"You don't need to apologize," she said, her shoulders lowering. "I know my recent activities have been so different from my usual ways that anyone would be concerned. I should thank you for bothering to say something."

Peter closed his mouth over the remainder of his argument. As his father used to say, when you've won the race, stop running it. "Thank you for understanding the reason for my blundering."

Bitsy inclined her head. "What can I do for you, then, Peter? I have a dinner for which I need to begin dressing soon."

Back to first names again, and she'd said "soon," rather than "immediately." She'd given him his moment, then. Peter smiled. "Do you have five minutes to admire the roses in your garden?"

Her mouth curved. "Certainly."

He almost wanted to begin singing, which would cause a whole other disaster. Instead, Peter joined her in the hallway, walking beside her through the back of the house and out to Dockering House's small city garden.

"I do adore summer roses," she said, bending down to breathe in the scent of some red ones.

"And I adore you, Bitsy. I've adored you since the moment I saw you on the dance floor at Almack's for your first waltz."

"Goodness. You remember that? I felt so awkward, as if I might end up on the floor at any moment with my skirt flung over my head."

He laughed. "I would never have allowed that to happen."

"Still, that was the first time we met, and you were lucky I didn't step on your foot. I can't believe you instantly adored me, Peter. You have more sense than that."

Oh, this was going well. "'Who ever loved that loved not at first sight?'" he quoted deliberately.

She grinned, as he'd known she would. "You quoted the Bard," she accused, pointing a finger at him. "Now you must give me a soliloquy."

Peter took her hand. It felt like he'd been waiting his entire life for this moment. He'd certainly practiced enough for it. "'I do much wonder that one man,'" he began, "'seeing how much another man is a fool when he dedicates his behaviors to love, will, after he hath laughed at such shallow follies in others, become the argument of his own scorn by falling in love: and such a man is Peter Cordray.'"

"That's supposed to be Claudio, is it not?" she asked quietly.

Of course she would know that. A clever girl, she was. "I said what I meant to say. Bitsy, marry me. You'll make me the happiest man alive."

Bitsy smiled. "You are a very nice man, Peter Cordray. That is why I know you'll understand that I need a little time to consider. I've—It sounds silly, but without Galahad, I feel like I'm missing an arm or a leg. I'm not whole. Not yet. And I can't give you all of me when part of me hasn't yet been recovered."

And the damned dog *still* managed to ruin things. "I don't mean to be cruel, but you know with each passing day the likelihood of you finding him becomes less, my dear. Allow your heart to be happy about an impending marriage, instead. The rest of you will follow along."

"You're correct, of course, but it wouldn't be fair to you for me—or anyone else—to view you as simply taking the place of my dearest pet. I would never insult you like that. Give me some time to grieve, at least. Then ask me again."

His brother had been correct. Arthur had said the best way to win her over would be to be the one to find her bloody dog and return it to her. To be the hero, rather than the idiot having to stand patiently while she decided if accepting a husband took priority over missing a pet. Peter nodded, his jaw clenched hard. "Of course, Bitsy. I should have waited to ask you for your hand. It's only that every time I see you smiling at another man, or dancing with him, I want it to be me."

"Thank you for your patience, Peter." She squeezed his hand, then tugged her fingers free of his. "A month or two won't make such a very great difference, will it?"

A bloody month? "Of course not."

He left through the garden; they had no good news to share with her parents, so walking back through the house and having to keep a pleasant smile on his face seemed useless. Why did nothing go the way it was supposed to for him?

Galahad hated him, so he'd gotten rid of Galahad. Now she wouldn't agree to marry him because she missed Galahad. And he couldn't return the damned poodle to her because he'd ordered it drowned. He'd shot himself in the foot, the knee, and the groin.

Swinging up on Shadow, he turned for home. The only hope he had was that Bly hadn't yet gotten rid of one or both of the dogs, but he'd given the order two days ago. Still, the thief had seemed reluctant to harm the animals.

Peter stopped. Two days wasn't so very long. Perhaps Jimmy Bly hadn't yet gotten up the nerve to toss either one into the Thames. And either one would do. He could convince her that Lancelot was Galahad if it came to that; she'd taken Woriton's dog home once already without realizing it wasn't hers. Then she would be happy, the replacement dog would have no reason to bite him, and they could be married.

Pulling up the gelding, he turned south, heading for the last place he'd met with Bly. He'd said their business was finished, but they'd also set up a signal to let the man know Peter wanted to meet with him. It might not be too late. He could still win this.

CHAPTER THIRTEEN

JIMMY BLY WASN'T CERTAIN WHY HE CONTINUED TO RETURN TO the Covent Garden alley to look for a sign that Cordray wanted to see him again. He'd been paid, and the fancy gentleman had said their business was finished, but then again, the fellow might want to know for certain the dogs had been done away with as he'd ordered, and he might be willing to part with a quid or two for the answer. Or there could be another dog that needed to go missing, and at least forty more quid to do the deed. Maybe fifty.

Well, the dogs hadn't been drowned, and the longer Jimmy spent in their company, the less he even wanted to think about their intended demise. In the two days since his last meeting with Cordray, he'd begun to seriously consider giving the lads over to Sally, so she could add them to her act. She would appreciate that, and as the fair spent half the year well away from London, Cordray would have no reason to believe anything in his plans had gone awry.

But now Cordray had left a mark and nine lines beside it on the brick wall in the alleyway, so the fancy man wanted something. Nine o'clock tonight, and before then Jimmy meant to come up with a convincing story to explain how he'd disposed of the poodles.

Lying was a tricky thing, though. He could lift coins from a man's pocket without anyone being the wiser, but he'd never been much good at lying. None of the stories he'd told Sally about the dogs had convinced her for a single moment. A smart woman, Sally Pangle was. And a pretty one. The idea of her getting dragged deeper into this mess than she already was gave him the shakes, but he would for certain be better off if she helped him invent a pair of deaths that made sense and wouldn't trip him up in the telling of the tale.

She wasn't at the Rookery today, though; her fellow fair workers were deciding on their acts and demonstrating them to Mr. Arnold Happley before they set their traveling schedule for the autumn. Lancelot and Galahad were alone in his room, and he hoped no one got curious enough at the sounds coming from inside and tried to open the door. Keeping the lads from being noticed had been difficult enough without those flyers Lord Woriton had put up. And unless he meant to pretend that he hadn't seen Cordray's marks, he'd have to invent the story of their demise all on his own.

That flyer had offered a hundred quid for returning one of the poodles. That meant possibly two hundred quid for returning them both. That was more money than he'd ever seen together in one place, and if not for the agreement he'd made with Cordray and the threats of hangings, he might have been considering a way to get the lads back where they belonged without him being blamed for taking them.

He found another butcher's shop half a mile away from home and bought another three pounds of beef, and some mutton for chitterlings. Lancelot had taken a liking to them, and mutton was a damned sight more affordable than beef. It was nice to have someone about who liked his cooking, even if the someone had four legs and a tail.

When he returned home both dogs were thankfully still there, curled up together on his bed. "Enjoy that while you can, because

I ain't giving up my bed tonight," he said, setting his supplies down so he could cook dinner for the three of them. That done, he sat in his chair. The poodles strolled up on either side, wagging at him. "Sally's taught you a thing or two, hasn't she?" he mused, tossing them bits of beef and mutton. "I reckon I could join the fair myself with the two of you. Leave London behind me. What do you think? Jimmy Bly and His Amazing Poodles? Or maybe we'd be Lad, Louie, and James? James is my formal name, you know."

Lancelot wagged his tail, while Galahad woofed. Good dogs, they were, and even Galahad had been behaving himself once he realized no one was going to hurt him. Having Jenny and Bob and Pickle about had helped; he didn't know if the dogs could talk to each other, but something had convinced the big poodle that he was safe there.

He waited until the church on the corner rang its bell eight times, then cleaned up the room and left the dogs to take over his bed again. One thing he knew for certain: He wasn't doing anything else for Cordray unless the fancy man paid him up front. No working for half and hoping nobody changed the conditions for him receiving the blunt.

A pair of crates on one side of the alley made for a nice perch, giving him a view of anyone coming and going at either end, and keeping him out of the sticky mud made up of horse dung, dirt, rainwater, and piss. The alleyways in Mayfair were much nicer, but the likes of Cordray didn't want to risk being seen there with the likes of him.

"Bly? Where the devil are you? Bly!"

Jimmy watched as Cordray crept into the alley, keeping to the shadows along one wall like a rat afraid of lamplight. He could pretend he'd never gotten the message. He could stay where he was and just hide there until Cordray grew tired of waiting for him and left. It wouldn't take long; places like the alley in Charing Cross made the fancy man nervous.

"Bly! Damnation."

He sighed. "I'm here."

Cordray jumped, making a high-pitched squeaking sound as he whipped around, and Jimmy hopped to the ground, mud sloshing up over the tops of his shoes. "Why didn't you say so?" Cordray barked.

"I just did. What do you want now? I thought we were finished."

"So did I. Things change." He folded his arms over his chest, then changed his mind and stuffed his hands into his coat pockets. "The poodles. Did you drown them?"

"Of course I did. Tied a stone around each of 'em so they wouldn't float, and tossed them into the Thames."

Cordray uttered a curse. "You're certain neither of them could have survived?"

Jimmy puffed out his chest. "You hired me to do a job. I done it." That sounded believable, if he said so himself.

"I need a dog."

Cordray clenched both his fists, and Jimmy took a step backward. If it came to a fight, it wouldn't matter who'd started it or who won. It would be him dragged before the magistrate, no doubt about it. "Wouldn't the lady suspect something if you suddenly got yourself a dog with her still missing hers?"

"Not a dog for me, you imbecile."

"Then you're going to have to explain it better. And mayhap stop insulting me, or whatever you want me for is going to cost you double."

It was satisfying, seeing Cordray's expression tighten, his cheeks go red as he realized he'd talked himself into a corner. The fancy man could go and hire himself another thief, but fancy folk didn't care to wander among the rabble looking for the worst of the worst. It ended badly, more often than not.

"I wonder what would happen to you if I called for a Bow Street Runner right now?" Cordray growled, narrowing his eyes.

"I'd get arrested," Jimmy said, keeping his voice level and matter-of-fact, as if just the mention of the Runners didn't make him break out in a cold sweat. "And then I'd sing a song about a fellow calling himself Cordray, who hired me to steal a dog from a young lady and drown it."

"You bastard. You wouldn't dare."

Shrugging, Jimmy dug his hands into his coat pockets. "I'm not the one who started this conversation. And you still ain't told me what you want from me."

"I want you to find me a dog," the fancy man stated, anger in every stiff muscle across his back.

"A black poodle, I assume? To replace the one you had me murder?"

"Yes. Precisely that. Will you do it?"

If he said no, Cordray *would* be able to find someone else to do the job. It could even happen that this thief got hold of one of the boys, or Jenny. There weren't that many black poodles in London. If they'd been in Prussia, now, he imagined poodles filled every street. But where the devil would he find a fourth one?

"I'm getting impatient, Bly."

"I'll find you another black poodle, Cordray. For fifty quid."

"That's outrageous. I could purchase two horses for that."

"It's the price of a poodle, these days. Especially with the Duke of Woriton posting flyers all across Charing Cross offering a hundred-quid reward for his poodle back. And fifty quid for information."

"He posted flyers? Damn it all. I saw the advertisement in the newspaper, but you lot generally can't read, can you?"

"Generally not, but enough of us do to make it interesting."

"Fine. Fifty pounds, then. Half now, and half when you've handed me a live black poodle that could pass for Galahad."

Jimmy had decided he wanted his money up front from now on,

but he could see that he'd already pushed Cordray about as far as he could. And even twenty-five pounds on top of what he'd already gotten off the fancy man already made him richer than all of his neighbors. "Let's see the blunt, then."

"I'm not jesting, Bly. And I need it in two days. I'll meet you here then. If not, I will hunt you down and take that money out of your hide."

"I may not be able to read, but I hear just fine, Cordray. Two days, one poodle, here. And then you'll give me another twenty-five, in addition to the twenty-five you're giving me right now."

"Yes, yes." Pulling the blunt from his pocket, Cordray handed it over. "Two days," he repeated.

"You going to tell me why you suddenly want a third poodle after you had me kill two of 'em?"

"Because the chit requires her poodle back before she'll agree to marry me. I will present it to her, she will say yes, and then you will remove it again before she realizes she's been tricked."

That seemed like a dastardly thing to do, take a lady's dog, order it killed, trick her into thinking she had it back, and then taking it away again. It was no business of his, but the entire mess just sat wrong with him. He'd ask Sally's opinion, though; she had a better sense of right and wrong than he did, and she'd be back at the Rookery tomorrow. "Then I'll see you here in two days."

Michael swung down from Romer and tied off the gelding in front of the butcher's shop. Despite his idiotic desire to shove in every door in East London and demand to see the residents' pets, he'd equipped himself with just a pencil and paper, and his map. Brute force might have been satisfying, but logic would still serve him better—to a point.

The point where reason gave way to punching had moved closer yesterday afternoon. Elizabeth had flirted with him. *Him*. And he'd liked it so much that he'd kissed her before he'd come back to his senses. Thank God he *had* remembered what a well-ordered, science-driven life he lived. Because he'd wanted to do more than kiss her, to brush her hair from her face, to sit with her over luncheon and talk about . . . nothing. He'd wanted to dance naked with her in his study, and have her in his bedchamber, and wake up beside her in the morning, and she was a basketful of warm, bright chaos and feeling.

She shouldn't have pretended to be interested in the melting temperature of lead or the recombination of chlorides. No, she'd *been* interested. He'd heard a plentitude of questions from bored, uninterested people, and those weren't the questions she'd asked. That didn't matter, though. Speaking scientifically, she was a positive and he was a negative. The two had no business being together. They were incompatible; that was their nature.

Swearing under his breath, he pushed open the shop door. "Good morning."

The butcher looked up from hacking a side of beef into sections. "You again? What do you want now? I've told you everything I know."

"About that." Michael pulled a flyer from his pocket and unfolded it. "Have you seen this?"

The butcher's right eye twitched. "I've seen it. What of it?"

"It's my flyer. I'm the Duke of Woriton."

"Th . . . Well, I figured you was, after those flyers showed up, but I still don't know why you're here."

"I wonder what your customers would think if I began complaining that you sold me a pound of beef doused with laudanum?" Michael asked matter-of-factly.

"What? I did no such thing. You brought that into my shop. It wasn't doused with anything, the last time I saw it."

Michael set one hand flat on the counter. "And the last time you saw it, to whom were you handing it?"

"I told . . . Heh, you're a clever one, ain't you?"

"You're the one who can give me a simple, honest answer and receive fifty quid."

The butcher took a look around the shop, then stabbed his knife into the wooden block in front of him. "Rats don't live long here-abouts," he said, wiping his hands off on a cloth.

"Then don't tell anyone you've spoken to me. I certainly won't mention it."

"I said too much about cuts of beef the other day, didn't I?"

"You offered more information than we asked for," Michael said, nodding. "You didn't attempt to sell us anything, and in fact, you tried to send us to a different butcher's shop."

"I figured." The butcher sighed. "All I know is a fellow calling himself Jimmy started coming in a week or so ago and asking for my best cuts of beef. I never seen him before, and it didn't seem like it was for him. Could be nothing."

"Which direction did he come from or head toward?"

"East. There's a lot of east even from here, though."

That corroborated the information he'd noted on his map, and Michael nodded again. "Description?"

"Are you giving me this fifty quid, or just threatening my business?"

As a rule—or as a habit, he supposed—Michael didn't chat much. Not with people who didn't share his interests and weren't of a scientific bent. The fact that he enjoyed talking with Elizabeth continued to surprise him. But over the past few days he'd had more conversation with just . . . people than he had in his entire life, and he'd begun to find it interesting. Yesterday, chatting with a few hundred people, none of whom he had anything in common with, had been . . . fun, for lack of a better word. Yes, part of it had been because Elizabeth had a sharp wit and a keen sense of humor and she'd been just as involved as he, but it wasn't just that.

He pulled the money from his pocket and set it on the counter. "Description?" he repeated.

"Skinny, brown hair a bit raggedy, a small scar here," he said, running a finger along the back of his left hand. "I'd say five and twenty, maybe a bit older. And the last time I saw him, he was buying double the meat he'd started with."

Double the meat might well mean double the dogs. "When *is* the last time you saw him?"

"About twenty minutes before you and the miss came to visit me."

That figured. They'd nearly run head-on into their quarry. At the same time, they might as well have missed him by a hundred miles. One man in an ocean of people did not make for good odds. But he had part of a name, now, and a general description. "How was he dressed? Like a laborer?"

The butcher shrugged. "I couldn't tell you what he does. Not from what he was wearing. A thin brown coat, whitish shirt, brown trousers, worn shoes, and a brown cap."

"You're an observant fellow," Michael commented, making notes on his map.

"A man comes out of nowhere and starts buying expensive cuts of beef from me and tins of biscuits from the bakery, and I notice."

"Tins of biscuits?"

He gestured with his chin down the lane. "Ask the baker. I just seen the tins under his arm."

"Thank you," Michael said, folding up the map again.

"All this for some dogs?" the butcher asked, freeing his knife again.

"Not for the dogs. For the lady. Two ladies, actually."

He left the shop and went to visit the baker, from whom he extracted a very similar description. "Jimmy" wasn't precisely an uncommon name, and without a surname it didn't help much at all. The only benefit was that the thefts seemed to have been perpetrated by one man, and not a group of ne'er-do-wells, and that a different poodle, one trained to do tricks, seemed to live in the same area.

Three large black poodles would be easier to find than one, and with that in mind he headed east, dismounted halfway through Smithfield, and after leaving Romer in a street urchin's care, started walking. Up the streets, down the streets, asking every passerby if he or she had spotted a large, curly-furred black dog, by itself or in the company of two smaller white dogs.

Nine streets on, he began to find answers, people who'd seen a large, fluffy black dog, in the company of two little, fluffy white dogs who did tricks. Marking the map as he went, he continued on for another four streets, where the mentions began to decrease again. Going back to the densest area of affirmative responses, he headed north, then south, asking his questions.

Four hours later he had the likeliest location for at least one big black poodle within two streets in either direction. Somewhere among the run-down shops, workhouses, warehouses converted into individual rooms to let, amid the mud of poorly packed streets and the filth of rats and cats and dogs and pigs and chickens all chasing after the same scraps, was at least one black poodle and two little white dogs. And unless he'd read every clue wrong, this was also the most likely place for two other large black poodles to be held.

Now was the time he could begin kicking in doors and demanding answers—except for one thing. Unless his first guess netted him a dog thief, said thief would know that someone was close on his tail. He could flee, or worse, he could kill the dogs if they were indeed still alive and *then* make a run for it.

To correct for this imbalance, he needed more people to help him search, or a better way to go about it. Bow Street would be helpful, except that they'd already expressed their lack of interest in finding stolen pets for citizens. He could hire some ne'er-do-wells to assist, but one of them could well warn their chosen target.

This would take some planning and thought, and for once he would have welcomed another opinion. A specific, female opinion. He didn't need to be able to read minds to know that she was presently annoyed with him, or that keeping his distance was better for both of them. For God's sake, she could be betrothed by now. At the same time, this was about her dog and his aunt's dog, and they were still partners, she'd said, until this chapter had been closed.

Going by that logic, the sooner they reached the end of this, the better. And not just for the dogs.

When he returned home, he went upstairs to change out of the clothes that smelled very accurately of his time spent close by the Thames and the canneries and tanneries that squatted along its banks. He wanted to head out again and collect Elizabeth for the next part of this search, but knew quite well how full her calendar was. The odds of simply driving over to Dockering House and finding her there and available were worse than abysmal. Worse, he might find her home, after all, and celebrating her betrothal.

"Your Grace?"

He looked up from his cup of tea. Huston stood in the library doorway, silver salver in his hands. That either meant a letter, a bill, or a calling card. Generally, he would take the time to deduce which it was, but this afternoon that seemed a silly way to waste time. "What is it?"

"A letter has arrived," the butler stated, not moving. "From Lady Mary. Your aunt."

"I know who my aunt is, Huston. Hand it over."

The butler walked forward and lowered the tray. Stifling a sigh, Michael lifted the folded missive and broke the wax seal to open it.

He read through the short letter while Huston waited, doom on his face. For once the butler had the right of it.

"Your Grace?"

"Aunt Mary's friend's husband, the one who's allergic to dogs, has taken ill. She is therefore returning to London early, and will arrive to take charge of Lancelot in three days' time."

"Saints preserve us. What are we going to do?"

Pushing to his feet, Michael finished his tea and pocketed the note. "*We* are not doing anything. *I* am going to call on Elizabeth Dockering. Have the curricle readied."

"I thought you had a picnic with your friends today, Bitsy," her mother said, looking up from her correspondence.

Elizabeth hefted the basket she carried over one arm. "I did; I sent word an hour ago to Anne that I wouldn't be attending."

"So you're going weeding in the garden, instead?"

"Mama, I just . . ." Elizabeth trailed off. "I just feel a bit melancholy," she said. "I don't wish for company. Especially company that expects me to laugh and be witty and flirtatious."

Her mother set aside her letter and stood. "Perhaps it would have been easier on you if the Duke of Woriton hadn't been about to keep you hoping for a better ending than the one we all knew was likely to come."

Ah, Woriton, her other reason for melancholy. One she couldn't even explain without sounding like a madwoman. "Michael did more to help me find Galahad than anyone else. He spent hundreds of pounds looking for clues and interviewing possible witnesses."

"It may seem kind of him, but I've heard that his aunt dotes on her dog. No doubt he had as much reason to want to find the poodles as you."

"So he wasn't doing it for me, you mean? I'm aware of that. We were partners."

"You 'were.' You're not partners now? You've given up, then?"

She flipped her free hand. "Oh, I don't know. He has research he needs to do, and he's giving a talk at the Philosophical Society in just a few weeks." Elizabeth sighed. "I think you have the right of it, Mama. Going about with him looking for clues has only managed to allow me to postpone feeling sad. Today, I want to go be by myself in the garden and weed."

"Very well, my dear." The viscountess kissed her on one cheek. "I adored Galahad, too. A young lady never had a more fierce and loyal protector. I wish you and Woriton had been able to find him."

That made her want to cry, so with a nod, not trusting her voice, she grimaced and turned for the rear of the house and the small garden that lay between the main house and the stable. Galahad had been missing for a week, now. Lancelot, for longer than that. She and Michael had been offered a cat, several black mutts, and a rooster as possible replacements. With the amount of money he'd offered, someone *should* have come forward with evidence. But that hadn't happened.

Nothing had happened, other than her realizing that her life was a great deal more frivolous than the duke's, and that she liked chatting with him and the way he listened to and valued her conversation. She liked looking at him, and when he looked at her, and she liked imagining his arms around her. She liked figuring things out with him, and handing out money to people who truly needed it, and going to have tea in very odd parts of town for a proper young lady. Places she never would have thought of going on her own. And she'd very much liked that kiss, even if he had claimed it was merely curiosity. *Bah.*

The trouble with a frivolous life was that a serious man didn't have time for it. Not for long. Even if he could be a great deal less serious than she'd expected upon their first, less-than-illustrious meeting. Even if she liked the way he smiled when he said something that made her laugh, that he knew to be funny. Even if she'd spent several nights dreaming about kissing him and a life spent in his company.

He'd made it clear that they were too different, that he didn't want to spend—waste—time doing the things she enjoyed. And however fascinating she found him, she wasn't certain she would be willing to give up all of her delights if that was the cost to be with him.

She almost felt like she was mourning two things, though: Galahad, and the loss of a very unexpected . . . something she'd almost discovered with Michael Bromley, the Duke of Woriton. And so yes, weeding seemed appropriate.

"Take a look at this."

She jumped at the sound of Michael's voice, nearly falling on her backside into the flower bed. "You startled me," she exclaimed, turning her head to see him standing a few feet behind her, his gaze on his meticulous map.

"Did I? I already drove through Hyde Park looking for you; you said you had a picnic today."

"I decided not to go. The garden needs tending to."

He glanced up from the paper to look about the garden. "This is one of those times I shouldn't comment, I gather?"

"Yes, it is." And it didn't matter if her garden was neat and well cared for. A garden always needed a bit of trimming and weeding. It was the nature of growing things.

"Very well." He held his free hand down to her. "Are you coming up, or do I need to sit on the ground?"

As he outranked her, technically she should stand. On the other hand, he'd asked—and she remained . . . unsettled by her reaction to that kiss. "I'm not moving."

With a slight nod he sat on the flat stone beside her, crossing his legs in front of him. Either he had no idea that dukes didn't do such things, or he didn't care. She decided it was probably the latter, but that didn't signify, either. It was just another way of keeping her mind from dwelling on the things she wanted to avoid.

"Look," he repeated, and turned his map so she could see it.

In addition to the X's and triangles he'd drawn yesterday, now the map was dotted with circles throughout Smithfield and part of Covent Garden. "What's this? More sightings?"

"Yes." Michael glanced up at her face. "I decided with the majority of reported sightings to the east of here, I should go explore a little. I asked everyone I'd met if they'd seen a black poodle, which I described so I wouldn't receive false information. As I worked my way east from here," and he indicated a spot on the map, "the sightings increased. I kept going until they decreased significantly, then returned to the middle of the heaviest sightings and went north and then south. As you can see, this area here is where the majority of the sightings occurred."

"Each circle represents someone who saw a black poodle?"

"Yes. All in all it isn't many, but mathematically speaking, a few is more than none. And farther out in every direction there *were* none."

She looked at it again. He must have walked for miles and miles this morning. "I thought you didn't like talking to people."

"I've been attempting to imitate your charm. It works surprisingly well; I can see why you've perfected it. By my reckoning, at least one black poodle resides or is being held here." He indicated the middle of the circles, approximately two streets broad in any direction. "It's not a small area, but it will be considerably easier to search there than it would be to hunt through the whole of London."

"I thought you were occupied with discovering a chlorine medicinal disinfectant."

"I have found that I can think about several things at once. And finding the poodles would seem to be more pressing." Michael tilted his head. "I'm aware that the dog most seen is likely to be the one that can do the tricks, but that one might lead us to Galahad and Lancelot. I think it's worth another look. Do you want to join me?"

Join him for another afternoon of clever conversation and adventure? Of course she wanted to. But then she would forget how incompatible they were and begin thinking thoughts that would only hurt her later again. "I am quite occupied at the moment," she said aloud, and snipped a daisy off its stem.

"Occupied with what, destroying flora?"

"You could just call it a flower, you know."

Michael blinked. "What are you angry at?"

"What makes you think I'm angry?" Elizabeth snorted. "I'm gardening. It takes concentration."

"You should be doing more of that, then. I thought it was the dead flowers to be pruned. Not the live blooms." He stood. "I'll see what I can accomplish, then. I had thought to benefit from your opinion and observations, but I also think haste is imperative." For a moment he continued looking down at her, his lean face impassive. "There is another issue, I suppose I should tell you. My aunt wrote me. She's coming back to London early. In three days, as a matter of fact. Good day, Elizabeth."

Oh, no.

He left her garden for the carriage drive. Then he would ride off on Romer and go spend the rest of his day as he had the first part of it—speaking to strangers and more than likely going places he shouldn't in order to find his aunt's poodle. And her poodle. The man was so single-minded he would probably walk directly into danger without even realizing it. Clearly he needed someone to at least make certain he didn't cause anyone to try to shoot him. And that way, accompanying him could have nothing to do with her bothersome physical attraction to the man.

"Oh, bother," she muttered, digging her trowel into the earth and scrambling to her feet. Lifting her skirt, she trotted around the corner to find him climbing into a pretty black curricle. A liveried groom sat on the rear perch, so he wouldn't precisely be alone, but that boy looked like a stiff wind might blow him over. "Wait a moment!" she called.

"Are you coming, then?"

"Give me a moment to inform my mother and fetch Peggy, and yes, I'll join you. One of the dogs you're taking all your time looking for is mine, after all. And we're still partners, are we not?"

He nodded, the slightest of smiles touching his mouth and making her heart beat faster. "We are."

Not bothering with decorum, she ran to the front door, slipping inside as Crawford pulled it open for her. "Mama? Peggy!"

"Good heavens, my dear," her mother's voice came from the morning room. "What's happened?"

"Nothing. The Duke of Woriton found some information that could lead us to Galahad, and his aunt is returning home much earlier than expected. I'm going with him to help search."

Lady Mardensea appeared in the doorway. "You said you wanted some time to yourself, to mourn. This is the opposite of that, Bitsy."

"If there's still even a small bit of hope, Mama, I can't do nothing."

Peggy skidded into the foyer from the direction of the kitchen. "Miss Bitsy?" she panted.

"Please fetch my reticule. We're doing another search with Woriton."

"We haven't given up, then?" the lady's maid asked.

"Not yet."

"Very well," her mother said, sighing. "But please tell His Grace that Lord Peter Cordray has proposed to you. You don't wish to lead anyone astray."

She was the one feeling like she was being led astray, every time Michael appeared. But she did understand what her mother meant. "I haven't accepted yet, but yes, I will inform him."

In fact, mentioning Peter at luncheon yesterday had been the only thing she could recall that had seemed to ruffle Michael. It wouldn't mean anything, of course, but she did want to know what he would say. He did keep reminding her of the virtues of curiosity, after all.

The Dockering House groom handed her up to the curricle's high seat, and then helped Peggy onto the rear perch with the tiger. "Are you certain you don't mean to change your mind again?" Michael asked, one eyebrow lifting.

"Just drive, will you?"

Chuckling, he snapped the reins, and the pretty black pair of horses jumped into a trot. "Not as comfortable as your barouche, but it's better for maneuvering on narrow streets."

"May I see the map again?" she asked.

He pulled it from his breast pocket and handed it to her. "I overstepped yesterday. I did not ask first, and I did not apologize for my behavior after. If you wish me to apologize now, I will do so—though as an experiment, I consider it among the most . . . interesting I've yet encountered."

Elizabeth scowled at the map for a moment. He missed subtlety sometimes, or ignored it, at least, but thus far he'd been honest with her. And certainly the only thing he'd actually promised was that he would do his utmost to find her dog. "I . . . behaved in a manner that encouraged you, and I was hoping for precisely that response. Not what you said about it afterward, of course, but I have yet to witness you replying to anything in an expected manner. Pray don't mention it again. I believe we've both had our curiosity satisfied."

She used that phrase deliberately, and had the satisfaction of seeing a muscle in his jaw jump. Good. Perhaps he'd been more affected than he pretended. She certainly had been.

"You expected me to kiss you? How could you, when I didn't anticipate doing so, myself?"

Behind them, Peggy gasped. "Miss Bitsy!"

Oh, good heavens. "I don't want to talk about it any further. At all. Ever."

"Very well. I do owe you a better answer to your question, however," he went on, clearly unconcerned by the maid's shock. "You asked my opinion about whether you conducted electricity, and I stated that opinions don't matter to science. That was not an adequate response."

She didn't want to talk about their conversation yesterday any more than she did about the kiss. The former hadn't gone as she wished, and then he'd embarrassed her. Hurt her, actually. "Michael, we're supposed to be looking for clues. What are you hoping to see?"

"Ah. Very well. This time we're looking to hire the woman with three performing dogs, I think." He leaned a breath closer to her. "If you were asking yesterday whether I find you attractive, I do. Perhaps too much so for the good of either of us."

She faced forward, her cheeks burning. The curricle continued moving, the only sounds the myriad ones from the streets and buildings around them. *He found her attractive.* And likewise, definitely. It just didn't change anything.

Finally, she glanced over at him. The corner of his mouth quirked. "That's the longest you've been silent since we met," he noted.

Oh! Now he wanted to tease her? Well, two could play that game. "If you want chit chat, I should inform you that Peter Cordray asked me in a very gentlemanly manner to marry him yesterday," she stated, smoothing out her skirt again.

The reins jumped in his hands, and the curricle veered to one side of the road, nearly colliding with an ice wagon, before he yanked the team back under control. "You said you had a good idea he meant to get around to it," he commented after a moment, his voice a little flat. "You accepted the offer, I presume?"

Now she had a chance to use his "curiosity" against him, but she didn't like the idea of tormenting anyone—even if he'd accidently informed her maid that they'd kissed. "I asked him for a little time to recover from Galahad's loss before I answer him."

"Do you think he'd care if he realized that you saw him as your replacement pet? Or would that be too damaging to his pride?"

If Michael had thought it, she probably shouldn't have said that very same thing aloud to Peter. It hadn't seemed to trouble the marquis's brother, though, so perhaps she'd worded it kindlier than she remembered. "I see him as no such thing. A husband is not a pet. Most of them aren't, anyway. I'm allowed a moment to breathe, am I not?"

"Of course, you are. Two moments, if you wish them." He cleared his throat. "Anyway, we need a reason for wishing to hire the dogs and their mistress."

"We're holding a grand party for my father, let's say," she suggested, considering. "We've already arranged for jugglers and acrobats, and then we glimpsed the harlequin and her poodles and were immediately entranced."

"Well done. I brought some coin for bribery, on the chance that anyone needs to be convinced. Let's do a little obvious searching first, though; it may flush her out of hiding. Some of the people I queried this morning may remember me, but I didn't give any reason for wanting to find a poodle. You have provided us with one."

She nodded, more than relieved that they were back to their

easy, enjoyable partnership. All she needed to do was remember not to flirt with him again, to not think too much about how very arousing that kiss had been, to remember that they had different needs and desires in life, and everything would go swimmingly.

CHAPTER FOURTEEN

"HE WANTS YOU TO DO WHAT?" SALLY TOOK THE LEADS OFF THE little boys and Jenny, leaving them free to run about Jimmy's room with the other two poodles. They'd all been spending more time here than in her own room, lately, and Jimmy, despite his lack of a legitimate job—or thanks to his illegitimate one—had been feeding the lot of them.

"Find another black poodle. From what he said, the young lady won't marry him while she's mourning her poodle, so he's decided to be the one to find Galahad and return him."

"Even though Galahad's drowned, as far as he knows."

"Exactly."

"That man's a menace."

Jimmy blew out his breath and dropped into his chair. "I don't disagree, Sally. I didn't even want to go meet him, except I didn't want him roaming up and down the alleyway, yelling for me."

"But you took his money. Again."

"I did. I'm a weak man. I wanted to talk to you about all this before I met with him, being that you're a better person than me, but

I had to decide on my own. And I decided I would take his money and then figure things out. So what do I do?"

"You're asking me?"

"Times like this, I remember how lucky I am to have someone like you in my life." He paused, his brow furrowing before he looked up at her again. "No, not someone *like* you. You. You grew up in the same life as me, but damn if you don't still see right and wrong, and always land on the good and fair side of things."

Her cheeks warmed. "Jimmy."

"No. You're my compass, you are, pointing true north and arguing with me until I head myself in that direction, too. So what do you say I should do, my compass?"

That was quite possibly the nicest compliment she'd ever received. It was certainly the most meaningful. "If it were up to me," she said, "I wouldn't let an animal within ten feet of that Cordray. And he's been nothing but trouble for you since the moment you met him."

"But I did take his money. Or half of what I asked him for. And we made an agreement. If word gets out that my word's no good, well, that ends with me begging for coins on a street corner."

Men. "Jimmy, don't give your word in the first place for something you don't want to do." Turning her back on him, she went to his little table and stove and put together five bowls for the five dogs. She didn't want to admit that the blunt Jimmy had taken in since he'd begun this nonsense had seen both her and her dogs fed better than she would have been able to manage on her own, or that her objections hadn't been over morality as much as they'd been about his safety.

He was spending a fortune, and would be to-let again by winter, but they'd all had more steak than she'd ever dreamed of, and she and Jimmy had been eating fresh peaches and oranges and had some very fine tea with sugar, and twice now he'd brought home fresh blackberry pies. She could see why he'd been tempted into meeting with Cordray again. That didn't make her feel any easier about it, though.

"He wants me to nab the third poodle away from Miss Dockering again after she agrees to marry him, so I can return that one without making much of a stir, at least."

"Except for poor Miss Dockering, who will have lost three poodles entrusted to her care, thinking each one is Galahad. She'll end up in Bedlam."

Jimmy frowned, standing to pace from one end of the small room to the other. "Then you tell me what I should do, Sally. I'm caught in the middle of this, and if I go to Bow Street, I'll be thrown in jail before you can call me a woolly-crowned sapskull."

"You could return the dogs."

For a long moment she thought he'd frozen like one of those statues railing at the heavens. His fist clenched, he glared at the ceiling, mouth agape. Then he turned to face her, his jaw snapping closed again. "They'd arrest me."

He hadn't said no, at least. "Explain what happened. Don't hand over the poodles until you've been given the opportunity to say your piece."

"Cordray could still send Bow Street after me. I know whose word they'd take, and for damned certain it wouldn't be mine."

"Sit down, Jimmy," she said, taking the room's second chair, which had sprouted cushions shortly after she'd begun calling on him regarding the dogs. Her chair, when she considered it.

Blowing out his breath, he pulled the other chair over to face her and sat down again. "I'm sitting."

"Now listen. Don't talk; just listen."

Jimmy nodded.

"You did something wrong. You've a good heart, but this isn't the first time you've burgled somebody."

"That was only me nipping purses and knuckling billfolds. Just enough to keep a roof over my head, such as it is."

"No talking," she reminded him, hoping she wasn't about to wreck what had been a nicely budding something that felt a great deal more intimate than friendship. "You stole two pets. Pets missed so much that a duke is willing to pay a hundred pounds to get one of them back. The man you took them for told you to drown them. He doesn't care about the animals, or about their owners, to be willing to cause that much pain. He's even courting the lady."

"You have the right of that, for damned certain."

"Woriton, at least, is circling closer and closer to finding you. All it would take is Widow Vixing getting a glimpse of one of the poodles and seeing the flyer, or anyone glancing up at your window at the exact moment Galahad decides to take a look outside. We aren't the only people living in the Rookery, Jimmy. We're only the least dishonest ones."

He snorted. "And that ain't saying much."

For a short moment he looked at the poodles, the three of them lying in a heap with Pickle and Bob tucked up against Lancelot. "They're good boys," he said finally. "Even Galahad's been behaving himself. That's thanks to you, but it doesn't change the fact that they deserve to go home. I won't be able to keep feeding 'em beef and oat biscuits forever. Lancelot's taken to chitterlings, but even I don't like those much."

"Then you'll go talk to Woriton? Or at least to Miss Dockering?"

"If I can figure how to do it without getting nicked."

Leaning forward, Sally put a hand on his knee and kissed him on the cheek. "My compass doesn't point north, Jimmy Bly. It points toward you."

His gaze lowered to her mouth. "Sally, you m——"

A fist pounded on his door. They both jumped, and all five dogs leaped into a barking frenzy. Cursing, Jimmy raced to his door and cracked it open. "What is it?" he asked.

Big Mickey Fife shoved his round face into the narrow opening. "Thought Sally should know," he grunted, "there's a fancy bloke and a pretty miss down the street by the tanner's asking for a harlequin and her dogs, looking to hire 'em for another rich bloke's birthday party."

"Thank you, Mickey," she called, standing. A well-heeled man and woman looking to hire her wasn't all that unusual, but everything these days made her suspicious—especially when it involved the dogs. Jenny, in particular. And even with all that in mind, she had a very good idea who it was down by the tanner's.

The big dockworker pushed farther into the room. "Hey, there's some papers going about saying they'll pay money for a black poodle. Is them poodles?"

"No," Jimmy answered smoothly. "These is water dogs. I use 'em for searching the Thames at low tide for trinkets."

"That's a fair idea, to have dogs do the digging for you." Mickey winked at Sally. "You get tired of this shake bag, you let me know, Sally Pangle."

Jimmy put a hand on the big man's forehead and pushed, then shut the door on him. "Shite in a bucket," he muttered, leaning back against the frame.

Sally gazed at him. "Poodles *are* water dogs, you know."

"I listen to you, Sally. I just don't always admit to it."

"You know who that is, just up the street," she said, hoping he was the man she believed him to be. Lord knew she'd been wrong before.

"I reckon I do." He took a deep breath, his shoulders lifting and falling. "Wait here with the lads. If I don't come back, will you see they get to where they belong?"

"I don't want you going to prison, Jimmy. You need to take the lads and get somewhere safe. Somewhere away from here, until we have a sound plan. I'll lure them away." Pulling the trio of leads off the hook by the door, she clicked her tongue. All three of her dogs crawled out of the pile and trotted up to her, sitting at her feet. One by one she put the leads around them, attaching Bob's to Pickle, and Pickle's to Jenny. "I'll head them north and west." She took a quick breath. "If you find a safe place, come back and see me tomorrow, so I'll know where you are."

"Sally, you don't h——"

"I know what I don't have to do. And what I need to do. Get going, Jimmy Bly. They could be climbing those stairs at any moment."

"Wait." Taking three steps across the room, he put a hand on her cheek and kissed her on the mouth. "My compass points at you, too."

Oh, my. Now she had an even better reason to do this, but the idea of deliberately turning herself into bait still made her shiver inside. If it went wrong, she could lose Jenny, Pickle, and Bob, and her job with the fair. This wasn't just about dogs, though; this was about Jimmy, and Jimmy and her, and, well, everything.

"Are you certain you haven't seen them?" Elizabeth asked with a warm smile, addressing the old woman selling half-wilted posies. "My father loves dogs. Now that I've heard of them, I can't imagine not hiring them for his birthday."

"I sell posies," the woman said, for the fourth time. "Buy a posy?"

Michael gave the old lady a shilling, and she handed him a yellow daisy with several petals missing. "Now, have you seen one big black dog and two small white dogs together?"

"Posies," she called, and shambled away up the street, squawking.

"She's the third one in a row to not know anything," Elizabeth commented, taking his arm as they moved a few feet forward along the crowded street. She'd been sticking closer to him the nearer they came to the sounds and smells and crowds close by the Thames docks, and Michael didn't blame her. It was loud, rank, and dangerous here.

"I shouldn't have dragged you here," he muttered, stepping between her and a leering drunk. "Enjoying your company is one thing. Putting you in danger is something else entirely."

"You enjoy my company?" She grinned. "Be careful, Your Grace, or the next thing you know you'll be going on picnics."

With her, he just might. "This isn't meant to be a lark. Not entirely, anyway." *Wonderful.* Now he'd begun to babble.

"Then let's continue with our business, shall we? We had fair luck until we reached Bartholomew Close. Now no one knows anything."

"I believe that's because everyone here knows something." He leaned his head close to hers, the faint scent of lemon in her hair welcome and heady after the odor billowing from the tannery. "Our harlequin is *very* close by, I'd wager."

"But if no one tells us where we can find her, it doesn't matter if we're standing on her toes."

Her reasoning made sense, as it always did. His map and grids could get them within a few hundred feet, but down here a few hundred feet meant myriad buildings and four times that many people. In addition, streets were barely streets, made of packed earth and with building corners intruding, or shacks put up, blocking the way, so that they'd had to leave the curricle behind.

He glanced over his shoulder to make certain her maid, Peggy, remained close by, as well. The poor woman looked miserable, but as long as they were all being proper, her presence remained necessary. Michael handed her the yellow flower. "With my compliments."

The lady's maid blushed, clutching it to her as if it were a shield. "Thank you, Your Grace."

"What are we going to do, Michael?" Elizabeth pressed. "Continue standing here and hope that she and the dogs will prance by?"

"I—"

A young lady turned the corner toward them, her gown a plain brown and yellow, and a lead in her hand. Behind her, all in a row, trotted a black poodle and two small white dogs, each attached to the one in front of it. Michael nodded his chin in their direction, and Elizabeth turned to look as, without so much as a glance around her, the woman continued up the street, turned right, and disappeared from view again.

"Yes, I think that's a good plan," he continued, putting his hand over hers where it rested on his arm. "Stay close to me. Are you up for a chase?"

"You found one female in all of London. There are moments you amaze me," she breathed, an excited smile curving her mouth. "Do try to keep up."

Oh, he would do better than keep up. Yes, he'd narrowed down the woman's location, but to have her trot by nearly on command? That trumped his precious science with a large dose of pure dumb luck. And he was happy to have a chase to give him a few moments to consider it all. However, as vital as the dog lady was to his theory of finding Galahad and Lancelot, his first concern was Elizabeth. He was not letting her out of his sight, even at the cost of their best clue. Or propriety. Michael grabbed her hand before they set off. "Do not let go."

"She's leading us away from somewhere, isn't she?" Elizabeth panted, as they wove among carts and people and buildings.

"No doubt. The poodles are probably being moved somewhere else, and she's providing the distraction—which does indicate that at least one of the dogs is still alive."

"I would suggest we split up," she commented, glancing over her shoulder as Peggy ran behind them, "but that seems a very poor idea."

"I can tolerate losing the dogs," Michael stated, tightening his grip on her hand. "Not you."

She glanced up at him at that, but he pretended to ignore her sharp look. He could explain his comment away if necessary—of course the life of a young lady was of more importance than that of an animal—but he preferred to let it stand. Let her wonder. If she suspected how dear she'd become to him, well, facts were damned facts.

The tail of the rearmost white dog flashed briefly into view, then whipped out of sight again behind a large coach. None of this altered the focus of his search, and that lay behind them back where they'd first caught sight of the woman and her pack. But he was also aware that a word with her could save him—them—hours or days of searching.

"We're not going to catch her," Elizabeth wheezed a minute later. "Or rather, Peggy and I are not. We'll wait here. You go get her."

Michael stopped when she did. "No."

"It's logical; you know that. Don't let our best clue get away."

"No. If she's trying to escape, then we won't see her again, and we can assume that she is part of the dog stealers. If she's trying to lead us away, she'll reappear once she's realized we're not following her." Aside from that, he was *not* leaving her or Peggy in the middle of Smithfield.

"But you said they could be moving the dogs at this very moment! All your work at tracking them here would be for nothing."

Rather than repeat his answer a third time, he turned them around, back in the direction from which they'd come. If this had been one of his experiments suddenly having unexpected results, he would have gone back to the beginning to see whether he had a pattern or a mess. Instinct told him this was a pattern, but the only way to find out for sure was to stop the chase.

"There she is," Elizabeth whispered a few moments later, her gaze down the left side of the street as they crossed. "She's looking for us, I think."

"Don't look at her. Let her chase us now, for a bit."

"I'll wager she didn't expect that," she commented, humor touching her voice.

If anyone had told him a fortnight ago that he would be leading a reverse chase through East London, he would have lost a great deal of money wagering against the odds of that ever happening. Yet there he was, holding hands with a woman who aggravated him and enchanted him in equal amounts, and he was having a great deal more fun than he could remember having . . . ever.

"Hello?"

"Ignore her," he muttered, increasing their pace back toward Bartholomew Close. Peggy continued to lag, so he reached back with his free hand and gripped her fingers as well. No doubt gentlemen didn't assist maids, but neither female from Dockering House would be left to get lost while he was about.

"Hello, miss? Sir? I've been looking everywhere for you," the woman called out, trotting closer with her menagerie behind her. "Are you the ones looking for trick dogs and a woman dressed as a harlequin?"

"Michael?" Elizabeth breathed.

They were nearly back to where they'd begun. He nodded, slowing. "Be careful."

She freed her hand from his, waving it at him from behind her back to tell him to keep his distance as she faced the woman. Evidently, he was too fearsome for direct conversation. He edged sideways and forward anyway, to keep them both in view.

"Is that you?" Elizabeth asked the woman. "Oh, there the dogs are. Thank goodness."

The black-haired female stopped a few feet away. "We've been chasing each other all over London, it seems."

"Have we? It's very crowded here, to be sure. How does anyone find anyone else?" Elizabeth smiled, and he realized he didn't need to warn her about anything. Talking to people, charming them, that was her forte. She'd charmed him, and even the devil himself wouldn't be much of a challenge after that.

"We're used to it here, I suppose," the woman said, glancing from him to her.

"Even so. I saw you the other night, dressed as a harlequin and your dogs doing the most wonderful tricks. I've been trying to find you—that is, *we've* been trying to find you—ever since." She put a hand to her chest. "Elizabeth Dockering. And this is Michael."

He could guess why she'd neglected to add the "miss" and "duke" business; the woman looked ready to flee as it was. Michael smiled at her, wishing he practiced the expression more. Until he'd met Elizabeth, he hadn't used it all that much. "Hello," he offered.

"We were just practicing," the woman said. "I wasn't begging."

"Of course not," Elizabeth gushed, all empathy now that they'd caught their quarry—or rather, allowed her to catch them. "Let me explain. We are putting on a birthday party for my father. He loves performances and animals. We've already arranged for a juggler and some acrobats. If your dogs are as marvelous as they looked the other night, we would very much like to hire you, as well."

"Goodness. I have an agreement with Arnold Happley and the Three-Seasons Fair, but this is our off season. We generally travel and perform once the gentry has left London for the countryside. Occasionally one lord or another will even lend us his property to set up our entertainments."

Hm. Was she implying that if he provided a location in the country for them to hold their fair, she would give him information about the poodles? She'd been coy thus far; nothing of what she'd said gave him any clues. And neither of them had said they owned property in the country. "That's interesting work you've found . . . I'm sorry, I don't know your name, ma'am."

She chuckled. "'Ma'am.' No one's ever called me that before, I don't think. It's Sally. Sally Pangle."

"Miss Pangle, then. Would western Wiltshire, for instance, be a good location for your fair?"

Elizabeth glanced at him. He was the one with property to his name, though; her father no doubt owned some, but she couldn't promise anything without the viscount's permission.

"Western Wiltshire? Well, that's close by the route we've been taking, the last few years. It could be grand for us, to add another location. I'd have to ask Mr. Happley, of course." She lowered her head a little, looking up at him from beneath her lashes. "Whyever would you do such a generous thing for me, Mr. Dockering? I don't know you."

"Yes, Mr. Dockering," Elizabeth said, a grin practically bursting from her lips. "Please explain it."

Ah. So he and Elizabeth were married yet again, and this time he'd taken her name, which she clearly found hilarious. Intriguing as all that was, though, they'd entered into the tricky part of the conversation. He wanted to push; it was in his nature to state what he required and observe the consequences. He could hear Elizabeth's voice in his mind, though, as clearly as he could see her standing there and looking at him. *Finesse.* Some things required finesse. "My interest is actually in dogs," he said slowly. "Poodles. Black ones, in particular."

For a single heartbeat she hesitated. "My Jenny isn't for sale, sir," she returned. "The four of us are an act."

"Poodles are rare here in London," Michael went on. "Discovering the whereabouts of two male black poodles, for example, would be worth a great deal to me. No questions asked."

Her mouth opened and shut again. "I'm sorry, I can't—"

"Don't fret, Sally," a tall, shaggy-haired man said, walking up to her. "None of this is your doing." He looked at Michael. "None of this is her doing."

"Then it's your doing," Michael said, releasing Peggy and coiling his hand into a fist. "Give me a reason I shouldn't flatten you right here."

The man took a step backward. "I've a story to tell, but I'd prefer to do it where folk ain't glaring at me," the man—Jimmy without-a-last-name, no doubt—said, "and where you punching me isn't likely to cause a riot. There's a tavern, The Blue Goose, three streets north and west of here. What say I meet you there in twenty minutes?"

Elizabeth, gripping Michael's arm so hard she was going to leave a bruise, stepped forward. "Please, if you have any infor—"

"Your two . . . friends are safe, Miss Dockering," he broke in. "I just know a few things that need to see the sunlight."

"We'll see you at The Blue Goose in twenty minutes, then." Michael nodded, pulling Elizabeth with him back in the direction of the curricle.

"But what if he doesn't come?" she whispered, craning her neck to look over her shoulder.

"Then we've a very good idea where to start looking again," Michael stated. "He could have demanded money before he met with us, or warned us not to bring in Bow Street, or not make an appearance at all. Instead, he told you the dogs are safe."

She stopped, turning to face him. "Do you believe him? Is Galahad truly alive, do you think?" she whispered, fiddling with his lapels and gazing up at him.

If she was a flower, he was definitely a bee. So yes, he was damned attracted to her. And while she also had thorns, he had a stinger, himself. That didn't mean they belonged together. Michael took a breath. She didn't care about how confident he was in the facts. She wanted something to hope for—and he damned well wasn't going to take that from her. "I think the odds of that have just improved a great deal."

"Whatever he wants for the return of the dogs," she said, shifting to grab his sleeve again and pulling him toward the carriage, "please pay it. I will reimburse you. I promise. I just don't—"

"Elizabeth," he interrupted, helping her up to the curricle's high seat and trying very hard not to catch her abrupt enthusiasm, "we are partners. If the dogs are in his possession, they are both going to be returned. I'm not leaving one of them behind."

"Now *I* want to kiss *you*," she gushed, twisting in her seat to keep him in view as he assisted the maid onto the rear perch. "Can you believe it, Peggy? We may have Galahad back today!"

She wanted to kiss him. Michael watched as she flitted from one emotion to another. He'd thought about little else since he'd lost his sanity and kissed her, and hearing her express the desire to repeat it despite the bungle of things he'd made afterward nearly made him forget what the devil they were doing. Even if it had been an expression, just said in general exuberance, it meant something. At the least, it meant that even a stodgy, ill-mannered nodcock like himself could change enough to be smiled at by a fiery fairy sprite.

Climbing up the wheel, he took his seat, wrapped the reins around his hands, and sent the team into a careful walk toward the tavern. He knew exactly where it was, because he'd passed by it thrice this morning as he'd narrowed down the area to search.

The appearance of the shaggy-haired fellow meant he'd been correct, that his theories and analysis of the information they'd gleaned from all the Bromley House visitors and all the pedestrians he'd stopped earlier in the day had brought him to precisely the right spot in all of London. That should feel . . . satisfying, he supposed, the way he felt when he'd proven a theorem about some chemical combination or other.

But it didn't. He'd reached the goal, but as a consequence of that, he was about to lose a very important thing that defied a definition, or even an explanation. He couldn't put it in writing, because he didn't quite understand it—probably because it wasn't about his mind. This trouble came from his heart.

Shaking himself, he turned up the street where the tavern stood. Facts, information, he knew what to do with those. They'd always served him well, and they would continue to do so. "I would like to ask a few questions about why he chose Dockering House for both of his thefts," he said aloud. "It may prevent future incidents."

"As long as you don't make him angry," Elizabeth said, still grinning and flushed with excitement. "You're very good at that, but he's the one who knows where Galahad and Lancelot are. Hopefully."

"I shall do my utmost not to anger the man who broke into your bedchamber and stole your dog," he said, lifting an eyebrow.

"You know what I mean. I just want our two boys back."

"Of course. And then your Season can proceed as it was meant to. You won't be mourning Galahad any longer, so I imagine you'll have an answer for Cordray."

Elizabeth sighed, her smile slipping. "Despite my teasing about him, sometimes I think it's just expected that he and I will marry because our bloodlines and familial circumstances are compatible. It's almost as if everyone already knows the ending of the story, and they—and we—are all just waiting for act five, scene three, wherein the marriage occurs. That none of the other circumstances or happenstances actually mean anything."

"Some people would be relieved to know their lives are as organized as a play, that they can do no wrong because the ending is already written and decided upon." He made a flowing gesture.

"Everything will happen as it ought." If that was so, her play hadn't been meant to include him.

"That sounds terribly dull, when you say it that way. But is that where I am?"

Generally, when someone asked his opinion, Michael gave it. Facts, as he often said, didn't lie. And neither did he. Even now, aware that he didn't like the idea of Elizabeth marrying Peter Cordray, saying those words aloud smacked of self-service and even jealousy. "I think," he said slowly, "that you're the only one who can answer that question. And if you don't like the answer, you're the only one who can alter the plot of your play."

"I'm not the only one even in my play," she stated, sighing, "but I take your meaning."

No, she didn't. Because if she had understood what he was saying, what he wanted to say, she would—should—be running in the opposite direction as fast as her feet could carry her. And so should he be, but there he sat. And there he would remain, for as long as he could make excuses to do so.

CHAPTER FIFTEEN

MICHAEL TOOK THE TAVERN'S ONE PRIVATE ROOM. THE COST WAS beyond ridiculous considering the beer-stained table, a straw-covered floor so trod upon it had been ground into a fine dust, and the fact that the "room" would seat six people comfortably only if four of them were absent.

Still, Elizabeth appreciated the gesture. The looks some of the inebriated men inside the main room sent her made her uneasy, and left her feeling badly in need of a bath, especially after the unladylike running about she'd done earlier. The shabby private room was the safest place for her in the building, and she knew he'd assessed that the moment they stepped inside, had done a mathematical formula about the drunkenness of the clientele, and had resolved that two pounds for a room smaller than her dressing room at home was acceptable.

"What if he doesn't appear?" she asked, sitting at the table but keeping her hands in her lap. The wood planking looked sticky, and she had no desire at all to test that observation. "We don't know his name. And Sally Pangle's name might not be Sally Pangle."

"If I'm correct, his name is Jimmy. Having a first name doesn't help much, except perhaps to confirm that he is indeed the man who began purchasing expensive cuts of beef from our friendly butcher just over a week ago."

"You spoke to that butcher again?"

Michael shrugged. "He had information, which I needed."

"And he just told you."

With a short grin, he checked the door one more time and sat opposite her. "I'm persuasive."

"Well, I'll admit that you can be charming on occasion."

"I appreciate that," he said. "Actually, though, with him I used threats."

Elizabeth snorted, covering her face with one hand. "The amount of effort you've gone to, Michael, just to find my dog, is astounding. And yes, I know you'll say you're trying to find your aunt's dog, as well, but I appreciate it. Very much."

She also appreciated having this glimpse into his life. It seemed almost unimaginable that they'd never met before the tangle at the park, and that sight unseen she'd put him in the category of old, stuffy, and odd—solely based on hearsay and rumors from her fellows. Because while he definitely had his eccentricities, he was neither old nor stuffy. In fact, once she'd pushed past the very thorny and very thick brick wall he kept around himself, she found him delightful. And charismatic. And compelling.

If they got the dogs back today, she supposed they would be finished with all of this, as he'd said. He would return to his chemicals and experiments and awards and scientific talks, and she would return to her dinners and parties. She could be a married woman by the end of the month if she wanted to be, and if she didn't, she could likely remain popular rather than laughable for another half a Season or so.

If not Lord Peter Cordray, though, then who? No one else had caught her interest, which she knew because she'd looked. Well, "no one" might not be entirely true. Elizabeth glanced at the tall, lean man seated across from her. Who knew that daydreams—and regular, nighttime ones—could be such glorious, heady things, and so painful at the same time?

In actual life, how long did fascination last? Would he tire of her asking stupid questions? Would she tire of never understanding what he was doing? Elizabeth made a face. Generally, she liked questions and seeking answers, but all of these were simply lunacy.

The tavern's proprietor barged into the room to hand over a wooden tray crowded with cheeses, a pot of tea, and a trio of mugs that looked more suited for ale. Elizabeth put a smile back on her face, because being grateful and thankful would serve much better than petulance or haughtiness.

Michael poured her a mug of tea, one for Peggy, and another one for himself, and she reflected that while she'd seen his self-confidence and his focus, not once had she seen him be either petulant or haughty. And he'd just poured her maid tea without a second's hesitation.

He took a single sip of his, and then set it aside. "I may want to take this with me for decomposition. I would like to know what the devil he put into it, and I cannot in good conscience allow either of you to drink it. Perhaps a wine would suffice, if he has a bottle that's never been opened."

She took a sniff and decided the cheeses looked more palatable. "How long do we wait?"

He pulled out his pocket watch and showed the time to her. "It's been fifteen minutes."

"Let's say ten more, and then I'll decide how hopeful I still am," she said, trying to smile. "Whatever happens, I shall need a long nap after this."

Chuckling, he dropped the watch back into his pocket. "You and me both. Though I may have to flee the country if I don't have

Lancelot standing beside me when my aunt arrives at Bromley House to collect him in three days."

"I can't imagine you being afraid of anyone."

"I'm not afraid of her; I'm afraid of breaking her heart."

Her own felt like it had been broken ninety-seven times since she'd first lost hold of Galahad that day, and for such a variety of reasons she couldn't even begin to name them. She could only hope that the last one would be the last time, but that didn't seem likely. "I hope you won't have to do that," she said aloud.

"So do I."

Oh, this was all so maddening. She liked Michael Bromley. More than she might have thought it possible to care for anyone. At the same time, she was fairly certain that these . . . feelings meant she'd gone mad. Or he had, which amounted to the same thing. She faced him. "Michael, I—"

The door to their tiny room opened again, and the brown-haired man, possibly named Jimmy, leaned into the room. "You're here," he said.

"Yes, we are. I would offer you some tea, but it tastes like rotten chicken feet." With a brief grin that was far more enchanting than he could possibly realize, Michael motioned their guest to the remaining chair.

The man eyed him. "You're in good humor. Am I about to be jumped on by Bow Street?"

"You said the poodles are well. That pleases me. Are they also in your care? Please keep in mind that if I catch you in a lie, I am *not* going to be happy."

"You been trying to catch me for days, it seems, and I'm still here."

Michael started to lean his elbows on the sticky table, then apparently changed his mind. "Yes, you are here. Right in front of me. Because I found you, Jimmy. It is Jimmy, isn't it?"

One of the man's eyes twitched. "It is. I reckon you got hold of that butcher. I knew he'd nose me out."

"I would feel better about all this if you'd come here with Lancelot and Galahad," Elizabeth put in, sending a glare of her own at Jimmy. "You haven't; does that mean you want even more money?"

"No." The man scowled. "I said I've a tale to tell you. It's all true, but I reckon you won't like it much. So the dogs are elsewhere to make certain you won't hand me to the magistrate after I've said my piece."

"A good move, strategically." Michael sat back a little, his gaze assessing. "You're wagering on our good faith, though, which we may not have. You did steal our dogs, after all."

"That I did. Wished I hadn't, though, nearly from the minute it was done." He blew out his breath. "Last name's Bly. James Bly. Or Jimmy, which is what most people call me. A fortnight or so ago, I was out fishing in some cove's pockets, and a fellow saw me doing it. Instead of yelling for the law, he asked me to help him out with something, and said he'd pay me for it. It sounded good to me, and better than being in shackles, so I agreed to take a dog from a certain room in a certain house."

"Who asked you to do this?" Michael asked, his voice flat.

"I'll get to that. He paid me, told me to keep hold of the dog for a few days, and then he'd decide what should be done with it. Then I'm to copy a ransom letter and deliver it, which I done, and then I'm to return the dog. But before I can do that last thing, he tells me to go back to the same house, to the same room, and take another dog just like the first dog. I make him pay me more, on account of it not being my fault that I took the wrong dog the first time. Anyway, taking the second one made an even bigger ruckus, so I couldn't return the first dog like the note said I would."

"I did think the timing was odd," Michael noted, and gestured at Jimmy Bly to continue.

"Then the fellow tells me to keep hold of both dogs, and he'll tell me what to do with 'em in a few days. By then I'd figured what the dogs ate, and damn if it wasn't expensive to keep feeding 'em, but I said I would because I couldn't let 'em starve. And that Galahad tried to eat me, until Sally calmed him down, so I didn't have to keep him locked up in the corner any longer."

This was taking a great deal of time to get through, but at the same time it fascinated Elizabeth to hear it all laid out so matter-of-factly, as if Mr. Bly were the hero suffering through all of it. "Go on."

"Aye. That went on for a bit, and all the while His Highness here," and he gestured at Michael, "getting closer and closer to finding the lot of us, and then the fellow arranges another meeting and tells me to drown both dogs in the Thames. That didn't sit well with me, they being the good boys they are, so I said I'd do it, but I didn't."

"Thank heavens," Elizabeth breathed, her heart pounding.

"I thought we was finished, but then he left sign so I met up with him again, and he asked me if I'd drowned the dogs, and I said I had. And then he cursed at me and told me to find him another black poodle that looked just like the lads and to give it to him, wait a few days, and then nab it again from the same place I got the first two."

Something in all this tickled at the edge of her mind. Immediately she dismissed it, because it would have been too horrible for words. Still . . . "When did this last thing happen, about you being asked to find a third black poodle?"

"Last night, as a matter of fact. That's when I told Sally that I wasn't doing anything else for that horse's arse, no matter how much he paid me. Taking a lady's dog because it didn't like him and telling me to murder it and then pretending to give it back to her so she'd think him a hero and then taking it away again when he didn't need it any longer? It makes my head spin, and makes me mad enough to spit nails, all at the same time."

"Peter Cordray," Michael said, before she could make herself utter the name.

Elizabeth stared at Jimmy Bly. "Don't just nod," she demanded. "Say the name of the person who hired you to do all of this."

"I—His Glory has the right of it, Miss Dockering," the dog thief said. "He only gave me one name, but it was Cordray. He was furious when he found out that you and the duke here had traded dogs and I took the wrong one. I don't know if you mean to marry him, miss, but he's a damned cur."

She stood up, striding the two steps to the window and wishing she had a much larger room in which to pace. "It doesn't make any sense," she muttered, twisting her fingers together. Every meeting she'd had with Peter, every conversation, every dance, every smile— she needed to think through each and every one of them again, trying to figure out how Bly could be wrong, or worse, how she missed such a basic and unforgivable flaw in a man's character.

"It does make sense," Michael said from his seat.

"Yes, yes, you and your logic. But I'm not talking about logic. I thought he cared for me. He said he did. He said he loves me and he asked to marry me. I've been considering it, you know. Seriously considering becoming his wife. How does it make sense that a man can claim to love me and steal my dog? And then order it killed?"

Michael stood up, shifting a chair aside to make room for himself beside her at the window. "I stand corrected," he said. "That does not make sense. None whatsoever."

"Oh, now you're just trying to humor me," she snapped, flipping a hand at him and wishing he, of all people, had not been there to see her so humiliated by a man she'd very nearly married. Why she didn't want him to know—well, she didn't have time to figure that out at the moment, but she didn't. "Are you worried I'll begin crying? I imagine logical men such as yourself hate tears."

"You have no idea what I hate, Elizabeth, or whom," he said, something about his voice making the hairs lift on the back of her neck and causing her to think that he did have something—or someone—very specific that made him angry. Dangerously so. "I will tell you it isn't tears, though."

Jimmy Bly cleared his throat. "If you wouldn't mind waiting here for a bit, I'd be pleased to go fetch both the dogs and return them to you. Seems you've been through enough. More than enough, and I'm ashamed of my part in it."

"Yes, that would—"

"No," Elizabeth cut in, facing the room again.

Michael looked at her, his brown eyes sharp and searching as he tried to decipher what she might be planning. A thrill ran down her spine; outthinking the Duke of Woriton wasn't something one accomplished every day. "Enlighten me," he said aloud.

Oh, this feeling was much better than the loss and betrayal Peter Cordray had caused her. This one was exciting. Arousing. Even without his mental capabilities, Michael Bromley was a handsome man. And she'd thought of something he hadn't—unless he'd already considered the entirety of possible responses and discarded them as ill-advised. Well, ill-advised appealed to her at this moment.

"Your friend, Sally Pangle," she said, turning to Mr. Bly. "Her poodle is a female, is she not?"

"Jenny? She's a bitch, for certain. Why is that—"

"You want Cordray to present you with Jenny," Michael interrupted. "You want him to tell you he's found Galahad, and have him give you Jenny."

"That's the beginning of what I want," she said, looking back at him again. "I want Peter Cordray to be embarrassed and humiliated and exposed for the lying, hardhearted blackguard he is."

Immediately behind her, Peggy gasped. "Miss Bitsy! All that scandal could dig its fingers into you!"

"I don't care. I am tired of playing someone else's game. And of being his pawn."

"When you consider it, though, Lord Peter *has* gone to a great deal of trouble to win you."

Elizabeth glared at her lady's maid. She understood the reason for the argument; most of the *haut ton* had by now assumed that she would eventually marry Peter. She'd more or less accepted it herself, even if she had been dragging her feet about it, hoping, she supposed, for some tall, handsome stranger to appear and make her heart beat faster before she settled into a predictable married life. And of course Galahad had never liked Cordray—a fact for which the poodle had very nearly paid with his life.

"Peggy, I refuse to admire his efforts when every one of them was about making things easier for himself, without a thought spared for me except to decide when I might be the most vulnerable and willing to accept his suit."

"When is Cordray expecting the replacement poodle to be delivered?" Michael asked, his fingers brushing hers as he returned to his chair. She didn't think it was an accident, and it made her wish for a moment just to lean on him.

"He gave me two days, so tomorrow night." Bly cleared his throat. "I reckon I can guess what you're planning, but Jenny is too important to Sally for me to risk her in Cordray's company for any length of time."

"What if you were to tell him that you found his poodle, but would bring it to Cordray House the next morning, yourself?" Michael said. "Elizabeth could send word that she wants to see Cordray directly after breakfast."

"*For* breakfast," she amended. "With friends present." Including the duke, whether he'd realized it yet or not.

Michael nodded. "Cordray would have Jenny for less than an hour before the time came to hand her over to Elizabeth."

"You're not going to try to stop me?" she asked, her attention turning to Michael again.

"People have attempted to stop me all my life, my dear," he said, a rueful smile touching his mouth. "I'm not about to do it to someone else. Not unless it involves your safety, that is."

He really hadn't tried to keep her out of any of this. In fact, he'd invited her along on some of their more questionable searches. She couldn't imagine someone like Peter Cordray allowing her to go walking through the slums of Smithfield, no matter the reason. No matter if the decision should have been hers.

In addition to that, he'd called her "my dear." Had that been a term of endearment between friends and partners? Or had he meant it in a more romantic sense? And why had that abruptly become the focus of her afternoon, just like his kiss had occupied her for the past days?

Shaking herself, she smiled at him. "Thank you. I could certainly use your assistance."

"Then you have it. What is your ending wish, though? Nothing Cordray has done is illegal, strictly speaking."

"I will settle for embarrassing him and ensuring that he ends the Season a bachelor. Then he can take the remainder of the year to decide whether he wishes to continue as the villain, or if he will hopefully make an attempt to improve himself."

"That's exceedingly optimistic of you, Elizabeth. While I can't fault your heart, I have to wonder what happens if he decides he's the wronged party in all this."

"You mean what happens if he decides to hurt me more than I've hurt him?"

"It's entirely possible. He's proven himself to be a vindictive horse's arse."

She sighed. "I will respond as is necessary. Next Season will be my last as a spinster, anyway, or it may become permanent. I doubt it will be as satisfying for him to bother an old, married woman." Of course, that still left her the task of finding a husband, one who made her think of marriage as something beyond simply the next step to take in her life. That wasn't for today, though.

Michael nodded. "Will you do it, Bly? This depends on you."

"When I decided to come out and meet you, my lord, I reckoned the odds of me ending up before the magistrate by the end of the day were too high to wager against. I'll help you. I should never have agreed to work for Cordray in the first place." He started to pick up his mug of tea, then changed his mind again. "I'm to keep the lads, then, until this is settled?"

"Actually, if you could bring them to Dockering House tomorrow evening before you meet with Cordray to tell him about Jenny's existence, I think that would suffice," Elizabeth said, the beginnings of her plan filling her mind. "Will this Sally of yours go along with our plan?"

"She ain't my Sally—not yet, anyways, but I'll convince her. So, all you need me to do is bring you the boys, talk to Cordray tomorrow night, and bring Jenny to him the next morning?"

"That's it."

"I don't know what you're planning, but I'm happy to see Cordray set on his arse, excuse my language. I'll do it. And so's you don't fret about the lads, you can find me at a place called the Rookery, on Maudlin's Rents. I have a room on the third floor."

Elizabeth faced him. "I don't know you, Mr. Bly, but I think you may be in the wrong line of work." Leaning over the table, she kissed him on the cheek. All the while she'd been fretting about Galahad, this man had evidently been feeding him the best cuts of beef *and* making friends with him. Thank heavens for small twists of providence.

The dog stealer blushed. "So Sally keeps telling me."

"Do you or Sally read and write?" Michael asked.

"Sally does."

"Good. After you speak with Cordray tomorrow night, please send me word." Pulling some coins from his pocket, Michael handed them over.

"I'll do that." Pocketing the money, Bly stood. "I'd best be off. Sally will be worrying about me, and unless I'm mistaken, you have some plotting to do."

"That we do. Thank you, Mr. Bly, for not making us chase you down."

He grinned at her. "You very nearly *did* chase me down. Of course, I could be lying to you about everything." With that, he slipped out of the room and shut the door behind him.

That took some of the air out of her lungs. "Please tell me that last bit was a jest," she said, sitting down again.

"Considering how much time I have left until my aunt returns, I am choosing to believe precisely that." The duke reached across the small table and took her hand. "This is your revenge. What do you have in mind?"

"Your Grace!" Peggy exclaimed, glaring at their joined fingers.

He looked up at the maid. "You missed the worst impropriety. It's a bit late to point out anything less at this juncture."

"But . . . I . . ."

"I only have the beginnings of an idea," Elizabeth said, grinning at both Peggy's discomfiture and Michael's unfailing logic. "I was hoping you would help me figure it all out. I don't generally engage in schemes and underhanded things."

"I suppose I should be flattered you think me that devious. I do have a few thoughts on the topic." Releasing her fingers, he stood again. "I would prefer we discuss it somewhere that serves a better quality of tea, however. My home, or yours?"

"Yours," she answered, hoping she didn't sound too eager. The things in his house—the books, the experiments, the man—fascinated her, and she hadn't yet had her fill. "I don't want to risk Peter Cordray calling on me before I'm ready," she went on aloud, just in case.

"That makes sense. Shall we?"

She took his offered hand. He helped her to her feet, and kept his grip on her fingers as they left the tiny room, made their way through the very dirty tavern, and returned to his curricle. Peggy made strangling noises behind them, but didn't object again.

Oh, she could get used to this, to the way he looked out for her while letting her do as she pleased, the way nearly every word out of his mouth challenged her thinking and her wits, to the way he not only looked at her, but *saw* her, to that slight, warm smile that touched his mouth and lit his keen brown eyes.

It could all be over the day after tomorrow. She would have Galahad back, he would have Lancelot, and Lord Peter Cordray would be dealt with. Her Season would continue, and with the added attention and breath of scandal, would be even busier than previously. And the Duke of Woriton would return to his solitary life of doing important things.

But that wasn't today. Today they were partners, and they had a scheme to conjure.

CHAPTER SIXTEEN

"WHAT DO YOU MEAN, YOU DON'T HAVE IT YET?" PETER CORDRAY looked ready to punch something, and Jimmy edged sideways, very aware that he was the only other person in the alleyway.

"I told you," he said, "the family goes out every morning for a walk together. It'll be simple to snatch the dog then, and bring it straight over to you. Besides, that's less time for you to have to worry over feeding it and being seen with it."

Narrowing his eyes, Cordray looked up the alley again, as if he expected a horde of poodles to come charging at him. "Don't think you can outsmart me, Bly. We've agreed on payment, and that is all you're going to receive. Try to cross me, you rat, and I'll see to it personally that you regret it."

It made a difference, Jimmy was discovering, to have a duke for a friend—or at least an acquaintance—when being threatened by a marquis's brother. Not that he'd have anything at all if this didn't go the way it was meant to, but unlike Cordray, the Duke of Woriton hadn't insulted him once. Not his education, not his rank, not his employment, such as it was. "I ain't trying to cross you. I'm just tired of meeting you in this alleyway."

"And I am exceedingly tired of your mouth. Be at my residence at nine o'clock tomorrow morning, Bly. Do not be late. I've already been invited to call on Bitsy for breakfast at ten o'clock. If you ruin this for me, I—"

"You'll make me regret it. I ain't being flip, Cordray. I know the rules. Nine o'clock. I'll be there. With the black poodle."

Cordray jabbed a finger at him. "You'd better be."

That last threat seemed to fill his quota, because he folded his pointing finger into a fist and stalked over to climb back on his horse. Jimmy waited until Cordray was out of sight, because he definitely didn't want the man following him. Not when he'd delivered two poodles to Miss Dockering an hour ago, and had another one waiting for him at home after he'd sworn he had none.

When he returned to his room at the Rookery, three dogs sat in a row, looking at him. Behind them, Sally snapped her fingers, and they rose up on their hind legs, gave one bark, and settled into a sit again. "The children are asking how your meeting went," Sally commented, around a mouthful of buttered bread.

"As well as can be expected," he said, shutting the door and crouching as Jenny and the two little dogs came wagging up to paw him and lick his face. Despite the trio, his room felt . . . empty. The two big lads were gone, back where they belonged, and damn if he didn't miss them. "I sent the note you wrote for me on to Woriton on my way back from meeting Cordray. Felt odd to give a lad a shilling to run to Mayfair without me having to see to it myself."

She snorted. "Don't get used to it, Jimmy. Paying boys to run your messages is a privilege neither of us can afford."

"I wouldn't be able to read it if you *did* have one sent to me."

The idea of affording things, though, had already begun to bother him despite the hundred twenty or so quid he'd made from Cordray's scheming. Nearly half of it was gone already, used to buy food for the dogs, a new dress for Sally, some good-quality tea, a teapot and two proper cups, and other treats he'd decided the lot of them, five dogs and two people, should have.

He had money to keep himself fed and sheltered for a good while if he returned to eating nothing but chitterlings and stale bread. After that, the easy ways to make some blunt would start whispering at him again. Sally would remember that he wasn't a good man, and she would stop calling on him for tea or dinner.

"Do you trust him with Jenny?"

Jimmy shook those thoughts out of his head. They weren't doing any good crashing about in there, anyway. "No. But he'll only have her for the time it takes him to get her to Dockering House and give her over to Miss Bitsy. The young miss promised she'd look after Jenny, and I'm to go collect her first thing in the afternoon."

"It still makes me nervous. If he realizes that Miss Bitsy knows what he did and is only looking to get revenge on him, he could do anything to Jenny."

"I'll follow him, then. To make certain she stays safe until she's finished playing with the rich folk."

"I . . . Thank you, Jimmy. I know you'll look out for her."

He cleared his throat. "I'm almost going to be sad, to have all this over with. It's been a good excuse to have you come calling, and you do lighten a room. Even this one."

Color touched her cheeks. "We'll still visit you. You're only a flight of stairs away, after all. And someone has to keep you honest."

"I will try to be that. I'll be looking for work starting day after tomorrow. Work that won't have me jumping at shadows or worried about the law every time I set a foot outside."

"Good. I'll give you all the help I can, until I leave in August."

And then she'd be gone until Christmastime, at the earliest. More than four months for him to keep himself from dipping into some rich cove's pockets and getting himself enough blunt to pay his rent for a few weeks. He smiled anyway, though, because despite all the evidence of his poor decisions, she hadn't yet given up on him. "Maybe by the time you come back to London I'll be amenable to shoveling horse shite for the fair, after all."

"You've too much wit to settle for that, but I'll see what I can find for you." With that she stood. "I'm going to go pretend to get some sleep and give Jenny a good trim so she can pass for a proper lady's poodle."

Nodding, he pulled open the door for her. "I'll come fetch her in the morning."

Sally put a hand on his shoulder, lifted on her toes, and touched her lips to his. "We'll be ready."

Damn. Jimmy put a hand on her hip and kissed her back. There were plenty of women about Smithfield willing to warm his bed for a price, but he'd slept alone since Sally Pangle had moved into the Rookery. She was the one for him, whether he ever made enough of himself to offer for her or not.

Maybe he should have kept the dogs, after all, just so he would have an excuse to keep asking her for her assistance with them. Living an honest life was going to be bloody tiring and even more frustrating, and that was for damned certain, but for God's sake he hoped it would be worth it. Sometimes a man just wanted one damned dream to come true.

Having the poodle delivered to Cordray House was a risk, Peter knew; if either his brother or his insufferable sister-in-law spied him receiving the dog from Bly, then his tale of searching for the animal for days would collapse. They might keep his secret from the rest of the *ton*, but they would remind him every day afterward of how he'd bought his way into a marriage.

Well, they had no idea what he'd actually done to secure Bitsy Dockering's hand, or that a little additional humiliation was tolerable. After all, less than one hundred fifty pounds when all was said and done to win himself a wife wasn't such a poor trade, anyway.

With that in mind, he went out to the garden behind the stable and sat on a half-empty barrel of apples to wait for the slippery Bly. He'd already accepted Bitsy's invitation to breakfast, so Jimmy had best deliver what he'd promised, and on time. The dog might turn out to be unnecessary; Bitsy had asked for a few weeks to mourn Galahad's loss, it was true, and while it had only been a few days since he'd proposed, blubbering over a damned dog for more than a day was excessive. Hopefully she'd now recovered herself. And if she meant to accept his suit this morning, then he would have a splendid gift to give her in return—a dog hopefully better-behaved than Galahad, and one that as far as she knew would *be* Galahad. If she hadn't yet made up her mind, the poodle would ensure that she did, and in his favor.

Moments where he literally couldn't lose were few and far between. As long as Bly showed, breakfast this morning would be one of them. The diamond of the Season for two Seasons now, a woman with friends and connections and the skill to utilize them, not to mention a very generous dowry from her parents, all now coming to him because he'd been bold enough to remove his largest obstacle—Galahad. And he was generous enough to replace the bloody animal with an improved version, albeit temporarily. Yes, the price he'd paid was well worth it.

He pulled out his pocket watch and opened it. Three minutes past nine. Bly was late. Any second now, his salvation would appear. If it didn't appear in the next five minutes, however, he was going to go out to look for it.

"I told you I'd manage it," Jimmy Bly's voice came, from just beyond the stable.

Peter shifted to cover his startled jump. "Keep your voice down."

Bly hunched lower. "My apologies," he whispered. "Just a bit relieved to have this over with." He continued forward, a large black dog on a thin lead pacing behind him. "Your replacement for Galahad," he announced.

Hopping down from the barrel, Peter stalked forward. "The fur cut is similar, but not the same."

"As far as your lady knows, the poor lad's been in the hands of thieves for near a fortnight. He's bound to look disheveled," Bly offered. "But he's close to the same size, I reckon, and he's a friendly one. Not likely to try to bite off any of your manly parts."

"Shut up." Peter grabbed the lead out of the thief's hand. "He'll do, for a quick moment, anyway. I want him gone, too, though, before the weekend. Bitsy will have me; she won't need a damned dog. Messy, smelly, loud things." He jerked on the lead, and the dog stumbled a little.

Bly put out a hand. "Take care, Mr. Cordray. There ain't another black poodle in London that I've been able to find, and you don't want that one hating you before you hand him off to your lady."

For God's sake, he detested being schooled by inferiors, but in this instance, Bly made a good point. Two of them. He reached into his pocket. "Twenty-five more pounds," he said, but pulled it back when Bly reached for it. "If you give me your word that you'll do away with this one after I have my betrothal."

Bly sighed. "I figured it would come down to me doing it for free. I agree, just so I can wash my hands of all this."

"I thought you would." Peter reluctantly opened his hand and let the thief take the money. "I never want to see you again. If you show your face in Mayfair after this, I'll see you hanged."

Bly pocketed the money. "I'd wish you luck, but I don't care to," he said, turning away. "You don't need it anyway, I suppose."

Peter watched him until he vanished around the corner of the stable. Then he looked down at the dog, sitting on its haunches beside the apple barrel. It was a close match, thankfully, though he imagined all black poodles looked the same. He did know they were a rarity to find in London, because he hadn't trusted Jimmy Bly to be telling him the truth. But he'd asked, and he'd looked, and the only thing rarer, it seemed, was a virgin on her wedding night.

"Ah, weddings," he mused, pulled the dog along behind him as he walked for the stable door. "I'll be having one, thanks to you."

He'd already had Shadow saddled, and swung into the saddle with the end of the dog's lead wrapped around one wrist. A coach might have made for a more spectacular moment, but he'd reasoned that a horse looked more sincere—as if he'd found the dog and then not taken the time to return home, have the coach readied, and be driven to Dockering House.

That did leave another problem: Bloody Woriton's flyers were still posted about Town even if the date they advertised had passed, and if the residents of Mayfair hadn't seen them, they'd seen the duke's damned offer in the newspaper. No doubt a line of hopeful liars still waited outside Bromley House hoping to catch His Grace and squeeze some blunt out of him. Peter hoped so, anyway. The madman deserved an endless line of disruption from his so-called experiments after he'd stepped on Peter's toes so thoroughly. But the poodle with him now, new Galahad, might create a stir among the common folk. He would have to be alert for anyone ready to cut the lead and snatch the poodle from him before he reached Dockering House.

He therefore kept to a trot, the dog as close to Shadow as the horse would tolerate. It seemed to know how to walk on a lead, at least, which in itself made it a better dog than Galahad. "No, no, no," he muttered to himself. This *was* Galahad. Forgetting that would be a disaster.

Two carriages stood on the drive at Dockering House, and he wove around them to deposit Shadow at the stable. "Have I missed something?" he asked, stepping to the ground.

A groom took charge of the gray. "My lord? Oh. No, my lord. Miss Bitsy's decided to have a breakfast this morning. She's been neglecting her friends, she said, and won't have it any longer."

"Ah." He hadn't expected an audience, but he certainly didn't mind one. The more witnesses to her joy and then her acceptance of his proposal, the faster word would spread, and the sooner he could begin collecting on some of those wagers made against him in White's wagering book.

A footman pulled open the front door as he reached it, his eyes widening as he spied the dog. "Good heavens," he breathed.

"Shh." Peter put a finger to his lips. "A grand surprise, don't you think?"

Silently the footman nodded, and led the way down the hall to the breakfast room. Chatting and laughter sounded inside, and Peter slowed. A statement before the grand reveal would do him better, he decided.

"Take the lead and wait here," he instructed the footman, handing the care of the poodle over. "And be silent."

"Yes, my lord," the servant whispered. "As the grave."

"Shut your mouth, then. For God's sake." Pushing past the footman, Peter opened the door and let himself into the breakfast room.

Bitsy sat at the head of the table, one hand over Anne Caufield's as the two ladies laughed at something. Anne's sister, Alice, sat beyond her sister, and both Tom and Geoffrey Hillstead were in attendance, as well. Their closest circle of friends, back together again after a fortnight of madness. This could only bode well.

His sense of satisfaction, the growing excitement beating into his chest, growled to a halt, though, as the man seated at the foot of the table turned to look at him. Woriton. What the devil was the duke doing at a lighthearted breakfast? The man couldn't make conversation to save his life.

"Good morning," he said anyway, sketching a bow that encompassed all of the guests and their hostess. "I'm surprised to see us all here, but glad of it. It's been too long since we all sat together."

"Hear, hear," Tom Hillstead seconded, lifting his cup of tea in a toast.

"We nearly gave away your chair," his brother added, indicating the one directly on Bitsy's right. His place of privilege, as it were. He and Bitsy would be trading places after today, though, him at the head of the table, and her to his right.

"I didn't expect to see you, Woriton," he drawled, signaling Crawford for a cup of tea but not moving yet toward his seat. He still had a surprise to deliver. "Don't you have some chemicals boiling somewhere?"

"Now, now, Peter," Bitsy said warmly. "We're all going to be good friends from now on."

Not bloody likely. Peter nodded. "As you wish, my dear."

Woriton didn't say anything, instead returning to what looked like a fine rabbit hash. Hopefully the bastard hadn't taken all of it; that dish happened to be Peter's favorite.

He cleared his throat. "I didn't know we would all be here, but I'm happy to have company to celebrate some very good news." Taking a step backward, he reached his hand through the doorway into the hall and grabbed for the lead. He felt only air. Moving closer, he reached out again, swung his hand about, and finally felt the lead against the tips of his fingers. *Imbecile.* Snatching it away, he pulled the dog around him and into the room. "I have found Galahad!"

Bitsy gasped, putting both hands to her mouth. She slid out of the chair onto the floor and held out her arms. "Oh, my!"

Peter shoved the dog with his toe, and it walked forward to lick Bitsy on one cheek. Disgusting, but Bitsy seemed to like it. "Wherever did you find him?" she asked, hugging the dog.

"While Woriton's been sitting about waiting for people to come to him, I've been out looking. Everywhere. I couldn't tolerate seeing you so distraught, Bitsy. Finally, I was able to hunt down a thief who apparently stole and sold dogs, and he still had Galahad in his possession. The man will *not* be troubling you again. You have my word."

"Oh, my," she breathed, her arms still around the animal. Belatedly he hoped it didn't have fleas. "Was there no sign of Lancelot, though?" she asked, glancing at Woriton.

"Sadly, no. Only Galahad. He recognized me immediately, but with this rescue, we seem to have become allies." Taking a deep breath, he sank onto his knees beside Bitsy on the floor. "We could add to the joy of this moment," he said, reaching out to take one of her hands, "if you would agree to marry me."

Anne clapped, squealing. One of the Hillsteads made a grumbling sound. It must have been Tom, as Geoffrey had been pursuing Anne all Season. Peter listened especially for Woriton's reaction, but the duke didn't make a sound. He'd likely realized he hadn't a chance the moment the dog had appeared, but a quiet groan or a curse would have been supremely satisfying.

Pulling her fingers free of his, Bitsy let go of the dog and rose to her feet. "How did you know this was Galahad, and not Lancelot?" she asked. "They are nearly twins, after all."

It felt stupid to remain on his knees, so Peter stood, as well. "He growled at me when he first saw me," he answered, wishing she would concentrate. Marriage was far more important than a damned dog. Thank the devil he'd already arranged for Bly to do away with this one, as well; now that he was free of Galahad, he wasn't about to allow another distraction into his life with Bitsy. "A man knows his enemies. It wasn't until he realized I was removing him from the thief's lair that he decided we might be friends."

What had he become, that he was now spending time spinning tales of what a dog was thinking in a completely imagined circumstance? It was ridiculous and demeaning, and he'd gone to too much trouble to be ignored for a poodle.

"You said you needed time to mourn, Bitsy," he went on, smiling. "Now there's no need to do so. Let us continue the celebration by announcing our engagement."

"Well, you see," she said, taking the end of the lead off his wrist, "I want to be certain I have all the facts straight. For instance, you've told me this is Galahad. I noticed, however, that this poodle, while of a similar size, couldn't possibly be Galahad."

"What?"

"Yes. He, you see, is a she. This dog is a female."

Behind him Alice gasped. "No, he isn't."

Bitsy lifted both eyebrows. "I assure you, this dog is female. Look for yourself. I did."

"I am not—" Swearing, Peter knelt again and went down onto his hands to look beneath the dog. *That damned Jimmy Bly.* He'd been sold a bill of goods. He'd failed to look the proverbial gift dog in the mouth. Jaw clenched, he stood again. He knew himself to be quick-witted, and this next moment would be his greatest test. "This means that Galahad is indeed lost," he said, lowering his shoulders. "I must have confronted the thief too forcefully, and he lied to me to save his own hide. All I can give you, then, is as near a perfect replacement as can be imagined."

"Idiot," Woriton muttered from the foot of the table.

"You cannot give her to me, my lord. She is someone else's beloved pet."

"Nonsense," he snapped, then rolled his shoulders. This was only a momentary setback. He'd very nearly secured her hand three days ago, when she'd had no dog at all. "Look at the extremes to which you and Woriton went to recover your animals. I've heard nothing at all about this one. Wherever it came from, they don't want it back."

"It's a nice gesture," Anne said, and he sent her an approving look. At least someone had retained their senses.

"Crawford," Bitsy said, petting the poodle on the head, "please ask Peggy to join us."

"You and the poodle are becoming fast friends already," Peter pointed out. "And this one isn't biting everyone and growling at everyone who dares pass by."

"So this one is better than Galahad?" She glanced down at the dog.

Don't go too far, Peter, he reminded himself. "No dog will surpass Galahad in your heart, Bitsy. I understand that. But surely you've room in that heart of yours for a new pet and a man who loves you madly."

"It is my opinion that any man who loved me madly," she retorted, her eyes narrowing and her voice not at all sweet, "would not hire someone to steal my dog—twice—and then order it drowned because it doesn't like him."

Peter blinked, certain he must have misheard something. "What are you talking about?"

Crawford returned to the breakfast room, the maid behind him. Had Peggy seen him talking to Bly? That made no sense. The servant wouldn't know Bly from the prime minister. It was far more likely that Woriton thought he'd caught wind of something, and the duke had decided to step where he wasn't wanted again to make as much trouble as possible.

Then the maid continued forward, two leather leads in her hands. Attached to those were two big black poodles, their coats disheveled and unevenly trimmed, but alike enough in size that they might have been twins. *Good God.* "The b—"

"You remember Lancelot, do you not?" Bitsy said, taking the lead the maid held in her left hand. "And I know you're acquainted with Galahad."

With the timing of a clock the second poodle growled, his ears lowering and his head dropping as he crouched. It all seemed a dream—a nightmare, rather—with past mistakes flying out of the walls and swirling around him while he desperately tried to keep his balance and form a coherent thought that would allow him to awaken and set everything back the way it had been before he'd stepped through the breakfast room door.

"How in the world did you find them?" he stumbled, then decided he should be startled and befuddled. "I looked everywhere! Thank God they're both safe. Whyever didn't you say anything, Bitsy? This is wonderful news!"

"We know it was you, Lord Peter," Bitsy said, loosening her hold a little on Galahad's lead. "You hired a man to break into my home and steal my dog. It so happened that His Grace the Duke of Woriton and I had exchanged dogs by accident earlier that day, so Lancelot was the one to be taken. And then I can only suppose you decided that me being frightened of losing my pet again wasn't enough, because you did it again. The second time you got Galahad."

"Bitsy, surely y—"

"I have to commend you for charming everyone in my family," she cut in again, "including myself. Galahad knew you were no good, though." She leaned down, patting his head. "Good dog."

"If I may," Woriton took up, twisting in his seat, "you considered returning Galahad after you secured her hand, then realized you would only be allowing an enemy into your own home. You ordered him—and Lancelot, who had nothing to do with this but the misfortune to be a poodle—drowned, to be certain nothing stood between you and your goal."

"You're mad," Peter sputtered. They couldn't have deciphered all this on their own. Bly had to have told them. Damned, damned Bly. He should have known better than to trust a bloody pickpocket.

"So then you proposed," Bitsy took up again, "but I told you I wanted some time to mourn Galahad's loss, since I genuinely thought him gone forever. I suppose that's what made you decide to have your thief friend find a poodle to replace Galahad. A pity you didn't think to check her undercarriage."

"I have no idea what you're talking about," Peter snapped, "but I am supremely insulted. I demand an apology, Bitsy, and most especially from you, Woriton. You've been attempting to step in where you're not wanted for weeks now." He glared at the duke, still sitting as coolly as if he'd been discussing a cricket match. "Don't you realize that she's the princess, I'm the prince, and you're the touched hermit who makes the sleeping potions? Go away and take your mad ideas with you, so I may explain myself to Bitsy."

"Are you hearing none of what I've said, Lord Peter?" Bitsy glared at him, her hands on her hips and her mouth a flat line. "I know—*know*—what you've done here, and I want nothing further to do with you. At least you've taught me that the next time my dog doesn't like someone, I should pay attention."

"That's ridiculous, Bitsy. You and I are perfect for each other. Do not let a filthy animal set you down the wrong path. In another year you'll be a spinster, and the number of your suitors will become as dried up as the rest of you. I am your one, best chance."

She opened her mouth, the skin of her cheeks turning gray. Damnation, he'd said too much again. Before he could decide how best to blame his anger on Woriton, the duke stood up.

"Miss Dockering has now had the opportunity to speak her mind about your actions," he said amiably, taking a step forward, "and she's done so quite thoroughly. And admirably. With your permission, Elizabeth," and he inclined his head in her direction, "I would also like to take a moment to inform Cordray how I feel about my aunt's Lancelot being taken, as that is a separate issue."

"Of course, Your Grace," she said, dipping in a shallow curtsy. "Thank you."

"Oh, good. More long words and scientific formulas, is it, th—"

A fist caught Peter square on the jaw. The room spun, darkened, and didn't align itself again until he had an odd view of the ceiling and the chandelier.

Then a face appeared above him—Tom Hillstead. "Let's get you out of here before Bitsy has you arrested, Cordray," he said. The other Hillstead arrived at his other side, and then he flew upright into the air, the room swirling around him again for a few seconds before it settled.

"I am not finished," he announced.

"You are," Geoffrey Hillstead stated. "And it would likely be in your best interest to leave London for the country for the remainder of the Season. Killing a lady's dog to gain her hand, Cordray? That's the lowest thing I've ever heard. I'm ashamed I ever called you friend."

"You have no idea how much planning I—"

"Shut it, Cordray," Tom interrupted. "You're not making yourself look any better. Leave London, or I may be tempted to show my displeasure the same way Woriton did."

Before he could figure out how best to retort to that, Peter Cordray found himself out on the street, Shadow's reins in his hand and three large black poodles barking at him through the Dockering House front window.

CHAPTER SEVENTEEN

MICHAEL ATTACHED THE TUBE TO THE TOP OF THE RECEIVER, AND the other end to the closed valve of his modified burner. "You may want to stand back a little," he said, glancing down at Lancelot, curled up on the floor at his feet.

The poodle glanced up at him, wagged his tail, and returned to his nap. Checking the fit one more time, Michael connected the negative wire of the voltaic pile to the metal rod set into a pool of water and lowered the receiver over it as the liquid began a light boil.

"I admit it's not very exciting," he commented, not certain why he felt the need to talk to the dog when he was more than accustomed to working in the study by himself—except for the fact that he'd spent much of the past fortnight in the company of others. Other. And he'd enjoyed it. "The result, though, will hopefully be a continuous supply of burning oxygen where I can control the temperature and volume of the flame."

Something tapped at his window, and he jumped. He'd had a blackbird nesting in the tree outside, and he did not want it flying through the half-open window to knock his vials of acids onto the floor. "Go away," he ordered, turning around.

"Of course, Your Grace," Jimmy Bly said, a smile dropping from his face as he stepped backward. "Didn't mean to be a bother."

"Not you, Bly," Michael said, pulling the wire away from the metal rod again and standing. "I thought you were a bird. Come around to the front door."

The lopsided smile reappeared. "I ain't a bird, but I'm not near fancy enough to come to the front door of such a grand house, either."

The entire idea of doors and social rank had always been ridiculous. "The front door is closer."

The man shrugged. "As you say, then."

A moment later Huston knocked on the study door. "Your Grace, your sign is displayed, but a . . . person has arrived to speak to you."

"Send him in," Michael said, shifting his stool back from the table and sitting again.

Bly opened the door and slipped inside, shutting it again before Huston could do more than glare through the opening. Lancelot stood, his entire rear end wagging as Bly crouched to ruffle his fur. "There you are, lad. You're a happy boy now, ain't you?"

"He seems to be under the impression that he's been on a holiday," Michael commented. "For which I thank you."

"I stole him, Your Lordship. Don't thank me."

"I'm not thanking you for the theft. I'm thanking you for the kindness you showed afterward. To Galahad, as well." Michael looked at the man for a moment. Kind deeds and the Duke of Woriton had been strangers for far too long. These past days had been eye-opening, to say the least. "Why the devil were you stealing dogs, anyway?"

Bly shrugged. "I tried working on the docks, but there's too many looking for jobs, and most with families they're trying to support. Worked for a blacksmith for a bit, but he wouldn't pay me unless he got paid first. I can't work for free. Dipping into pockets of well-to-do fellows seemed like it wasn't hurting anybody. Not much, anyway. When Cordray offered me forty quid to take a dog and mind it for a few days, it seemed like a gift." He snorted, straightening. "Shows what I know."

Hm. "You're good with the dogs. They like you."

"It didn't start that way. I thought Galahad would eat me. Took Sally showing me how to calm him before he started to trust me."

"How do you feel about horses?"

"Horses? I've never had much to do with 'em. Why?"

"Does Miss Pangle work with horses?"

Bly nodded. "On occasion. She has an act where the dogs ride about on a pony. Saddle and all."

"She seems to be a good influence on you," Michael commented, fiddling with an empty vial.

"She is one. If I had the means, well . . ." Jimmy trailed off. "Five mouths, even if three of 'em are dogs, are a lot to feed."

"I had my own good influence for a fortnight or so. Damnably inconvenient, all the introspection required, but I do miss it a bit." Or rather, two days after he'd last set eyes on Elizabeth, he missed *her.* Her influence, though, evidently remained. "If you're interested, there's a position open in my stable here. My man, Dobbin, would show you how to go about managing the horses and feeding, grooming, exercising, and riding."

"I . . . You heard me say I don't have much to do with horses."

Nodding, Michael stood. "I heard you. Are you interested?"

"Of course, I am. But—"

"Come along, then. I'll introduce you to Dobbin. The position pays twenty-five pounds a month. There's a bed here if you want it, or stay on at the Rookery."

He disconnected both ends of the battery and then led the way down the hall, through the kitchen, and out the side door to the stable. If any of his friends discovered that he'd hired the man who'd stolen his dog—or Aunt Mary's, rather—they'd think him mad, but most of them already thought that.

In the course of his search for Galahad and Lancelot he'd discovered that there were dozens of dog stealers in London, and he was fairly certain that not another one of them would have been as kind to the boys as Jimmy Bly had been. Sending a kind, thoughtful man with quick fingers, concerned about the well-being of the workers with whom he was competing, back into the wilds of East London was asking for a disaster to happen—probably to Jimmy. And he'd lately become fond of the idea of second chances; their rarity made them remarkable and unexpected.

Considering that Dobbin had no idea the stable needed a third groom, the man adapted quickly. As he introduced Bly to the horses and named off pieces of tack, Michael retreated to the house. It was an honest job, and it was up to Jimmy Bly to take it, and keep it.

"Your Grace, will any other possibly reformed thieves be stopping by today to use the front door?" Huston asked as Michael reentered the main part of the house. "I only ask because I'd intended to polish the silver today, but I don't wish it purloined."

"Polish away, Huston. Aunt Mary will be here at any moment, though, so I suggest you wait until after she and Lancelot have departed. You know she dislikes the smell."

"That I do. I had intended to wait until she came by to reclaim Lancelot. I'd never risk having Lady Mary seeing me in my shirt-sleeves."

Stopping in his doorway, Michael looked over his shoulder at the butler. "Good God, she might have to flutter her hands at you." He tilted his head. "Do we seem to have more chaos swirling about the house these days?"

Huston sighed, lowering his shoulders. "Thank you for mentioning that, Your Grace. I'd begun to wor——"

"I like it." Michael grinned. "It's less predictable."

"Yes. What I was going to say was that it was pleasant, having Miss Dockering come calling, even if the circumstances were less than ideal. I assume, though, that your alliance has ended?"

"She has Galahad back." Abruptly Michael wasn't interested in the conversation any longer. He had oxygen to produce, and a burner to try again before he moved on to the main component of his experiment. And the first twenty minutes of a talk to write. "I suppose it was pleasant, but I could do without any additional interruptions."

"Of course, Your Grace."

Sitting back down at his worktable, Michael drummed his fingers against the hard surface. Elizabeth's breakfast two mornings ago had been memorable for several reasons. Cordray, for example, would remember it as the moment his penchant for shortcuts and lies caught up with him. Elizabeth's other friends would remember it as the most gossip-producing meal of the Season. He supposed Elizabeth herself would recall it as the morning she'd stood up for herself and declined to play a crooked game of love and fidelity.

As for him, well, he'd finally gotten to punch someone over all this disaster, and it had been the man most deserving of a bloody nose. The entire time after the dog tangle in Hyde Park had been a surprisingly pleasant interlude, spent in the company of a clever, pretty, and unexpectedly fascinating young lady. Not that he was so old himself, but at nine and twenty, he'd become comfortable with, or at least accepting of, his bachelorhood.

Not that the theft of the dogs or meeting Elizabeth Dockering had anything to do with husbands or marriage. It was only that hoped-for matrimony had been an integral part of the episode. Perhaps he could incorporate something about unexpected and unlooked-for beneficial side effects of experiments into his talk next week. Thus far he had the information-heavy middle of the speech finished, and he'd written a very brief, very ineffective opening that he hadn't been able to stomach when he'd reread it last night.

He pulled his notes forward and wrote "humor" in the margin, to remind himself that a laugh made dry science more palatable. An explosion would be out of the question, because the audience would likely trample each other to escape the hall, but a funny anecdote, or relating one of those unexpected resul—

"Your Grace?" The study door rattled again.

"Oh, for God's sake. What is it, Huston?"

"Your aunt has arrived."

Indeed, Lancelot had already moved to the door, his tail wagging furiously. "So I see. Show her to the morning room. I'll be there in a moment."

He pulled Lancelot's lead from the shelf where he'd set it, and fastened it around the dog's neck. "Are you ready to go home, boy?" he asked, and the poodle barked.

"Oh, my sweet lovey," Aunt Mary cooed, as Lancelot bounded into the morning room ahead of Michael. The dog put his front feet on her knees as she sat in one of the chairs, licking her face and whining, nearly losing his balance, his tail wagged so hard. "Mama missed you! Yes, I did!"

"I'm sorry you had to return early," Michael commented, sitting in one of the chairs opposite her perch. "I know you were looking forward to a long visit."

She flapped a hand at him before she went back to cuddling the dog. "I enjoyed seeing Violet, but her husband is far more trouble than he's worth. I thought so before, but now I'm certain of it. That man had the nerve to greet me with a cat in his arms."

"And cats are . . . bad?"

"They're bad when you claim to be allergic to dogs. He was lying, that blasted Gerald. Or he wanted to make me jealous that he had his pet there and I didn't have mine." She slapped her hands on her knees.

"I hope he *is* allergic, and he procured that cat to tease me with, and Cleopatra is what made him ill. Ha! It would serve him right."

"Could you convince Lady Penderghast to come stay in London with you? It seems to me that her husband shouldn't be the one to have a say regarding whether the two of you are friends or not."

Mary Harris closed her mouth. "That's . . . You were paying attention to what I was saying?"

"Of course I was. I nearly always do."

"No, you don't. But I happen to approve of your reasoning, and I mean to use it when I write Violet. A holiday without Gerald about would be pleasant indeed."

"I'm glad I could help. Have you been home yet? Do you wish some tea?"

"I came straight here to fetch Lancelot. Tea would be lovely, if you're not too busy."

"I have work, but I am always happy to make time for you."

She raised her eyebrows. "You are?"

He had been quite neglectful in the past, hadn't he? Well, that was finished with. Elizabeth had never directly said it, but he had nevertheless understood the meaning behind some of her queries. Yes, it was important to chat with people from time to time, especially when he'd been spending his time supposedly attempting to help them. "I am. For you and for Lancelot."

His aunt blinked. "Oh yes, Lancelot. Did he give you any trouble? Did you take him out for walks as I asked?"

"I did. In fact, he met another black poodle in Hyde Park while we were out strolling. Miss Elizabeth Dockering's animal, Galahad."

"Galahad? To my Lancelot? That's quite a coincidence." She chuckled, then narrowed her eyes. "Dockering. The Viscount of Mardensea's youngest, yes?"

"I believe so."

"She's quite popular."

Michael glanced down at his hands. "So I've heard." The last thing he wanted was for his aunt to realize how fond he was of Elizabeth and create a shipload of fantasies that simply didn't account for reality. As far as Aunt Mary was to know, yes, he'd enjoyed making Elizabeth's acquaintance, and that was the end of it. Nothing about the way he almost wished one or the other of the dogs had remained missing so they could continue their search, or that the . . . overwhelming desire to kiss Miss Dockering again had ruined two experiments since then. His aunt wasn't to know anything about Lancelot being stolen, so the less said about the interlude, the better. He leaned sideways and rang the bell set on the side table.

The morning room door opened so quickly that Huston must have been resting against it. "Your Grace?"

"Tea for two, Huston. Bring the honey as well, if you please."

"Right away, Your Grace."

"And now you remember that I like honey in my tea? What's gotten into you?"

"Nothing has gotten into me. You know I adore you, and I missed you."

"You're certain Lancelot was no bother? Is that why you're happy to see me return?"

"Lancelot was a perfect gentleman. He didn't give me a moment's difficulty."

His aunt looked down at the dog, now lying at her feet. "Is that so, Lancelot? Were you a very good boy?"

The poodle sat up, went up onto his hind legs and put his front paws together as if he were praying, then lay down again, rolled over twice, got up again, turned a tight circle, and sat once more before putting his right paw up for a shake.

"I . . ." His aunt trailed off. "Good heavens."

Blast it all. "Aunt Mary, why didn't you tell me you'd taught him tricks?" Michael said, hopefully hiding his grimace behind a surprised smile and lifted eyebrows. "I would have had him practice them."

"I taught him to sit and lie down, Michael. Something of which you are well aware. This is new. Explain yourself."

For a moment he weighed spinning another tale or claiming ignorance, and both of those against telling her the truth. The first would take a great deal of sustained effort, the second she wouldn't believe, and the third, well, she wasn't likely to believe that, either. At least he would be able to maintain the story, because it was the truth.

The tea arrived, and he busied himself pouring a cup for her and one for him, adding two sugars and a spoonful of honey to hers. He handed her the cup and sat back.

"Michael Aldrich Bromley," she stated. "Speak."

"I haven't been middle-named in years, Aunt Mary," he said, taking a drink of tea. "And it didn't force me into compliance back then, either."

She glared at him, folding her arms across her bosom.

"Fine. You won't like it, and as everything turned out well there's no need for hysterics or recriminations or physical assault." Michael took a breath. "It began the day you left, when I took Lancelot out for a walk in Hyde Park."

He told her about the poodles getting tangled and one being mistaken for the other, about going to that blasted ball to inform Miss Dockering and then her returning home to find the dog that she'd thought was hers missing, the ransom note, the second dog being taken, the flyers he'd put out, their search of Charing Cross and Smithfield, Sally Pangle and her trained troupe of dogs, Jimmy Bly, and then their discovery that it had been Lord Peter Cordray all along, trying to steal Elizabeth's hand. When he'd finished with them returning Jenny to Jimmy and then to Sally, and him returning home with Lancelot two days ago, he picked up his considerably cooler tea and finished it off.

"That bloody blackguard," Mary burst out, gripping her teacup hard.

Michael lifted his brows again. "Aunt Mary! Such language."

"I am old enough to know when someone deserves profanity," she snapped, "and Peter Cordray certainly does. He told Mr. Bly to drown my Lancelot simply for being in the wrong place at the wrong time, which was no fault of his own."

"No, it wasn't," he agreed. "I did mention that I punched him in the face, though, did I not?"

"You should have thrashed him. And poor Miss Dockering! You're certain she's well?"

"When I last saw her two days ago she was fine, happy to have Galahad back and to see Cordray limping away. Elizabeth is a strong-willed woman. I doubt his duplicity has injured her any more than she told him it did."

"That's good to hear." His aunt set down her teacup. "Well, I've kept you long enough. I know you have a speech to prepare. And I'd like to get my Lancelot home and spoil him with biscuits for being so brave."

"He's actually taken a liking to chitterlings, I've been told," Michael commented, standing to help Aunt Mary to her feet.

"Not if I can help it," Mary commented, making a face. "Disgusting things, chitterlings." Leaving the room ahead of him, she accepted her shawl from Huston and pulled it around her shoulders. "As I'm back in London, I've decided to attend the Wincove soiree this evening," she announced. "I know you don't care to join me, but I always ask."

"I've a great deal of work to do, as you've already noted," he returned, nodding at her as she stepped out the door. "Have a good evening."

* * *

"*Huston, wait.*"

The butler nearly didn't hear Lady Mary Harris's whisper as he closed the front door upon her exiting Bromley House. He stood silent in the foyer, waiting as the Duke of Woriton strolled back to his study, straightened the "Do not disturb" sign, and shut himself in.

Huston cracked open the front door, to find the old duke's sister eye-to-eye with him. "My lady?" he whispered.

She took hold of the door, pushing past him and hurrying back to the morning room, Lancelot in tow. In the doorway she stopped, looking over her shoulder at him. "Well? Get in here," she breathed, and vanished inside.

Irregular didn't even begin to describe any of this, but the past fortnight hadn't precisely been usual at Bromley House. Gently shutting the front door, he tiptoed after her into the sunlit room. "My lady?"

"Shut the door, for heaven's sake."

Charles Huston shut the door, pressing his back against it. "My lady, this is completely—"

"Elizabeth Dockering," she said, in a more conversational tone. "What do you know of her?"

Oh, that. While he generally didn't gossip, Miss Dockering remained a topic of great interest among the Bromley House staff. He took a step farther into the room. "I know she's the daughter of Lord and Lady Mardensea, and that—"

"No, no. Not her biography. Has he called on her? Has she called on him?"

"Yes, to both. In the course of their search for the poodles, His Grace called upon her multiple times, and she's been here at least thrice." He frowned, considering. "Exactly thrice. And they've spent the day together on numerous occasions, hunting down clues and people they wished to interrogate."

Lady Mary sank down on the couch. "She's been here multiple times?"

"Yes, my lady."

"The first time didn't send her running screaming into the street?"

"No, my lady. I didn't take steps to eavesdrop, of course, but she seemed quite interested in seeing the study and some of his laboratory equipment. They luncheoned once in the garden."

"Sit down," she ordered, jabbing a finger at the chair where the duke had been sitting just minutes earlier, "and tell me what transpired. Everything, and exactly as it happened."

Charles inclined his head, carefully seating himself in the very comfortable chair. Thank goodness someone else had realized that the household was in disarray and wanted to know whether this was a good thing or a bad thing. Personally, he'd enjoyed Miss Dockering's visits. She'd brought more than a touch of civility to the house, something of which it was badly in need. And she'd coaxed Woriton *out* of the house, something of which the duke was badly in need. "This could take some time, my lady. There is a great deal to tell."

"Have a biscuit, then," she said, nudging the plate toward him. "I want to hear everything."

"Are you certain you wish to attend tonight, Bitsy?" her mother asked, pointing at the onyx earbobs her maid held in her left hand. "Those, Lois."

"I'm certain." Sitting on the edge of the bed, Elizabeth watched as Lois fastened the earbobs to the viscountess's ears and then held up two different shawls for her perusal. "I haven't done anything wrong, and if by chance Lord Peter Cordray or his brother are in attendance, I want to be there to be offended and surprised at Lady Wincove's lack of discernment."

That earned her a quick smile. "I was never as brave as you are, my dear, but I agree. Still, the next time you intend to expose a man for his lies and . . . ungentlemanly actions at our breakfast table, I do wish you would inform your father or me first. We might have wished to be there to add our scorn and dismay at the appropriate moment."

"I will be sure to do so, Mama."

Galahad trotted into the room, sniffed at her mother's waiting dance slippers, and curled up in front of the hearth. "He seems calmer, doesn't he?" the viscountess noted.

"Yes, very much so. I'm going to ask Miss Pangle some of her techniques for managing him. I don't want him returning to his skittish, wary ways if I can do anything to help him."

"It's astounding that the first time he was stolen and recovered nearly left us having to put him down, while the second time has seen him with better manners and an appetite for oat biscuits."

Elizabeth grinned. "I think we can blame that on Lancelot. Evidently, he adores biscuits."

Mentioning Lancelot made her think of Michael, and she sighed. They'd begun their acquaintance with insults, and ended it with a friendship that didn't seem at all sufficient. He was maddeningly direct and unconcerned over the things that were the center of her universe, and at the same time the hours spent in his company had been the most lively and enjoyable she'd ever experienced.

"What is it, my dear?"

Blinking, she looked up at her mother's reflection in the dressing mirror. "Hm? Oh, nothing. Just . . . pondering."

"Pondering what? I do hope you're not reconsidering your refusal of Peter Cordray."

Elizabeth straightened. "I certainly am not reconsidering him. What a horror that would have been. It's only that I had a very exciting adventure, and now that everything is back in place, it seems . . . dull."

The viscountess stood, gesturing Lois toward the door. The

maid departed the master bedchamber, pulling the door closed behind her. "The Duke of Woriton has baffled the *ton*'s matchmakers
and gossips for a decade now," she said, moving to sit on the bed
beside Elizabeth.

"What makes you think I was referring to Woriton? And why
is he so baffling, precisely? He's not some madman, despite what
Cordray said."

"He refuses to participate in any of the traditional forms of social
interaction and entertainment with his peers, and if he does make
an appearance, he insults and provokes them no end. He's tolerated
because he's wealthy; being the last male of his line means all the
various branches of the family have collapsed, which has delivered
him an awe-inspiring amount of money and property."

"I think he makes people feel like their lives are frivolous," Elizabeth mused. "He was just credited with discovering and proving
that chlorine can exist as a liquid. Did you know that? I wouldn't
have, except that the Duke of Sommerset told me. And Michael's
working to find an efficient way to use a chlorine or chloride derivative as a medical antiseptic. That could save lives. What have I
done to help anyone? I danced with Francis Henning, which made
his grandmother happy."

"Darling, you enter a room with a smile, and treat everyone as a
friend and worthy of your time and acquaintance. Not everyone can
do that, you know. You bring a smile and warmth and compassion
with you wherever you go. That is a very rare gift."

"Well, thank you for saying so, Mama." Elizabeth kissed her
mother on the cheek. "I just think there must be a happy medium
somewhere between complete frivolity and steely-eyed logic."

"In an ideal world, perhaps there would be. For now, you still
need to finish dressing for the ball. And keep your thoughts turned toward the future. You've thankfully lost your most determined suitor.
Unfortunately, though, I imagine several other potential beaux will

have been frightened away. And you still need to find someone with whom you can live . . . harmoniously." The viscountess squeezed her fingers. "I know you've become fond of Woriton, but—"

"But we are oil and water. Yes, I know."

The devil of it was, if anyone could find a way to combine oil and water, it would be Michael. Her parents had made little effort to dissuade her from her interest, because everyone—herself included—knew just how mad a match between them would be. With her reputation, her greatest usefulness to a spouse would rest in her ability to be a well-liked, much-admired hostess and companion. Michael made a mockery of most of Society's polite events.

But after seeing his completely different world, she and her frivolity were ready for a share of serious and important. Lord Steely-Eyed Logic, though, needed to come to his own conclusion about whether he would be better off with a bit of frivolity and warmth in his life. If he didn't, the positive and negative charges of their voltaic battery would never do whatever it was they were supposed to do. And he would never kiss her again, or hold her, or tell her that he loved her.

He did say romantic things, after all. He'd told her that light had a speed, and that the light of stars in the sky had traveled thousands of years just to be seen for that one moment. And he'd held her hand on occasion, and she didn't think that was just to be certain she wasn't stolen by some thief. And he'd kissed her. Didn't he realize how much she enjoyed his company? How much she looked forward to spending time with him? *Oh, bother.*

Occasionally she was a fan of irony. Finally falling for a man when she'd had men falling all over her for two years, and then watching him walk away without a single fond word at the end of their temporary partnership—no, today she was not a fan of irony. At all. Irony could go sit in a mud puddle, for all she cared.

CHAPTER EIGHTEEN

SALLY PANGLE SET THE THREE BOWLS DOWN FOR HER THREE dogs, then settled at her little table to eat her own dinner. No beef or oat biscuits tonight for her partners, though; as far as she knew Jimmy hadn't even returned home yet. And with no Society dogs to feed, her own dogs were well on their way back to scraps and bones.

It worried her that Jimmy remained absent. He'd mentioned last evening that his source of income, Peter Cordray, had been run out of Town and now he would be back to scrambling for rent money in a few months. For him that would mean trying to find a job toting boxes or making shop deliveries, attempting not to step on the toes of men who already made their money doing such things.

She didn't know what it was, that thing that made him think himself, his own comfort, was worth less than that of any man who had himself a wife and children, but it was also rather endearing. Still, a kindhearted thief could be hanged or transported as easily as a hardhearted one.

Jenny lifted her head from her food bowl and looked toward the door. A heartbeat later someone knocked. Keeping her relief in check until she was certain, Sally stood and walked over to unhook the latch and open the door.

"Good evening, Sally," Jimmy said, and put his palms on her shoulders before he bent his head to deliver a sound kiss.

Heat tangled along her spine. "What in the world prompted that?"

With a grin he let her go to glance beyond her. "Jenny, Pickle, Bob."

A trio of tails wagged and then the dogs returned to their dinner. "Well, you've nearly eaten me alive, so you might as well come in," she said, teetering somewhere between alarm and delight. "I'd begun to think you were out snatching someone's horse, or something. Now I'm even more worried."

"Funny you should say that," he said, still smiling as he held her chair for her and then sat down across her little table.

More alarm bells went off in her skull. "Why is that funny?" she demanded, handing him a plate with buttered bread and a quarter of a roasted chicken on it.

"Thank you. I'm half starved." He dug into the chicken.

"Jimmy Bly, I am going to punch you in the nose if you don't tell me why my mentioning stealing horses is funny."

"You are an angry woman, Sally Pangle."

"Only where you're concerned."

He set down his fork. "I went to see Woriton this morning, to inquire after the dogs. He invited me into his house through the front door, and we chatted like we were old friends."

"Through the front door?" She narrowed her eyes. "Woriton seemed like a good sort. Tell me he didn't put you up to stealing someone's horse."

"He did not. He offered me work. Steady work, at his stable. Working with his horses, learning the trade." Jimmy snorted. "Can you imagine me, a groom at a fancy house?"

"Woriton knows you don't have any experience with horses?"

"I told him so, straight up. He told me not to mind that, as long as I was willing to learn." Jimmy cleared his throat, then reached across the table and grabbed her fingers. "I reckoned I could ask you for a few pointers, if you're willing to help me."

"Of course I'm willing to help you." Legitimate work. From a good employer. A tear ran down her cheek. "I'm very happy for you. Is it what you want?"

"I think it is. He mentioned that he liked how good I was with the dogs. I told him I had you to thank for that." He squeezed her hand. "I have a job, Sally. A good one. Twenty-five pounds a month."

"That's very generous of him."

Jimmy smiled again, his eyes looking as damp as hers. "He liked that I was kind. Have you ever heard such a thing? And I can room at Bromley House, or here. I think I'll stay here, though, at least while you're in London. Because a husband and wife should lodge together, don't you reckon?"

He'd said it. He'd said the words. Well, not precisely, but she knew what it meant. Still, a lady hopefully only had reason to hear those words spoken once in her life, and she wanted them said clear and unmistakable. "You have to ask me," she whispered, shaking.

Taking her other hand as well, he leaned over the table. "Sally Pangle, I've been in love with you for a damned long time. I didn't know how I could do anything about it, though, when I couldn't find honest work. But now I have, and so I can. Will you marry me, Sally?"

"Yes, I will marry you, Jimmy Bly. I've been in love with you for a damned long time, too."

He smiled, leaned in, and kissed her once more. Heat trailed along her insides, desire she could finally feel without having to chastise herself about it. She laughed against his mouth.

"What's so funny?"

"I'm happy. Do you think we might find a place closer to Bromley House, where we and the dogs have a spare room or two?"

"Widow Vixing won't be happy, losing two tenants at once," he commented, and kissed her again. "We may have to leave in the middle of the night."

Sally laughed again. "Our next adventure."

"There's no one I'd rather have one with, my sweet Sally."

Michael read through the paragraph he'd written, crossed out the middle sentence, read it again, and then marked out the entire thing. "Damnation," he muttered, crumpling up the paper and throwing it into the fireplace.

Generally, he thought himself a fair hand at explaining scientific matters, but now whenever he wrote a sentence, he imagined Elizabeth listening to it and how she would react. That paragraph would have made her yawn, he was certain. It might even have put her to sleep.

She wasn't a scientist, of course, and he was going to be speaking to scientists. At the same time, dull was dull. And while he wouldn't have given any of this a second thought before, as long as the information he wanted to convey was delivered, now he seemed to be spending an inordinate amount of time fretting over nonsense.

He began again. "Look, for example, at this candle. It provides light, but three disparate elements are required for it to do so. Firstly, we need fuel, a substance that can be burn—"

"You have a caller, Your Grace," Huston said, appearing in his open office doorway.

"It's past time for visitors. And the dogs have been recovered. There is no more reward forthcoming. Feel free to use any of those, Huston, and cease interrupting me."

"It's Lady Mary, my lord."

"Twice in one day?" He sighed, pushing back from the desk. "Show her in. And she'd best not be here to complain about Lancelot's manners."

"I am not here to complain that you were able to recover my precious lovey," his aunt said, sweeping into the room.

He looked at her. "You're dressed for a party."

"I told you I would be attending the Wincove soiree." She shifted a little, the movement swirling out the bottom of her dark blue skirt and making the silver threads sewn into it glitter.

"Hasn't it begun?"

"Yes."

"But you're here, and not there."

"I require a man whose arm I may hold."

Michael picked up his pen again. "Take Huston."

His aunt huffed. "I will not take your butler to a soiree. If I meant to do such a thing, I would take my own. Taggert, at least, can dance."

He set down the pen. "And how, pray tell, do you know that?"

"Because I taught him. Now go get dressed. I can't make an appearance with you garbed like a field hand."

Glancing down at his rolled-up shirtsleeves and open waistcoat, Michael frowned. "I am working. A speech does not write itself, you know."

"Work tomorrow. Tonight, you're escorting me to a party."

Suspicion made him narrow his eyes. "Why, precisely? I've never escorted you to a party before."

"Of course you have."

She sounded so sure, he had to go back and reconsider his statement. "I don't think I have, Aunt Mary."

"Then you are a poor excuse for a nephew, and you will do so now."

"You didn't answer the 'why' of it, I notice."

"Because I'm asking you to, Michael. For heaven's sake, go get dressed."

"Fine, if it'll make you stop nagging me."

On another evening he might have refused, but his damned speech was going nowhere, and in the very back corner of his mind it occurred to him that Elizabeth might be in attendance. He could ask her how Galahad was recovering, if nothing else. And seeing her might help inspire him and his writing.

As he climbed the stairs, he wondered what she would think if she knew that she'd become his muse, and that she had been very critical of his efforts thus far. More than likely, she would say that he'd portrayed her with admirable accuracy.

Jarrett appeared, uttering a whimper as Michael straightened from digging into his wardrobe. "Please, my lord, allow me to se-lect some items for you."

"Just make it quick, Jarrett," he ordered the valet. "It's a waste of time to begin with. Extending it only makes it worse."

Dark gray trousers, black shoes, a black and green waistcoat, and a black coat later, Michael eyed his reflection in the dressing mirror as the valet tied his cravat into a ridiculously intricate knot. He looked passable, which was good enough, as far as he was concerned.

"That'll do," he said, standing and pushing the valet's hands away from his cravat.

"But I need to tuck the ends into the knot," Jarrett protested.

"It's fine. Go away. I won't require you when I return, which will hopefully be in under an hour."

"Yes, my lord."

If he was able to return quickly enough, he would have an-other few hours to work tonight before he retired to bed. It wasn't enough, but he had only himself to blame for putting the speech to one side for as long as he had. Himself and a pair of missing poodles, and an enchanting young lady who wouldn't want to be a part of his life even if he thought of her romantically, even if he'd always stated that romance was for fools without better things to do.

"You should be wearing a cravat pin," his aunt observed as he returned downstairs. "Something jade."

"I am not going back upstairs for something as useless as a pin." He gestured her toward the door. "If we're going, then let's be off. I will still have a speech to write after you've swirled about the Wincove ballroom."

Huston pulled open the door, and Michael handed Mary into her coach before he followed her inside. He had a suspicion that she was matchmaking again, despite the fact that she'd declared herself out of that business five years ago when he'd rejected all of the seven women she'd shoved in his direction. He shuddered at the recollection. Being expected to remember who liked what, or whether the dress so-and-so had worn the previous week was more or less flattering than the one she'd chosen for that evening, reciting facts about the weather, pretending to be interested in whatever the latest scandal might be—he would rather have run naked through Haymarket at noon on a sunny day.

"This is one of my favorite soirees every year," Mary observed, fiddling with the end of her shawl. "Not terribly crowded, the ballroom opening onto the garden so one might even waltz on the terrace, all the young people dancing and smiling. It almost makes up for me having to return from my holiday early."

"Yes. Sounds lovely."

"I know sarcasm when I hear it, Michael."

"Good. I would hate to think I'd wasted the effort."

She glanced at him, then turned her gaze out the window. "Was there anything about the past fortnight that you enjoyed?" she asked. "I know you went to great effort and expense to find Lancelot and Galahad, but was it all unpleasant?"

"I suppose not," he conceded. "It was amusing having horrible tea in the world's smallest private room at the world's seediest tavern."

Mary chuckled. "I can imagine."

"I mean, I've dined with professors and lecturers at less than reputable establishments, but this one was truly horrible. Elizabeth went to stomp about the room, and she could only manage three steps before she came up against the window."

"Stomping definitely requires space."

"Evidently so." He smiled as he recalled. "And I will say that having half the residents of Charing Cross and Smithfield lined up outside the house and being able to give most of them some coin for their troubles—Elizabeth said it was the most fun she'd ever had, and I have to admit there was some satisfaction in knowing I'd provided the means for more than a few families to eat well that night." He shifted a little. "I meant to ask Elizabeth if she knows of any reputable charities to which I might give money on a more regular basis."

"That would be good of you. I donate to several charities. I'd be happy to pass along their names to you."

He nodded, sinking back in his seat. No matchmaking thus far, and she'd offered actual useful information. "Thank you. Yes, do."

"Of course. And I want to thank you again for hitting that ridiculous Peter Cordray. Any man who would abuse an animal, or order it abused, has no business becoming a husband."

"I have no argument with that. Even aside from his other disqualifications, in pursuing Elizabeth he was like a rock and she a whirlwind, flying circles around him in everything from manners to intellect."

"Well, the rock has evidently fled London, and has been disowned by his brother."

"I'm glad to hear it. He has no business being anywhere around Elizabeth. I imagine she'll sleep better, knowing he's gone."

"I certainly would. What a villain." She tapped his knee with her fan. "What you did was a very good deed."

"Hopefully it's what any other person would have done under the same circumstances."

"Any other person wouldn't have done so, and don't pretend you think otherwise, nephew."

Michael shrugged. "It happened, and I was there. It's over with now." And the sooner he could forget all of it, the better off he would be. The better off his speech would be, and the better off his experiments would be. No more distractions. It had been a fine, very fine, interlude, but it had reached its conclusion.

"So it is. I'll stop pestering you for details about it, then."

Thank God for that. Now she only needed to change her mind about needing him to escort her to the party, but he didn't bother to hope that would happen. No, he'd put in as little time as he could manage, make his escape, and either borrow her coach or hire a hack to return him home. One unpleasant evening, finished.

The street outside Dorsett House, the London home of Lord and Lady Wincove, was packed with vehicles and horses, along with a good share of pedestrians stopping to ogle the sights. Michael stepped down from the coach and helped his aunt to the ground. "I'm here as your guest," he muttered. "Leave it at that."

"Oh, very well." She handed her invitation over to the butler. "Lady Mary Harris and guest," she said, as the thin man took in the two of them.

They followed him to the ballroom entrance, where he stopped. "Lady Mary Harris," he announced in a booming voice, "and His Grace Michael Bromley, the Duke of Woriton."

"Dammit," he muttered.

"Perhaps no one will notice," his aunt said, half dragging him toward the back of the room. "I'm in need of some refreshment."

He walked with her, ignoring the curious, speculative looks

of the other guests. Evidently word had spread about his part in Cordray's flight, because generally all he received was a few stares and a bit of condescending muttering. Tonight, though, one young lady even fluttered her fan at him, as if recovering a pair of lost dogs made him a romantic hero.

Another one dropped her dance card just as he passed. He stepped on it and continued on his way, until a third young lady stopped directly in front of him. "Your Grace, I have one spot left on my dance card. Would you be so kind as to take it?"

"No," he said, and walked around her.

"Michael," his aunt chastised. "Behave yourself."

"I am behaving no differently than I usually do," he pointed out. "You're the one who insisted I come." He tugged his arm free of hers. "Why am I here, actually? You're practically carrying me through the ballroom; you're more in need of an anchor than an escort."

"I wanted to see you out and enjoying yourself," she burst out. "Is that so horrible?"

Matchmaking it was, then, the clever old woman. "I was enjoying myself. At home. Writing my speech. Good evening, Aunt Mary." He inclined his head.

"Michael, don't—"

Turning on his heel, he headed back for the door.

"Oh!" his aunt exclaimed from behind him. "Oh, dear!"

He suspected another trap, but turned around anyway. Aunt Mary lay on the floor, one hand flung over her eyes. Even as he acknowledged that, firstly, she was probably feigning fainting and, secondly, she'd outflanked him by being willing to make a spectacle of herself, he returned to her side, knelt down, and helped her sit up. "What the devil are you about?" he muttered.

She grabbed his hand. "You abandoned an old woman with rickety knees," she whispered back at him. "What did you expect would happen? Help me up."

Michael lifted her to her feet. Mary Harris was fairly petite, so he could ostensibly have carried her either to a chair or better yet out of the ballroom, but with the amount of spleen she'd developed, she might well have turned that into a wrestling match. "There," he said, shifting her hand to his arm. "Better?"

"Oh, yes. I'll be fine in a moment. Let's head to the refreshments, shall we? Perhaps I need a bite to eat. I have been traveling nearly all day, you know."

Well, now he was nearly convinced that she did need him to help steady her. "Tell me you ate dinner."

"What, dear? I can't quite recall. Actually, I think some fresh air would serve me better."

They changed direction yet again, heading for the open terrace doors leading out to the garden as music began behind them. He nearly ran into someone, and lifted his head to glare. Just beyond Lord Oakley's round face, he spied another, much more familiar face. *Elizabeth.*

She'd worn a deep red gown, covered by a white lace woven through with black beads. The effect was that of rippling starlight, and he stopped, mesmerized. Red ribbons curled with her honey-blond hair, while rubies hung from her ears and a single one rested at the base of her throat. *Stunning. Utterly stunning.*

They weren't partners any longer, and so he had no excuse to approach her at all. But he wanted to. He wanted to talk with her, just sit and look at her, and other, more heated things that hadn't crossed his mind for some time until he'd met her. None of that made him a match for her. The problem, very simply, was him.

She turned and saw him, her green eyes widening. "Michael."

Aunt Mary released his arm and shoved him at Miss Dockering, the minx.

Now it all made sense, but he couldn't even bring himself to be annoyed. Instead, he sketched a bow. "Elizabeth. How are you this evening?"

"Better, now that you're here. Dance with me, will you? Every man seems to fear that I'll expose them for the cowardly fiends they are."

Elizabeth Dockering without a dance partner was practically a crime. He didn't need to be a paragon of Society to know that. Michael nodded. "Of course."

He reached out his hand, and she put her fingers in his. Even through her red gloves he felt sparks, electricity crackling between them. He knew what caused a flow of energy: a completed circuit, positive to negative. *A completed circuit.*

"What are we dancing?" he asked, walking with her to the cleared terrace and glad for the breath of cool air coming from the garden.

"A waltz, I'm afraid."

That was serendipitous. "I'll manage it."

Putting his free hand on her waist, he turned her in to the steps. Other couples had taken to the floor in a riot of colors, but other than noting their relative orbits in order to avoid a collision, he ignored them. Her fingers were warm, and they tightened around his as he drew her a breath closer.

"How goes your speech?" she asked, looking up at him, eyes the color of sweet, fresh clover meeting his.

"It's rubbish," he answered. "Too wordy, too erudite, and very, very dull."

"I would be happy to volunteer as your audience. I have never found your explanations dull."

He took a breath, when he felt like he hadn't been breathing in a very long time. Years, even. "With our mutual business completed, I thought you would be happy to be rid of me."

"Michael, I . . ." She trailed off. "You're serious, aren't you?

No, I would not be happy to be rid of you. I find you and your work fascinating, in fact."

"Do you?" he murmured.

"I thought I'd made that rather clear."

"You do have a reputation for being polite, you know," he reminded her, even though he should likely have kept his mouth shut and for once simply accepted a miracle.

Green eyes smiled. "I'm never polite with you."

"No, I don't suppose you are," he mused. "You wouldn't mind spending more time in my company, then? This speech may take me another week to finish. It wouldn't be as exciting as walking through Covent Garden, or a footrace through Smithfield."

The smile reached her mouth. "No, I wouldn't mind," she whispered.

Good God. Keeping his one hand on her waist and the other around hers, he stopped dancing. "I have come to know some things about electricity," he said, hearing his voice shake a little. "Sparks, positive and negative charges, how it can force elements together or break them apart. And I feel electricity when I'm around you, Elizabeth. It's as if you are the positive half of energy, and I'm the negative. We work best when we're together. Or I work best when I'm about you."

"You could use some frivolity and warmth in your life," she said, tears welling in her pretty eyes. "And I want—I *want*—more gravity in mine. I think we are both better when we're together."

"As a researcher," he took up, his heart pounding like a blacksmith's hammer, "I've found that any one moment could be the difference between success and failure. I don't want to miss my moment with you, Elizabeth." He didn't even have a damned ring, but he didn't care. Michael sank down on one knee, ignoring the gasps and several crashes happening in the widening circle around them. "I adore you."

"Michael," she breathed, a tear running down one cheek now. She didn't look unhappy, though. Not at all, and he'd already learned her expressions, what she seemed to be feeling when she made them. And at this moment she was . . . happy.

"I can't say I adored you the day we met," he went on quietly, "because you annoyed the devil out of me, but even then I couldn't stop thinking about you. I've never stopped thinking about you from that first moment. I haven't much experience with love, but I believe it should feel like this. Like I . . . Like I've known you forever, but I could spend a hundred lifetimes learning who you are. I don't want to be without you. Will you do me the very great honor of becoming my wife?"

She nodded, more tears joining the first. "I can't even talk," she quavered, and sank down to throw her arms around him. "Yes," she murmured. "You are the best man I've ever known. Yes, yes, yes."

Michael tilted her head up with his fingertips and kissed her. Sparks, indeed. Lightning, thunder, all the heavens clanging about and making chaotic, glorious music. Because of her. "I love you."

"I love you, too. And I love that every time I see the night sky, I imagine how very far every bit of starlight has traveled to be there at that moment, when I'm looking up. You made stars more beautiful and more precious than I already thought them. And you make my life better, just by being present in it." She kissed him back.

He stood, drawing her up with him. "To starlight, then. And electricity. And poodles."

With a laugh, she pulled his face down and kissed him again as they ignored the stir of Lady Wincove gasping and fainting into her son's arms. "To poodles."

EPILOGUE

JIMMY BLY OPENED THE DOOR OF THE SMALL HOUSE ON Bryanston Mews in Marylebone and stepped inside. His coat smelled faintly of hay and horses, and he shrugged out of it, hanging it on one of the pegs by the door.

"How is she?" he called, bypassing the small front room for the kitchen at the rear.

"Better, I'd say," Sally answered, looking up from where she sat on the floor in the corner between the stove and the larder, Jenny and a pile of blankets beside her.

"Good. Dobbin doesn't know a dog physician, but he gave me a few names of fellows he says he'd trust with Woriton's horses." He pulled the note from his pocket. "And the duke himself said he'd pay any bill for her care. And Miss Bitsy said to get her whatever she needs and not to worry about it."

"Thank you for doing that. And thank them for thinking of Jenny, even while they're planning a wedding." She smiled at him. "She's fine, I think. Come take a look."

He was relieved to see his wife's smile—since Jenny had slunk into the corner and refused to emerge last night, she'd been too worried to sleep or eat, which had made him the same. Sighing, he put a hand on her shoulder and leaned down to give Jenny a pat, only to freeze and yank his fingers back in surprise. "What the devil?"

"Puppies," Sally said, chuckling. "Six of them. I had no idea what was afoot until the first one came popping out."

Jimmy knelt beside her, bending down to gently lift one of the tiny black balls of fur. "Six of them," he marveled. "Your act will be famous all over England, now."

Pickle and Bob trotted over, did some sniffing, and wandered back to their half-empty food bowls. "We've gone from being a family of five to one of eleven." Sally kissed the puppy in his hands, and he set it down beside Jenny again.

"They look pure black. Who do you reckon the papa is? Galahad, or Lancelot?"

"Oh, Jimmy," his wife said, sliding onto his lap and putting her arms around his shoulders, "did I ever tell you Jenny's full name?"

"What? No. What is it?"

"Guinevere. So whether it's Lancelot or Galahad, it's perfect."

AUTHOR'S NOTE

SOME OF MICHAEL BROMLEY'S WORK, INVENTIONS, AND DISCOVER-ies are based on those of Michael Faraday, arguably the most famous scientist in England during the Regency period. As I researched information for this story, I was surprised by the advances that were continually being made, and by the people making them. Michael Faraday began his career as a bookbinder, and discovered his affinity for science as he read the books he'd been tasked with binding.

One of the first and most influential of those books was *Conversations on Chemistry,* by Jane Marcet, first published in 1817—and which happens to still be in print to this day. It was from that book and its myriad illustrations that I learned how to make a voltaic pile and several other devices helpful to my story.

So I owe thanks to both Michael Faraday and Jane Marcet for their contributions to science and to my little romantic comedy.

ABOUT THE AUTHOR

A native and current resident of Southern California, SUZANNE ENOCH loves movies almost as much as she loves books, with a special place in her heart for anything Star Wars. She has written more than forty Regency novels and historical romances—including the Scandalous Brides and Scandalous Highlanders series—which are regularly found on the *New York Times* bestseller list. When she is not busily working on her next book, Suzanne likes to contemplate interesting phenomena, like how the three guppies in her aquarium became 161 guppies in five months.